WEEKENDS
with the
SUNSHINE
GARDENING
SOCIETY

WEEKENDS

with the

SUNSHINE GARDENING SOCIETY

SOPHIE GREEN

hachette
AUSTRALIA

hachette
AUSTRALIA

Published in Australia and New Zealand in 2023
by Hachette Australia
(an imprint of Hachette Australia Pty Limited)
Gadigal Country, Level 17, 207 Kent Street, Sydney, NSW 2000
www.hachette.com.au

Hachette Australia acknowledges and pays our respects to the past, present and
future Traditional Owners and Custodians of Country throughout Australia
and recognises the continuation of cultural, spiritual and educational practices
of Aboriginal and Torres Strait Islander peoples. Our head office is located on
the lands of the Gadigal people of the Eora Nation.

 A catalogue record for this
book is available from the
NATIONAL LIBRARY OF AUSTRALIA   National Library of Australia

ISBN: 978 0 7336 4942 4 (paperback)

Cover design by Christabella Designs
Cover images courtesy of Shutterstock
Author photograph courtesy of Jen Bradley
Part heading illustrations by Sophie Green
Typeset in 12/16.25 pt Sabon LT Pro by Bookhouse, Sydney
Printed and bound in Australia by McPherson's Printing Group

 MIX
Paper | Supporting
responsible forestry
FSC
www.fsc.org   FSC® C001695

The paper this book is printed on is certified against the
Forest Stewardship Council® Standards. McPherson's Printing
Group holds FSC® chain of custody certification SA-COC-005379.
FSC® promotes environmentally responsible, socially beneficial
and economically viable management of the world's forests.

*In memory of my grandfather, a lifelong gardener.
And for my parents in honour of their years of
weekends in the garden, raking leaves, pulling out weeds
and creating beauty.*

MARCH 1987

PIGFACE

CHAPTER ONE

Noosa Main Beach is the same yet not. Eternal but changed. There is still the view that takes in Fraser Island on a clear day; the shoreline still curls around towards the national park on one end and is truncated by the breakwater at the other. Over that breakwater there are rougher waves and braver surfers. Here, hugging into the lee side, there tend to be more gentle, rolling waves that can turn vigorous on certain tides but usually welcome timid swimmers.

The beach has been fortified by rocks and sand has been pumped in from the river that empties beyond the breakwater. If this hadn't been done erosion would have caused this beautiful, bright stretch of sand to disappear. Noosa Heads, locals say, is being loved to death. Everyone wants it to look perfect so they can have their perfect holiday. Time and tides – and some people's opinions on the form the shoreline should take – have other ideas. So every now and again the beach washes away, the rocks are exposed, and the tourists ignore that because sand will be brought in to cover up those rocks and everything will look perfect again. But the locals know what it used to look like. Cynthia knows. Or, more truthfully, she remembers. Because she hasn't been home – not properly – for fourteen years. Even though she was twenty-five then she thought she may never return. Not because she doesn't love the place but because she wanted to leave it behind. She had a new life and it wasn't in Noosa. Or Australia, for that matter.

A child squeals close by and seagulls bustle around the sand. One of the lifesavers folds his arms and squints as he regards two swimmers between the flags who look like they're about to be outside the flags. His mouth opens; there's a warning coming. The swimmers, as if intuiting that they're about to be told off, change course and move back between those flags that promise safety, protection. Lifesavers. *Life savers.* What a concept. It would be nice, Cynthia thinks, if someone could come along and save her life. Or, rather, rescue her from it because it feels like her feet have been pulled from under her.

She digs her toes into the sand and waits for the wave that's coming towards her. When it arrives the water is warmer than she expected. It's reassuring. These are the waves she grew up with. This is the sand she knows.

She hadn't expected to feel reassured when she came back. She'd thought she may feel disappointed in herself for scurrying home from Los Angeles instead of staying to deal with the end of her marriage. She suspected she'd feel superior to the Noosa locals who'd stayed put while she went off to have the sort of life – and lifestyle – she'd always believed more suited to her than anything on offer in the fishing-shack town she'd left behind. Noosa isn't that town any more, though. It's busier and has the patina of a place that is well loved: lots of smiling visitors, rotating frequently, and the wear and tear that comes from so many different humans passing through, along with the new coats of paint on buildings that signal that the town is being tended.

As a child and teenager and young mother here Cynthia never quite understood what Pat, her first husband, called 'Noosa magic', and she still didn't understand it all those years she was away. Now, though, with this sea foam on her feet and these gulls and this breeze, with those rocks leading the way around the coast to the bush beyond, and the sky that is the most gentle shade of blue she's ever seen, she wonders. Perhaps there is magic here. And if there is, she needs to find it. Along with some fortitude and forbearance.

Cynthia jumps as a hand is placed on her shoulder.

'Missed it?' her father says, his voice croakier than it sounded on the phone during their long-distance calls.

'No,' she says, and it's both a lie and the truth, because she has and she hasn't at differing times.

Her father peers at her and nods slowly, like he's figured her out. Then again, he always has.

'Sure,' he says. 'Well, the house missed you.'

'You mean the house misses Mum's housekeeping,' she says wryly.

The state of the three-bedroom, one-storey dwelling at Little Cove, almost within sight of where they're standing now, suggests her father hasn't lifted a finger since her mother died five months ago. Not that Cynthia knows what he's been doing or not doing, because she couldn't come back for the funeral.

She had visited, once, after her mother was diagnosed and before they knew how serious her illness was. No one told Cynthia it was terminal; if they had, she would have come home and stayed until her mother died, then dealt with the mess of her life in Los Angeles later. For as much as she and her mother weren't close, they were connected, and while Diane always seemed to live at one remove from everyone around her, Cynthia loved her. Loves her still. Yes, everything else could have waited because, as Cynthia knows now, we have so few chances to stand witness to the biggest changes in the lives of those we love.

'Could be,' her father admits. 'I'm not that good at keeping things tidy. Doing washing.'

'How would you know?' she says playfully. 'You've never tried.'

'I don't expect you to do it,' he says gruffly.

'Course you do.' She pats his hand. 'I don't mind, Papa. I came back to spend time with you.'

He peers at her again. 'Uh-huh. And Odette, of course.'

'Yes, of course,' Cynthia smiles tightly.

Odette, her daughter, had been the ever-present witness to the unpleasantness – to put it mildly – of Cynthia's second marriage and, as soon as she turned sixteen, she told Cynthia she wanted to move back to Australia to live with her father. It wasn't as if Cynthia could claim that life in Los Angeles wasn't worth leaving. She'd wanted to leave it too, but sometimes marriages aren't that straightforward.

They had been so close. But Cynthia failed Odette, or she felt she had, by not protecting her from what was going on, so she didn't call her that often. Didn't write. She wanted Odette to be happier than she had been all those years away from her father. Except those years of living apart made Cynthia unhappier than she has ever been, and now she feels so disconnected from her daughter it's as if they're former colleagues who shared a terrible boss and all they have in common are war stories they don't wish to repeat. She doesn't know how to talk to Odette any more, let alone how to be her mother.

Cynthia has to reacquaint herself with that role, however, because what has really brought her back to the place of her youth is that Odette, still in her own youth, has announced that she's two months pregnant and planning to keep the baby. Cynthia plans to disabuse her of that notion. Odette has so much life ahead of her – and Cynthia is more aware of that than most. She was nineteen when she became pregnant with Odette.

Her father probably knows Odette better than Cynthia herself does these days. He also probably knows that while his daughter is pleased to see him, the real motive for her return is to try to talk his granddaughter out of becoming a mother. He won't say anything about that, however. Minding his own business has been Wilfred's life credo.

'I suppose I should call her,' Cynthia says.

Her father nods slowly. 'Yep.' He glances out to sea then back to her. 'But first I have some fresh prawns and some bread from the junction.'

'Don't tell me Sid's bakery is still there?'

'No. But the bread's good.' He pats her shoulder. 'Come on. Time to go home.'

Cynthia takes one more look at the sea and thinks about coming back for a swim later. Those LA beaches just weren't the same as this glorious expanse. She wants to plunge into the salt water just so she can turn around and look at the shore, revel in the beauty of it, and try not to think about how many years she could have been enjoying it.

'Yes, Papa,' she says. 'It is.'

CHAPTER TWO

Lorraine slams the Wettex down on the sink and exhales loudly. 'Terry, I have told you a *million* times that when you go to the shops you need to take Simon with you!'

'I don't want to,' her eldest son replies.

'I don't *care*. I don't have time to watch him all day, every weekend – I need your help. Plus he loves going with you.'

'Yeah. That's the problem.'

Terry glowers at her. He's fourteen and riding the messy wave of puberty, alternately loathing her and wanting her to tell him that life will turn out okay. Ha! She'd like someone to tell her that too.

'Mike, say something,' she mutters as her husband enters the kitchen.

'Mate,' he says, ruffling Terry's hair.

'Dad, stop it!' Terry looks mortified then mildly pleased.

'Why?' Mike chuckles and winks at Lorraine. 'It's too much fun seeing your reaction. Darl, did you hear about Howard sacking Andrew Peacock? Can't believe it – I thought that bloke had nine lives.'

'Why – because he's had an affair with Shirley MacLaine?' she mutters.

Mike chortles. 'Yeah, probably.'

'Terry, where's Simon now?' Lorraine turns fully away from the sink and puts her hands on her hips.

Terry shrugs. 'Dunno.'

'Could you *find him*?'

'Why do I have to hang out with that little creep?' Terry says just as his brother walks into the room.

Lorraine sees Simon just in time to also see his face crumple. 'Darling.' She yanks off her rubber gloves and throws them on the kitchen bench before going to her youngest and giving him a hug. 'Terry didn't mean it,' she says softly, kissing the loose curls on the top of Simon's head then glaring at her teenager.

'Yeah, I did,' Terry snickers. 'He follows me around. It's embarrassing. My friends think he's a loser.'

Mike chuckles again.

'Michael, it's not funny,' Lorraine says just as Simon starts to sniffle.

When she waited five years after Terry was born to have another child it was because she needed to get used to the idea of one kid before she added another. She didn't stop to think that her eldest child would be a teenager while her youngest was still in single digits, which is like parenting two different species instead of one.

'What is happening?'

Mike's mother, Cora, has joined them, wafting through the doorway. Cora likes to waft. She once told Lorraine that she'd read in a magazine that a lady should look elegant when she walks; her interpretation is to waft all over the house, day and night, until she finally retires to her bedroom. Although she probably wafts in there too. Lorraine wouldn't know. Cora keeps the door closed unless she wants the room vacuumed, when she leaves it open. Presumably as an invitation to Lorraine to do that vacuuming.

Cora's all right, really. She just used to have a maid or a cleaner or something back when Mike was growing up in Toowoomba. Now that she's living in Cooroy with grown-up Mike and his wife, she thinks Lorraine is that maid. And Lorraine, not wanting to rock the boat or her marriage, goes along with it. So she probably only has herself to blame. She shouldn't have let Cora move in when Mike's father died. That was the original mistake.

'It's fine, Cora,' Lorraine says, stroking Simon's head as he continues to sniffle.

But Cora has spied the tears on Simon's cheeks and is now wafting in his direction. 'My poor baby,' she murmurs, kissing his cheek. Simon's her favourite. Which Terry knows. It hasn't helped with Terry's attitude towards his brother.

'Honestly, Cora, it's fine.' Lorraine looks pointedly at Mike, who is, inconveniently, looking in the fridge.

'Where are the snags?' he asks, presumably of her.

'In the freezer,' she snaps. Where he put them when he brought them home from the butcher.

The ringing phone on the kitchen bench gives her an opportunity to step back and observe the scene playing out before her: teenage son looking at her like he wishes she'd disappear into a hole; husband's head swivelling from side to side as he continues to look in the fridge, not the freezer; nine-year-old son sniffing as his grandmother squeezes him into a hug.

'Hello,' she says curtly into the receiver.

'Lorraine?'

'Yep.'

The voice on the line sounds vaguely familiar, which means it's probably one of the school mothers wanting her to make toffee for the fete or whatever it is that's coming up. There's always something. Fundraiser, fete, dance, teacher leaving.

'Hi,' the voice says.

Lorraine frowns. 'Yeah. Hi.' Who does this joker think she is?

'It's me.' The voice is meek now.

'Who's me?'

'Cynthia.'

That makes Lorraine pause. Cynthia Scheffer used to be the best thing in her life. The funniest, smartest, trendiest person she knew at school; the most daring of them all even after she had Odette. So daring she up and left for Los Angeles with that surfer she met after he caught a wave off Tea Tree Bay and found her sitting on the rocks, almost as if she was waiting for him. Because she was. She'd spied him waxing a surfboard in the car park nearby and decided he was a better prospect than her husband. Or maybe she just wanted to force a change. Either way, Pat never saw it coming.

Now that Lorraine has been a mother for fourteen years, she understands the desire to force a change. But that change took Cynthia far away from everyone who loved her and, after an initial letter-writing spree, she stopped contacting Lorraine, and eventually Lorraine stopped trying to contact her.

And the clincher was that the surfer didn't last but Cynthia stayed over there, with Odette, and married some film producer or whatever. So Cynthia's dad told Lorraine when she saw him fishing round at Noosaville one day. After that they started catching up for tea every now and again; they'd always got on when Lorraine was a teenager. Less so Lorraine and Cynthia's mum, who was a little stand-offish. Wilfred hasn't said a word, though, about Cynthia coming home. Which, given the lack of STD pips or international dialling noise, she must be.

'Hello, Cynthia,' Lorraine says in the most formal voice she can muster.

She glances at Mike, who was privy to her tears when Cynthia stopped writing back. Now he's shut the fridge door and has that look on his face he gets when he's worried that the dog has pooed on the neighbour's lawn. He leans his head to one side, holding her gaze. She knows what it means: *Are you all right?* He can be sensitive sometimes. Usually when it counts. That's why she puts up with having his mother in the house.

She smiles at him. Yes, she's all right. Cynthia may have broken her heart but Mike and Terry and Simon glued it back together.

'How . . . how are you?' Cynthia says, her voice soft.

'Fine. You?'

'I'm . . . back.'

'Yep. Gathered that.'

Lorraine hears a sigh. 'I haven't been a good friend.'

Lorraine makes a face into the phone. Useless but satisfying.

'You've been no kind of friend,' she says, although her voice is calm. She's just saying the truth, isn't she? No need for drama.

Silence for a few seconds. Then another sigh. 'No, I haven't.' More silence.

'But I'd love to see you,' Cynthia goes on.

Lorraine thinks about that. What would it be like to see Cynthia again? Would she want to kick her in the shins? Or would she – more likely, she believes – want to wrap her in a hug then go back to the way things were? Because she's never had another friend like Cynthia. No one who has encouraged her to be herself as much as Cynthia did. Lorraine knows now that friends like that are so rare that a person needs to be prepared to overlook some dodgy behaviour from time to time. Because we all make mistakes. Which doesn't mean she's going to let Cynthia off the hook straightaway. Lorraine isn't a pushover. Much. Not in this case, anyway. She still loves Cynthia – you don't stop loving someone when you've been as close as they were – but she's not just going to forgive and forget. That's for people who watch daytime soaps and think life is as easy as saying a few nice words.

'I'll have to think about it,' she says, even though she already has. 'I have a lot on.'

'Of course.' Cynthia sounds relieved. 'I'm at Dad's if . . . you know . . . you want to call.'

'Yeah, all right.' Now it's Lorraine's turn to pause. How do you end a conversation like this?

'I'd better go,' she says eventually. 'Things to do.'

'Okay.'

'Ta-ta.'

She hangs up in time to see Simon stick out his tongue at Terry and she braces herself for whatever's coming next.

CHAPTER THREE

The garden is a mess. Elizabeth knows this. It's imposs-ible to not know it because she sees it every day. This medium-sized back garden that was once ordered and cared for – that was loved – is now unruly. There is leaf litter in the beds. There are sticks on the grass. The bushes that need pruning haven't been pruned in a while. Flowers have fallen and started to rot.

Jon wouldn't approve. 'Never let a weed go unremoved,' he liked to say. She can only imagine what he would make of what his beloved project has become. But he's not here. He hasn't been here for three months. Is it three months? Maybe it's four. Maybe it's two. Maybe it's an eternity.

That's something Elizabeth has discovered about grief: it causes time to change shape. Grief this profound, this paralysing, is not something she's had to deal with – not in such a major way. At thirty years of age she's lost grandparents and she's grieved them. But they weren't people she spent every day with, or had a child with. There's a special kind of grief for those people.

She'd lived such an ordered life until this; no doubt that's one of the things Jon liked about her when they met, as he was a man who liked an ordered garden and a pressed tie and a clean shave. He never said and she didn't ask, and now she can't ask because he is dead. And because he's dead he can't see the disorder in his garden and in his wife.

'Mum-my,' comes Charlie's singsong voice from the back door.

Elizabeth turns her head towards it. 'Yes, darling?'

'What's for lunch?'

Lunch. Elizabeth hasn't thought about it. That's another thing about grief: it sucks up all the other functions of life, like eating. If it hadn't been for her mother regularly appearing with crustless cheese sandwiches and chicken vol-au-vents at key times, Elizabeth wouldn't have eaten for weeks. Her mother seems to have developed a predilection for cocktail food – or perhaps it's that she thinks Elizabeth will only eat things that can be picked up in one hand. It's surprising cabanossi hasn't made an appearance.

So while Elizabeth hasn't thought about lunch, her mother will have. There will be something covered in Glad Wrap in the fridge, because her mother dropped round this morning, as she does every morning, sometimes with Elizabeth's father in tow. They have both helped her more than she knew she would need to be helped.

In the week after Jon died, for instance, her father was brilliant: capable, commanding, helping to organise the funeral and making sure guests at the wake were looked after while Elizabeth sat limply in a chair and tried to remember the names of people she hadn't seen in years. She and Jon had known each other since high school but they'd lost touch with most of their high-school friends – those same people who drove up the Bruce Highway from Brisbane to kiss her on the cheek and pat her hand and say they were so very, very sorry. She wanted to ask them why they weren't so sorry that they didn't visit Jon in the two years he was sick; years in which Charlie was discovering the world and Elizabeth tried to manage a boy looking outwards and a husband whose illness made him turn inwards. If her parents hadn't packed up their lives in Brisbane to live nearby, Elizabeth would have faced it all mostly alone.

It had been Jon's idea to move to Noosaville when he took up a job at the council. Being a civil engineer would take him places, he told her, and it took them up the road to the Sunshine Coast. They both loved it and chose Noosaville as their home, with its charming houses and the river so close they could hear the swish of boats. Elizabeth walked Charlie in his pram by the river, over to Hastings Street in Noosa Heads and back again. Long walks, soaking in the sun, looking at birds, enjoying the slow pace of this small community.

Her parents chose Sunshine Beach as their home. Not too much of a drive from her, and she couldn't blame them for preferring the ocean to the river. A lifetime in Brisbane has probably inured them to rivers. But she still likes them.

Except Elizabeth hasn't walked by that river in months. Not since Jon started ailing and she had to spend her time by his side. Not had to. Wanted to. Or sometimes had to. Caring for someone who is seriously ill, then terminally ill, is an act of love but often, too, of service. There are minutes, hours, days when you have to take a breath and rededicate yourself to the task. For task it becomes. Even love can be a task. Ask any parent.

Elizabeth smiles weakly at her son. 'Lunch, um . . . I'm sure Granny left us something delicious. Would you like to go and check?'

He looks at her as if he'd rather *she* go and check, his little nose wrinkling, his thick titian-coloured fringe almost covering it. She needs to take him for a haircut. Something else to add to the list of things she's been neglecting.

Charlie's glance moves to the garden bed over Elizabeth's shoulder and now his forehead is wrinkling along with his nose. 'What's wrong with that?'

He points to something and Elizabeth turns to see a wilting hydrangea.

Another weak smile. 'It just needs a bit of attention.' *Don't we all.*

'Is it dying?'

His eyes are bright and she sees only innocence there, but what he has said makes her breath catch. The plant *is* dying. Because his father, the garden's caretaker, has died. There's a parable or something in that, isn't there? Or there should be. If she reads her Bible again, the way she's been meaning to ever since Jon died – all the way through, knowing there will be succour in it if only she can sit down and *focus* – maybe she'll find it. But for now there's only a dying hydrangea and no way to explain it other than neglect.

That's what she told Reverend Willoughby when he stopped by to see her last Sunday. She hadn't turned up to church again that morning and he was worried about her, he said. He has been very kind to her since Jon died, even though she's been slack about her church attendance. She supposes it's his job, but she appreciates it nonetheless. He's checked on her and his wife has brought food. Small gestures that have meant a great deal.

When he visited he glanced around the garden and raised his eyebrows, then muttered something about sending someone to give her a hand. But Elizabeth doesn't expect anything. That's something else about grief: even an expectation of getting out of bed in the morning seems grandiose.

'Maybe,' she says to Charlie and stands. 'But I'll give it a water and see if it recovers.'

'Okay,' he says cheerfully and smiles at her.

Charlie's good humour has been the one thing that has brightened Elizabeth's days. He's old enough to know his father has gone but young enough to still live in the moment. Events are measured in how many sleeps away they are, and Charlie has no concept of dwelling in the past. That's a punishment Elizabeth gets to keep to herself.

'Come on,' she says, holding out her hand to him. 'Let's go and see what's in the fridge.'

He grins and takes it, swinging on her arm.

'Mu-um,' he says.

'Yes, darling?'

'Can we go to the park?'

Elizabeth closes her eyes and inhales. He's been asking to do this every day for weeks now. But outside, beyond this house, is a world she's not ready for yet.

'Maybe,' she says, as she does every day, and his smile tells her that the answer is good enough for him. For now.

CHAPTER FOUR

The din of a restaurant kitchen as service ramps up is something Kathy is used to. That slight nervous anticipation of the hours ahead – not knowing what sort of people are going to walk through the door, whether they'll be pleasant customers or the sort who complain at the drop of a hat, the tightrope walk of making sure all the meals come out on time and to the right people – is also something she is used to. What she is not used to is being answerable to someone else about how the restaurant runs. Kathy's been in charge of staff for so long that she no longer knows how to obey. Which may turn out to be a problem because, despite her years of experience and her most recent job being that of restaurant manager, the only job she's been able to find at short notice in the supposedly burgeoning hospitality industry of Noosa Shire is as a waitress with occasional bartending duties at a nice little establishment by the river.

The restaurant has a view. That's something. There are houses on the opposite bank, and boats between them, and pelicans most days, all of which they can see through the glass that forms the entire front of the restaurant. The view can be seen from the banquettes too, which are new enough not to show signs of wear and tear, and from the tables that are large enough to accommodate main meals and side dishes – not something Kathy takes for granted after working in tiny Melbourne establishments where they were lucky to fit the bread basket on the table along with the meals. What she didn't have in Melbourne were the biting midge things that manifest at sunset for anyone who decides that a stroll along the riverbank would be a good idea. This isn't the lifestyle Kathy aspired to when she left Melbourne and moved here two weeks ago.

Two weeks of scrambling to find a decent place to live and a job that pays her enough to cover the rent. She supposes she could have allowed more time but time isn't usually a component of snap decisions.

A year ago, in a flush of romantic love, she and her beloved, Jem, had decided that the Sunshine Coast seemed like the ideal place to live with its eternal summer. Or, rather, not-Melbourne weather. Kathy had visited once and found it bright and bustling with promise: there were businesses opening, and homes with front and back gardens. At that stage Kathy was living in a narrow place in Carlton North with some paving out the front, a couple of square metres of fading lawn out the back, and a huge deciduous tree that covered everything with leaves in autumn. It was her former marital home, which was likely a factor in her daydreams of living elsewhere.

A month ago, Jem had announced that Kathy was no longer wanted as another paramour had been found. A younger, firmer individual whose breasts still bounce and who may, one day, want children. At fifty-four and with two grown-up offspring of her own, Kathy is beyond having babies. She'd been pleased about that, for a while. Until the point where her inability to have more children became the rationale to break her heart.

She knows that wasn't the real reason, though. It was the convenient reason. There were others, hinted at earlier when Kathy hadn't been prepared to up-end her life to do what Jem wanted to do, which was to move to Warrnambool and farm sheep. Freezing bloody Warrnambool, where the winds come in off the Great Southern Ocean and everyone is pleasant and community-minded to make up for it. Kathy used to have holidays in Warrnambool, back when she was married and her children were young. A long time ago. So she hadn't wanted to make that particular change, yet here she is with an up-ended life anyway. At least this version is the one she chose.

'Hmm, only half-booked,' Hans, the restaurant's co-owner, says, scrutinising the reservations book.

'It's a Tuesday,' Kathy says lightly. 'I think a lot of the tourists go home on Tuesday.'

He nods and narrows his eyes at her, like he's trying to work out if she really knows anything about it. True, she isn't familiar with the area yet. But she knows hospitality and its rhythms. How there are certain weeks of the year that are dead quiet, and it's the same weeks each year and has nothing to do with school terms or full moons or even the weather. They're just quiet. Sometimes she wishes a scientist or someone would do research on it so she can find out why it happens.

'If we were to close one day a week,' Hans says, looking at her sideways, 'which one would you choose?'

Kathy wonders if this is a loaded question: if he's about to ask her to cut back on a day of work. Or maybe he genuinely wants her opinion.

'Wednesday,' she says, because she's been chatting to the kitchen staff about the busy and quiet times. 'That's the dead day in the week.'

Hans raises his eyebrows. 'You would not do this in Melbourne,' he states.

'No,' Kathy agrees. 'But that's a completely different scene. Melbourne has a lot of business lunches throughout the week. From what I understand of this place, the tourists go home on Tuesday and the next ones arrive on Thursday. It's all about long weekends.' She smiles to show that she's trying to be helpful.

He didn't have to hire her, this young man with slicked-back hair and an Hermès belt. She's a generation older than the rest of the staff, and she knows from friends who used to be colleagues that finding work at their age is almost an impossibility. At fifty-four, apparently, she's too old to be useful. But not to Hans. He was almost apologetic about having only a waitressing job to offer her and promised he'd promote her as soon as he could. She didn't tell him that this was the only job she was offered and while it wasn't what she'd hoped for she wasn't in a position to be picky.

'I think you are right,' he says. 'I have talked to the other owners about only doing dinner service on this day.' Another sideways glance. 'This will not affect you.'

His reassurance is kind.

'Okay,' Kathy says. 'Let me know if you need a hand with anything.'

She doesn't know why she said that. Does it sound condescending?

'I appreciate your experience,' Hans says quietly and closes the reservations book. 'Would you like a coffee before the hordes arrive?' He grins, presumably so she knows he's being ironic about those hordes.

'Thank you, yes.'

He gestures to a table that has been set for lunch service, as they all have. 'Espresso, yes?'

She nods then sits at the table. She'll drink two or three espressos to get her through the day, then at night she'll unwind with half a bottle of whatever she picks up on the way home. Although she has to remember that bottle shops aren't as thick on the ground here as they are in Melbourne, and businesses close early. It's still a small town. Or a collection of very small towns.

'I'll be only a minute,' Hans says, and heads for the espresso machine.

Kathy was impressed when she saw the machine the first time she was here; she thought only Melburnians appreciated good coffee. Hans, as it turns out, has an Italian mother and an appreciation of coffee accordingly.

As she hears the machine hissing away, Kathy glances towards the river. No, it's not a bad view. At least when she ran away she ran to something picturesque.

'Thank you,' she says as Hans places the tiny cup and saucer in front of her. She waits for him to make his own coffee and they both knock them back in one gulp.

CHAPTER FIVE

As they emerge from the church the sun feels warm on Elizabeth's cheek and she closes her eyes briefly. It feels comforting to know the sun is always there. Whenever she has a bad day – and they are more frequent now than at any other time in her life – she tries to find sunlight, just for a few minutes. Her mother told her once that she did it as a child too – she'd find Elizabeth lying on the grass in their back garden, face up, eyes closed. It's one of the things Elizabeth likes about living in this part of the world: sunshine is so frequently available, and on the days when there is rain it often clears quickly. That's life in the subtropics, as her father likes to say.

Today the sun on her face tells her that she's not only managed to make it out of bed but outside too. And not just outside the house but all the way to church. She needed it today. Needed the reassurance that there is something bigger than her, bigger than what has happened to her. There is a small segment of her brain that acknowledges that the only way she can come back to life is to realise that she is but one small part of a much greater whole, and in that context her woes are not so great.

She takes Charlie's hand and they start down the steps.

'Elizabeth,' says a familiar voice behind her and she turns around.

'Reverend.' She smiles.

He puts a hand on her shoulder. 'How are you?' His head dips – that unconscious display of sincerity that Elizabeth never noticed before in others but now sees regularly.

She smiles again. It's hard to know what else to do. She's always believed in politeness and believes it would be impolite to inflict her sadness on others. The reverend knows she's sad – that's why he checks on her – so asking about her wellbeing is perfunctory. Yet that's *his* politeness and she accepts it as such. Except what she really wants to do is ask him: 'When you feel like screaming – when each day can become an exercise in trying to sew the threads of your life together only to see them fall apart anew – how are you meant to act?'

How am I meant to be now?

It's not just missing Jon – that's a given. How can she not miss a man who, even at his worst, was thoughtful and considerate, never wanting to impose on her – although it was inevitable. He was a kind, understated man who was serious when needed and lighthearted when appropriate. When they were teenagers Elizabeth thought him boring, with his Bible study and his manners. It wasn't until they were older and she'd experienced more of the world and its people that she realised the qualities Jon had were rare. He was a true friend, to her and others; he was steadfast and solid. She loved his voice, which was deep, right until the end. She loved his hair, which was thick and dark brown, and he never minded when she ran her fingers through it and messed it up, teasing that he couldn't do it to her because curly hair wasn't made for running fingers through. As his physicality faded she was still attracted to what she remembered of the man he was, and she loved the man who remained, until he didn't.

Now she has to reconstruct a life not only around Jon's absence but one that includes it, because that absence will be a central fact of Charlie's existence. Elizabeth may feel better in time; she may even marry again. Who knows? But Charlie's father is gone forever. That's not something she knows how to manage.

Everyone who gave her well-meaning advice about having a baby failed to mention what to do if that baby's father died.

'I'm . . . here,' she says, because it's all she can think of to say, with the sun warming her cheek and her son's hand in hers, with the memory of hymns sung fresh and the reading still in her mind.

It was from Corinthians: *For our light and momentary troubles are achieving for us an eternal glory that far outweighs them all. So we fix our eyes not on what is seen, but on what is unseen, since what is seen is temporary, but what is unseen is eternal.* She's sure the reverend chose it for her, to remind her that her sadness is temporary, even if it lasts for the rest of her life. The Bible has not always provided comfort for her, but it finds her at the most important times. Or perhaps she finds it.

So she is here. Seen and temporary.

The reverend pats her shoulder. 'Sometimes I think that's all we can ever know to be true,' he says, his voice deep and reassuring.

Then he crouches down next to Charlie. 'And you, young man – how is school?'

Charlie shrugs and rolls one of his feet to its outer edge, as he tends to do when he's feeling shy. 'S'all right,' he says, then glances up at his mother. He's only in kindergarten and still ambivalent about something that takes him away from home five days a week.

Reverend Willoughby chuckles and stands. 'I think that's all we can ever know to be true about *school*, too.'

He smiles at Elizabeth. 'I hope we'll see you next Sunday, Elizabeth, but if you are ever not here, please know that our thoughts will be with you.'

She nods quickly. 'Thank you, Reverend.'

Charlie tugs on her hand.

'That's my cue,' she says, and as she turns to go the reverend lifts his hand in half a wave and something about it makes tears catch in Elizabeth's throat. He looks like he cares – that's probably what has triggered her emotion. When people express care these days she can unravel just a little, almost as if she's so grateful for their care that she feels overwhelmed by it.

Charlie lets go of her hand and skips ahead, stopping to pluck a dandelion growing in the nature strip. He picks up an empty drink can and inspects its insides.

'No, Charlie,' Elizabeth says warningly. 'You don't know where it's been.'

He drops it, but skips back to present her with the dandelion, grinning before he pirouettes away. As his head turns he looks so much like Jon that this time it's her heart that responds, jerking in her chest, and the tears in her throat turn into a sob.

What she didn't expect about grief – if one can ever expect anything – is how physical it is. How much her hands long to hold Jon again. How her skin wants to touch his. Before, when it was abstract, she'd thought of grief as an experience of emotions and of the mind: thoughts turning turbulent, sadness becoming a state of being. Yet it's her body that tells her how much she is missing Jon. There are actual pangs, sometimes – pains in her abdomen, or her leg, or her neck.

'What's wrong?' Charlie says, coming back to take her hand as they near the house and its garden and all the evidence of his life that Jon left behind.

What's wrong? For Charlie, most days are fine. He still has her, and the day-to-day details of his life haven't changed much. It's not for her to try to make him see the world differently.

'Absolutely nothing, my darling,' she says, pushing open the gate that leads into the garden and following the path to the back of the house. 'Now, how about some morning tea?'

Charlie looks just as thrilled as if she'd said the Easter Bunny was about to visit, and it's in moments like these that Elizabeth starts to believe that, just maybe, there truly is absolutely nothing wrong.

CHAPTER SIX

It is almost impossible, Cynthia thinks, to not see the baby in your grown-up child. To not remember the first time you saw her, so tiny, her features indistinct yet uniquely hers. It seems like last week that Odette was so small. Now she is nineteen, and while Cynthia knows exactly how that time passed and where, this fact seems unreal. Her daughter is nineteen. An adult. She is not that baby any more. Sometimes, though, Cynthia wishes she were, just so she could cuddle her. Just so she could whisper in her ear that everything is wonderful, like she used to do. An incantation for them both.

While Odette's hair is different to how she kept it in Los Angeles, Cynthia would recognise the shape of her head anywhere. She sees it now from the back as her daughter sits on the verandah, looking out through the trees at the side of the house to the ocean beyond, although it's not that visible any more. Cynthia's father used to keep the trees trimmed so the view was clear; since her mother died he seems to prefer that they provide a screen for him instead. She's going to talk to him about it, because that view really shouldn't be denied.

As Cynthia steps on the threshold between sitting room and verandah, the wood creaks and Odette's head turns. Cynthia watches her daughter's expression range swiftly from surprise to consternation to affection to annoyance.

'Mum,' she says flatly.

'Hello, baby.'

Odette presses her lips together. She used to like it when Cynthia called her 'baby'; maybe she doesn't now.

'You didn't say you were coming.' Odette's eyes stare into hers. They're harder than they used to be.

Maybe that's because she's cross at Cynthia or maybe it's just what happens to pretty girls after years of being subjected to the needs and wants of the men around them. Armour has to be developed, and that flint is part of it.

'I . . . wanted to surprise you.' Cynthia's smile is as big as she can make it.

'You did.'

Odette glances to the side gate, which is now being opened by Pat. Cynthia hasn't seen Pat, Odette's father, since . . . well, it's been years. He last came to Los Angeles when Odette was fourteen, and two years later Odette was living with him in Noosa. Cynthia and Pat spoke on the phone – they'd always done that – but their conversations had become more strained after Odette's return because Cynthia would try to tell Pat how to be Odette's parent, which he didn't appreciate. Still, they'd remained civil.

Cynthia tried so hard to make her marriage to Max work, partly to show Pat that she wasn't the problem. She'd left him, yes, and she'd left the surfer she left him for. But her second husband had come along when she was in her early thirties and in a better position to know what she wanted. Although not, as it turned out, to exercise better judgement. Maybe she and marriage just aren't made for each other. It doesn't matter if Pat thinks that too; she has to keep reminding herself of this. His opinion on anything except Odette is irrelevant.

Their eyes meet as he puts a foot on the bottom of four steps leading up to the verandah.

'Cyn,' he says, smiling. 'What a lovely surprise.'

28

Cynthia turns to Odette and raises an eyebrow. *See*, she wants to say, *some people can pretend to be happy I'm here.*

'Nice to see you, Pat.'

Now she's the one surprised as he kisses her cheek. He smells the same: Old Spice and salt water. The scent does what scents tend to do: evokes memories. For a few seconds she's a teenager again and so is he, and Odette is a speck of stardust waiting to come to earth.

But he doesn't look like a teenager; nor does she, of course. He has a healthy beard with the odd fleck of silver and his thick brown hair has similar traces of ageing. And she – well, just before she left Los Angeles she marched into her hairdresser's and asked for her shoulder-blade-length locks to be cut off. She was severing her marriage and it seemed appropriate to do the same to the hair that her husband had insisted she keep 'long and luscious'. Just thinking about that makes her shudder. So she looks properly middle-aged now even though she's only thirty-nine. She feels it too, given that Odette may be about to make her a grandmother.

'What do you think about our girl, huh?' Pat says, gazing at Odette with adoration. He was besotted from the second she was born; Cynthia had never been able to fault his devotion as a father. Nor as a husband, really.

'I think she's wonderful, as always,' Cynthia murmurs.

Odette glares at her. 'Is that why you hardly ever call me?' she snaps. 'And now you think you can show up and be my mother again.'

Cynthia starts to protest, except that would suggest she thinks Odette has said something wrong – and she hasn't. She is trying to be Odette's mother again, because Odette still needs her; because everyone needs their mother even when they think they don't. But clearly she was foolish to think that sixteen years of being a mother could outweigh the past three years of barely being there for her daughter, no matter the reason.

'We're going to be grandparents.' Pat beams and nudges Cynthia, obviously trying to save the day. 'While we're still young enough to run around after the kid. Pretty good, right?'

Cynthia wants to ask Pat if he's ever anything less than cheerful, but now is not the time. Besides, she knows the answer: *rarely*. Looking on the bright side of life has been his credo for as long as she's known him and probably longer.

'Mum doesn't want me to have it,' Odette says, with another glare at Cynthia. 'I don't hear from you for weeks, then I call to tell you I'm pregnant and all you can do is ask me if it's too late to get rid of it.'

Cynthia blanches, because that's not exactly how the conversation went. And the reason she hadn't spoken to Odette for weeks was because she was spending all her energy trying to work out how to leave a rather terrifying man without her entire life imploding.

Pat frowns. 'What? I thought you'd be thrilled.'

'If you recall, Pat, I wasn't thrilled when I was pregnant at that age.'

'But look how it turned out!'

He gestures to their daughter and Cynthia can't disagree. She's also acutely aware that in wanting to tell Odette that she's too young, she's admitting the same thing about herself.

'It'll be fine,' Pat continues. 'She's got me, she's got your dad.' He glances at Cynthia. 'And you, if you're sticking around.'

Is she? Cynthia can't see beyond this week. Once she made the decision to leave her husband and LA, she could only think as far ahead as seeing Odette and her father. Waiting for the financial settlement of her divorce has put her in limbo, but that's only part of it. There's also the fact that she doesn't know where she belongs any more. She always thought she belonged with Odette and Odette with her, but that had changed three years ago. Of course, twenty years ago she thought she'd always belong with Pat. Life is change. That's all she knows now.

'I'll see,' is what she tells Pat.

'How's Fred?'

Pat has always called her father Fred even though his name is Wilfred and his friends call him Wilf. Her mother always used his full name.

'He's managing, I think.'

'I haven't seen him for a couple of weeks. Should pop round more often to check on him.' Another glance in her direction. 'If that's all right with you.'

Cynthia frowns. 'A couple of weeks?' She has imagined them not seeing each other for years. Neither of them has mentioned the other.

Now it's Pat's turn to frown. 'Yeah? We go fishing.' He looks away again. 'For ages now. Since . . .'

'Since we left, Mum,' Odette pipes up, sounding cheerful, as if she's forgotten that she's angry with Cynthia. 'They're mates.' She looks quite pleased about it. And there's no reason, really, why she shouldn't be.

'Oh,' is all Cynthia can manage as her idea of how her world has worked is dismantled.

'I've brought mussels,' says Pat, holding up a heavy plastic bag. 'Fred'll be happy. Is he here? We'll pull some lunch together.'

Pat heads inside the house without waiting for an answer, leaving Cynthia to stare at the back of Odette's head once more.

'We should talk,' she says, her voice tentative.

Odette sighs heavily. 'Not today, Mum.' She stands and walks towards Cynthia, who wonders what she's going to do.

'I missed you,' Odette says, biting her bottom lip. 'And I love you. But you can't make me change my mind. It's my body, Mum. It's my baby.'

Cynthia remembers a very similar conversation when she was Odette's age, standing in this very house, probably not too far from this spot. Her mother was sitting on the couch, her hands in fists, and her father was standing behind it, his arms folded.

Pat was next to her, with his arm around her waist, and she'd felt protected, safe – with him, and in the decision they'd made together to become parents.

'This is ridiculous,' her mother had said, her face twisting in a way Cynthia had never seen before.

'Why, Mum?' she'd said, feeling Pat's fingers squeezing her, comforting her.

'Because your whole life will be ruined!' Her mother was almost puce and Cynthia felt like she'd been slapped.

Distress was etched into her father's face too, but Cynthia didn't know if it was because of what her mother had said or because Cynthia wanted to make him a grandfather.

'So . . . having me and Kit ruined your life?' she said after a few seconds had passed.

Her mother huffed and tightened her fists. 'Not ruined.' Her eyes squeezed tightly shut then she opened them again. 'I wanted you both. But things were never the same.'

Cynthia remembered her mother needing time alone on weekends when she was young and she never knew why. Her brother Christopher, known as Kit, would take himself off 'exploring' and their mother liked that, but Cynthia wasn't allowed to do the same because she was a girl. Instead, her mother would tell her to stay in her room then she'd disappear for hours. Their father would be around sometimes, but mostly Cynthia was trusted to look after herself. It was no wonder, she realised years later, that she'd attached to Pat like a limpet when he'd made it clear that all he ever wanted was to be around her.

Now their daughter is giving Cynthia the opportunity to either be like her own mother or not. To be supportive or not – except Cynthia's definition of support is to encourage Odette to not limit her options. When Cynthia was Odette's age, *wife* and *mother* were the main paths a young woman could take. But Odette doesn't have to be constrained by that any more, and

Cynthia can't help wanting to remind her of that. So maybe she's not so different to her mother.

'I know it's your baby,' she says to Odette. 'But you're still *my* baby and I want what's best for you.'

Odette's eyes are hard again. 'That's why you married Max, is it?'

'Darling, that's –'

'Leave it, Mum,' she snaps.

'Cyn!' Pat calls. 'Mussels!'

Odette gives her one last glare then goes inside.

As Cynthia follows her she imagines, for a second, that she sees her mother sitting on the couch, her hands still in fists, and feels the cold chill of family history come over her.

APRIL 1987

BEACH FLAX LILY

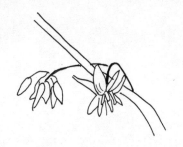

CHAPTER SEVEN

Another Sunday morning has come and gone without Elizabeth making it back to church, so when she hears a knock on the front door later in the day she takes a deep breath and prepares to explain herself to Reverend Willoughby.

'Who is it?' Charlie says from the sitting room floor where he's leafing through a picture book and giggling at the illustrations.

'I don't know, darling.' Elizabeth pushes herself off the couch and walks slowly towards the door. 'I'll find out.'

'Yoo-hoo!' comes a decidedly not-Reverend tone from outside.

Elizabeth frowns as she peers through the pane of clouded glass that is meant to let in light but really just stops her from clearly seeing who's on the other side of the door. She can make out two shapes, both female, one taller and darker-haired than the other. They seem harmless, so she opens the door but keeps her frown just in case she needs to ward off busybodies.

'Hello?' she says to a stocky-looking older woman of around five foot three wearing a T-shirt that says *Painters and Dockers*, and a slender woman a few inches taller, dark hair in a bun, pearls around her neck and a pale blue linen shirt rolled up to just below her elbows.

'Are you Elizabeth?' the shorter one says.

She guesses they're from the church – where else could they be from? – so she has no reason not to own up to being herself.

'Yes,' she replies.

'Great.' The shorter woman puts her foot across the threshold and Elizabeth, sensing that she'd be powerless to resist, steps back.

'I'm Shirley,' the woman says. 'Call me Shirl. Everyone does.' She jerks a thumb to the woman behind her. 'This is Barbara. Call her Barb. Everyone does.'

Barbara glides in after Shirley. 'Hello, dear,' she says. 'We're here about your garden.'

'Rev sent us,' Shirley explains.

'Who?' Elizabeth's forehead tightens and she realises she hasn't stopped frowning since she heard the knock, so she forces herself to relax.

'Rev Willoughby,' Shirl says with a snort. 'You know.'

'We're here for your garden,' Barbara says again.

Now it clicks: the reverend said he'd send someone to help her. There was no further discussion, though. No notice. No *warning*, which Elizabeth clearly needed since these two ladies have turned up meaning business and she doesn't even know them. She's not been comfortable with strangers lately; they require too much work by way of politeness and small talk and explanations about Jon's death.

'Rev gave me a ring,' Shirley says, putting her hands on her hips and glancing around the room. 'He said we should look in on Elizabeth who lives on Elizabeth Street. I said that would be easy to remember.' She grins.

It's been a while since Elizabeth has said her address to anyone. When Jon found the house he believed its location meant it was destined to be their home; he didn't reckon on his wife having to put up with jokes from almost everyone she gave her address to.

'Nice place,' Shirley continues. 'I knew the previous owners. Couple of blokes. They tricked it out. Chintz and whatnot. You're a bit more . . .' She nods slowly. 'Refined.'

'My husband's taste,' Elizabeth says.

The house is the way Jon wanted it, which is the way she wanted it. It's a dedication she made, to herself and to him, over the past couple of years.

Shirley's face drops. 'Sorry, pet. I didn't mean to bring him up.'

Elizabeth can tell Shirley knows all about Jon. All about his death, that is. Which means Barbara must too. For a second Elizabeth feels exposed, to think these strangers know something so personal. Then she feels relieved, because she doesn't have to break the news.

'You didn't,' she says. 'I did. But I don't . . .' She frowns again. 'I don't know what you can do about the garden.'

'Well . . . everything!' Barbara smiles and there is kindness and radiance in it.

'We're the Sunshine Gardening Society,' Shirley says, looking quite pleased about it.

'Sorry – the what?'

'We're a society of lady gardeners who give people a hand,' Shirley says. 'Been going on since the fifties. There's just the two of us at the moment so we're a bit flat out. When we heard about you, though, we decided to drop some of the other jobs. Temporarily, that is. This is a good project.'

Elizabeth thinks over what she's said. If this garden is a project – and she doesn't deny that it would be – they'd be here for a while and paying for gardeners isn't something she can contemplate. She doesn't have an income, and the payout from Jon's life insurance will barely cover her and Charlie's living expenses. Not even once she finds the job she's determined to get because she must: she can't live like this forever.

'Oh . . . I . . .' She swallows, trying to figure out how to say it without being rude.

'We're volunteers,' Barbara says, smiling again. 'Just in case you're wondering.'

'I . . . I was.' Elizabeth smiles weakly in return.

'We only work on weekends,' Shirley says. 'And since there's just the two of us it'll be slow. Unless . . .' She arches an eyebrow. 'You'd like to help us with it?'

'I don't garden,' Elizabeth says quickly.

Shirley chortles. 'I didn't either. Come on, let's see what we're dealing with.'

'Hi,' Charlie says, appearing at Elizabeth's side. He can be shy sometimes yet he's visibly curious about these strangers, his mouth open and eyes alight.

'Hello, young man,' Shirley says. 'I'm Shirl. Who are you?'

'Charlie.' He dips his head then grins, looking up from underneath his fringe.

'This is Barb.' Shirl nods towards her companion. 'Would you like to come to the garden too, Charlie?'

He nods, still grinning, and Shirley looks enquiringly at Elizabeth.

'Through here.' Elizabeth leads them towards the kitchen, which has glass doors instead of a wall looking out onto the garden.

Shirley whistles. 'She's a big 'un.' She glances at Barbara, who is smiling enigmatically.

'What a treat,' Barbara says. She holds out her arms in a slight V. 'It's been beautifully organised.'

Elizabeth looks and sees only mess.

'Was it like this when you moved in?' Barbara goes on.

'No. It was a jungle then. My husband . . .' Elizabeth's voice catches as she remembers the glee on Jon's face when he saw it, his excitement as he told her everything he could do with such a great big plot of land. 'My husband cut that all back then designed the garden he wanted. He was out here a lot.' She smiles but it's brief, because while the memories of Jon bring her joy, the remembrance of his absence means it's short-lived. 'He was sick for a couple of years. It became harder to look after it. And I . . .' She shrugs limply.

Shirley puts a hand on Elizabeth's shoulder. 'You were looking after him.' She nods at Charlie. 'And him.' Now she's patting slowly. 'Not so much yourself, though.' It isn't a question.

'Now, why don't you tell us about the garden?' Shirley prompts.

Elizabeth gazes at Jon's great project, then slides open one of the glass doors so they can all go outside.

There are steps leading from the kitchen down to a patio, and beyond it is a lawn, mostly weeds now, with two long rectangular garden beds on each side and a shorter bed at the far end. She knows the names of the plants, because Jon would tell her: mandevillas, begonias, gardenias, gerberas, pansies and petunias, hydrangeas, hibiscus, zinnias. Colourful plants, meant to bloom together and create something beautiful. Jasmine climbs up the fence to her left, bougainvillea in the back corners, and down the right a row of camellias provides privacy from the street, as there's only a low fence. Where the camellias end there's a gate, then another length of fence before another gate, which leads to the entrance of the house. Incongruously, a gum tree stands against the fence, a relic of whatever this land looked like before. Of all the plants and trees in this garden, only the gum is in good shape.

'Jon loved colour,' Elizabeth says. 'Everywhere. Paintings on the walls, bright curtains. So he wanted a garden with lots of colour.'

'That explains the pansies and those pink hibiscus,' says Shirley. She squints. 'And what are those – zinnias?'

Elizabeth nods.

'This will look spectacular,' Barbara breathes, 'with some TLC and time.' She catches Elizabeth's eye. 'With your permission, of course. We will only return if you want us here.'

There'd been days when Jon was so weak he could barely make it to the bathroom but he still wanted to be in this garden. He'd try to pick up the hose or the watering can and Elizabeth would pretend that he was strong enough to keep the garden alive.

She'd tell herself that it was a sign he was improving, even though she knew that was impossible. This garden represents all of Jon's hopes and ambitions and also his decline. She feels so conflicted about it she can hardly bear to look at it, yet she knows that the last thing she can do for him – her last way to love him – is to take care of it, if only to show Charlie that she won't give up on something his father wanted. And so that Charlie can have this garden to remember him by.

Yet it's such a big task. Too big, perhaps, even with help. These last few years have taken so much from her and she's not sure if she has the wherewithal to rebuild this garden as well as her own life.

'I can't ask you to do that,' she says, offering these kindly women an easy way out.

'You're not,' Shirley says, looking amused. 'We're forcing it on you. Rev's orders.'

'How do you know him?' Elizabeth says. It didn't occur to her to ask before.

'He was very good to me,' Barbara says, 'when my son died.' She looks at Elizabeth meaningfully.

Elizabeth goes to say *I'm sorry* then stops herself, because Barbara will know, as she does, that it doesn't need to be said. They understand each other.

'Far be it from me,' Elizabeth says instead, 'to go against the reverend.'

She glances at Charlie, who looks quite pleased as he skips around the patio.

'So we'll see you Saturday,' Shirley says gleefully. 'Goody – I love a big project. And Barb's a whiz at garden design. She'll know exactly what's going on here. See ya, Charlie!'

Shirley is back up into the house before Elizabeth knows what's going on.

Barbara squeezes Elizabeth's arm and follows her. 'Don't worry,' she says over her shoulder, 'we'll bring everything we need.'

As the front door closes behind them Elizabeth stands in the doorway between the kitchen and the sitting room, looking at it. She doesn't know what to make of what just happened, or whether to thank the reverend or chastise him for it.

When she feels a breeze at the back of her neck, though, she wonders if it's Jon, reminding her to accept help, the way he did in those last days. That breeze finds her in all rooms of the house, even with all the doors closed. It's one of the mysteries of her life after his death. That and the way he visits her in dreams, holding out single-stemmed flowers, smiling, healthy. She never had those dreams when he was alive.

'Charlie!' she calls, although he could be deep in the garden by now. Sometimes she finds him sitting on the stone seat down the far end, talking to the air. Or to his father. He has told her more than once that Daddy is in the garden.

When she hears no movement she walks back to the kitchen and, looking out, sees him on the bench, cross-legged, smiling to himself, and decides to leave him there.

CHAPTER EIGHT

Oh, this is awkward. Waiting to see your former best friend who you haven't seen in yonks. It feels like waiting for a first date. No – like waiting to give birth.

Giving birth was not an experience Lorraine enjoyed. 'Just go with it,' the midwife had said to her when the contractions really kicked in. *You go with it!* Lorraine had wanted to yell back. *You go with it right out the door and take the bloody contractions with you, and the baby too while you're at it!* By that stage Lorraine had realised it was too late to change her mind about having a baby, and while she didn't regret it she had really, really wished she could come back and do the birth thing some other time. Or have someone else do it for her. And the worst bit was that by the time she got pregnant with Simon she'd forgotten how bad the first birth had been and she got to do it all over again.

'Get you anything?' says the waitress in this little coffee shop in an unremarkable shopping area near the Ken Rosewall Tennis Centre courts on Hastings Street. Not that long ago you would have been able to see the river from the street. It was one of the features of the place: beach on one side of Hastings, river on the other. When she was a kid there were people living in tents on this side of the street, right next to the river. Looking back, she can't believe it happened, because imagine it! Just living here, on one of the best pieces of land in the country, in a tent! She also remembers the bull that someone up on the hill owned. Big fella. Used to take up a position in the middle of the street and intimidate people into not passing by. That was the pitfall of living in a tent: no protection against the bull.

The tents are long gone now, as are most of the original buildings, and these days the beach side of the street has apartment buildings no more than three storeys high and the river side has the courts and some shops, and it's not so easy to turn your head one way to see still water and another to see waves.

The waitress is giving her a look, which is how Lorraine knows she's let her mind wander off.

'When my friend gets here, thanks,' she replies finally. Her friend. It just slipped out. Who knows if they'll be that again.

It was her mother who had urged her to call Cynthia after a few days. Rose had always liked Cynthia and used to say she was good for Lorraine because she did her homework on time and didn't get detention, unlike Lorraine's other friends.

'I'm sure she has a valid reason for not writing back,' Rose said. 'She was always so correct about things.'

By that Rose meant that Cynthia wrote thank-you notes and always cleaned up after herself when she visited. Normally Lorraine couldn't stand goody-two-shoes but Cynthia wasn't one of those, not really – she just liked to cause a minimum of fuss, she said once. If she did things properly there was no fuss. *No fun either* was what Lorraine always wanted to say, but she didn't because she really did love Cynthia and knew she was lucky to have a friend who would put up with her being a bit hopeless about time and deadlines and things like that. There was just so much to do, wasn't there? People to chat to, trees to look at – Lorraine could get distracted by anything if you gave her a chance. The teachers used to say she was a daydreamer. Well, that stopped as soon as she had Terry. Can't daydream with a baby because they need you too much and they die if you don't take care of them properly.

'Lorraine?'

She blinks herself back to the present and looks up to see Cynthia standing with the sun behind her and a nervous smile.

And she should be nervous: Lorraine hasn't forgiven her, not by a long way. Cynthia is going to have to come up with some serious grovelling if that's to change. Rose might have talked her into meeting up but that's only the first step. Because the truth is Lorraine's been feeling abandoned by the person who's known her the longest outside of her family.

She squints into the light. 'What happened to your hair?'

Probably not the sort of hello Cynthia was expecting but what else do you say to someone when you haven't seen them for years and you don't want to be too friendly because you want them to work for it?

Cynthia's smile falters. 'I cut it.'

'I can see that.' Lorraine stands. 'But you've always had it long.'

More faltering. Uncertainty. Cynthia's eyes half-close then open. 'Um . . . hello? Maybe we could start there.'

'Oh. Yeah.' Even if she's trying to make Cynthia work for it there's no need to completely forget her manners. 'Hello.'

They stand looking at each other, and it's only now that Lorraine thinks Cynthia could have made any number of remarks about how *she* looks – wider, saggier, her dark brown hair streaked with grey, bags under her eyes, and she's not even forty yet. Those kids are sapping the life out of her. Them and her mother-in-law and life in general. Why is there always so much to do? This afternoon she has to go over the books for Mike's business, and tomorrow she has to help him out by mowing some lawns because he's double-booked himself and Mr Someone from Eumundi needs a gutter cleaned. Odd jobs, that's Mike's trade, and he's good at it. Too good, given the amount of work. At least they're not worrying about money. Just time. There's never enough of that.

Cynthia smiles, and it's one of those sad smiles people have when they're about to say something you won't like or that they'll regret. That's how it always is in the movies, anyway. Lorraine doesn't smile sadly at people. Come to think of it, she doesn't smile much at all. Too busy to smile. Or maybe she doesn't feel like it. She hasn't stopped to figure that out.

'I've really missed you,' Cynthia says, and she squeezes Lorraine's forearm.

'Is that why you stopped writing?' Lorraine snaps.

Oh, that was mean. She knew it as she was saying it. So why did she say it? No need to be so short with Cynthia just because she's not ready to be best friends again. Yet. She's tired, that's it. No filter when she's tired. Mike always says: *You should take a breath before you speak, darl.* To his credit, he cops her barbs at him on the chin; it's the things she says to other people that he warns her about. She should take more care, she knows that. Before her life got so busy she used to be nicer. Or maybe not nicer. Kinder. More considerate.

'Yes,' Cynthia says, and her chin lifts a little. 'Actually, it was.'

Lorraine frowns. 'That makes no sense.'

'Shall we sit?' Cynthia gestures to the table.

Lorraine nods and sits heavily.

'Every letter from you reminded me of what I'd left,' Cynthia says softly. 'And I couldn't afford to doubt that I'd made the right decision. I'd put all my eggs in that basket and . . .' She looks away and shrugs, then smiles ruefully. 'They were getting scrambled. It was easier to try to forget that you were here and I couldn't see you. I thought if I stopped writing you'd eventually stop too.'

'It worked,' Lorraine says, then huffs. 'You duffer.'

Cynthia's eyes widen. 'Duffer? Me?'

'Yeah.' Lorraine tries smiling. It doesn't feel so bad. 'So . . . it wasn't the right decision, I'm guessing? Given you're back.' No point pussyfooting around it.

'It was for a while.' Cynthia gazes towards the river and sighs. 'Until I met my second husband. Max. I think I'd stopped writing to you by then so you wouldn't know his name.'

Lorraine shakes her head: no, she didn't know it. Wilfred has never mentioned it.

'He was wonderful,' Cynthia says. 'Charming. Good-looking in that film-industry way.'

Having no idea what that means, Lorraine frowns.

'Tan, teeth, layered hair,' Cynthia explains. 'His teeth cost more than his car.' She laughs bitterly.

'So . . . what? Too charming in the end?'

It's a risky thing to say – maybe even a little mean – but if Cynthia's going to tell some sob story about how her life just wasn't perfect enough so she left it, Lorraine's going to jump into the river. Or push Cynthia into it.

'Too violent,' Cynthia says, and it's so blunt – so *there* – that Lorraine gasps.

'What?' she says. 'With you?'

Cynthia nods, tight-lipped. 'It's why Odette left. She couldn't bear it any more. Nor could I, but . . .' Another faraway gaze. 'It can be hard to leave when your friends are all the same people and everyone thinks he's just such a good guy.'

As Cynthia looks back Lorraine sees no sadness in her eyes, only strength, and she remembers anew that this is the woman who stood up to her own mother when she was pregnant, who insisted that everything would work out. Which it did. Until it didn't.

'So it's taken me this long to get away from him,' Cynthia says. 'I could have walked away with nothing – that would have made it quicker. But his life – his work – was made better because I was in it. All those parties I put on, all those wives I socialised with just so he could make his connections.'

Her nostrils flare. 'He fought me for a while. Trying to make me stay, actually. His line was that if I just stayed I wouldn't have to leave with nothing. But I never intended to leave with nothing, because I deserved something.' Another flare. 'I deserved *everything*, especially after what he put me through.'

Lorraine nods, and feels both a mild thrill that her friend was so feisty and sadness that Cynthia didn't trust her with any of this.

'So how did you get away in the end?' she asks.

'Luckily he met someone else.' Cynthia laughs again and it's hard-edged. 'Not lucky for her, because who knows what he's doing to her. But lucky for me. She wanted to marry him and have his babies, he said, so suddenly he wanted the divorce done quickly.'

She sighs again, although this time it sounds like she's letting go of dead air.

Lorraine considers what to say next.

'You could have just told me what was going on.' She nudges Cynthia. 'We were *mates*, Cyn. We told each other everything.'

She remembers their late-night confessionals during high-school sleepovers, Cynthia's brother yelling at them to shut up, the two of them sneaking out into the garden on warm evenings to sit under the giant palm tree and gossip about boys and teachers.

'I would have understood,' she continues. 'Whatever you were going through, you could have told me. Maybe I could even have helped. I swear, if Mike had heard about this he'd have been on a plane so fast to get you out of there.'

A few years ago Mike had learnt that one of his best mates was beating up his wife. He was round there like a shot, telling the bloke he was going to call the cops and the wife that she could come and stay. The couple are still married but as far as anyone knows he isn't hurting her any more.

Cynthia smiles. 'I'd have liked to see that.'

'Yeah, well . . . the offer's always open.'

'Thank you.' Cynthia swallows. 'Anyway, that's the past. I can't dwell on how many times I failed to get away from him.' Her laugh is tight, forced. 'I'll drive myself mad if I do that.'

Lorraine nods slowly. 'Yeah, I guess so.' She sits back and crosses her arms, as she likes to do when she's pondering something. 'So, what do we do now? Do we just become friends again?'

'Do you . . .' Cynthia raises her eyebrows. 'Want to? I'd understand if you don't. It's fine. Honestly.'

'Hold your horses, princess.' Lorraine cocks an eyebrow of her own.

She used to call Cynthia *princess* at school, because the boys used to treat her like she was one. But there was never any jealousy between them, about anything. Lorraine always loved and admired her friend, and she knew Cynthia felt the same about her.

'We need some rules,' Lorraine goes on. 'Don't cut me out ever again.'

'Agreed.'

'Don't think I won't understand what you're going through, because I probably will.'

'Okay.'

'Right.' Lorraine nods once. 'Sure, let's be friends again. I've never had another friend like you. I think I'd like having you back.'

'Really?' Cynthia looks like she may cry, and Lorraine feels vaguely flattered.

She grins. 'Yep.' Ah, that's where her smile was all this time: waiting for a friend. 'Just don't take off overseas again because I might get used to having you around.'

Cynthia's face clouds briefly. 'I . . . I don't know if I'm staying.'

'Sure you are.' Lorraine nods again, like she's decided the matter. 'This is where you belong.'

'Maybe.' Now Cynthia smiles. 'Thank you.'

'No need to thank me. Now – are you eating? I could do with a cheese toastie.'

Cynthia laughs breezily and Lorraine remembers that sound from when they were carefree.

'Me too,' Cynthia says.

And they spend the next few minutes deciding whether to have ham or tomato on their toastie, and the minutes after that working out when they can catch up again, and finally Lorraine feels like she'll have something to look forward to that can keep her going through the flurry of her life.

CHAPTER NINE

'That was a good day today, Kathy.' Hans smiles down at her, slightly stooped.

Kathy always wants to tell him to stand up straight. That's what she's told her son for years. Once Grant hit puberty and shot up above his classmates he started stooping, like he was apologising for being taller than them. Kathy – all of five foot four – wanted to say that *some people* would give an eye tooth to be tall, so Grant should embrace it. Instead she told him to stand up straight, put his shoulders back, let people talk up to him. It didn't work. He's twenty-eight now and the stoop is part of who he is. Maybe it's not too late for Hans, though; she could start working on him. Once she knows him a little better.

'Yes, it was.' She smiles. 'I love it when it's busy.'

Hans nods vigorously. 'Many happy customers. That makes *me* happy.'

Kathy runs a hand through her hair, some of which has escaped from her tight ponytail. No matter how careful she is about slicking it back, strands make their way out of the elastic. She hopes she hasn't looked too messy; her standards have always been high when it comes to how she presents on the job. Then she yawns. One of those yawns that come upon a person with little notice and make them look rude.

'Ooh, sorry,' she says, clamping a hand over her mouth. 'Guess I'm more tired than I thought.'

'Please, go home,' Hans says. It sounds abrupt but his face is soft.

Kathy is getting used to how clipped he can be when interacting with staff, and she knows it's just his manner.

'Rightio,' she says and walks towards the broom cupboard where the staff keep their bags.

'What are you doing tonight?' Hans says as he sorts the receipts at his desk.

She shrugs. 'Dinner. Telly. Nothing much.'

He glances up. 'Alone?'

She pauses. He's not yet asked about her personal life, nor has she about his. Have they been working together long enough for them to become familiar? Or even on the way to being friends? She likes him; they get along. They could be friends. Certainly she should make some friends here. But friendship means trading information and there are some things she still needs to hold on to. She has no intention of lying to him, though.

'Yes,' she says. Then thinks she may as well return the favour. 'You?'

His eyelids flutter and he looks a little abashed. 'Yes. But that is for the better – I have more to do here, then I think I will fall asleep straightaway.'

Adjusting her handbag to a more comfortable spot on her shoulder, Kathy smiles. 'See you tomorrow.'

'Wait! I forgot.' Hans turns in the direction of the kitchen as Kathy does as instructed. She knows what he's doing; he's taken to doing it every afternoon.

'Here.' He returns, triumphant, with two takeaway containers. 'Chef put some food aside for you.'

'Now, Hans, I'm sure that's because *you* asked him to do that.'

'Better than it goes to waste,' he says matter-of-factly.

Kathy hasn't yet worked out why he's so kind to her but she suspects it's because she reminds him of his mother or something. She can only hope that Grant is as gracious to older women.

'Thank you,' she says, holding the containers aloft like trophies before she tucks them into her voluminous bag and heads for her car, parked two streets away where all the staff park.

The drive home to her little house in Noosa Junction is quick. Every drive around here is quick. Melbourne, with its criss-crossing roads and spread-out suburbs, seems like the most difficult place in the world compared with the Sunshine Coast, where if something is a ten-minute drive away everyone thinks it's a major inconvenience.

Walking to the front door Kathy notes, again, that the bushes in the front garden need watering. They never seem to get much rain so they require extra attention, but she's just not in the habit of it yet. Same with the back garden. It's not as if either garden is huge, so it wouldn't take her long to water. She just has to remember to do it. And she doesn't want to do it now, when she's tired.

So instead she goes inside and walks to the kitchen and puts the food in the fridge. Osso bucco and mashed potato by the look of it. She'll enjoy that tonight.

First, though, she's going to have a drink. It may be only 4 p.m. but she's been on her feet for hours and she deserves a little treat. Even if she knows that starting at four means she'll be drinking for longer than she should. One glass of wine turns into half a bottle. Sometimes almost a whole bottle. Or that's how it seems to go. Not every day. Some days. Most days, if she's honest.

She's made the excuse to herself that she needs the comfort, because she's on her own and everyone needs something, don't they? The danger is in the fact that it's threatening to move beyond comfort to companionship, and that's because she hasn't made any friends here. If she had somewhere to be at night she wouldn't be drinking. She's just so *bored* of herself and wine makes her less bored. And boring.

After two large glasses, and with the osso bucco warming in the oven, she does what she usually does at this point in the bottle: she pulls out her most recent photo album. She has a few albums with photos of Grant and his sister, Michelle. Older albums feature their father, Owen. But none of them appears in this newer album. It's reserved for Jemima. Or Jem, as she liked to be called, except Kathy always preferred her full name. It sounded so lovely.

It was the shock of Kathy's life when she fell for Jemima. There she was, married thirty years, fond of Owen and he of her. They were companions; that's how she learnt the habit of not being alone. They liked to go rock'n'roll dancing from time to time, and to the pub on Sundays. He liked the cricket, and she could tolerate it. She liked the tennis, and he didn't mind it. Their older middle age was nice. They had made plans for retirement, when it came.

Then Jemima started working at the restaurant Kathy was managing and from the moment they met Kathy knew she was in trouble. The way Jemima smiled at her – it made her feel something she hadn't felt ever. Giddy. *Lovestruck*. She used to think that was a ridiculous term. Only teenagers get lovestruck, and when she was a teenager the boys hadn't impressed her enough for that. It was only once she met Jemima that she realised why that might have been the case.

Jemima was younger than her by twenty years and infinitely cooler. She had a sharp haircut and clothes that looked like she spent time thinking about what she wore but not so much time that it was a preoccupation. And she was fun. She laughed a lot and Kathy laughed with her.

It took all of Kathy's self-control to not let on that she was attracted to Jemima, that she thought about her all the time when they weren't together, and that when they were in the same place at the same time all she wanted to do was gaze at her. Not because she was worried about what it meant – it felt so *normal* in some ways that Kathy couldn't believe she hadn't worked out before that she wasn't really attracted to men. But first of all because Jemima was so much younger and she knew it was ridiculous to even think romantically about someone that age; also because she was Jemima's manager; plus she had no idea if Jemima was attracted to women herself. Or, if she were, that she'd ever consider Kathy as a prospect. Kathy had never considered herself as any kind of prospect, not even when Owen asked her to marry him.

One night she and Jemima were both closing up and Kathy had told Jemima she could go home, she didn't have to stay.

'What if I want to?' Jemima had said, stepping a little closer to Kathy, who had the credit-card receipts in one hand and half a glass of wine in the other. A little tipple while closing up had been her ritual for a while.

'Um,' Kathy had said, because what else *could* she say? She was flustered, with Jemima standing next to her, looking at her with those big brown eyes, smelling of some perfume Kathy couldn't identify because she wasn't the perfume-wearing kind herself, but it was rich and slightly cloying and to this day when Kathy smells it on some other woman she can remember how she felt as Jemima took the receipts and the wine out of her hands, put them on the table, and kissed her.

Thrilled. That's how she felt. And relieved. Because Jemima liked her back.

Or that's what Kathy thought at the time. Because after she left Owen and moved in with Jemima, after they had several glorious months together and Kathy felt like the world was brighter and wider than she could ever have imagined, Jemima left her for someone else. Someone around her own age. And Kathy never knew if Jemima had ever cared for her, or if she was just a way station while Jemima looked for the person she really wanted to be with.

That's when Kathy fled north, driving from Melbourne to Noosa, crying most of the way. Somewhere past Tenterfield she realised that perhaps it didn't matter if Jemima had never loved her back, because the way Kathy felt was all she could ever know, and that was all that was important. She loved Jemima; she loves her still. That is what she knows to be true, and that's what she can hang on to.

It doesn't comfort her, though. At night, after work, when she's at home alone, trying to focus on a book or do a crossword, trying to not think about Jemima and how much she loves her, there's no comfort.

That's another reason why she's been drinking. Wine lulls her into thinking that everything's all right. She knows it's a falsehood; she knows that in the morning it won't be all right. But, oh, she gets those few hours of forgetting and right now that's what keeps her going. That and the idea that maybe, one day, she won't need to forget any more and Jemima will be just a nice memory.

It's a good dream. She'll wait to see if it becomes real.

CHAPTER TEN

'When did you move here?' Cynthia says, squinting out through French doors at Von's neat back garden.

Von walks slowly towards her, using a cane. When Cynthia left Australia Von was upright and strong; so was her father. Now both of them take longer to move around and enjoy it less. Old age is no fun, Cynthia has decided.

She can see pigface and beach flax lily in the garden beds. Her mother used to grow the same flowers, always a fan of natives and less fond of flowers from the northern hemisphere. 'Not our kind,' she would say whenever Cynthia asked why there were no camellias or azaleas or roses in their large garden.

On a trellis by Von's side fence there are tomato and passionfruit vines, and a bird bath next to a garden seat. The whole thing looks like a lovely haven. The house itself has the same feeling to it: a small weatherboard cottage painted white, with white interior walls and cane furniture, books and lamps and cut flowers in vases.

'Six years ago,' Von says, putting one hand on Cynthia's shoulder when she arrives. 'The children thought I should have a smaller place. Never thought I'd live in Tewantin.' She shrugs. 'But it'll see me out.'

'Nonsense!' Cynthia chides. 'You're not going anywhere.'

Von smiles wryly, her eyes almost disappearing inside folds of skin that she's had as long as Cynthia has known her but which have grown more pronounced. 'I will eventually,' she says. 'We all do.'

'I suppose so.'

'No suppose about it. Death is our only certainty.'

Von moves towards the couch.

'I don't remember you being this gloomy,' Cynthia says as they both sit.

'That's not gloom! It's fact.' Von sighs as she manoeuvres herself deeper into the cushions.

Cynthia nods towards the upright piano in the corner of the room. 'Are you still playing regularly?'

Von was her piano teacher from the age of six, and even when Cynthia decided it was no longer cool to play she still came to see Von, in her old house with her dead husband's paintings all over the walls and her ferocious cats. The cats are long gone, and so are the paintings, it seems. Perhaps Von's children, Bede and Audrey, have claimed their inheritance early.

'Of course. Are you?' But the look Von gives her shows she already knows the answer.

'I haven't had time.'

Von raises her eyebrows. 'We can all make time for the things that are important.'

'I guess that's true.' Cynthia looks out to the garden again and sees a brush turkey slowly plodding across the lawn. 'You have a visitor,' she says.

Von cranes her neck in response. 'Oh yes, they love scratching up my garden when it's nesting time,' she says with irritation. 'I've tried everything to get rid of them. But they were here first, so I understand why they're so tenacious.'

Cynthia smiles. 'You're fairly tenacious too.'

'This is true.' Von props her cane against the couch. 'Now, what's going on?'

'What do you mean?' Although Cynthia knows Von can read her easily, she doesn't want to give in that quickly.

Von waves a hand. 'I know you're happy to see me and you wanted to visit to say hello, et cetera, but since the second you walked in you've looked like there's something you want to say and you're not sure how to say it.'

'Do you think I'll be that perceptive when I'm as old as you?' Cynthia teases. They've never taken each other too seriously.

'Watch it.' Von picks up the cane and shakes it in Cynthia's direction. 'These days I come with weapons.'

Cynthia laughs, relieved that their dynamic hasn't changed, then she presses her lips together in a determined line, ready to make her confession.

'My daughter is barely speaking to me,' she says.

'Oh, you too,' Von says, her eyes twinkling.

'What do you mean?'

'Your daughter is a teenager, Cynthia. It's her *job* to not speak to you.'

'A *pregnant* teenager,' Cynthia mutters.

If there's a flicker of surprise on Von's face, Cynthia fails to catch it.

'Oh, her too,' Von says quietly.

Cynthia's mouth drops open. 'Von!'

'Hm – what?'

'That's not very nice!'

'But it's the truth.' Von shrugs. 'One hesitates to say, "Like mother, like daughter . . . "' Her eyes twinkle again. 'I'm teasing. But you have to admit it's a little bit funny.'

'No, I don't. It's outrageous.'

'And yet when your parents had this same reaction to you, I recall that you were very upset.'

It seems like no time has passed since Cynthia told Von she was pregnant, knowing that of all the adults in her life Von was bound to be the one not to judge. Von had eloped with her husband when neither of their sets of parents approved of their match; they'd moved to Queensland, far from their entrenched social circles in Melbourne, and pursued a life of art and music. Von was a bohemian before Cynthia even knew what the word was, and she was fierce in her approval of people who did things outside the norm. *That's where the fun is*, she'd said to Cynthia once. *That's where life's rules are tested and changed, and how we create beauty and invoke joy.* Cynthia has tried to be as audacious in her own life but she knows she fell back into conventions: marry the man with the good career, have the properly cared-for house, look a certain way, be a certain kind of person. Not that it brought her contentment, or peace. Instead it's brought her back here.

Yet she named her daughter after a swan princess because she loved *Swan Lake* so much as a child. Her life had once been full of art and music – before she'd decided that to fit in with everyone else it needed to be about the beach and boys – and she had wished that for Odette as well. How can she be so surprised, then, when Odette has decided to live up to her namesake and free herself from what she perceives as restrictions on her life?

'Still, that was different – that was *me*. I should be allowed to have other rules for my daughter.'

Cynthia knows she's on a losing wicket with this argument, but she also knows she's applying a double standard to Odette and feels the need to justify it. To herself, if not to anyone else.

Von nods slowly. 'Yes, I tried that. That's why Audrey stopped speaking to me. But we're fine now. And you and Odette will be too.'

'I can't imagine you not approving of one of your children.'

Audrey and Bede were grown-ups by the time Cynthia met Von, both strong-willed and making their ways in the world but staying in close contact with their mother even as they flitted around Australia and other countries.

'It was a silly thing.' Another wave of the hand. 'As I said, we're fine now.'

'How did you manage it?' Cynthia says.

'I realised I needed to focus less on myself and more on everyone and everything around me, which helped to put matters into perspective. My daughter's life was her business, and it always will be, and my concerns were trifling in the scheme of things.'

Cynthia knows that what Von says is true: Odette's life is her own business. Yet she can't help wanting to tell her to think carefully about what she's doing, to weigh up all the factors. But then what if she decides to do the very thing Cynthia believes is wrong?

No one told her that parenting would involve conundrums. She thought it would be cute smiles and toddler giggles and some parent–teacher nights she didn't want to attend.

She feels Von patting her hand. 'I've lost count of how many times you've wandered off since you arrived,' Von says.

'I'm so sorry!' Cynthia shakes her head, trying to get herself back in the present. 'It's just . . .'

She breathes in, and it sounds ragged because she wants to cry. Here, in the secure presence of a woman who has loved her for decades, she feels something inside her letting go.

Another pat on her hand. 'Out with it.'

'I've been calling her every day. Several times a day. I saw her once the other day and she was civil to me but now she won't call me back. All I said was that I don't even know who she's pregnant *to* and I want to meet him. How did it come to this point, that I don't know something as important as *that*?'

'Because Odette is a woman,' Von says firmly. 'And as much as you may want to know details about her life, she doesn't have to share them.'

'But –' Cynthia stops, and that ragged breath turns into half a sob.

This time Von takes her hand and squeezes it. 'Have you stopped to consider that maybe she doesn't want you to meet him – and that might be more to do with him than you?'

No, Cynthia hasn't considered this, because even if that were the case shouldn't Odette tell her anyway?

'You're not going to solve this by thinking about it, or even talking about it,' Von continues. 'I think you need a distraction. A hobby.'

Cynthia blinks. 'A hobby?' She's not a person given to hobbies, a term which, as far as she's concerned, denotes crochet, pottery and life-drawing classes, none of which has ever interested her.

'Yes. Or something more like a project, perhaps. Something you can focus on.' Von pauses. 'I know just the thing.'

She takes hold of her cane and pushes herself off the couch.

Cynthia wants to help her but she also doesn't want to offend her – Von is a proud woman and she may not like Cynthia implying that she is in need of assistance. So Cynthia watches as Von walks over to the dresser placed between two windows and yanks open a drawer. She extracts an old scrapbook and tucks it under her arm before making her way back to the couch and sitting heavily.

'Here.' Von proffers the scrapbook and Cynthia takes it, opening it to the first page and some clippings from *The Noosa News* dated 1969 and 1975. She turns the next pages over and sees photographs, some with Von in them, all of them showing women wearing gardening gloves and big smiles.

'What's this?' she says.

Von smiles proudly. 'The Sunshine Gardening Society.'

'I have no idea what that is.' But Cynthia wonders why not, when clearly it was something Von was involved with for years.

Von gives her a funny look. 'I was one of the founders. In, ooh . . .' She scrunches up her eyes. 'Nineteen fifty-four. We were a small group. Mothers. Our children were in the same year at the primary school, and our husbands . . .' Her smile is sad. 'I was lucky with mine but the war did him no favours. Some of the other women had a terrible time. Those men – they were damaged, but they wouldn't speak of it.' She shifts her cane further along the couch. 'We needed something positive to do. And we wanted *beauty*. Do you know what I mean?'

Cynthia isn't sure she does – not in the way Von seems to mean it.

'We all need beauty and passion in our lives, don't we?' Von is animated now, sitting a little further forwards. 'Otherwise why are we *here*, Cynthia? What is the purpose of it all?' She doesn't appear to want an answer.

'Some of us got talking. We liked gardens but we couldn't grow anything we wanted to. This climate,' she gestures towards the French doors, 'isn't conducive to several types of plant. Or flower. So we swapped tips about how to grow things. Then we started hearing about the occasional person who needed a hand with their own gardens. The elderly.' She snorts. 'Probably younger than I am now. Or a young mother who had her hands full. We thought we could do some good.' She gestures to the scrapbook. 'So we became the Sunshine Gardening Society. And it's not what you think – one of the founders lived in Sunshine Beach. Just as well, or we might have been the Peregian Gardening Society, which doesn't quite have the same ring to it. And we quietly went about our business, helping out locals, then the council. We were quite the thing.'

'I . . .' Cynthia smiles weakly. 'I had no idea. How can I not know this about you?'

Von gives her that funny look again. 'But your mother was in it,' she says. 'That's how we met. She joined after I'd been in it for a while. We were happy to have her. She was younger than the rest of us, and she was passionate about native plants when none of us knew much about them.'

This revelation makes Cynthia's stomach drop. Her mother? In a group with Von? How could she not know *that* too?

'I can see you're confused,' Von says. 'Diane never told you, clearly.'

Cynthia shakes her head.

When Cynthia was a teenager and spent most of her weekends on the beach, her mother would occasionally insist that they go for a walk, just the two of them, into the bush on the Noosa headland, where she'd point out native trees and flowers. Cynthia barely paid attention – partly because anything her mother was interested in was inherently nothing she liked. Moreover, it wasn't really the sort of information her adolescent brain wished to take in. But she wishes now she had.

She wishes too that she had come back more than once when her mother was sick, instead of being wrapped up in her Los Angeles life. She was trying to polish the veneer of her existence, going to parties, being bright and sparkly and winsome, letting everyone think she was fabulous and charmed. It was a shallow existence, and meanwhile the substance of her life was here. As Odette seemed to have detected on her own, right before she moved back. At least Odette had been close by as her grandmother ailed. Cynthia had let them both down. Except no one had told her how sick Diane really was. When she called – infrequently, yes, but often enough to make it clear she wanted a report – her father said her mother was 'fine, just fine'. The last time he said that was a week before she died.

'But you probably never *asked*, dear,' Von says. 'We mothers like to have our secrets – as I'm sure you know – but we get away with so many of them because no one ever *asks* what we get up to in a day. When your children and your husband think you're just their servant, they overlook you.'

'I didn't –'

'You did,' Von says firmly. 'We *all* did. We take them for granted, our mothers. But they were people too. You and I are people too, are we not?'

Regret grabs hold of Cynthia again. She never spent the time she should have with her mother. Now, there might be a way to redress that.

'So you think I should join this Sunshine Gardening Society?'

Von nods. 'I do. And I can put in a word. They need members. Everyone's so busy these days. No time to help anyone else.'

'You're not a member any more?'

Von gestures to the stick. 'Not for a while. But I know what's going on.'

Cynthia laughs. 'I would never suspect otherwise.'

Von shuffles to the edge of the couch. 'Come on – I'll show you my garden. Get you used to the idea.' She looks up as Cynthia stands. 'Because mine is one of the gardens you'll be working on.'

Cynthia laughs again. 'Ah – an ulterior motive.'

This time she gives in to her impulse to help and offers her hand to Von, who takes it and hauls herself to standing.

'Always,' Von says, squeezing her hand, 'and never.'

Cynthia keeps hold of her old friend as she leads the way to the French doors and out into the sunshine.

CHAPTER ELEVEN

The first day Shirley and Barbara arrived to work in Jon's garden, Elizabeth thought she may explode with worry. She was grateful for the help, yet the second Shirl brandished her trowel Elizabeth felt a weight of responsibility for ensuring that the garden be taken care of the way Jon would do it, if he were here.

Not to mention that she would be spending time in the company of strangers. She's never been one to be overly familiar. Or casual. She's always been slow to make friends and slower still to lose them – or so she thought. Jon's death appears to have swept a few of them away on a tide of not wanting to witness her grief. So instead of friends in the garden there were strangers, prodding the dirt with tools and pulling at branches, and she wanted to yell at them and say it was like they were poking and prodding Jon – except she knew she was being melodramatic, even if it was just in her own head.

That first day Elizabeth mainly watched and tried to catch whatever it was Shirley and Barbara were muttering to each other. That's when they weren't reminding her to call them Shirl and Barb. Which she just can't. Not yet. Nicknames are for friends, and they're not her friends. They're kindly neighbourhood ladies who feel sorry for her and her half-orphaned child.

Charlie seemed delighted to have them there. Shirl gave him jobs, and he was so agreeable about doing them that Elizabeth wondered why she'd never thought of it.

Now they're back for their second Saturday in Jon's garden, and Shirley is standing in front of her looking fairly smug. Today she's wearing a T-shirt with Jimi Hendrix on it. Elizabeth is barely aware of who that is. Or was. She's more inclined to Ralph Vaughan Williams with a side of Gustav Holst.

'Got a new helper,' Shirley says.

'Oh?' Elizabeth glances around the garden and sees only Barbara.

'Name's Cynthia.' Shirley holds out a pair of gloves. 'Brought these for you. Noticed you didn't have any last time.'

Elizabeth blushes. She does have gloves – Jon's gloves. But last time she didn't feel she could put them on. It would be presumptuous in a way she can't explain to anyone else.

'Thank you,' she says, accepting the gift.

The side gate opens and a blonde-haired woman steps through it, looking hesitant, although her face relaxes when she sees Charlie with his fingers in a pile of dirt.

'Cynthia?' Shirley says, moving towards her.

'Yes.' Cynthia's smile drops a little, almost as if she's nervous. Elizabeth understands.

'You found the place okay?'

'Yes, thank you, Shirley.' A glance towards Elizabeth, then Barbara, then back to Shirley.

'Like I said on the phone, call me Shirl.' Shirley looks pointedly at Elizabeth. 'Everyone does.'

'And I'm Barbara. Although I like to be called Barb.'

An extended hand, a kind smile. Elizabeth has decided that kindness must be Barbara's way of life.

'This is Elizabeth,' Shirley says, closing the gap between them and nodding as if to encourage Cynthia to come closer.

'Hello, Elizabeth.'

There's a flicker of something in Cynthia's eyes and Elizabeth wonders how much Shirley has told her. She would prefer that Cynthia isn't here out of pity; that would be an extra responsibility. So often these days Elizabeth feels as if she has to live up to the ideal of a grieving woman. It brings its own special exhaustion.

'Hello.' She smiles as warmly as she's able to.

Cynthia gestures towards Shirley's gift. 'Nice gloves.'

'They're new,' Elizabeth says.

'Did you bring some?' Shirley asks Cynthia, who holds up a fairly battered-looking pair.

'They were my mother's,' Cynthia says. Her face changes expression for a second, then she's composed once more.

'Oh yeah.' Shirley squints. 'I remember her.' She glances towards Barbara. 'Remember Diane, Barb?'

Barbara turns around from the plant she's been examining, her eyes wide. 'You're Diane's daughter?'

Cynthia nods, her lips pressed together.

'I was sorry to hear that she died,' Barbara says.

'Me too,' Cynthia replies.

Elizabeth doesn't know how to interpret that. Cynthia is here holding her mother's gloves yet it sounds like she wasn't with her when she died. What kind of relationship must they have had? Not one she'll be asking about today, obviously. If ever. She'll keep wondering, though. People interest her, even if she rarely lets on that this is the case.

'Right,' Shirley says with authority. 'New gloves, old gloves, all gloved. That's important. Don't want us getting cut on anything unexpected. So, Cyn – can I call you that?'

Cynthia frowns but nods.

'You're with Barb. Lizzie, you're with me.'

Elizabeth wasn't given a say about her own nickname and she doesn't think it would help anyway. Shirley does what she wants – Elizabeth knows this already – and what she wants right now is to work on Jon's garden.

'Master Charles,' Shirley says, and Charlie looks up, grinning. 'You're on rubbish duty.'

'This is my son,' Elizabeth explains to Cynthia.

'Hello, Charles,' Cynthia says.

'Charlie,' Elizabeth says. 'Usually he's Charlie.'

Cynthia simply nods in response then puts on her gloves. 'Well,' she says to no one in particular, 'I know nothing about gardening so I'll need some direction.'

'I don't either,' Elizabeth says, relieved that she's no longer the only novice.

'That's fine,' Shirley says, 'because Barb and I are good at giving orders.' She winks at them. 'And here's the first one.' She hands each of them a pair of secateurs. 'Cut where we tell you, all right?'

Elizabeth takes the secateurs and considers the fact that she's about to cut into plants Jon put in the earth himself. That feeling of explosive worry rises again – how will she know if she's doing the right thing?

'I can hear your brain whirring,' Shirley says under her breath as Cynthia wanders towards Barbara. Her eyes are bright as they meet Elizabeth's. 'Just stick with me, you'll be fine. I won't be doing anything Jon wouldn't have done if he was half the gardener you say.'

With a grateful smile Elizabeth stands back as Shirley explains their task for the next little while. Then she cuts where she's told and hands the litter to Charlie, who races off to deposit it in the big bag they're using for all the garden refuse, before skipping back to Barb and taking the next lot from her.

CHAPTER TWELVE

Yet again – *yet again!* – Terry hasn't taken the rubbish out to the big bin. It's his one job. Well, his one inside job. He has outside jobs. Mowing and whatnot. Mike's so busy with other people's lawns that he forgets their own most of the time. But garbage and lawns are not hard jobs for a teenager, and Lorraine is trying to teach Terry to be responsible. How do the youth learn to be grown-ups if they don't take *responsibility* for something every now and again?

She didn't like doing jobs either when she was young, but her parents insisted and eventually she saw the value in them. Especially once it came time to run her own house and she already knew how to do everything. She doesn't want Terry growing up to be some woman's burden because she and Mike cosseted him. He has to learn how to run a house. Maybe she needs to tell him that it will actually make him *more* attractive, because who doesn't love competence? It's what attracted her to Mike. He could fix things. Build things. And because of all that activity he had – still has – a really good body. Muscular. Straight of back. He's a good-lookin' rooster too. Maybe she needs to remember that the next time he gets on her nerves asking where his keys are when he's the only one who uses them.

Back to the rubbish. She has a mind to tell Terry off. But now the phone is ringing and she knows the thought will evaporate, because she just has too many thoughts to keep track of.

'Hello?' she says distractedly.

'Hi, Loz.'

Loz. That means it's Cynthia. That's what she used to call her. Obviously they're back on old terms. That suits Lorraine. They had such a good time the other day – after she decided to forgive Cynthia, if not forgive and forget, although the forget part will probably take care of itself. She walked away hoping Cynthia would decide they could be best friends again, and god knows Lorraine's missed having that in her life. Sure, she's friends with some of the school mums but it isn't the same as knowing someone so well you don't really need to explain anything. Plus each time she socialises with the school mums they're all so worn out they're yawning after two glasses of house white.

'Cyn,' she says. 'Nice to hear your voice. Thought you may have decided to go back to your LA mansion after you realised that Little Cove house isn't getting any bigger.'

Lorraine can't resist teasing her; she never could. Cynthia was always a cut above everyone else at school – more graceful, more gracious, more cultured – and Lorraine saw it as her role to keep the playing field level. Well, as level as she could. No amount of teasing Cynthia made her become like the rest of them. Until she got pregnant, and then she was worse than everyone else in the eyes of a few.

'You're as hilarious as ever, obviously,' Cynthia says, and there's a smile in her voice. 'How's your day going?'

Lorraine is about to launch into her usual list of irritations and errands then stops herself. Does she really want Cynthia to know how unglamorous her own life is? Because she was only half-joking about the LA mansion: if she could live in a fancy house and have someone else do the housework for her, she'd jump at it.

Ah, stuff it. Cyn's going to find out eventually, because Lorraine isn't much of a liar and even worse at playing poker.

'My day has been spent washing the clothes of one grown man, one grown woman, a teenager and a child,' she announces. 'Plus making a stew, taking bookings for Mike, mopping the floors and figuring out if I know how to paint the walls.'

There's a pause on the line. 'So do you?'

Now Lorraine pauses too, because that was the task she was in the middle of when she got distracted by Terry not taking out the rubbish, then Cynthia rang.

'Not sure,' she admits. 'But if you know anything about it, feel free to help me.'

'I don't.'

'Right. Long shot anyway.' Lorraine fakes a sigh. 'How's your day going? No, wait, don't tell me: you read the paper at leisure, made a pot of tea then decided to read a book.'

'Again with the hilarity. No – I was clearing out some stuff.'

Lorraine thinks about this. 'Is that some kind of code for Odette getting rid of the baby?'

There's another pause. Longer this time. Lorraine considers the possibility that she's overstepped.

'Nothing like that,' Cynthia says quietly. 'I believe she's still with child.'

Cynthia hasn't told Lorraine much about Odette and her situation, but Lorraine remembers how fraught it was for Cynthia at the time. As much as Cynthia loved Odette when she was born – as did Pat – being a young mother was hard. Lorraine often thought that Cynthia had put her dreams and plans on hold, even if she never complained about it. Or maybe moving overseas in pursuit of that fella was her way of complaining.

Thinking about Cynthia leaving Pat reminds Lorraine that she hasn't yet told Cynthia that she and Pat are friends, kind of. That is, Pat and Mike are friends. They met completely separately from Lorraine, at the Noosa Surf Club, and Lorraine felt awkward about it but she can hardly deny Mike his friends. And she and Pat might have then consoled each other over the fact that Cynthia had cut them both out of her life. So she knows that Pat is over the moon about Odette's baby and that he hopes Cynthia will be too, eventually. And she really should say something to Cynthia about that but is now the time? On the phone? Lorraine can't see her face. She needs to see her face so she can work out if Cynthia is cross.

'Fair enough,' is what she says instead. 'So what was the stuff?'

'It was from a garden. I've joined the Sunshine Gardening Society.'

'The what?'

'It's a gardening society. Named after Sunshine Beach. Von told me about it.'

'Von!' Lorraine smiles into the phone. She remembers Von well with her naughty sense of humour and her strict rules about piano practice. A real one-off, as her mother would say. Strident and outspoken before that became the fashion for women for a few years in the seventies. But ever since Nancy Reagan and Hazel Hawke came to prominence, everyone expects women to put up – silently – with men doing silly things like using the word 'bum' and cackling about it on national television. And mostly they do. Lorraine is willing to bet Von doesn't, though.

'Yes, I saw her the other day,' Cynthia says, 'and she told me about this society she founded. Or helped found. In the 1950s. Local women doing the gardening for people who need it. Sort of like good works. Actually, I suppose they are good works.'

'Wait.' Lorraine is having a memory and hoping it will fully form before it slips away again. 'Wait . . . I think I know about them! My mother-in-law said something once about how when Mike was young and his father had taken off, she needed help around the place and these ladies came and raked up her leaves and pulled out her weeds. They'd have to be the same group, right?'

'Where did Mike grow up?'

'Cooroy.'

'You mean he grew up in Cooroy and you're living there now?'

'Yes . . . why? You're back in Little Cove.'

If Cynthia thinks she's going to get away with implying that Mike doesn't get around much or something, she can have a dose of pot-calling-kettle-black from Lorraine.

'All right, all right. It was worth a shot.' Lorraine swears she can hear Cynthia smiling.

'Nice try,' she says. 'So, yeah. Cooroy. Not the same house he grew up in. But I wonder if Von helped his mum back then?'

'You can ask the gardeners yourself.'

'What do you mean?'

'Well, I've gone twice now and I like it. It's . . . rewarding. We're helping this young woman whose husband has died. He built this wonderful garden but it's fallen into ruin. She's working on it too, but we could do with another pair of hands.'

'I don't have time,' Lorraine says quickly. Because it's true. She can barely take care of her own place – why should she take care of someone else's?

'I know. But I'd like you to make time. I think you'd enjoy doing something that's not for your husband or your boys. And it would be a way of spending time together.' Cynthia pauses. 'I really have missed you.'

'Good.'

Now it's Lorraine turn to pause because she feels a bit emotional. How silly. Cynthia ignores her for *years* and now she says one nice thing and Lorraine turns to water.

'I'll think about it,' she continues.

'Well, I asked Shirley about it and she said you can join us next Saturday at ten at Elizabeth's house. That's the place I was talking about.'

'Who's Shirley?'

'One of the ringleaders. You'll like her.'

Lorraine grunts. 'Saturday, you say?'

'They've always met on weekends because the original members liked the idea of their husbands being forced to watch their children. If it was a school day they couldn't do that.'

'Cute,' Lorraine says, even though it's not cute, is it? It's a bit sad. At least she can rely on Mike to look after the kids, even if he once looked away long enough for Terry to light a match and set fire to some newspaper.

'I'll think about it,' she repeats.

She can't just say yes, even if she quite likes the idea of helping other people. It's good to do volunteering, isn't it? Her mother's always done some. Reading to the elderly or whatnot. Of course, now her mother's heading for elderly herself. Lorraine bites her lip as she thinks about how long it's been since she visited her mother. Too long. Almost a fortnight. Normally she's in Rose's pocket at least once a week. So she needs to get over there. Her mother could've fallen on her head for all Lorraine knows. Eumundi's not far enough away for distance to be the excuse. Running around like a headless chook is the excuse.

But Cynthia gives her the address anyway, and Lorraine writes it down because she knows – of course she knows – that she's going to be there, and Cynthia knows her well enough to know that she hates missing out on things – that's what her mother has said about her for as long as she can remember. Now that Cynthia's told her about the Sunshine Gardening Society Lorraine will start thinking about it and wondering what they're like and what they do, and before she knows it Saturday will come around and she'll find herself kneeling on someone's grass and getting stuck into some pruning. No good at saying no, that's her.

'You think about,' Cynthia says cheerfully, 'and I'll buy you some gardening gloves.'

'Your choice,' Lorraine says.

'I know.'

Lorraine can hear Terry coming in the door – she knows the footfall of every member of her family, including Cora. Come to think of it, she hasn't heard Cora's for a while. Is she out? Lorraine didn't check when she came back from the shops.

'I have to run,' she says into the phone.

'I understand. See you next weekend.'

'I'll think about it!'

She hears Cynthia laughing as she hangs up the phone.

CHAPTER THIRTEEN

It's deep enough into autumn that Kathy is prepared to try walking to work, although the risk of ending up sweaty is ever present because the restaurant is at least half an hour away on foot. She could drive – she usually does – but she's told herself that fitness is important, not least because she's getting older and she wants to be able to move through the world without too many aches and pains if she can avoid them. One of the waitresses, Leesa, is fond of preaching the benefits of exercise. 'It's so fun!' she says, and she seems to not just believe it but embody it, always asking for the dinner shift so she can spend her days jogging and canoeing or something.

Kathy can't remember the last time she had fun. Maybe before she had Grant? When she had Michelle she was twenty-four and she felt young and zippy; she and Owen would hire a baby-sitter or leave Michelle with Owen's mother so they could go out to dinner or to the theatre. After Grant was born Kathy felt deflated almost constantly, never quite recovering from giving birth because she already had another child to look after. Owen was fine – he still went for drinks with the boys after work and played footy on weekends. He couldn't understand why Kathy was so tired, and she couldn't be bothered pointing out that his job finished at 5 p.m. on a Friday each week whereas hers took up most of her waking hours seven days a week.

That's when they started to fracture a little; them and pretty much every other couple she knew with young children and a mother trying to manage on her own. One of her friends had extended family living in the house and Kathy was so jealous of the extra people available to watch children while housework was done. Owen's mother was always keen to help with the kids, but Kathy never felt she could ask her to do it too often lest her mother-in-law judge her for trying to skive off. Judgement is one of a mother's constants, keeping company with the other: self-judgement. She and Owen held it together for a long time, though. They weren't close but they were comfortable with each other. No doubt he's wondering what happened given things had hummed along the same way for years. When she left him Kathy didn't tell him about Jemima specifically, only that she'd fallen for someone else.

So she's at a stage now when she's prepared to reintroduce fun, or a version of it, into her life, and if Leesa thinks exercise is the way Kathy will give it a go. And if it doesn't quite take she'll look for something else.

Walking is the simplest way of exercising, so that's why she's chosen it. Everyone's made to walk; not everyone is made to run, or to do aerobics or Jazzercise. She went to a Jazzercise class once and that was enough – the teacher kept saying, 'Find that beat!' and Kathy simply could not. Ergo, walking is perfect: it's hard to stuff it up.

It's a good idea for her to start slowly after several years – decades – of not doing anything other than housework. Not that hauling a vacuum cleaner around isn't work. As she sets out she discovers her first mistake however: the sun is ahead of her, which means it's beating down right on her, and she's reluctant to put on the cap she's tucked into her bag because then her hair will look terrible when she takes it off. It's not that she's vain – no more than most – but she likes to look professional at work. Maybe she should turn back. Get the car.

No. She can't give up. It's just sun. She'll be warm, that's it. There's enough time to walk slowly.

So that's what she does, along Weyba Road, with Noosa Sound to her right, past some ritzy houses and some older buildings that will probably be torn down and replaced by ritzy houses. Everyone wants a water view.

As she walks she thinks about going out with the other staff earlier in the week. It was everyone's night off because the restaurant was closed and Hans thought it would be nice for them all to head to a bar. He meant well but Kathy had said it was a busman's holiday, which wasn't a phrase Hans had picked up when learning English so then she had to explain it, which was awkward.

Just as she'd finished she felt a nudge at her elbow. 'Hey Kathy, wanna go to the movies tomorrow night?' It was Mitchell, one of the bar staff from the restaurant. He was younger than her son but kept acting like he was interested in her romantically – or something akin to it. Sometimes she let him run with it, mainly because he could be an unstoppable force, and also because it was good to use her flirting muscle every now and again.

'What are you seeing?' she'd asked.

'*Top Gun.*' He winked at her.

'Is that still running? I thought it came out months ago.'

'It did. But it's so popular they keep it on.' Now he was grinning like the movie was the best idea he'd had in eons.

'I've seen it,' she said, and grinned back.

'Worth another look.' He wiggled his eyebrows and Kathy laughed.

'Learn to take "no" for an answer, Mitch.'

'Didn't hear ya say it.'

'Okay.' She leant towards him, her lips close to his ear. '*No,*' she breathed.

He shrugged and winked again. 'Can't blame a bloke for tryin'.'

'Off you go, Mitchell,' Hans said seriously.

'Yes, boss.' Mitchell gave him a mock salute and turned back towards Leesa, who was, Kathy thought, a more appropriate match for him.

Hans had frowned. 'I will say something to him.' But Kathy told him she was sure Mitch did it as a joke.

Actually, she wasn't sure – the look in his eyes appeared to be genuinely lascivious – but she wanted Hans to think she was. Mitchell didn't deserve to get into trouble. Plus, his cheek made her smile, and it's making her smile now as she remembers it. Even old ducks like her enjoy some appreciation from time to time, and it doesn't have to mean anything. It's probably better if it doesn't.

The memory has carried her a fair way along and now she's in Noosaville. The restaurant is only a few minutes away and the sweat patches under her arms are nothing that a couple of minutes in the air con won't fix.

She turns onto Elizabeth Street and hears voices – female, one of them louder than the others – then a gate opens and three women step onto the footpath, right in her way without noticing.

Kathy stops and considers going around them, but that would put her in the gutter and there's a car there, making it difficult to manoeuvre.

'Lizzie, I'm telling you,' says a short, robust-looking woman wearing a Beatles T-shirt, 'a little beach flax lily in the corner there will bring a nice pop of colour.'

A young woman with long curly hair is biting her bottom lip. 'I'm not sure,' she says. 'I don't know enough about natives to say.'

The Beatles woman sighs then glances up and sees Kathy. 'Sorry, love,' she says. 'We're in your way.'

'It's fine,' Kathy says, even though it isn't really, but it's the polite thing to say.

The trio shifts closer to the gate and Kathy gives them a tight smile as she passes.

'There's no rush to decide,' says the other woman – or Kathy presumes it's her because the voice is different, but they're behind her now and she's hardly going to turn around to check. Not until she's at the end of the block, that is, when she risks a backwards glance and sees the Beatles woman opening the back door of the car and putting something inside. Then, to Kathy's mortification, she waves.

With a quick wave back, and a quicker turn of the head away, Kathy scurries across the road towards the river and the safe haven of her workplace. She thinks about the woman and her beach flax lily on the walk home later that night, though, as she passes the house and sees one light on and hears what she's sure is a Beethoven piano concerto coming out of a slightly ajar window.

CHAPTER FOURTEEN

'Y ou don't have much experience,' says the woman – Sherry, Elizabeth thinks her name is – looking up at her while her finger taps the scant CV on the desk.

Elizabeth wants to say that motherhood is experience. She has to be a world-class organiser as well as housekeeper, cook and counsellor. Being the wife of a terminally ill man brought its own sort of experience too. More organisation. Tolerance. Learning of medical jargon – she had to remember Jon's medications and his doctors' names, keep track of his appointments, and keep everything running at home. But you can't put that on a CV. No one would accept it as valid experience. Yet is there any experience more important than managing a small child into life and a grown man out of it? If only there were a job title for that. Elizabeth would be set.

'Not in this sort of work, no,' she says. 'I haven't been a doctor's secretary. But I have, um, I mean, I do know a fair amount about doctors.'

'Oh?' Sherry has small eyes and big glasses that she keeps perched below her eyes, so Elizabeth isn't sure what their purpose could be.

'My . . . my husband was sick. For a couple of years. He had a lot of doctors. We went to a lot of appointments.'

'Oh, right. And how is he now?'

Elizabeth should have foreseen that question, because it's not as if she hasn't been asked it a lot lately. By shopkeepers and random people in the neighbourhood who haven't seen her for a while. So she'll give Sherry the same answer she gives them.

'He's dead.' Then she tries to smile in a reassuring manner, because people on the receiving end of news like that tend to want you to make it all right for *them*, as if it's not making her feel wretched having to say it. Knowing she'll have to say it for years. If not forever.

Sherry blinks. 'Oh,' she says. 'Right.'

Now Elizabeth plays the one strong card in her hand. 'So I really need the work. I have a son and I need to provide for him.'

She should add something, so it doesn't sound all too selfish. 'And I want to work,' she goes on. 'I have skills to offer.'

Sherry looks at her enquiringly.

'I've had to deal with a lot of challenges,' Elizabeth says. 'I feel I can handle anyone and anything. And I can type.'

Thank goodness her father suggested she learn to touch-type while she was at university, saying it was useful. He'd learnt it while he was in the army, and swore it helped him get promoted because he could pitch in and handle correspondence deftly when others could not.

Sherry looks momentarily pleased. 'We'll have to give you a test,' she says.

'Of course.' Elizabeth hopes she looks relaxed as she smiles. She doesn't like tests, but she's confident in her typing ability.

'And you can work the hours?'

Those hours are ten to five, four days a week, and Elizabeth isn't entirely sure she can manage them, but that's why she's heading to her parents' place after this, to ask if they can help.

'Yes.' She swallows. 'Absolutely.'

Sherry waves her into what looks like one of the doctors' rooms and plonks an Olivetti on the desk and a set of headphones on Elizabeth's ears. They're attached to a cassette player and, without any warning, Sherry presses 'play' and Elizabeth hears a recorded monotone, likely a doctor, dictating a letter.

Fifteen minutes later the dictation test has finished and Elizabeth sits back, hoping she hasn't made too many mistakes.

'We'll let you know,' Sherry says as she ushers her to the door and Elizabeth wonders if that's true.

Still, it would be a good idea to talk to her parents about looking after Charlie even if she doesn't get this particular job. She will have to work, at whatever job she can find, and it's more than likely that job won't fit neatly into school hours.

During the short drive from the medical practice in Sunrise Beach to her parents' house in Sunshine Beach, Elizabeth mentally runs through her to-do list for the rest of the day. She wakes up with a list in her head and never reaches its end. Items drop off as they're completed then more are added. It's entirely possible she'll have a to-do list in her head until the day she dies, and that feels somewhat like a torture. The ever-renewing, never-vanquished list. For just one day – that's all she dares hope for – she wishes she could be list-free. Or maybe she wouldn't know how to function without it.

She's noticed, much to her surprise, that the only time she doesn't think about the list is when she's gardening. There's something about putting her hands in the earth that sucks her worries out of her brain, almost like magic. Not that she believes in magic. If magic were real, wouldn't Jon be alive? She prayed often enough, and prayers are incantations in their own way.

'Hello, sweetheart,' her mother says with a wide smile as she opens the door to Elizabeth. Her parents live in a slightly run-down, one-storey weatherboard house that they're slowly renovating – her father likes a project – but it's as full of warmth as they are.

As her mother hugs her she pats Elizabeth's hair, as she usually does. It's a ritual, checking that Elizabeth is still there. They almost lost her once, as a child, when she ran out from a footpath – too fast for her father to catch her – and straight into a car, and ever since then her mother has carried out these discreet checks. When she was a teenager Elizabeth hated them. Now they're the most reassuring thing she can imagine.

Her mother walks slowly down the hall. She's stiffened with age, despite Elizabeth's exhortations that she keep mobile, go for walks, maybe take up golf.

Her father, sitting at the kitchen bench, springs up. That's what golf has done for him: kept him nimble. Why can't her mother see that?

'Hello, love,' he says, kissing her cheek, grabbing her arm. Again, to check. They both do it. They don't know how to not do it.

And Elizabeth can hardly talk: when Charlie was a baby she used to bend over his cot and put her cheek next to his mouth to feel his breath. Just checking.

'How did you go?' Her mother pats the stool next to her father's, indicating that Elizabeth should sit.

'Good, I think.' She sits obediently and puts her handbag on the bench. 'She gave me a typing test.'

Her father looks triumphant. 'Bet you did well.'

'I don't know yet, Dad.' She glances quickly at each of them. 'If I get the job I'll need you to give me a hand with Charlie. It's four days a week, and while I could take him to school I wouldn't be able to pick him up, because I'd finish at five. And school holidays . . .' That's only just occurred to her: what will she do in the holidays?

'We can do it,' her mother says firmly, nodding at her father. 'We'd love to do it.'

Her father pats her hand. 'We sure would.'

Although Elizabeth is used to her parents' generosity, she's never taken it for granted, and sometimes she can't fathom how she can be so lucky to have them help her the way they do. Her brother's back in Brisbane, probably feeling neglected because their parents came here to be with her and Charlie. And Jon, before he died.

'Don't worry about the holidays,' her mother says. 'We can put Charlie to work. Your father needs help with the renovations.'

Elizabeth laughs. 'I think he'd love that.'

'He probably won't once he's been painting all day,' her father says with a wink, 'but I'll go easy on him.'

'Thank you,' Elizabeth says and she feels tears in her eyes. Their kindness often makes her weepy. Or maybe she's just generally weepy. Most days that to-do list in her head is accompanied by a low tide of tears sitting in the rims of her eyes. 'I'm lucky to have you.'

'Nonsense,' her mother says. '*We're* lucky to have *you.*'

At that moment their Maltese terrier, Snowball, trots into the room. He always takes his time arriving, like he wants to make Elizabeth wait for his affection.

'Snowball will be happy to have Charlie here more too, won't you, boy?' Her father bends down and picks up the dog, tucking him under one arm. 'Come on, let's head for the garden,' he says to Elizabeth. 'I've got a nice clivia to show you that I just planted.'

Elizabeth stands and follows him. Her father loves his garden as much as Jon loved theirs. Elizabeth is yet to tell him about the Sunshine Gardening Society, because he's been hinting for a while that he'd like to work on Jon's garden. It's not that Elizabeth doesn't want him there but that she feels he's done more than enough to help her. Now she hopes he won't be upset that Shirley and Barbara see more of the garden than he does.

She'll have to tell him about it one day. Maybe when it's ready to be seen again. For now, though, she'll enjoy her father's enthusiasm for his clivia, and maybe take some mental notes about the plants, just to add something else to that eternal, infernal list.

MAY 1987

COAST HONEYSUCKLE

CHAPTER FIFTEEN

Cynthia leans against her car outside Elizabeth's house on a clear and mild Saturday morning. As she looks towards the house she can vaguely make out Elizabeth near the windows on the street side, her head bowed slightly along with her shoulders. She's a little mystery, that one. Cynthia has tried to draw her into conversation a couple of times, not about anything too serious – she's mindful that she doesn't know anyone in the Sunshine Gardening Society well yet and doesn't wish to be intrusive. However, the very fact of them working in Elizabeth's late husband's garden begs enquiry. It also seems like the polite thing to do: while the man may no longer be on this earth his presence is felt, if only because Elizabeth says Charlie looks so much like him.

So last weekend Cynthia asked, gently, if Elizabeth could tell her something about Jon. She could almost hear Shirl and Barb hold their breath as they waited for an answer.

Elizabeth sat back on her haunches in front of the petunias and smiled vaguely. 'He was thoughtful,' she said. 'And considerate.' She frowned. 'Maybe they're the same thing. Are they?'

Cynthia, recognising it for the stalling tactic it was, shrugged and smiled and said nothing. If Elizabeth didn't want to continue, she wasn't going to force her.

'We met at high school,' Elizabeth said softly, not looking at any of them. 'And we were in fellowship group together at church.' Then she laughed. 'My friends thought he was boring because he took his Bible study seriously and he was really well mannered.'

She paused and glanced briefly at Cynthia, almost as if looking for permission to go on.

'I don't think manners are boring,' Cynthia said. 'Imagine the world without them?'

Elizabeth nodded slowly. 'That's what I always thought too. I liked his manners.' She smiled. 'I loved them, actually. He was kind to people. To me. I know not every husband is kind to his wife.'

Cynthia knew that too, but said nothing because this wasn't her story.

'And he took his responsibilities towards me and Charlie seriously. He used to say he had to provide for us and protect us. My friends thought that was old-fashioned but . . .' She paused. 'It made everything easier. For me, having a baby, knowing he was going to look after us – I could just focus on Charlie and not have to worry about other things.'

She stopped and Cynthia heard her breath catch. Because, of course, as time went on and Charlie grew, Jon wasn't able to provide and protect. Instead it was Elizabeth having to do that. Or someone else. Cynthia doesn't know enough about her family and friends to speculate.

'He sounds like just the sort of man you deserve,' was what she said in response. Then Charlie came running up to his mother holding a snail and the reminiscence was over.

Elizabeth has gone from the window now, and Cynthia hears a car pull into the street, the engine stop and the door slam.

'Sorry, sorry! I'm here!' Lorraine bustles towards her, running one hand through her hair and flapping the other. 'Sorry, got caught up.'

Just then the gate to the garden opens and Shirl steps out. 'G'day, Cyn,' she says. 'Didn't know you were here.' She looks Lorraine up and down.

'I was waiting for Lorraine,' Cynthia replies. 'And this is Lorraine.'

'Right.' Shirl raises her eyebrows. 'Got some gloves?'

'Cynthia has them.'

Cynthia brandishes the pair she had promised to buy.

Shirl looks down at Lorraine's legs. 'Shorts?'

'I couldn't find the pants I wanted.' Lorraine looks guilty. 'Are shorts bad?'

Shirl shrugs. 'Not if you don't mind dirty knees. Hat?'

Lorraine proffers a beaten-up maroon cap bearing the XXXX logo.

'All right, then.' Shirl holds open the gate. 'Follow me.'

Cynthia follows Lorraine into the garden and sees Barb writing in a slender notebook – one she usually brings with her, presumably to keep records of anything they plant. Or not. Cynthia has no idea.

'This is Barbara,' Shirl says, gesturing.

'Call me Barb.' She extends a hand to Lorraine. 'Everyone does.'

'Hi, Barb!'

'Shorts?' Barb says.

'Been through that,' Shirl mutters.

Barb's smile returns. 'Oh. Right. Well – just keep an eye out for leeches.'

'Leeches!' Lorraine looks horrified.

'In certain kinds of weather they turn up. Probably not today. But if you keep wearing shorts . . .'

'I won't.'

'Good. Right. Well.' Barb half-turns away, glancing around, then turns back. 'We have some work to do here. This garden belongs to a young lady called Elizabeth and her son, Charles.'

'Elizabeth and Charles?' Lorraine retorts. 'Like the Royal Family?'

'I guess so.' Barb remains serene. 'Elizabeth's husband, Jon – not Philip, please note,' she winks at Lorraine, 'died not that long ago, and he was ailing for quite a while. The garden was his passion but it's showing us the story of his decline. As you can see . . .' Another half-turn and a glance around. 'It holds its design but it needs a great deal of care.'

'Natives,' Shirl says, as if something has been decided, although Cynthia has no idea what.

'Shirl, we talked about this,' Barb says quietly.

'Where there are weeds, pull 'em out and put in natives,' Shirl says firmly. 'Everyone knows the weeds don't grow back if you put the natives in.'

'Not *everyone*, Shirl.' Barb sighs. 'And it has to be right for the garden. This garden is of an English style. I think there are some roses round the other side of the house too. *Natives* won't work here. *As discussed.*'

'Make the *whole thing* natives!' Shirl declares, using both arms to gesticulate.

'Shirley! It's not our decision to make. And please don't use the opportunity of a new member to start this campaign again.'

There's a noise from the direction of the house and Barb's face softens as she looks towards it. Elizabeth is walking down the steps, looking so defeated that Cynthia wants to scoop her into a hug and tell her everything will be fine.

'Hello, I'm Elizabeth,' she says to Lorraine as she arrives on the bottom step.

'Hello, Elizabeth.'

Lorraine's vim has less vigour than it did before Shirl's rant and Cynthia wonders if she's reconsidering her decision to come today, even if she is, as she insists, just trying it out.

'Lorraine is joining the Sunshine Gardening Society today,' Barb says, looking proud.

Cynthia glances at Lorraine, whose eyes widen. She hopes Lorraine doesn't think she's railroaded her.

'Oh, I –' Lorraine starts, then stops as Barb stares at her. 'I'm, um, happy to be here.'

'As are we all,' Barb says.

'Enough chatting. Let's make a start, girls,' Shirl announces. She pulls gloves from her pants pocket and puts them on. 'Cyn, you're with me. Lorrie, you're with Barb. Lizzie, you can float. All right, let's get on with it.'

Lorraine looks like she's panicking, so Cynthia smiles in an effort to be reassuring, puts on her own gloves and gestures to Lorraine to do the same.

'What am I meant to do?' Lorraine whispers.

'Whatever Barb tells you,' says Cynthia. 'Don't worry – it'll be more fun than you think.'

With an expression of dismay, Lorraine nevertheless does as Shirl tells her and an hour goes past before Cynthia even thinks to check on her. When she does, she finds Lorraine with dirt on her knees, a grin and her hat pushed back.

'How are you going?' she asks.

'Great! I like weeds!'

Cynthia glances at Barb, who raises her eyebrows.

'Really? What's so good about them?'

'I mean, I like pulling them out.' Lorraine brings a gloved hand to her cheek and rubs, leaving dirt behind. 'There's this really satisfying thing that happens when you yank and the whole lot comes out.'

'Indeed.'

'Don't you like it?' Lorraine squints up at her because the sun is behind Cynthia's head.

'I can't say I've experienced it too often because I'm not as successful at weed pulling as you are.' She smiles mischievously. 'And obviously that means you'll have to come back and do the weeding that I'm just not capable of.'

Lorraine wags her head from side to side. 'We'll see.'

Another glance at Barb yields more raised eyebrows.

'She's a natural,' Barb murmurs.

'A natural woman,' Lorraine snorts. 'Sorry – I like the song.'

Cynthia smiles and brushes the dirt off Lorraine's cheek. 'I'll leave you to it, natural woman.'

She keeps smiling as she heads back to Shirl, who is chatting to Elizabeth about native grasses while Elizabeth's eyes glaze over.

CHAPTER SIXTEEN

Lorraine pauses and pushes her hair back with her forearm. Even though winter is on its way the days are still warm enough for her to sweat. They're not in Elizabeth's garden today, which Lorraine was surprised about, except Shirl said they need to let it 'rest' for a while. Or maybe it's Elizabeth who needs to rest, because she's not here today. They're in Von's garden – Lorraine was tickled pink when she found out she'd get to see Von again after all these years.

Last weekend, after they'd weeded Elizabeth's garden for hours, Lorraine could have wrung herself out. When she got home Mike took one look at her, grinned and said, 'My very own wet T-shirt contestant, eh?' She'd wanted to chastise him but it was kind of funny, and at least he didn't say anything about her dirty knees. Shirl had been right: the shorts were a bad idea. And Cynthia had been right too, in that Lorraine enjoyed the gardening, and the company of the others, so she's decided to return. Just to see if she still likes it.

'So Mike and I were, you know . . .' Lorraine says to Cynthia, who's working beside her.

'No,' Cynthia says, leaning further into the garden bed to pick up some leaf litter. 'I don't know.'

Lorraine sits back on her haunches and glances over each shoulder. '*You know.*'

Cynthia too sits back and raises an eyebrow. 'Oh. *In flagrante delicto?*'

'In what-now?'

'You were rooting.'

'Cyn!' Lorraine's cheeks turn pink and she looks around again, but Barb and Shirl seem to be discussing some spiky plant on the other side of the garden.

Cynthia laughs. 'You made me say it. I gave you the nice, polite Latin way out and you didn't take it.'

'I didn't even know you knew what that word means.'

'Me? The teenage preggo?' Cynthia winks.

'Anyway.' Lorraine reaches in to grab some leaf litter of her own then puts it in the big garbage bin situated between them. 'Cora walked in.'

'Walked in on you?' Cynthia's nose twitches.

'Yep. Didn't knock. Didn't say "yoo-hoo".'

'Does she normally say "yoo-hoo"?'

'Shut up. You know what I mean.'

Lorraine briefly closes her eyes as she recalls her mortification at seeing her mother-in-law standing in the doorway while Mike was nuzzling her neck. And more besides. Gah!

Cynthia starts to smile and stops. 'Sorry. It's awful, I know. But it's a little bit amusing too. So what happened?'

'I had to tap Mike on the shoulder to get him to stop.'

'You mean she didn't walk out immediately?'

'No. I think she was in shock.' The sight of Cora's face is something Lorraine is going to try hard to forget but she suspects she never will. 'Not half as much as I was, though.'

'And it's never happened before?' Cynthia gets up and indicates that they should move on to the next patch of litter.

'A couple of near misses. Anyway, she said she wanted to tell us that she was taking Simon to church.'

'But you're not religious.'

'Exactly.'

In fact, Lorraine suspects Cora invented the excuse on the spot, almost as if it was the worst thing she could think of to say to Lorraine at that exact moment. Because they've had this out before: Cora wanting the boys to be raised Greek Orthodox and both Mike and Lorraine insisting against it.

'So I said she couldn't do that and now she's not speaking to me,' Lorraine continues.

'Maybe she's embarrassed that she walked in on you. Did she see a boob or anything?'

Lorraine has to stop and think about that. 'She could have. But who cares! She walked in! And she didn't walk out straight-away! Honestly, it's almost like she wanted to watch, the perv.'

Lorraine turns to put some litter in the bin and almost bangs into Shirl.

'How are you going?' Shirl says.

'Making progress,' Cynthia says, smiling sweetly. Cynthia likes Shirl, Lorraine can tell, because she always does what Shirl says and smiles when she does it.

'Good. Barb and I are going to have a chat to Von about this cactus thing.' She points to the spiky plant.

'You don't want it here?' Lorraine asks.

'It doesn't *belong* here.' Shirl looks offended, but Lorraine reckons it's because of the cactus, not her. 'It'll spread its rotten spawn everywhere if we don't yank it out and we can't have lots of little cacti everywhere. No, no.' This is accompanied by a vigorous shake of the head.

'No, no, what?' It's Von, calling from the edge of the garden, her hearing clearly better than Lorraine would have thought for a woman her age. Rude of her to think it, but at least she didn't say it.

'This cactus.' Shirl points. 'Where did it come from?'

'You've seen it before.' Von pokes her cane into the grass as if she's making a point.

'Have I?'

Shirl looks to Barb, who raises her hands and shrugs.

'I don't remember it,' Shirl says.

Von sniffs. 'It didn't grow overnight, Shirley. I know it's been a few weeks since your last visit but I can assure you it was here then.'

'Some leaves have fallen from those,' Barb says, indicating the plants next to the cactus. 'Perhaps it's more exposed than it was.'

Shirl looks unconvinced.

'Good to know that your one-woman war against everything that isn't a native plant continues.' Von's expression is one of amusement.

'I'm not the only woman,' Shirl says defiantly. 'You've been round the traps long enough to know that, Vonnie.'

'True.' Von looks towards Cynthia. 'Your mother was of the same inclination.'

Cynthia nods. 'I know – she liked her native plants.'

'Wait – what?' Lorraine says.

'Um . . .' Cynthia frowns. 'I forgot to tell you – Mum was a member of the Sunshine Gardening Society.'

'When?'

'For years,' Von says.

Lorraine thinks about Diane and what she remembers of her hobbies, and can't think of anything. She never smiled much but she made a great sponge cake. Cynthia was always available on Saturdays because . . . because her mum was out and her father and Kit went fishing or something. So that's when Diane must have been gardening. How did Lorraine not know about it? Cynthia never said anything.

'I had no idea,' Lorraine says.

'Nor did I.'

Cynthia looks sad about that and Lorraine supposes you would be if you found out your mum had this whole part of her life that she kept a secret. It would feel like being lied to. Not that

Lorraine shares everything with her kids, but at least she told them what she was doing today.

'She never said anything?' she asks Cynthia.

Cynthia shakes her head.

'Almost like she was a druggie or something, trying to hide it.' Lorraine makes a face. 'Are we doing something naughty here?' She looks at tightly done-up Barb and Shirl with her Midnight Oil T-shirt and her dirty old slacks and starts to laugh. 'I mean, if the cops turn up they might arrest me for wearing shorts while gardening.'

She points to her legs, which are bare because she forgot to buy the pants to wear just for gardening. Skirts and dresses are more her style, so she doesn't have trousers handy.

Shirl's mouth twitches and Lorraine wonders if she's cracked her.

'Good to know your sense of humour is as well developed as ever, Lorraine,' Von says approvingly. 'And good to see you again, full stop.'

'You too, Von.' Lorraine turns back to the garden bed. 'I've missed you, as weird as that sounds.'

'Not at all,' comes the authoritative tone from behind her. 'I'd miss me too.'

Lorraine snorts and pulls out a weed.

'This is turning out to be fun,' she mutters to Cynthia, who looks almost relaxed, which is unusual for her.

'That's because it is,' Cynthia says softly.

'It may even be fun enough to help me forget that my mother-in-law walked in on me having sex.'

Lorraine hears a noise and turns to see that Shirl is standing close enough to have heard every word. Whoops.

'All true, Shirl,' she says.

'Sorry to hear that, Lorrie.' Shirl shakes her head then moves in the direction of the unfortunate cactus, picking up her machete on the way.

Lorraine has a brief thought of buying her own machete and displaying it next to her bedroom door, like a warning sign to Cora, but Mike would probably just think it's a new tool for his business and put it in the shed.

'So is that why you joined?' she asks Cynthia.

'Hm?' Cynthia is scrabbling around near the fence.

'Did you join the society because your mum did?'

Cynthia's back is to her so she can't tell if she's planning to anwer or not.

After a few seconds Lorraine hears a soft word: 'Partly.' Then Cynthia turns around and Lorraine sees that her face is half crumpled and she feels bad for asking.

'Sorry, Cyn,' she says.

'For what?'

'For asking.'

Cynthia shakes her head quickly. 'Nothing to apologise for. I mainly joined because Von told me to. But also because I wanted to understand Mum better.'

'Makes sense.' Lorraine pulls on another weed and makes a face when it breaks off halfway up the stem. 'I don't think she was hiding it from you. I think she just wanted something for herself. And I understand that.'

Cynthia smiles gratefully. 'As do I.'

'Bloody weed!' Lorraine holds up her limp trophy.

'I thought you loved weeds?'

'Shut up.'

'Okay.' Cynthia grins and turns away, while Lorraine digs her fingers into the dirt, hoping to find some roots.

CHAPTER SEVENTEEN

At certain moments Cynthia notices the ways this house has changed and the ways it hasn't. There are photos of her mother in frames – in the living room, in the bedrooms – but the other traces of her life are gone. Her sewing is no longer piled in a basket in the corner. The novels she was always reading aren't stacked on the little stool next to the couch; in fact, the stool has gone too. Her cookbooks have vanished, as has her apron. All of this happened while Cynthia was elsewhere and it's only now that she's here, seeing the evidence of it, that she realises she may never forgive herself for not being here when Diane died.

A dog is barking somewhere close and Cynthia thinks of something else she missed while she was gone: the death of the family pet, a Jack Russell called, appropriately, Jack. He was the successor to the previous Jack Russell, named Russ.

She thought that moving away, separating oneself from one's family, was what had to happen as a person grew older. When she became a mother she was still young, or so she felt, despite the responsibilities that arrived when Odette did. She wasn't ready to leave behind the structure of her original family life, even though her relationship with her mother had never been particularly close; and it was that structure she tried to replicate in her own little family, without questioning whether or not it suited her.

Then, in her mid-twenties, she felt the constraints of it all as shackles. She adored Odette, but motherhood was holding her back, as was marriage. Everything in her life was geared to someone else's needs and her own were never acknowledged. Indeed, she wasn't sure if she had them any more because it had been so long since they'd been expressed. The American surfer was just an excuse; an opportunity. What was really going on was that she wanted to leave, wanted to see who she might become if she wasn't stuck in what she perceived to be the rut of her life.

Pat was a casualty of that. Pat who is just now climbing the back steps to the house and sliding open the glass door, smiling at her like the old friend she guesses he probably is. Old friend and other parent of her only child. Severance from him, no matter how much she had thought it imperative, was impossible. They always had to deal with each other to raise Odette, whether she was in the US or here.

'Good morning,' he says as he closes the door then turns around to face her, his hands tucking into the pockets of his light-weight jacket. A sailing jacket, that's what it looks like. Although she doesn't think he sails. He's always been a surfer, and in her experience those types don't tend to exist in the same body.

'Good morning.' She smiles. She's expecting him – he called and said he'd like to come round and have a chat.

On hearing this her father decided he needed to go fishing, which made Cynthia think Wilfred knows what Pat wants to talk about. It seems odd, the two of them communicating regularly and her knowing nothing about it. But she has no right to know, even if it rankles a little.

She pushes herself up from the deep couch, her thighs telling her that they're still recovering from Saturday squatting in Von's garden. No one told her that gardening could be so physical, although if she'd given it a second's thought she probably would have realised.

Pat kisses her cheek; today he smells like salt water and Imperial Leather.

'Good to see you,' he says. 'Shall I make us a cuppa?'

Cynthia knows she should be the one suggesting that, but these days he's more familiar with this house than she is.

'That would be nice,' she says, and follows him into the kitchen.

He moves between kettle and cupboard, extracting mugs and a teapot, boiling water and pouring it over leaves, while he makes small talk about the waves and the tides. Subjects he's aware she has no interest in, and that's when she knows he must want to talk about something serious. He's softening her up.

He nods towards the living room. 'Let's sit.'

They arrange their mugs on the coffee table, and Cynthia stays perched on the edge of the couch while Pat sits back.

'So,' he says. 'Odette.'

'Mm?' Cynthia raises the mug to her lips even though she knows the tea is too hot yet to sip.

'You still haven't had a proper chat.'

It's not a question. Obviously Odette has been talking to him. Cynthia still isn't used to the fact that her daughter prefers Pat as a confidant.

'Me and Odette?'

'Yeah. Since you got back. You haven't spent any time alone.'

'I've called her a few times,' Cynthia says, terse. 'But given how quickly she's got off the phone – if I get to talk to her at all – I've had the distinct feeling she doesn't want to talk to me.'

Pat registers surprise. 'That's not true,' he says, his face softening.

'No?' Cynthia attempts a sip of tea to stall for time – wondering if this is some kind of ambush by her ex-husband to tell her she's a bad mother – and burns her tongue as a reward. She winces and puts the mug down.

'She wants nothing more than to talk to you, Cyn.'

Now Pat puts his mug on the side table and slides to the front of the couch, angling his body towards hers. For a second Cynthia thinks he's going to take her hand and she's surprised to realise that she wouldn't mind.

'But she's so ... *angry* with me.' She almost gasps at the truth of it.

'She's not. She's ... confused.' He shrugs. 'A bit scared. She thought you'd judge her.'

'Me?' Cynthia's laugh is bitter. '*Me?* Of all people?'

'Yeah, that's what I said.' He raises his eyebrows. 'I said you and I wouldn't judge. That we understand. But I guess she needs to hear it from you more than she needs to hear it from me.'

'I don't judge her,' she says. 'I'm just worried for her. Because I know ...' She exhales and it's ragged, and she has to watch herself here because she doesn't want to say anything to offend Pat.

Now he really does take her hand and it's as warm as she remembers.

'You know how hard it is to be a young mother,' he says, and squeezes. 'I remember. I was there.'

'Because you were responsible for it,' she says, taking back her hand, irritated that he's speaking like an observer instead of a very active participant.

'I remember that too.' He smiles benevolently, like he forgives her for being irritated, which is, of course, even more irritating.

'Look, Odette just wants to make her own decisions and be supported by us,' he continues. 'She knows you love her. She's just not sure if you approve of her.'

'Well, of course I do! She's wonderful!'

Pat tilts his head to the side and looks at her. 'Have you told her that lately?'

'She won't let me!'

He takes both of her hands this time and Cynthia feels her shoulders relax, the way they used to when her father pinched her cheek and told her he was pinching away her worries.

'If I organise for the two of you to get together,' Pat says, 'will you try to start with that?'

'Will you be there?'

'If you want me to be.'

'You know her better than I do. It would make sense.' Cynthia doesn't want to admit that she's nervous of being alone with her own daughter.

'You still know her, Cyn. Just like I still know you.' He grins. 'We go back, you and me. We're family. And Odette is the family we made. So we have to make this right. She needs us. Both of us. And this may sound familiar, but she's not that good at admitting she needs help. Or when she's wrong.'

Cynthia's eyes widen. 'What are you implying?'

Pat lets go of her hands and holds up his own in surrender. 'Nothing whatsoever.'

He picks up his mug. 'Tea's cooler now.'

'Unlike my temper, is that what you want to say?'

'Nah.' He shakes his head. 'That's trickier than anything I would say.'

Which is true: even when she was leaving him he never punished her verbally, even if she might have wished he would. That was the paradox of the situation: she wanted to leave him but wanted him to not want her to leave. All these years later, she knows that's because it wasn't him specifically that she wanted to leave. It was her life. Except, as she found out, her life went with her.

'You've always been a kind man,' she murmurs, but he doesn't say anything in response, and they sit and drink their tea in silence.

CHAPTER EIGHTEEN

There are skills Elizabeth is sure she has: organisation, acuity, punctuality, the ability to make decisions and stick to them. What she's not sure of today is where they've gone to.

She managed to deliver Charlie to school on time but somewhere between there and her new workplace she lost time. Perhaps it was when she was sitting in the car hyperventilating because she's about to be in an unfamiliar situation while still in the midst of widowhood, which is the most unfamiliar situation of her life and also a term she wishes did not apply to her.

Or maybe it was when she decided to take a walk around the block before going in, attempting to calm herself. Except she was sure that she had time for both the hyperventilating and the walk. When she parked the car outside the surgery – which looks like it was once a house on this little street in Sunrise Beach – she had fifteen minutes spare. Now, as she's bustling through the door, still breathing hard, sure that she looks as flustered as she feels, she's five minutes late.

'Good morning,' says a woman behind the desk with a tight-set perm and pearl studs in her ears. 'Name?'

'I'm Elizabeth. I'm, um . . . starting today.' She looks around for the woman who interviewed her but can't see her.

'Oh, yes!' the perm says. 'Doctor Lopes mentioned that. I'm Olive. We'll be working together in the mornings. You spoke to Sherry, right?'

'Yes.'

Olive smiles the kind of smile Elizabeth's grandmother used to make: tight lips and no eyes, like she's smiled so many times in her life that she's out of enthusiasm for it and won't engage more of her face than she needs to. When her grandmother did it, Elizabeth thought it was because she didn't like anyone much; later she realised it was because she'd spent her life appeasing others and by the time she was eighty simply couldn't be bothered any more. Perhaps Olive, too, is tired of appeasing everyone who walks through the door.

Elizabeth considers apologising for being late – that would be the polite thing to do – but Olive doesn't seem to have noticed so she lets it go.

'So your son is in kindy?' Olive says.

'Yes. Charlie. I just dropped him off.'

'And who's getting him after school?'

She says 'school' as *skeewwwl* and Elizabeth wants to giggle because that's how her granny used to say it. Her father's mother, not her mother's mother, the tight-smiler. *Are you off to skeeew-wwwl?* Granny would say when Elizabeth hopped up on her bed to say good morning. She took it for granted, having her grandmother in the house all the time. What she wouldn't give to have someone living with her now, not to help with Charlie necessarily but to help her not feel so lonely. If Granny were still alive she would be sorting Elizabeth out, bossing her around, straightening her skirt, telling her to change her earrings, asking her if she's eating enough. Elizabeth has tried to do that for herself but it's not the same.

'My parents will pick him up,' she replies.

'Oh?' A raised eyebrow. 'Does his dad have a busy job?'

Here it is. The moment Elizabeth knew would come, when she has to explain all over again that Jon is dead, then she has to make people feel better that they've asked her about a husband who is dead, then she has to put aside the sadness that inevitably arises for her whenever this exchange occurs – because Jon is dead, because he's staying dead, because this sadness is permanent and all she can do is try to shove it to the side from time to time, even though other people keep yanking it back to centre. She's considered having a badge made: *My husband is dead.* Just to pre-empt. And so she doesn't have to talk about it.

When she's with people who know her she can put thoughts of Jon to one side of her brain and just get on with living. Charlie doesn't ask about him much – which is a good and a bad thing – and her parents understand how she feels, so she rarely has to talk about Jon. Talking about him is what really makes her sad because she has to use past tense.

'He doesn't have a dad any more,' Elizabeth says. 'My husband died a few months ago.'

Olive's eyes widen and her mouth opens, then she presses her lips together and sniffs. 'Good on you, duck, getting back to things. To a job. I lost my Morrie when I wasn't much older than you and it took me *years*. I was that sad.' She sniffs again. 'Didn't have any kids, though, so at least I didn't have to worry about that. Still . . .'

She looks into Elizabeth's eyes for a few seconds, and while normally Elizabeth would find that uncomfortable, this time she doesn't. In fact, she feels relief, warm and comforting, flood her body and an overpowering sense of, for once, being in the right place at the right time. What were the odds that her new co-worker would understand her circumstances? That she wouldn't have to *explain* anything?

'It's not easy,' Olive says at last. 'So good on you.' She wriggles her chair-on-rollers to the side a little and pats the empty chair next to her. 'This is where you'll sit.'

Accepting the invitation, Elizabeth moves around behind the desk and puts her handbag underneath it before sitting down and smiling tentatively at Olive.

A door to Elizabeth's left opens and a man whom she presumes is Doctor Lopes sticks his head out.

'Olive?' he says. 'Is Mrs Toshiya here?'

'Not yet,' Olive says, tight-smiling in the doctor's direction.

He looks at his watch.

'You know she's always late,' Olive mutters.

'Yes,' he says. 'But *I'm* not.'

He notices Elizabeth and offers her a big smile. 'Hello,' he says cheerfully. 'I guess you're Elizabeth.'

'Yes.' Elizabeth stands up to greet him and self-consciously runs a hand down her skirt. This one always wrinkles. She should have worn something else.

'I'm Marco,' the doctor says, extending a hand.

'But call him "Doctor Lopes" around the patients,' Olive says, giving her a look that Elizabeth deciphers as one of irritation at the doctor, not at her.

'But Marco is fine when they're not around,' he says, giving Olive a look of his own. 'Very pleased you could join us, Elizabeth. Olive will show you the ropes.'

'So to speak,' Olive says under her breath.

'Call me when Mrs Toshiya arrives,' Marco says to Olive, then he nods to Elizabeth and closes his door.

'Like I wouldn't,' Olive huffs. 'Honestly.'

Elizabeth isn't sure whether to laugh or be worried that she's entered a hostile workplace.

'Family,' Olive goes on. 'Nightmare to work with.'

'Oh . . . ?' Elizabeth tries to calculate who Marco could be to Olive.

'My stepson,' Olive says. 'Met his father on a holiday. He was a widower. Marco was almost a teenager. His father's a hunk, let me tell you.' She rolls her eyes. 'Marco got the brains.'

Now Elizabeth can't help but laugh, because Marco is actually quite good-looking with his thick, chocolate-coloured hair and heavily lashed brown eyes.

'Anyway,' Olive continues, 'he's pretty much my son since I raised him from twelve but he *really* knows how to push my buttons. Insisted I work for him because no one else was good enough, then he drives me mad! But I'm scaling back, I told him.' She gives Elizabeth a proper smile. 'That's why you're here.'

The circumstances hadn't been explained at the interview; Elizabeth had presumed she would be replacing her.

'Sherry probably didn't tell you that,' Olive says, reading her mind.

'No. I thought I was . . . I thought someone was leaving.'

'Sherry and I work together – she'll be in later. I open up and she closes up. So I'm going to cut back on my days – once you're ready, I mean. For a little while we'll all be on top of each other, but Marco'll enjoy that.' She shoots a glance at the closed door. 'More attention for him. And for Doctor Blakeney. She'll be in later. Doctor Simpson too. And we have a nurse who does vaccinations for kids – that kind of thing. Lots going on!'

Elizabeth half-smiles and tries to process what the job will entail: looking after three doctors as well as a nurse and all their patients. She's spent months talking to hardly anyone, and in the space of a few weeks she's had strangers in her garden and now she'll be meeting strangers in her work. Hopefully her brain doesn't crumple in on itself with the sensory overload.

'It'll be a fair bit to take on,' Olive says, patting her hand. 'But I'll help you. You'll be right, duck.' She gives her the most genuine smile Elizabeth has seen since she arrived. 'Now, let's start.'

Olive picks up a sheaf of papers and swivels in Elizabeth's direction, and Elizabeth takes a deep breath as this new part of her life without Jon properly begins.

JUNE 1987

PRIMROSE
BALL WATTLE

CHAPTER NINETEEN

Why oh why oh why did she drink so much last night? Hangovers really should be banned. They take all the fun out of drinking. Not that Kathy is having that much fun, because at the rate she's going it's less like drinking and more like gulping. She really needs to slow down.

Or not. Who cares if she drinks too much? Quite clearly she doesn't or she'd do something about it.

Although she did see her neighbour – Boris or Barry, she can't remember his name – frowning in her direction when she clink-clinked out with the empty bottles this morning. What did he expect? It's a Saturday. Of course she's going to put out the empties after a week spent doing whatever-she-pleases-thanks-Boris-or-Barry. Because she's an adult and she can.

An adult who's acting like a teenager trying to get away with as much bad behaviour as possible.

She puts a hand over her face as she remembers cracking onto the woman working at the bottle-o last night. She was three sheets to the wind by then and the woman was trying to suggest that perhaps she didn't need to take home more grog, so Kathy asked if she could take the woman home instead. Luckily the woman had laughed. Probably because she's heard it before. What she didn't know is that Kathy hasn't tried it before.

Since Jemima left her she hasn't even drunkenly attempted to pick up anyone, male or female. She's almost felt cloistered within herself; not asexual so much as scared of what may happen if she gives permission to that part of herself to roam free in the world. So she's a little shocked by her own actions last night. What is she, a sleaze? She used to hate it when men tried something like that on her, and she'd be mortified to think her son is doing it. If he is. She doesn't know, because she'd never discuss it with him. Yet here she is, well past ripeness, trying to pluck an innocent party from the vine.

It makes her wonder what's lurking within. Perhaps she's been lying to herself about what sort of human being she is. All these years of believing she's polite and considerate, when the first chance she gets she's . . . *loose*.

But at least she is out trying to get healthy this morning. Again. Trying to reinstate the fitness regime that hasn't quite established itself. That's positive. That's something a responsible adult person does. A person who respects herself and is trying really hard to respect others when she's not too blotto to be in control of what comes out of her mouth.

A big walk is what's in order. Up the hill from Noosa Junction, past the holiday rentals and time-share apartments, and down towards Noosa Heads, along Main Beach up to the breakwater, then around the river's edge on dirt tracks until she reaches a small beach she has to cross, stepping carefully across sand that's being swallowed by the incoming tide.

She emerges onto a patch of grass that looks like it could do with a mow. There's a sign saying *Riverside Park* – well, yeah, what else? – and some trees with branches lopped off, clearly some time ago given the wounds don't look fresh. In fact, they look like vandalism, although she's no expert.

Ahead of her is a couple with a dog that's off leash. A kelpie, by the looks. Now the kelpie's heading in her direction, probably to round her up. People should really keep their dogs on leads.

'Oi! Lorraine!' calls the male of the couple over his shoulder, and the dog stops and lifts its head.

So does a woman who, Kathy can see now, is part of a small group bent over a garden bed, gardening tools next to their knees. The woman seems to work out that the man is talking to the dog, because she laughs and says something to the smaller blonde woman next to her.

Then she glances in Kathy's direction and smiles. It's such a nice smile. Welcoming. Almost like she knows Kathy.

Now she's nodding and waving like she *does* know Kathy. But Kathy doesn't know her. Or doesn't think she does. She really needs to cut down on the booze if her memory is this bad.

'Hello!' the woman – Lorraine, presumably – calls.

'Hi?' Kathy calls back but she doesn't walk any closer.

'You work at that restaurant on the river!' Lorraine shields her face with her hand, just as Kathy feels the warmth of the sun on her neck.

'Oh. Yeah,' she says.

'I'm Lorraine! My husband and I had dinner there a week or so ago. Anniversary.'

Kathy briefly closes her eyes to try to find the memory, and there it is: a pleasantly rowdy couple who seemed to enjoy each other's company, and the food and the wine. They were in the last sitting and Kathy left before they finished their meal because her shift was over.

'Right,' she says. 'Hi. I'm Kathy.'

Then she wonders what comes next: having made the acknowledgement, should she leave? No. Lorraine is being friendly. Kathy needs to be friendlier to people like Lorraine or she's going to be stuck at home alone for the rest of her life.

She walks towards the group. 'What are you doing?'

'We're the Sunshine Gardening Society!' Lorraine says and the blonde woman next to her raises her eyebrows. 'This my friend Cynthia.' She pats the blonde's arm. 'And this is Shirl, and Barb.'

There's a quick lift of the head from Shirl and Barb, and Kathy immediately recognises the robust shorter woman who wore a Beatles T-shirt the last time she saw her and now wears Crosby, Stills & Nash.

'G'day, love,' says the woman. 'I'm Shirl. That's Barb. Still walking, are you?' She winks.

Lorraine looks confused. 'Do you know each other?'

'No,' Kathy says, at the same time as Shirl says, 'Not know, per se, Lorrie – Kathy came across us outside Lizzie's place the other day. We were taking up the footpath, weren't we, Kath?'

Kathy laughs nervously, because she can't believe Shirl remembers her in that much detail. Surely she comes across a lot of random people? 'It was fine,' she says. 'So the Sunshine . . .' She can't remember the rest.

'Gardening Society.' Lorraine beams. 'We're volunteers. We look after some council areas. Some private gardens. Only on weekends. Saturdays, mainly. It's fun!'

She looks meaningfully at Kathy.

'Nice,' Kathy says.

'I remember you said you'd just moved here,' Lorraine returns.

'Did I?' Kathy can't remember that either. Normally she's not so chatty with diners. This Lorraine must have disarmed her.

'I ask a lot of questions,' Lorraine says. 'Bit of a chatterbox.' She laughs.

'I can attest to that,' says Cynthia.

Shirl glances in Kathy's direction again. 'Do you garden, love?'

'Oh, well . . .' Kathy is about to say no but that's not true. She hasn't been gardening since she moved here, but she and Owen had a lovely garden at their place in Carlton North. It was narrow but abundant with all sorts of plants that they enjoyed tending. Part of that comfortable lifestyle of theirs. Since she left him Kathy hasn't once thought about the fact that the end of the marriage meant the end of getting her hands in the dirt, being amongst nature. Instead she's been living indoors. Not a healthy lifestyle choice for many reasons, as she's discovering.

'Yes,' she says. 'I have done a bit of gardening.'

Shirl looks satisfied, like she's had a hunch confirmed. 'I have a spare pair of gloves,' she says, tugging something from a back pocket. 'Want to join us?'

'Oh.' Kathy looks down at her clothes – old shorts, a daggy T-shirt from a long-ago holiday destination. Not exactly fit for company, although she supposes anyone who's passed by her in the past hour or so has seen what she's wearing.

'Shorts aren't ideal,' Barb says, and Kathy notes her sensible long taupe slacks. 'But we can overlook that. If you'd like to join us, of course.' She smiles as if she doesn't mind one way or the other.

The day ahead holds nothing but reading the newspaper, indulging in regret and waiting for when the sun will be over the yardarm. Kathy has no good excuse to refuse these ladies. And what's the harm in putting on some gloves and picking up a trowel? If she doesn't like these women she doesn't have to see them again.

'Sounds good,' she says. 'What would you like me to do?'

'Here.' Shirl tosses the gloves to her as Lorraine shifts a little to the right.

'We're putting in some potted colour,' Lorraine explains, gesturing to some small plants on Cynthia's other side. 'Preparing the beds first.'

Kathy watches then copies, and before she knows it an hour has passed and she hasn't thought about Jemima or Owen or her children or anything else much at all, as the banter back and forth between the women keeps her distracted – and entertained. It turns out Shirl is a local bridge champion and has been trying to convince Barb to be her playing partner for years – except Barb has no interest in cards. And Lorraine and Cynthia have known each other since high school, which Kathy finds amazing since she made precisely zero friends in high school.

'So you'll come back?' Lorraine says as she gets to her feet, frowning. 'Ouch. Stiff.'

'Um . . . yes,' Kathy says, making a snap decision, because what else is she going to do on a weekend apart from work at night?

'Great! Karras is my last name. Look me up in the book and I'll tell you where we are next Saturday.'

'Okay.' Kathy stands up too, and smiles at each of the Sunshine Gardening Society members in turn.

'Always happy to have new members, Kath,' Shirl says. 'Lorrie, help me up.'

Lorraine pulls Shirl to a standing position, while Cynthia almost springs to her feet.

Barb remains on the earth and pushes her sunglasses further up her nose. 'Until next time, dear,' she says.

Unsure whether to stay longer or take off, Kathy looks uncertainly at Lorraine.

'We're about to go,' she says. 'You don't have to stay while we pack up. It's your first day – and you didn't even know you were going to do this! You can choof.'

'Oh . . . thanks.' Kathy looks around, unsure where to head to now. The past hour contained the closest thing she's had to peace of mind in what seems like years and she's not so keen for it to end. Yet she can't stay: she's not friends with these women.

The walking path by the river beckons and so, with a quick smile and a wave, she heads in its direction. As she walks she repeats Lorraine's last name to herself, determined to remember it so that once she's home she can check the phone book and make that call.

CHAPTER TWENTY

A hard, fast downpour has kept Cynthia and her father trapped in the house this morning. She'd told him she'd like to go for a walk in the national park, since they live on its fringes, and it would be better for her to have company when she's in there. Sometimes there's no one else around and while she's not scared of nature, she is scared of strange men.

Pat told her there's a huge marijuana plantation in the park. Not that he's seen it, just that 'everyone knows'. The sorts of people who have the chutzpah to grow and guard a huge marijuana plantation on Crown land are not the sorts Cynthia wants to encounter on a walking trail when she's on her own.

When she mentioned this supposed plantation to her father he simply raised an eyebrow and said, 'So?' Which she took as confirmation that the crops are there and the locals are looking the other way, because not much gets past Wilfred. The marijuana was not, therefore, the reason she gave her father when she asked him to accompany her on a walk, since he doesn't care about it. Instead she said she'd like to spend time with him, which is true. She just left out the part where she wants to ask about Odette and Pat and what her father has seen and heard from them both over the past few years.

Odette breezed in and out last night, ostensibly just to 'see Pa' although she slung a 'How are you, Mum?' in Cynthia's direction.

Cynthia had never felt so grateful for a scrap of affection. But she didn't let on, instead answering, 'Fine, thank you, darling.' She may even have seen a little smile from her daughter – although if one existed she probably owed it to Pat. The other day he called to say he'd talked to Odette about the three of them meeting up soon.

Pat likely knows the father of Odette's child but Cynthia doesn't even know his name. While she quite likes the idea of her daughter as the Madonna, because that's easier than thinking of Odette having sex, she knows there has to be a boy – a man, even – somewhere. Or not, because the lack of mentions of him makes Cynthia think he's not planning to be present for Odette or for his child, which is another reason Cynthia worries for her daughter.

It's in moments of contemplation such as these that Cynthia really misses her mother and simultaneously realises how much trouble she caused her, and how hypocritical she is being about Odette's pregnancy. Yet she feels unable to resist the hypocrisy. Her conclusion about it all is that being a parent is hard. No wonder she didn't try it twice.

Which is not entirely true. What she's never told anyone – not even Lorraine – is that when Odette was one year old she fell pregnant again then lost the baby. It wrecked her for quite a while. Sometimes she thinks that's the real, subterranean reason she left Pat: she didn't want to be reminded of losing their second child. He didn't know about the baby, either, but she made him pay for it.

'What's it to be?' her father says as he limps towards the couch.

The limp is new – and Cynthia is glad she's seen it now rather than halfway into the national park.

'What's wrong with your leg?' she asks.

Her father makes a face. 'Fell down the back steps.'

'When?'

'Just then.'

'What were you doing outside? It's raining.'

'Did I ask you to nag me?' He's glowering.

She glowers back. 'I'm not nagging. I'm *asking* because I'm *interested* in your welfare. But if you'd rather I don't take an interest, fine, I'll stop.'

She feels like stamping a foot to emphasise her point but that would be childish.

'Your mother nagged,' he says, but there's a wistful tone to it.

'Because she cared.'

He sighs and nods. 'That she did.'

Slowly he manoeuvres himself around the couch and sits down heavily next to Cynthia.

'I care too, Papa.'

'I know you do.' He pats her hand. 'A man just likes to do things his own way sometimes.'

Cynthia glances over to a framed photo of her mother that's displayed on its own, almost like a shrine, next to a pot plant that Cynthia is sure was in that same spot when she left years ago. In the photo her mother is sitting in the garden, two flowers in her hand, her head thrown back, laughing. She looks relaxed. At home.

'Is that the same peace lily Mum bought when Odette was born?' she says, gesturing to the plant.

Her father nods slowly. 'It is.'

'I can't believe it's still alive.'

Her father gives her a look. 'You mean you can't believe I've kept it alive since your mother died.'

Cynthia's cheeks feel hot. 'No.'

'I don't mind,' he says lightly. 'Not known for my green thumb.'

'All right, then . . . Yes, I didn't think you'd be able to keep a plant alive that long.'

'Just needs a little care and also to be left alone every now and again.' This time his look is freighted with meaning.

'Like you, you mean?' She laughs. 'Are you trying to tell me that you and the plant are kindred spirits?'

'Could be.' He shifts in his seat. 'Not walking, are we?'

'Not with your limp.' Cynthia's gaze goes once more to the photo of her mother. 'Von told me something the other day.'

'How is that old warhorse?'

'Old? Warhorse? You can hardly talk.'

He smiles, and inside the wrinkled face of this elderly man Cynthia sees her handsome father.

'True,' he accedes.

'The old warhorse is well,' she says. 'Still living with her art and her music. And you know how I've been going out every Saturday? I've joined the Sunshine Gardening Society. Von told me about it because she was one of the founders.'

Her father says nothing. Is it possible he didn't know his wife was in the same group? They were so close. But Cynthia's curious, and now that she seems to have become a member of the society simply because she keeps turning up every week she wants to know more about it, especially about her mother's role in it. She could ask Von, but her father is the more direct route – or so she believes.

'She said Mum was in it.'

Wilfred's eyes half-close. 'Did she now?'

'That's how they knew each other.'

He nods slowly. 'Yes, you may remember your mother going off on Saturday mornings from time to time.'

'I thought she was seeing friends,' Cynthia says. 'Although I guess that was also true.'

'She needed a break,' her father says, his tone sharp.

Searching her memory, Cynthia can't recall her mother ever expressing dissatisfaction with home life or acting as if she needed time away from them. Yet Cynthia also never expressed dissatisfaction with Pat and look what happened there. Perhaps she learnt to be a good actress from her mother. Although in her experience all women have sophisticated acting skills, usually acquired when they want to escape the presence or clutches of an intrusive man without him taking offence and becoming more aggressive as a result. Or perhaps it starts earlier than that, with the pressure to be a 'good little girl', while little boys are allowed to get away with tantrums and small acts of violence because 'boys will be boys'. There's a continuum of behaviour there, on the girl and boy side, but she feels too wearied by a lifetime of trying and failing to be a good girl to examine it more closely. Because leaving Pat made her decidedly not a good girl, and it was her mother who pointed it out first and most often.

'Were Kit and I that horrible?' Cynthia says. She remembers her brother could be a handful, always wandering into the bush and not coming home for hours.

'Not really,' her father says. 'But she had . . . troubles.' He looks down and Cynthia sees that he's kneading his fingers.

'Troubles?' She can't remember any. Her mother was always steadfast and capable; not full of joy, necessarily, but dependable, the way a child wants her mother to be. Always there when Cynthia needed her. The sort of mother Cynthia tried to be and, at a certain point, realised she'd failed to be when Odette moved back to Australia.

'Sometimes she wasn't right in the head,' her father says gruffly. 'You know?'

Again Cynthia scours her memory, trying to match something to what her father has said. Then it comes to her: being woken at night by the sound of glass breaking; muffled sobs, not from the next room but somewhere beyond; her father's voice low, almost a monotone.

And something else: weekends when her father would take her and Kit on adventures, as he called them. She never thought to ask why her mother wasn't with them, because of the way these adventures were presented: Papa in charge, taking them to camp in the hinterland, or to Fraser Island on the barge.

'No,' she says softly. 'I didn't know. But I remember you took me and Kit away sometimes. Was that to give Mum time to herself?'

He nods. 'Time to garden. With that society.' There's resignation in his voice.

Cynthia thinks of what it's been like for her these past weekends, the sense of satisfaction she's had from doing something literally earthy. Helping people as well as making places beautiful, helping to create an environment in which plants can flourish. Learning about the ecology of the area she grew up in, how there is grassland and wet heath and all sorts of things. Different weeds and how to spot them. Insects and their place in the ecosystem. All of it knowledge that connects her to her world and to other people in a way she has never contemplated before. And the best part is that it has come to her without effort: all she has to do is listen to Shirl and Barb as they impart their wisdom while she and Lorraine dig and tug and plant. For anyone who is having troubles, who is feeling detached from the joys of life, the appeal of this activity is plain. Because, as Cynthia realises, she needed it too.

It makes her heart break to think of her mother feeling so separated from her husband, her children, her life, that she needed to join the society, but it also makes her glad to know that the structure was there to support her.

'Did it help?' she asks Wilfred.

His eyes now meet hers and his hands are still. 'Well, she stayed.' His mouth turns down briefly. 'She was going to leave. All of us. But she stayed.'

Cynthia sees that the downpour has stopped, and soon the sun will probably come out, because the rain often visits in short bursts then disappears. It's a pattern she knows so intrinsically that she can almost tell the weather by observing her body: the tug of a headache as the barometric pressure rises, the sense of her joints almost oozing once the rain starts.

126

She has the strong desire to go outside and run her fingers over the wet grass, to feel the same earth her mother did all those years when she was clearly experiencing something Cynthia had no idea about and which she is ashamed she didn't recognise. Her mother wanted to leave them. To not be here. Which could mean either not here in this house or not here on this earth. She is sure her father has deliberately left that vague.

It's not as if Cynthia doesn't understand the impulse, because she did take herself away. Perhaps she subconsciously knew what her mother was thinking of all that time. Perhaps she did it on her mother's behalf, without fully understanding it. It's not so hard to believe that a mother and a daughter can understand things about the other without them being expressed. Cynthia will never truly know, though, because the past is as mysterious to her as the process that causes a seed to become a plant.

'Maybe we should go for that walk, after all, Papa,' she says. 'While it's sunny. If you're not still limping.'

'I reckon we could,' Wilfred says, and he puts his hands on the couch to push himself up. 'It'll be nice to be outside.'

As he stands he tests his feet. 'Right as rain,' he says, then winks.

Cynthia takes his arm and escorts him out the side doors to the garden. Her mother's garden, with all the secrets she poured into it. Perhaps one day, Cynthia thinks, she will dig them up.

CHAPTER TWENTY-ONE

'Terry!' Lorraine knows she's shouting into the void, because Terry probably isn't even in the house – he's impossible to keep track of these days. But it's worth a shot. His job this morning was to rake the garden. He's not supposed to go off skateboarding with his friends until he's done it, but there's debris on the lawn and not a rake in sight.

It's not as if Lorraine is giving him these jobs to punish him – she and Mike are run off their feet with their various commitments. The other day Cora suggested that perhaps Lorraine had taken on too much with the Sunshine Gardening Society and Lorraine had surprised herself with how cross she'd been in response.

'That is *my time* for *me*,' she'd said. 'Mike gets time for himself even with all the work. Just check his TAB receipts – he manages to put bets on the ponies when it suits him.'

'He works hard!' Cora objected, which really riled Lorraine, especially because Cora didn't take the bait about the betting.

When Lorraine married Mike he was paying back gambling debts – to his mother, because she'd paid them off for him. He swore it would never happen again, to both of them, but he slipped after each son was born. Then he begged for forgiveness and, as far as either of them knew, he'd stayed away from it for almost as long as Simon's been alive. So either that's true or he just hasn't been leaving the evidence in his pants pockets for Lorraine to find when she does the washing. Because that's how she discovered it the other day.

'And I don't work hard?' she flung back at Cora, whose nostrils flared. 'The gardening is important to me,' Lorraine carried on. 'I get to see my friend *and* we're doing good works.'

'You're a mother,' Cora had said sniffily. 'You are not supposed to have time for you.'

'Well, that's your generation, Cora,' Lorraine had snapped back. 'You sacrifice yourself to your kids and your husband, then you take it out on everyone else as soon as you get the chance.'

They'd stood blinking at each other, Cora looking like she'd been slapped and Lorraine feeling both sheepish about what she'd said and proud of it too, because Cora's sanctimony really gets under her skin.

Then Mike walked in and Cora burst into tears. Manipulation *par excellence* of the sort that can only be pulled off by someone who feels powerless. Of course, Mike's used to it and didn't immediately take his mother's side, but things have been awkward since – between Mike and Lorraine. Cora's been carrying on as if everything's lovely. Probably because she's enjoying the fact that Mike and Lorraine are tetchy with each other. Or maybe Lorraine is just being ungenerous.

'*Terryyyyyy!*' she tries again.

'He's not here,' comes Simon's small voice from the next room.

Lorraine walks in and sees her youngest son curled up on the couch, book in hand, looking forlorn. He's been like that a lot lately and Lorraine is starting to think it's because it gets him attention from Cora, who fusses over him as if he's some nineteenth-century orphan with consumption.

'When did he leave?' Lorraine makes herself ask this gently because it's not Simon's fault that Terry isn't here.

'Um . . . when the cartoon finished.'

Lorraine looks at her watch and sees that it's almost a quarter past nine, which means the cartoon probably finished at nine, given what TV programming is like. So Terry could be halfway to Noosaville by now if he's on his skateboard.

'You work him too hard.'

Lorraine jumps at the unexpected voice. Cora's. Naturally.

'He doesn't work at all,' Lorraine mutters, not turning completely towards her mother-in-law because that would be an invitation to Cora to keep talking.

'He's a boy,' Cora says. 'He wants to play.'

'Simon is a boy. Terry is a teenager. I had plenty of chores to do at that age.'

Although Mike probably didn't, given Cora's opinion about adolescents and work. It's a wonder Mike is so hardworking now.

'But you give Simon little jobs too.' Cora's face shows her disapproval.

'He *likes* them, Cora. Don't you, Si?'

Simon gives her those pathetic eyes he's been perfecting and Lorraine feels the queasiness that comes with thinking that your kid is betraying you to your enemy.

'Sometimes,' he says feebly, like his arm is being twisted.

Great – Cora's got to him too. Lorraine is being sidelined in her own house. Perhaps she should just leave them all to it and see how far they get when she's not there to pack their school lunches and organise haircuts and dentist appointments and presents for birthday parties. Not to mention the things she does for Mike, some of which can't be mentioned in company.

'Fine. You don't like them,' Lorraine says tersely and chews the inside of her cheek, like she always does when she's tense. Then she starts to breathe noisily, like she's blowing into bellows, and that's how she knows she's really stressed, because it's what she used to do before exams when she was at school.

'Are you all right?' Cora says, although Lorraine can't hear a skerrick of concern in her voice.

'No.'

She doesn't want to deal with this today. Doesn't want Simon to take his grandmother's side. Doesn't want Terry skiving off. Doesn't want Mike to be out working. It's Sunday. They should be spending time together as a family. It's been weeks since they've had Sunday lunch together, and Lorraine loves it when Mike lights the barbecue and throws on some snags and onions to make his famous-in-his-own-mind sausage sangers. Used to love it. She can't remember the last time he did it.

That's it. She's getting out of here. Cora can watch Simon. Simon would probably prefer that. If Terry comes back, Cora can tell him there's absolutely nothing for him to do because if Lorraine asks her to say he has a job she won't. She just wants to be the cool grandma. And what Lorraine needs right now is the non-cool grandma. She needs her own mother.

'I'm off,' she says.

'Where?' Cora says.

'Somewhere.' Lorraine isn't going to tell her anything. None of her business.

'Where, Mum?'

Simon's doing the consumptive thing again and for once Lorraine finds it annoying instead of cute, and it's really not great, is it, when you think your own kid is annoying? If she'd been doubting her desire to get out of the house for a while, this convinces her.

'*Somewhere*, Si.' If she uses the shortened form of his name she doesn't sound so harsh. That's what she tells herself, anyway. 'Nana will stay with you.'

She picks up the car keys and her handbag, and before she can blink she's pulling up outside her mother's house because Eumundi is just down the road. Even though Lorraine told Rose it was 'hicksville' when she bought there, she's happy about its proximity now.

'Mum,' she calls as she opens the back door and drops her bag on the kitchen counter.

'Hello, Loll,' Rose says as she walks hesitantly into the room. She twisted her ankle a couple of weeks ago and still won't tell Lorraine how.

'Nothing to worry about, Loll,' she'd said. Loll is what Rose has always called her. Short for Lolly, because Lorraine was, according to Rose, the sweetest little girl. As Lorraine likes to remind her, that was a long time ago.

'Still hurting?' she says, kissing her mother on the cheek.

Rose nods. 'Bit. What are you doing here?'

'Don't take this the wrong way but I think I want to drop my family out the window.'

Her mother arches an eyebrow, probably because she's heard this spiel before. 'All members? Or just Cora?'

'How dare you imply that,' Lorraine says drily, picking up a Red Delicious apple from the bowl her mother always keeps on the kitchen table and taking a bite. 'Actually, Terry and Simon today.' And Cora too, of course, but as her mother knows that goes without saying.

'What have they done?'

'Terry's not doing his chores and Simon is taking Cora's side on things.'

The latter isn't entirely true, but there's less drama in the truth and Lorraine is feeling dramatic.

'That's to be expected. Cora doesn't have to discipline him.' Rose smiles and pats Lorraine's cheek. 'You were the same with my mum.'

'Really?'

'And she indulged it. Wanted to be your favourite.' Rose shrugs. 'She was always a little competitive with me.'

'Good thing you don't compete with me.' Lorraine takes another bite and chews noisily. 'Or with Cora.'

They're both silent then. Rose has every right to be upset about the amount of time Cora gets to spend with their mutual grandchildren relative to how often she sees them, but she's never made a fuss. Lorraine knows that's not because she doesn't care. It's because she doesn't want to cause trouble within Lorraine's marriage. Except Lorraine has often thought she's letting her mother down by not insisting that the boys should see Rose more, even though that would mean her and Mike trying to find time to make it happen. Rose doesn't drive; never has. Cora doesn't either.

Lorraine couldn't stand to not be able to get in the car and zip off when she needs to, but that generation relied more on the menfolk to get them around. Or maybe it just wasn't that common for girls to drive. She really should ask her mum one day. But not today. Today she wants to wallow a while longer in feeling upset about her kids not behaving the way she wants them to.

'Cora loves them,' Rose says quietly. 'As do I. But sometimes we think going easy on kids is how we should love them, when the opposite needs to happen. Structure is good for young people.'

'Yeah, but how do you keep them in it? They usually listen to Mike but he's so *busy*, Mum.'

'Can't he cut back on work?'

'We need the money. Feeding five is expensive.'

And now it looks like he's placing bets too. She hasn't broached it with him yet and isn't sure how – because Cora's right, he does work hard and part of Lorraine thinks she shouldn't tell him what to do with money when it doesn't affect the rest of them. What's a couple of bucks here and there? That's all the receipts added up to.

'Plus he wants to build onto the house so Cora has more room,' she adds.

She and Mike had argued about that. Why should Cora get more space when their bedroom is the smallest in the house? Mike had said, 'We don't need much space to hold a whole lotta love,' and Lorraine had wanted to whack him. Softly, but whack him all the same, because how corny can you be? Even if it's true. He's always been good at giving her a good time. As he would say, 'It's one of my only talents.'

'So where do they think you are now?' Rose says.

'Who knows? Don't care.'

Rose's telephone rings and she walks slowly into the sitting room to answer it. 'Hello, Cora,' Lorraine hears her say, but doesn't catch the rest.

Once the call is over Rose comes back into the kitchen. 'That was Cora. She guessed you'd come here. Simon's crying. He thinks he upset you so much you left.'

'He's right,' Lorraine fires back, then she sighs. 'I'd better go.'

Her mother nods and squeezes her arm. 'Always here if you need me.'

'Same.' Lorraine kisses her cheek. 'Love you, Mum.'

'Love you too.'

As Lorraine starts the engine she realises that she may have only seen her mother for a few minutes but she feels a hundred times better. That's the power of being with someone who loves you unquestioningly.

It's probably what her children feel about her, too, even if they don't quite know it. She should try to honour that. Although Terry still needs to rake the lawn.

CHAPTER TWENTY-TWO

It occurs to Elizabeth that she's come to enjoy helping the ladies of the Sunshine Gardening Society as they work to remake Jon's garden so it closer fits his ideal. While gardening wasn't a love Elizabeth and Jon shared, being involved in his garden does help keep him close. Sometimes when she's digging up a garden bed, she can pretend that he's just in another part of the garden and if she turns around she'll see him. Although that's also the reason she feels a twinge of fear each time the ladies work in her garden – Elizabeth knows she will let herself imagine all sorts of things because she so badly wants them to be true. By doing something Jon loved she knows she can't bring him back, but she can tell herself that maybe he approves from wherever he is, or that he's guiding her somehow. Those would be fairy stories, however, and as much as she believes in Heaven and Hell she does not believe in any kind of afterlife that would bring her in contact with her husband once more.

Oh, but she wants to. And that's part of why she struggles some days to reconcile her faith with her reality.

The Bible provides guidance for all sorts of circumstances in life but she can't find exactly the one to help her now. There is nothing about what to do when you lie in bed at night and wish with your entire body and mind to hold your husband once more. Nothing to tell her what to say to comfort their son when his body is shuddering with sadness and he cries so much he coughs. Offering the phrase 'Daddy is in Heaven now' doesn't work because she has no way of proving it's true. She and Charlie have to take it on faith – literally. Which may be fine for her but her son is too young to understand. He wants to know where Heaven is and whether they can visit.

That fear is something Elizabeth simply has to live with, however, so today she will once more roll up her sleeves and let her forearms get dirty.

Shirley has turned up with a potted native that is a something-wattle, saying, 'It'll look beaut, promise!' amongst Jon's pinks and reds. The other women are arranging themselves in various spots around the garden. Right then, with them in place, Elizabeth feels like the garden is being so well taken care of that she could crawl back into bed and it wouldn't matter one bit.

Why does no one tell you that grief is so *tiring*? That it wears you down so you feel exhausted to the point where you're sure your rawest nerves and emotions are exposed to all. At the very time you need strength, it isn't there. If Elizabeth didn't believe that God's design for everything is perfect, she would be inclined to think that in this there has been a malfunction: the grieving human needs to be wired differently.

'Cat got your tongue?' Shirley says.

'Hm?' Elizabeth has the sensation of Shirley's question pulling her down a long tunnel and out into fresh air. She's had that feeling somewhat regularly of late.

'I asked how your job's going.'

Shirley's smiling in such a way that she doesn't seem offended that Elizabeth has basically been standing there ignoring her. It's then that Elizabeth notices she's wearing a T-shirt that says *Big Brother and the Holding Company*, whatever that means.

'Oh.' Elizabeth pauses to swallow and think. 'It's interesting. I think it will be fine.'

'You said it's with Doctor Lopes? Over at Sunrise?'

'Yes. There's Doctor Blakeney as well. And Doctor Simpson is in one or two days a week.'

'Old Bob Simpson, eh?' Shirley smiles mysteriously.

'He keeps talking about retiring,' Elizabeth says, 'but Olive says he won't be able to afford to go on cruises as often if he stops working. And he likes cruises, apparently.'

Elizabeth can still see the look on Olive's face as she shared this information *sotto voce* after Doctor Simpson walked past them – she made it seem as if going on a cruise was the naughtiest possible thing a person could do and Elizabeth had to stop herself laughing out loud. Which surprised her, because she hasn't been laughing much lately.

'Who doesn't?' Shirley says, then she picks up the potted native. 'All right if we put this in?'

Elizabeth feels resistance rising within her; then a wave travelling from another direction reminds her that Jon isn't here, and while she wants to honour him perhaps she has to let things change. For her own sake.

'I guess so,' is the compromise she reaches.

'Bewdy.'

It's too much, however, to actually watch the plant go in, so Elizabeth wanders deeper into the garden.

There's no Barbara today, but Cynthia and Lorraine are here – and there's someone new.

'Hello, Elizabeth,' Cynthia says, beaming. 'I thought Shirl was going to keep you all day.'

Elizabeth smiles weakly, because she had wondered the same thing. 'What are you doing?' she asks.

'We're pruning these shrubs.' Cynthia gestures to the hydrangeas. 'Shirl said winter is the time to cut them.'

'Really?' Elizabeth should know these things, because she'll have to maintain this garden once these ladies have moved on to other projects. The prospect makes her feel slightly weak, but also spurs her to the conviction that she should train Charlie to do it.

'How have you been, Elizabeth?' Lorraine says, gloved hands on hips, her sunhat halfway down the back of her skull. She always looks as if she's in the middle of great movement, her hair and clothes slightly awry.

Elizabeth finds it endearing – she was brought up to be so proper all the time and quite often that can feel like living inside a corset. She longs to be unlaced and unconfined but she won't let herself.

'Pretty good,' she says, and it's a fair approximation of the truth. Today she feels slightly better than yesterday, and yesterday she felt slightly better than the day before. 'What about you?'

'I want to kick my mother-in-law in the shins and lock my teenager in the attic. Not that we have an attic.' Lorraine smiles, and Elizabeth can't tell if she's serious about what she's said.

'You have a tough mother-in-law too?'

It's the new woman, who is older than Lorraine and Cynthia. Her face is lined in a way that suggests she frowns more than she smiles, and her shoulders are stooped, just as Elizabeth knows hers tend to get when she's feeling low.

'I would say they're all like that,' Lorraine says, 'but my mother is lovely to Mike – and Mike'd say the same. This is Kathy, by the way.' She points her elbow to the newcomer.

'Hi, Kathy, I'm Elizabeth.'

'Pleased to meet you – and to spend time in your garden. It's going to be lovely once we're done.'

'Thanks. I can't claim any credit for it.'

Elizabeth sighs and glances around at the thick stands of flowering shrubs and the smaller plants dotted between them. Jon crammed this space with as much colour as he could, and while he was alive Elizabeth spent hardly any time out here. What a waste. What a shame. She didn't appreciate her husband's passion until he died.

'I heard.' Kathy's gaze is direct and unsentimental, and Elizabeth likes it. She's really sick of pity, which still appears before and after church on Sundays – when she makes it there – and when some of her friends phone her.

'Your husband had a good eye,' Kathy goes on. 'We'll make sure it's kept up to his standard. Although, of course, only you can tell us that.' She smiles briefly then bends down to brush twigs off her pants.

'How did you come to join the gardening society?' Elizabeth hasn't asked this of any of the others, but it seems appropriate given Kathy's just shown up in her garden.

'We co-opted her,' Cynthia says. 'She was walking past when we were in a park and before she knew it we'd made her a gardener.'

'I'm new to the area,' Kathy explains.

'So she needs some friends. That's the real reason she joined.' Lorraine winks at Kathy then adjusts her hat. 'Anyway, we should get back to it. I'm sure you don't want us hanging around all day.'

'Take as long as you need, honestly.' Elizabeth feels a twinge of disappointment that their conversation is over so soon. 'And I have lunch for you when you're ready.'

'That's so kind,' Cynthia says, tilting her head to one side. 'You're very thoughtful.'

'Trying to be,' Elizabeth murmurs, but she takes her leave before Cynthia can reply and heads back to Shirley to get her orders for the day.

JULY 1987

BROAD-LEAVED GEEBUNG

CHAPTER TWENTY-THREE

The breakwater on Main Beach wasn't here when Cynthia was a child. There was the stretch of sand starting at the Little Cove end – just around from Little Cove itself – and going all the way until . . . Well, some days you couldn't see the end of the beach because it would be lost in salt haze. But it was far. Hours and hours if a person had a vehicle that could drive on sand.

On a clear day you could see Fraser Island beyond the point where the beach finished. Cynthia thinks of those weekend adventures with her father and Kit, driving – on roads – all the way to the barge then leaving the car behind. Once they were on the water it always felt like anything could happen, then they'd step off on the island and the magic really began.

They'd camp overnight and listen to the noises of frogs and birds and insects. Papa would make up stories about what all the creatures were doing. They were never scary: in his tales the frogs were beneficent rulers of a vast kingdom of lifeforms, organising communities and negotiating with the birds about who could go where at what time. He knew a lot about the trees and the plants on the island and which creatures would prefer this tree or that. It made the whole place seem alive with energy and history; it was special. And she can't remember the last time she went there.

Now Cynthia knows those adventures were undertaken to give her mother time to herself, or with the Sunshine Gardening Society.

On the weekend, while they were in Elizabeth's garden, Kathy had asked how long the society had been going and how many gardens they'd tended, and Shirl said something about the local council holding an oral history – transcribed – of the society. But when Cynthia asked how she might go about getting a copy of it Shirl went vague and said that she'd never actually seen the document, just heard about it.

It's hard for Cynthia to avoid the conclusion that the Sunshine Gardening Society is more akin to the Sunshine Secret Society – and she can't say she dislikes the idea. In a world where so many women's lives are always on display – as they move from parents' homes to marital homes, always serving, always observed – it makes sense that they might use good works as an opportunity to share secrets. Or to keep them. It seems the women of the society past and present might have kept her mother's secrets, and as much as Cynthia feels indignant about that she understands it too.

Today, there's a light morning breeze and it's cool. Winter is here. The sunlight is paler than in spring and summer, and the colour of the water has changed accordingly. Cynthia won't be swimming in the ocean until winter is over, even if the days are pleasant.

'Cynthia,' calls the voice she's been expecting, and she turns to see Pat walking slowly across the rocks clad in a fisherman's jumper, bermuda shorts and docksiders. Behind him walks their daughter, in a long cotton dress and an almost-as-long woollen cardigan.

Both of them seem to have dressed to have an each-way bet on what the temperature will turn out to be. Or maybe the bet is on what this meeting will turn out to be. Pat wasn't sure if Odette would come, just said he wanted to try to bring them all together.

'Hello, Pat,' Cynthia says once he's a couple of metres away, his hair ruffling in the breeze.

He's grinning at her like everything's fine, like Cynthia's father hasn't been nagging her to 'talk to your bloody daughter' even though, as Cynthia has reminded him, her bloody daughter doesn't want to talk to her.

Yet here is Odette, all nineteen years and rounded belly of her, hair cropped and dyed blonde, the dark roots even longer than they were last time Cynthia saw her, eyes as big and brown as they have always been. Out here in the light – which may be more muted than in summer but which conceals nothing – it's as though she's seeing Odette for the first time in years. And she's still so young. Too young to be a mother.

Cynthia is sure she never looked that young, perhaps because it feels like five lifetimes have passed since she was Odette's age. She's changed countries and lives. Her father once told her that time can change shape and she believes it now. One year can be a different length from another, depending on what happens.

Now enough time has passed that Odette's baby will have fingernails and eyelashes, which means it's becoming a person. A person Odette will need to care for, who she will love as much as Cynthia loves her. That shock of recognition that Odette is about to experience the same transformation that took place when Cynthia herself became a mother is enough for Cynthia to know that as much as she thought a different outcome was preferable, what is happening now is inexorable and, ultimately, good.

Odette will become a mother; Cynthia needs to let her.

'Hello, darling,' she says. Because Odette will always be her darling, no matter what goes on between them.

Odette's lips part and Cynthia guesses that she's probably wondering whether to reprimand her for being so familiar or to call her 'Mummy' the way she used to.

'Hi,' is what she says.

'You look well.'

Odette rolls her eyes. 'I feel gross.'

'Have you been sick?'

'Not for a while. I'm just . . . big. I don't like being big.' Odette glances at her father, who has kept his body angled towards Cynthia this whole time.

'I understand,' Cynthia says, then she too looks at Pat. 'So, the breakwater?'

He smiles and shrugs. 'I like it. We can see everything. And no one can overhear us.'

'In case we . . . shout? Is that what you mean?'

Pat's expression changes to something more hangdog. 'I've never shouted at you.'

That's true: he hasn't. Never shouted, never even seemed to be annoyed. Cynthia stood before him fourteen years ago and said she was leaving him and taking their daughter and he still didn't raise his voice to her. Afterwards she wondered if she'd wanted to get *something* out of him. Some sign that he cared. She didn't know, then, that temper doesn't necessarily denote affection; that people – men – show their love in different ways. It was naive of her.

'No, I'm the shouter,' she says, because that's also true.

Odette smiles briefly. 'Me too.'

Pat turns and looks out to sea for a minute or so. When he turns back his expression is serious. 'I can't have my two best girls not talking to each other,' he says. 'Especially when I can't figure out a good reason why.'

'I'm happy to talk to Odette,' Cynthia says quickly.

'You judge me!' Odette says almost over the top of her.

'I do not!' Cynthia can hear how loud she sounds and resolves to dial it down. 'I just *worry* about you.' Her eyes meet Pat's. 'It's normal for a parent to worry,' she continues. 'Especially when their child is about to become a parent themselves.'

'Wilf says they didn't judge *you*,' Odette says churlishly.

'Oh, he's Wilf now, is he?'

'Sometimes.' Odette folds her arms above her belly and steps closer.

Cynthia thinks back to the day she told her parents that she was expecting. She doesn't remember judgement so much as outrage, and at that time they seemed to be the same thing.

If her father remembers it differently – well, that's how memory works. She can't say he's wrong. She can't say *she's* wrong.

She takes a breath. 'My father may not think he was judgemental. And I don't think I'm judging you, whereas you think I am. So who knows where the truth is. But I'm not.' Another breath. 'I am concerned that you'll be doing this on your own and that's a hard, hard road.'

As I well know, she wants to add, except Odette could then say – truthfully – that Cynthia became a single mother by leaving Pat. Pat never left her.

'Ash is still thinking about it,' Odette mumbles.

Ash is, Cynthia guesses, the baby's father.

'He shouldn't have to think about it, darling,' she says sharply. 'Your father didn't. If this Ash doesn't want to take responsibility it's probably better that he leaves you alone.' She swallows the hard lump of hypocrisy that's lodged in her throat. 'As much as I wish that weren't the case. You deserve better.'

She glances at Pat, who looks a little wretched, and takes that to mean he feels the same way she does.

Odette's shoulders relax and she looks at her father. 'Dad said you miss me.'

Pat raises his eyebrows to Cynthia and she knows it's him admitting that he may have massaged Odette into the meeting today. As if Cynthia minds – their daughter is standing here and not telling her to get lost. That's a victory.

'I miss you every day that I don't see you,' Cynthia says. 'You are part of me – I can't not think about you. I can't not miss you. And I don't mean this to sound condescending, but once you're a mother you'll understand that better.'

Odette puts her hands on her hips, like she's squaring up to Cynthia.

'I hope I didn't kick you from the inside the way this baby is doing to me,' she says, and Cynthia smiles with the relief of something that sounds like an actual civil sentence.

'You did,' she replies. 'But I didn't mind.'

She wants to hug Odette – squeeze her so tightly that she can feel how much she is loved. But that's not the cool thing to do once your child is past childhood, so Cynthia keeps her arms by her sides.

'I didn't mind because I wanted you so much,' she says.

'I want this baby too!'

'I know you do.'

'Ash said he wants to see me this weekend.' Odette's voice trembles a little. With hope, Cynthia imagines, even if she doesn't feel it herself.

'That's good.'

'I've told Odette that you and I will help her with the baby,' Pat says. 'Whether Ash is involved or not.'

'We will. I will.' Cynthia smiles at him with gratitude.

'I just don't want you to lecture me, Mum.'

That hurts a little, but it's not as if Cynthia didn't use a similar line to her own mother. 'Who says I will?'

Odette rolls her eyes. 'History says you will.'

'Odette!' Cynthia tries to feign outrage except her daughter is telling the truth, and she is rewarded with a small smile. 'I just want what's best for you. Even if it doesn't seem like it.'

Before Odette can say anything more, Pat positions himself between them. 'How about a walk on the beach back to your place? I wouldn't mind dropping in to see your father.'

'Sounds good.'

Cynthia follows them as they step carefully over the stones, towards the sand, and watches as Pat puts his hand on Odette's shoulder.

Maybe one day Cynthia will be able to do that again. Today, though, she'll take the walk and anything else Odette is prepared to offer her and count herself lucky.

CHAPTER TWENTY-FOUR

The bottle of shiraz is half-empty and Kathy isn't sure how that happened. She remembers uncorking it then letting it breathe for a little while – the sommelier at the restaurant is always going on about letting red wines *breathe*. Of course, the sommelier is mainly interested in wine being its best whereas Kathy is mainly interested in drinking it for the effect. She tries, though. Working in hospitality, she needs to at least pretend to consider things like wine breathing.

Partly the wine-breathing routine is how she kids herself that she's not drinking more than she should. If she can resist it for fifteen minutes, that makes her not desperate. If she can look at that bottle opened and not touch it for a while, she doesn't have a problem. Which is about as plausible as her reasoning that not keeping wine in the house means she's not developing a very bad habit that she's using to ward off sadness and grief – and, prob-ably the biggest factor of all, loneliness. She kids herself that it's a temporary measure and that she'll feel less sad about Jemima soon, even though rationally she knows that dulling the pain, whichever means she chooses, is not the same as dealing with it. It's just delaying the dealing.

She is well aware, too, that kidding herself has been an almost lifelong pursuit. She kidded herself that she was content being married to Owen. When she met Jemima she kidded herself that this was the first and only time she'd ever been attracted to anyone female when she distinctly remembers having crushes on at least two female classmates. At the time she thought it was just what teenage girls did, and because she spent years – decades – without meeting a woman she was attracted to she thought that was that.

Except she's also kidding herself there. She had a friend, Denise, and they were as close as anything; then Kathy found herself thinking about the way Denise smelled and how pretty she looked with her new haircut, and when Denise actually asked her one day if she was in love with her – suggesting that she didn't mind if Kathy was – Kathy was so offended that she broke off the friendship. Except she wasn't really offended, just mortified that she'd been so transparent.

She wondered for months afterwards what might have happened if she'd admitted it. Because she *was* in love with Denise. In her mind it was a capital-R Romantic love – she idealised Denise and told herself that she wanted to be like her, so sophisticated and accomplished, so she was in love with the paragon and it had nothing to do with desire. The truth, however, was that it was small-r romantic and Denise knew it even if Kathy wouldn't admit to it.

It was the first time someone had seen her and her wants more clearly than Kathy could see them herself. The next person to do it was Jemima. The person after that was, in a different way, Lorraine, who had identified something in Kathy that day in the park, and by inviting her to join the Sunshine Gardening Society has given her a reason to think the world a rosier place than she has of late.

Not that it's so rosy Kathy won't have maybe just another half-glass of shiraz. She still needs a crutch and this is the one she's chosen.

Then the phone rings and she jumps, knocking her glass over on the coffee table and the wine with it. She swears, torn between wanting to mop up the wine immediately and answer the phone. No one calls her at night. Who's ringing her this late?

'Hello?' she says, sounding cross.

'Hi, Mum,' says an equally cross voice back to her and Kathy swears under her breath. Michelle. Who has not once called her since she left Melbourne. Why now?

Kathy doesn't want another confrontation like the one they had when she said she departed for Queensland and Michelle told her she was running away from her problems. Which was, yes, okay, correct – but that didn't mean Kathy wanted to hear it.

'Hi, sweetheart,' she says, because a mother has to at least pretend to be affectionate even when she's not feeling it. 'How are you?'

Kathy realises this sounds lame because it's the sort of question you ask when you're talking to someone regularly, not when you've been ignoring them because they don't approve of you and 'your choices', as Michelle and her brother termed it. *We don't like your choices, Mum.* Yeah, so? What if Mum doesn't like them either but feels as if they aren't choices so much as inevitabilities?

'So now you care how I am?'

Michelle's voice is loaded with disdain and it makes Kathy sigh, because her grown-up daughter seems to think Kathy should still be taking her children into account with every decision she makes about her life.

'Of course,' Kathy says, trying to keep her voice neutral. No sense in poking the bear. 'Just because I don't live in Melbourne any more doesn't mean I don't care.'

'You don't ring me.'

Kathy takes a slow breath so she doesn't take the bait. 'I'm sorry, Michelle, I know I've been slack.'

It's always better to show penance even if you don't really feel it. Time is saved because it's what the accuser wants.

Michelle huffs in response. 'Are you drunk?'

'What?'

'You've been drinking.'

'It's Friday night, Mich. I'm allowed to unwind.'

'Grant said you were drunk the other night too.'

Kathy has a vague memory of her son calling her after she'd finished a bottle of something, but she didn't think she was drunk so much as chirpy. Not that she can admit to not really remembering their conversation because that would be proof of what he told his sister.

'Then I guess I'm a failure as a mother.' When penance doesn't work, sometimes admitting defeat can do the trick.

'Don't be so *dramatic*.' Another huff, then Michelle sighs. 'We're just worried about you.'

'I'm fine,' Kathy says and she realises that, in some ways, she means it. She has a job, she has activities, she's still trying to commit to getting fit. Effort is being made.

'Then why did you leave?'

There's a tone of hurt-little-girl and Kathy understands, even if she doesn't want to give in to it. Michelle is more than old enough to be responsible for her own feelings.

'Because I wanted to change things. And I have.'

'By drinking every night?'

'It's not every night,' she says before she can censor herself, and she's rewarded with a minute's silence on the phone line.

'It's not good to drink alone,' Michelle says finally.

'I know. But, honestly, I'm fine. Or I'm getting to fine.'

More silence. Then, 'When will you be fine?'

Now it's Kathy's turn to pause. She thinks about her life now. The week just gone. The week ahead. Work is going well. She likes her co-workers; Hans is funny and kind. And she really likes the Sunshine Gardening Society. When she's in Elizabeth's garden, in particular, she feels useful and capable. That's not a feeling she's had for a while. If she keeps being a member of the society she's fairly sure she'll be fine. Or one of the ladies will make sure she is, because if Lorraine's not asking her direct questions, Cynthia is gently prying, trying to find out if she's settling into Sunshine Coast life, whether she has hobbies, what she likes to do during her free time when she's not gardening. Their interest has made Kathy think she *should* do more with her life than work and sit at home. So she's getting there. She just needs to change this one bad habit.

'I'm working on it,' she tells Michelle. 'Promise.'

'Can I come and visit?'

'Why would you want to do that? I thought you were mad at me.'

'I miss you, Mum. Grant does too. Even Dad does.'

Good old Owen. He's probably still never said a bad word about her.

'Do you want to visit so you can stop me drinking at night?' Kathy asks.

When the kids were teenagers she used to insist on picking them up from parties so they wouldn't be tempted to drink. Michelle is now probably turning this monitoring trick on her.

'That's one of the reasons. But the main one is that I'd like to see you.'

'Then I suppose you can.'

'Great.' Michelle sounds relieved. 'I'll work out some dates and let you know.'

'Okay.' Kathy smiles into the phone. 'It'll be good to see you.'

'You too. Bye, Mum.'

'Bye, sweetheart.'

Kathy looks around the living room, which is hardly welcoming to her let alone a guest. Next time she sees Shirl she'll ask where she can buy some cushions or something. Shirl strikes her as the sort of person who'd know that kind of thing, given she seems to know which person grew up in which house and who was related to the mayor and whose uncle used to be a minister in the Bjelke-Petersen government and where so-and-so's restaurant used to be.

She pours the last of the wine down the sink, tidies up the kitchen, and turns out the lights as she takes herself off to bed.

CHAPTER TWENTY-FIVE

Lorraine isn't sure how she feels about going to someone else's garden. They've mostly been working at Elizabeth's place the past few weekends, with the occasional detour, and she was starting to feel a sense of ownership about it, almost like it was *her* garden. After they'd yanked out weeds and pruned bushes and cleaned up leaf litter, the design of the garden became clear and with it the reward of their work: beauty. The place looked marvellous, and the blooms weren't even blooming yet.

'Gardening's great!' she told Mike one night. 'Once you can see how all the plants and whatnot work together, it's like creating a space for people to just enjoy looking at. And it's nice to be around all that nature.'

Mike gave her a funny look. 'Yeah. Why do you think I do it as a job?'

'But you never talk about it. You talk about the handyman stuff, not the gardening stuff.'

'Because I get better stories out of the handyman stuff.' He'd sat back in his chair and lit a cigarette.

Sometimes, later at night, the two of them sit in the kitchen and have a quiet drink and a quiet smoke, out of the range of Mike's mother, who particularly doesn't like smoking. Obviously Lorraine has never revealed to Cora that she's smoked for years, and she's invested in a lot of minty chewing gum to hide that fact. Living with Cora has meant both Lorraine and Mike have had to cut back, though. Or Lorraine has. She's pretty sure Mike smokes while he works, but he's outside a lot of the time so it doesn't seem to stick to his clothes. Lorraine can't smoke in the house while Cora's awake. So night-time it is, after the kids have also gone to bed. It's become their little ritual, hers and Mike's, and usually they can sort out most things that way – although lately Mike's been needling her a bit about how she's 'upset' Cora and Lorraine hasn't taken it too well. She's been tempted to ask him about the TAB receipts except that might look like tit for tat.

'I suppose that's true,' Lorraine said as he inhaled. 'You manage to hammer your thumb quite a bit.'

'Or maybe I just tell you I do.' He raised an eyebrow. 'For laughs.'

'Ha ha. How is it funny when I just think you're clumsy?'

She'd winked at him and he'd given her a peck, and they'd enjoyed their ciggies and their drinks and gone to bed happy.

Tonight she'll tell him that they aren't at Elizabeth's any longer because they've become victims of their own success and fixed it up so well that they won't need to go back for a little while.

Now they're at a place at Castaways Beach. The owner died and it's been years since his children visited, so they didn't realise that he basically lived in a jungle. A neighbour rang Barb and asked if the Sunshine Gardening Society could help. They'd helped the neighbour a few years before and she'd kept the number.

Lorraine knows they're in for an interesting time of it when Shirl turns up with her machete. She's looking forward to seeing her wield it on the vines that are clogging up most of the front garden.

'Where's young Charlie today?' Shirl says to Elizabeth.

'With my parents,' says Elizabeth. 'He spends a lot of time with them.'

Barb smiles benevolently. 'That's good for the boy. And I'm sure they enjoy it.'

Elizabeth smiles quickly in response then looks around. 'What would you like me to do?'

'You can pick up whatever we cut off and drop it in the wheelbarrow,' says Barb.

Nodding in answer, Elizabeth stands back and waits as Shirl starts hacking.

Lorraine decides to be friendly. It's a character trait of hers – some would say defect. Like her teachers. They always told her parents she was 'too ready to make friends' because she talked in class a lot. But her parents never tried to change her, and being ready to make friends was how she and Cynthia buddied up, so Lorraine has never thought of it as a defect. Hopefully Elizabeth won't either. Lorraine hasn't had a chance to chat to her much before, mainly because Elizabeth tends to work alone in her own garden and she's a little stand-offish, if Lorraine is being honest. Which Lorraine understands. Grief and all that. Not that she's been through anything as bad as Elizabeth but she tries to understand.

'So, a kid-free day?' Lorraine asks as she also stands back. Her instruction from Shirl is to wait until a passageway has been cleared then they'll all get in and do what they can.

'Yes.' Another quick smile. 'My parents are happy about me doing this. They said it's good to get out and do something a bit different.' Her eyes cloud over.

'Must be tough,' Lorraine says, 'when it's just you. No time for yourself. I'm lucky because my eldest is old enough to watch his brother – when he can be bothered. And my mother-in-law lives with us.' Lorraine's trying to focus on the positives of that.

'Oh? You're brave.'

Lorraine glances sideways at Elizabeth, trying to work out if she's joking. 'Yeah,' she says. 'Maybe. Probably.'

She thinks about Cora tut-tutting her way around the kitchen while Lorraine cooks dinner, and how she'd like to yell at her to get out yet restrains herself. Is that bravery? Or martyrdom?

'I could never live with my mother-in-law,' Elizabeth says, folding her arms, although Lorraine notices she is clenching and releasing her fists.

'Is she close by?'

A quick shake of the head. 'No. Thank goodness. After Jon died she wanted me to put Charlie in a boarding school – that's what she thinks of me as a parent.'

Lorraine ponders the idea of putting Terry in particular in a boarding school and finds it quite appealing. Not that they can afford it. And it's not like he'd get a scholarship. Oh well, another dream denied.

'Did Jon go to boarding school?' Lorraine asks. She's never had this much of a conversation with Elizabeth so she doesn't know if she's crossing some kind of line.

'Yes. And he hated it. Which she knows.' Elizabeth gestures in Shirl's direction, clearly wanting to change the subject. 'She's making progress.'

'God love her, she's a little Trojan,' Lorraine says with a laugh. 'And that's my cue. I'll bring you back some good rubbish.'

'Thanks.'

Lorraine starts wading into the garden, past Shirl's fallen vines, then turns to look over her shoulder. Just to check on Elizabeth because she feels like she should.

Elizabeth is standing just as she left her, those fists still going, only now her lips are pressed together and Lorraine could swear that she looks like she's about to cry. Crying probably comes with the widowhood territory, though, so Lorraine shouldn't worry about it. Except she does. And she decides that Elizabeth will definitely be the next friend she tries to make.

CHAPTER TWENTY-SIX

This is as cold as winter here will ever get, Cynthia thinks, as she takes Von's arm and steers her onto the path that accompanies the river. In that respect she's swapped one temperate place for another, although that's where the comparisons to Los Angeles end. Her former home is a company town, and everyone seems to be from somewhere else – as, of course, she was – and trying to get something. Trying to beat others to roles, to jobs, to projects. Everyone is your friend and no one is. Or maybe Cynthia just didn't know how to make friends there, nor have the opportunity because Max always wanted her to be at his beck and call – which included throwing parties and holding dinners so he could network with people in the industry. None of those parties benefited her; if anything, they made Max more determined to have her do more for him, because her greatest talent, it seemed, was making him look good. And there was no one she could talk to about it.

All those years she missed Lorraine like a limb, but she let her go. After a few letters Cynthia didn't answer she felt like it was too late. Now she knows it wasn't. That, most likely, it would never be. She's so grateful to Lorraine for taking her back.

Grateful too that Von is still alive and they can spend this time together – although Cynthia has resisted Von's heavy suggestions that she return to playing piano. While she may have the time to practise now, she doesn't want to inflict that on her father. She remembers what it was like when Odette wanted to learn violin; her ears can sometimes feel like they're still recovering.

'So,' she says, tightening her grip on Von's arm as they near a broken-up bit of path, 'what have you been up to?'

'Apart from being old?' Von's tone is wry but Cynthia knows there's some truth to it: she hates being old.

'Wasn't it you who told me that being old is just a state of mind?' she says.

'My knees have other ideas.'

Cynthia laughs. 'I guess they're entitled to – they've done a lot of good work over the years.'

'Now, I know what *you've* been up to,' Von says in a school-mistressy tone, 'given you're a valued member of the Sunshine Gardening Society.'

'Am I?'

'So Barb tells me.' Von arches an eyebrow. 'I get reports. Don't ever presume that I'm not keeping tabs on you.'

Cynthia laughs. 'I wouldn't dare.'

'So I'm guessing that's why we haven't had a social visit for a while. A person could come to feel neglected.'

Cynthia glances at Von to see if she's joking but can tell straight-away that she's not, and she feels immediately contrite. Between Lorraine and Odette and Pat and her father and the society and her soon-to-be-ex-husband's lawyers negotiating the divorce via fax, it isn't so much that Von has slipped her mind as that she hadn't noticed how much time had passed since she visited.

Not that she has a good reason to not visit. After years of separation from these people she loves, she should take greater care – and not take them for granted.

'I'm sorry, Von. I really am. I don't have an excuse.'

'No, you don't. But I accept your apology.'

Von nudges her and Cynthia knows they'll be all right.

'Are you doing anything about those knees?' she says.

Von shrugs. 'There's nothing to do. They're worn out. I know it's good to move them, but at the same time it hurts to do so. A slow walk with you is fine, though. As long as we amble rather than trot.'

'No trotting, I promise.'

Cynthia turns her face towards the water, which is glistening with sunlight. There are houses behind them but none ahead and hardly any across the water. She can't see the ocean beyond the opposite shore but she knows it's there. Right here, though, a small boat putt-putts past and birds are wading in the shallows.

'That's a black-winged stilt,' Von says, pointing to a black-and-white bird with long legs. 'And there are some terns there too.'

'I didn't know you like birds.'

'*Like* is a strong word.' Von presses her lips together. 'I'm aware of birds. As they are aware of me. We have an uneasy truce.'

'That makes it sound like you've had a bad experience!' Cynthia says, laughing.

'Pooed on the head twice, and those terrible cockatoos keep stripping my trees.' Von shakes her head slowly.

'You can't blame all birds for that.'

'I can and I will.' Von's face softens. 'My son was a bird-watcher when he was a teenager. His father or I would go with him just to make sure he didn't get lost. He had a tendency to become wrapped up in what he was doing and lose track of time and his surroundings.'

'So no birdwatching now?'

'I don't think so. His children's sporting activities keep him busy. Saturdays, Sundays, after school . . . I can't recall his life being so hectic when he was young.'

Von looks ahead and her eyes narrow. 'Well, this is interesting timing.'

'What?'

Cynthia sees a woman around Von's age, a little bit rounder and shorter than Von, with a blue rinse and perm, a cardigan sporting a brooch, and shoes with a heel high enough to be at odds with the walking stick she's using.

'Tilly,' Von says flatly, although loudly enough for the woman to hear.

'Vonnie!' Tilly leans heavily on the cane as she walks towards them. 'Vonnie! How have you been?'

'Unbelievably well,' says Von, and Cynthia has to stop herself laughing at what is clearly a show of bravado. She's quite sure she's never heard of a Tilly but there's some story here.

'You?' Von asks.

Tilly holds up the cane. 'Getting used to this.' Her gaze turns to Cynthia.

'This is my friend Cynthia,' Von says. 'You may remember her mother, Diane. From the society.'

Now Cynthia feels a jolt of something like shock at meeting another person who knew her mother through an activity that she was ignorant about. These are people who knew her mother in a way she never did, and never can. People with whom Diane wished to share something that she didn't wish to share with her husband and children.

'Oh, Diane,' Tilly says in a slightly condescending tone. 'Poor Diane.'

Poor Diane?

'Why . . .' Cynthia clears her throat, trying to work out if she really wants to ask this question. 'Why do you say that?'

'She was so unhappy,' Tilly says with a sigh.

'Not all the time,' Von says tersely.

'But Cynthia would know that!' Tilly smiles as if she's delivering good news.

Now Cynthia hears herself gasping, almost as if a space has opened up in her chest and let air out. No, she didn't know that. There's so much she didn't know about her mother – which her mother didn't want her to know.

'I didn't even know she was in the society,' Cynthia says softly.

'She just needed some time to herself,' Tilly says. 'We all did! Husbands, children . . .' She closes her eyes and presses her lips together like she's trying to wish away a bad fairy. Then she opens her eyes. 'You get sick of them, don't you? Always wanting something!'

Then her smile drops; possibly she's realised that Cynthia is one of the children she's talking about.

'Anyway, we loved our husbands and children,' she goes on. 'We just needed to feel like we were doing something good – for ourselves and for others. And we did enjoy it, didn't we, Von?'

'We did,' Von agrees.

'And we made some lovely gardens. I sometimes wonder what happened to them after we finished – but it wasn't our job to keep going back. We just had to provide enough help for people to try to help themselves. You know?' Tilly nods quickly, her eyes drifting away towards the water.

'Did my mother help herself?' Cynthia says quietly.

'She did,' Von says firmly. 'And the time she needed to spend with us was never about not wanting to be with you.'

'Oh, never!' Tilly says. 'I didn't mean that!'

But she did, of course. It's not as if Cynthia doesn't understand, either, only that she wishes she could talk to her mother about it, to understand *her* better. Even though she knows that regret is a road one should never travel down too long. It ends nowhere good, as her father says.

'I think we'll keep walking, Matilda,' Von says sternly. 'Nice to see you.'

Tilly looks slightly crestfallen, but Cynthia imagines she'll bounce back. Rather than saying anything to her, however, she offers a wave.

She and Von continue along the path in silence.

After a few minutes Von says, 'Perhaps I should start to educate you in the plants of the local area. Although I hear Shirl may be trying to impress that knowledge upon you already.'

Cynthia relaxes and laughs. 'She doesn't always use names, and I don't always remember them anyway.'

'Very well. If you would like to come and visit me again next week we can begin your education.'

Cynthia thinks about the week ahead and almost says she won't have time to visit – but of course she will. Her brain may be crowded with wondering about her mother and thinking about Odette becoming a mother herself, mixed in with occasional fretting about her father growing older, but she has time to see Von. And it would be of benefit to her – and, if she flatters herself, to Von as well.

'That would be a pleasure and a privilege for me,' Cynthia says, then she and Von keep on their merry way.

CHAPTER TWENTY-SEVEN

Watching Charlie play in her parents' garden after church, Elizabeth can almost believe that everything is the same as it ever was, that Jon is about to walk into the room behind her, put his hands on her shoulders and ask if she'd like a cup of tea or something else.

He took care of her, and he would say she took care of him too. When he was ailing he apologised for the fact that he would never be able to reciprocate the care she was giving him; that she was going to have to manage on her own after he was gone. She almost said no, he took care of her in his own way. But by then it wasn't true, and she knew he was right: the scales had tipped permanently towards him. It's not as if his death tipped them back, either, or changed the balance, because how do you weigh grief? Elizabeth can't even work out the shape of it, let alone how to measure it.

Some days it feels like a blob sitting on her chest when she wakes up, and as soon as she moves to get out of bed it slithers off to the sides of her body and clings to her while she tries to move through the day. Other days it's like a mist around her; there's nothing she can grab at, so she can neither pin it down nor throw it out. At times she can be feeling quite okay then it manifests in the way Charlie laughs, so like Jon. Or when Jon's mother calls and tries to give her orders about Charlie, and Elizabeth wishes her husband were here to fend off the one person who can dismantle her, no matter how much she tries not to let it happen.

When Jon was dying, and especially once Elizabeth contemplated having to manage the house and garden on her own, she thought about moving back to Brisbane. That way her parents could return to their lives and she could reconnect with the place and people she knows best. What has stopped her is that Jon's mother, Gladys, is there and Elizabeth knows that means Charlie will have to see her more than he does now. Which means Elizabeth will have to see her.

'She means well,' her parents keep saying, but Elizabeth isn't sure that's true. Gladys means to *control*, that's for sure, and if Charlie is within her orbit she will attempt to control more, knowing that Elizabeth abhors confrontation.

Jon was always good at standing up to his mother, because it had been just the two of them for a long time. Jon's father – eerily – had died when Jon was not much older than Charlie. Elizabeth knows she should see her mother-in-law as a source of potential support, because she understands exactly what Elizabeth and Charlie are going through, but she can't bear to. The thought of being anywhere near that woman feels like fingernails on a blackboard.

Maybe that's because Elizabeth can't bear to see her own grief displayed on someone else – because for sure Gladys is grieving as much as she is. It's been appalling enough to lose a husband. Elizabeth doesn't want to think about what it would mean to lose a child. She can never let herself entertain even a skerrick of an idea of it, because it would undo her.

Hearing footsteps behind her, she turns to see her mother entering the sunroom and smiles.

Drawing alongside, her mother smiles herself as she sees Charlie in the garden. 'He's doing well,' she says. '*You've* done well, darling. I don't know how you've coped with everything, but to see him happy . . .' Her mother's eyes have tears in them as she turns towards Elizabeth. 'It's a miracle.'

No, it's not, Elizabeth wants to say. Partly because she's not sure she believes in miracles any more. She prayed for one when Jon was dying. Prayed hard. Went to church more often, dropped to her knees in the kitchen, in the bathroom, in the laundry, tried to bargain with God. It's not that she thought Jon was more worthy of a miracle than anyone else. She just had to try. Except he was, wasn't he? This man who gave so much love to her, to his son, to her parents, to everyone around him? He was never unkind; he was generous. These are traits that should be common but they're not, which to her mind made him special. And because he was special he should have been saved. The world would be so much better with him in it.

No doubt everyone thinks that when their loved one dies, but Elizabeth knows it's true because the world seems so harsh now he's gone. Even when people do nice things for her – like those funny ladies in the Sunshine Gardening Society – she slips back into misery. She's not sure how to get out of it.

'I'm lucky,' is what she says to her mother, even though she doesn't believe it. People like to hear things like that, though. Especially when they care about you. It's the paradox of love: those who love you want to support you in your darkest hour, yet your darkest hour causes them so much pain that they'd rather not know, and you know they'd rather not know so you keep it to yourself, wondering how long you can stand it.

'Charlie's a good boy,' Elizabeth goes on. 'He's stayed pretty cheerful.'

'You have undoubtedly helped with that.' Her mother's smile is soft. 'Come on – your dad has lunch ready.'

Elizabeth waves to Charlie to beckon him inside, and she sees him nod, drop the ball he's been playing with and head for the side passage that will take him into the kitchen. He bounces inside, tufts of hair sticking up, almost like he's electrified, and grins as he sees his favourite sandwiches on the table: Vegemite and cheese.

'Thanks, Grandpa!' he says as he picks one up.

This, Elizabeth thinks, is where she finds the odd moments of light these days: in Charlie's happiness in ordinary things. He loves insects, he loves flowers, he loves sandwiches. He coos at dogs and runs after birds. His world is right here in the present moment, and Elizabeth wishes she knew how to live that way rather than residing so constantly in the past.

'You haven't said much about your job, darling,' her mother says as she cuts into her more grown-up meal of quiche.

Each day when Elizabeth picks up Charlie from her parents' place, she tends to run in and run out. They don't chitchat about her work. If they talk about anything it's Charlie, and sometimes Elizabeth thinks to ask her parents about what they've been doing.

'I like it,' she says, and it's the first time she's realised this.

'Well, that's good!' Her father grins and shows his crow's-feet.

In Elizabeth's mind he's always had them, but she supposes he was young once, like her. One day she'll have crow's-feet and Charlie won't ever remember her without them, and that will be a privilege of growing older in the way Jon never can.

'You said something about Olive, early on,' her mother prompts.

Thinking of Olive makes Elizabeth smile. 'She's entertaining. The other day she brought knitting. I said I couldn't imagine she ever needs to wear wool around here, it's so mild. She said she was knitting a jumper for her dog.'

'What sort of dog?' asks her father.

'A greyhound.'

He nods. 'Skinny breed. I can understand the need for wool.'

'I want to know where she got the pattern,' her mother says.

'I think she's making it up as she goes.'

Elizabeth pictures Olive sitting at the desk, telling Doctor Lopes he's eating too many of the staff biscuits as she knits one, purls one. Moss stitch, she said it was. It looked laborious and didn't give Elizabeth the urge to knit.

'And the doctors?' her mother asks.

'They're pretty good. Olive and Doctor Lopes bicker, but she's his stepmother so I suppose it's allowed.'

'What's this Doctor Lopes like?' Her mother is looking at her expectantly, and Elizabeth knows why: she thinks Elizabeth shouldn't spend too long on her own, that it won't be good for her. So she'll be thinking that Doctor Lopes might be a romantic prospect.

'He's fine, Mum,' she says in a knowing tone. 'Not interested in me.'

'I bet he is,' her mother says.

'He's not.'

'How do you know?'

'*Mum.*' She nods in Charlie's direction.

'He won't understand,' her mother mutters. 'Besides, you're too lovely to stay on your own for long.'

'*Mum!*' Elizabeth says again, and sighs heavily. 'It's not just Jon I'm getting over. It's his illness.' She glances at Charlie, because maybe he won't understand this either but maybe he will, and she's either scarring him for life or she's saying something he needs to hear. 'Watching someone be sick like that, for so long . . . It's like we have to recover from the grief of witnessing that. And then the grief of him dying is separate.'

She breathes raggedly, feeling herself getting upset. She hardly ever lets herself cry, and certainly not in front of Charlie. Or her parents. They need to think she's strong too. She shouldn't be their burden. As her mother pats her forearm Elizabeth hiccups to hide a sob.

'We understand, darling,' her mother murmurs. 'We know you're going to grieve for a while.' Then she throws her hands in the air. 'I guess I thought you should have a little fun as well. You deserve it.'

Elizabeth sniffs back the rest of her tears and fakes a smile. 'I don't think that's true. Does anyone really deserve it?'

'Of course they do!' her father says. 'And you more than most. All you've been through.' He shakes his head. 'It's not right.'

There's silence for a few seconds, broken only by the sound of Charlie chewing.

'I miss Dad,' he says quietly, eventually. 'But it's okay, Mum. You don't have to miss him forever.'

He grins, like he's said nothing serious at all, when what Elizabeth feels like saying in reply is, *What if I want to miss him forever?* Because she knows, truly, that there's an ease to grieving. Her excuse to opt out of all sorts of things is built-in and unassailable. She doesn't have to try to re-engage with life; not really.

'Tell us about this gardening club,' her mother says.

Changing the subject is something they've all become good at. When it becomes too heavy they talk about something else. Elizabeth can't say she minds.

'Society, Mum,' she says. 'It's the Sunshine Gardening Society.'

'Lovely! What do you do?'

For the next few minutes Elizabeth regales them with stories of Shirley and her machete, Barb and her immaculate hairdo, Lorraine and her mother-in-law. She doesn't know as much about Cynthia and Kathy so there's little to relay.

The distraction works, and by the time she's ready to take Charlie home Elizabeth's mind is on plants and she finds herself looking forward to next weekend.

CHAPTER TWENTY-EIGHT

'Hello, Cora.' Lorraine's mother is thin-lipped as she smiles her way into the living room.

Lorraine hovers nervously behind her, fully aware that Rose and Cora barely get on at the best of times. But with them both living on the Sunshine Coast it seems ridiculous to not have a family gathering from time to time, even if the kids pronounce the idea *boring* because everything is *boring* and they're *bored*.

'Then read a bloody book!' Lorraine had shrieked at Terry the other day after the umpteenth 'I'm *bored*' emanated from his metal-filled mouth.

Braces. They're the latest thing she's had to organise and pay for. Mike's started doing some fishing in the early mornings to supplement their income because it turns out that a teenage boy can eat three times as much as the rest of the household and still say he's hungry, plus he needs things like braces, plus he grows out of his clothes and shoes every three months.

Lorraine can only hope that Simon will grow the same way, so the gear she now has stashed away in the shed will fit him. Although he looks like he may be shaping up to be a small fella. Which doesn't bother her but it will probably bother him. He's insecure enough as it is these days.

Anyway, telling Terry to read a book didn't work because apparently books are *boring*. He'd grabbed his skateboard and slunk out of the house, ignoring her demands to tell her where he's going. It's a weird sensation when your son is now taller than you and therefore just slightly intimidating when he's brooding.

She tried to ask Cora what that felt like when Mike grew but Cora cluck-clucked like Lorraine had a problem for even thinking it was weird.

Lorraine wanted to tell Cora that it's weird she can live in this house with all its expenses and not contribute one single sou. But she didn't. Because if you want a peaceful life you don't say things that are going to antagonise an elder. Or anyone. Which means you just push down your feelings and let them take root and grow like a clump of ugly old weeds which then need to be pulled out . . .

Yeah, doing all this gardening has got her thinking. She's really shoved her problems with Cora deep, deep down – but that hasn't helped. They're still around. It's just that now they're all tucked up inside her, growing, and they're definitely weeds, not some bush that's going to sprout pretty flowers. She's started to think about what to do with those weeds; even mentioned them to Cynthia the other day.

'You're asking me, the person who let her mother die while she stayed overseas and didn't even come back for the funeral?' Cynthia said.

She had tears in her eyes but that wasn't going to stop Lorraine. 'So why didn't you?' she said.

'Because when I left Max I left pretty much everything at the house.' Cynthia's face fell. 'Including my passport.'

'Well, that was silly.' Lorraine likes to call things as she sees them.

'I didn't know I'd need it!'

'Not right then, maybe, but you would've eventually. I mean . . . you're here now, right?'

Cynthia sighed. 'He finally let me back in to pack everything up. But it was too late. For Mum.'

Then she looked like she was really about to cry so Lorraine had changed the subject. Not that she's afraid of Cynthia's tears but she knows Cynthia is.

Later, Lorraine remembered what Shirl had said about replacing weeds with natives so the weeds don't grow back. But what's the human equivalent? What can she plant in her own life to stop these Cora weeds growing?

Then she realised she was trying to be a bit tricky with herself and maybe she should just stop worrying about it. That's when she thought it was time to get her mother over for a lunch, so at least there's one person on her side in the house. Mike is on her side most of the time, but when it comes to Cora he's torn. Rose, at least, will never betray her.

So here her mother is, trying not to show how much Cora irritates her, but Cora can tell and even seems to be enjoying it.

'Hello, Rose,' she says, offering her own thin-lipped smile in return. 'Nice to see you.'

Rose holds up the cake she's brought. 'I've made a quince cake.'

'Yum!' Lorraine declares, because she loves her mother's cakes.

'Quinces are for poor people,' Cora mutters, then smiles as if they haven't all heard her.

'What are quinces, Mum?' Simon asks.

'Fruit, Si.' Lorraine glares at Cora. 'And they're delicious in a cake.'

'Yum!' he says and Lorraine could kiss him.

'G'day, Rose,' booms Mike as he walks into the room. He grabs his mother-in-law and plants a noisy kiss on her cheek. 'Quince cake? Yum!'

Mike takes the cake and walks into the kitchen, and Lorraine wants to kiss him too. She is so conscious of her mother being the second-run grandparent because Cora gets all the time with the kids. Or time with Simon, because none of them sees Terry much any more.

Yet here is her eldest, loping into the room looking positively gleeful.

'Hi, Gran!' He wraps his arms around Rose and holds on for a good few seconds.

Who is this boy? Lorraine hasn't seen him for months. But maybe her mother has . . . Maybe that's where Terry goes when he disappears for hours on end. Wouldn't her mother tell her, though? And if not, why not? Are they conspiring against her?

Gawd, she really has to stop being so paranoid. She's convinced Simon is ganging up with Cora, and now it's Terry with her mother. Although if it turns out they're all against her she'll feel smug about being right.

'Why don't you sit down, Mum?' she says, making a mental note to raise the subject of Terry later.

Rose goes to sit in the armchair near the window, but Cora makes a noise and Rose looks up. 'Hm?'

'I sit there,' Cora says.

Rose looks at Lorraine, and Lorraine can interpret that look: *You must be kidding me.* No, Mum, she's not kidding you, she's declared ownership of the chair and none of us can get near it.

'It's all right, Mum,' Mike says as he re-enters the room. 'Rose is our guest. She can have the armchair.'

Cora's face looks pinched and Lorraine wants to do a victory dance, but then she realises: Rose is the guest, Cora is the resident. This power imbalance is never going to change and Lorraine is the one who'll be trying to negotiate truces for the rest of these women's lives.

Although the imbalance tilts a little in the other direction as Terry goes and stands next to Rose, one arm on the back of the chair, almost as if he wants to sit on the arm but isn't sure how that would look.

Something else Lorraine realises: Rose hasn't remarked on how tall Terry is now. The last time she saw him – as far as Lorraine knows – was a few months ago and Terry's grown about ten centimetres since then. They measured him against the wall. Which means they've definitely been hanging out. Her own son and her own mother, meeting up without her and not saying a word.

She wants to feel upset. Instead she just feels a little sad – Terry probably goes there to have uncomplicated love and support at a time when his mother is often yelling at him to do his chores. But that's Lorraine's job, isn't it? She has to turn him into a functional adult. There are no rainbows and moonbeams in that. Grandmothers get the rainbows. And the smiles and hugs that go with them. Lorraine can feel herself working up to some kind of tantrum about it all, but she has to hold it together.

'So what do we reckon about Hawkey getting back in?' Mike remarks and Lorraine groans. Her mother is decidedly not a Labor voter, which Mike knows but always seems to forget, and any mention of Bob Hawke – or, worse, Paul Keating – tends to send her into a rant about how he's going to ruin the country.

'I like his hair,' Cora says.

'Can't argue with that.' Mike pats his own close crop. 'It's a good mane.'

'Have you been playing bowls, Cora?' Rose says as Cora makes a show of not liking her seat on the couch.

'No.' Cora pulls a face. 'My hip.'

'Oh.' Rose widens her eyes in Lorraine's direction, something else Lorraine can interpret: *I'm trying here.*

'Mum's been swimming a bit, haven't you, Mum?' Lorraine says, trying to gee things along.

'Ooh yes, at Noosa Main Beach.' Rose beams. 'There's a pack of hooligans who swim *quite* a way out. I'm not brave enough for that, but I enjoy what I do, up and down the beach.'

'In the ocean?' says Cora. 'You will be eaten by sharks.' From the look on her face Cora isn't joking.

'*Jaws* isn't real, Mum,' Mike says, chuckling. 'Anyway, who's for a softie? Rose?'

'I think we need wine,' Lorraine says, risking Cora's opprobrium. Her mother-in-law thinks only alcoholics drink at lunch.

'Good idea! Riesling okay for you, Rose?'

Her mother nods approval as Cora's nostrils flare.

'Gran, I made a book for you!' Simon says to Rose, then he hops to his feet and runs off in the direction of his bedroom.

More nostril-flaring from Cora, but this time Lorraine doesn't care. She's touched that Simon would do something like that and, by the look on Rose's face when he returns, so is she.

It feels like a small victory, although Lorraine isn't sure over what. Cora isn't her enemy, not really, even if it feels that way sometimes. But as she watches Terry keeping up his sentinel stance and Simon almost sitting on Rose's feet, she wonders what they sense, her boys, and it makes her proud of them all of a sudden. Proud and a bit weepy, and she doesn't want anyone to see, so she quickly puts down her glass and hurries into the kitchen.

And when Mike comes up behind her and wraps his arms around her, kisses the nape of her neck and tells her that he loves her, she can almost feel some of those weeds shrivelling up and dying. Even if she knows that tomorrow a few more will probably spring up.

AUGUST 1987

WHITE BEARD

CHAPTER TWENTY-NINE

If this weren't Queensland Cynthia would want a fireplace in this house, just for days like this when it feels so cold that she wants to stay curled up on the couch, her feet in socks and a scarf around her neck. Except it *is* Queensland and winter isn't a recognised season here, so she opts for the socks only and a blanket over her knees as she gazes out at the fading afternoon light on the garden. She missed these colours when she was in Los Angeles, just as she missed the beaches and the birds and trees.

There's nothing she misses about LA, which is why she left so much behind – she didn't need to bring that life with her here. Besides, if she'd tried to pack up everything she owned there it would have taken longer to leave, which would have meant more time in which her ex-husband could behave even more badly.

The sound of the back door opening and closing tells her that her father has returned from the job he said he had to do. She turns her head and sees him walking slowly towards her with something tucked under his arm.

'Did you finish your job?' she asks.

'Mm-hm,' he says, and places something rectangular wrapped in calico on the coffee table in front of her.

'What's that?' she says, sitting forwards.

He gestures towards it. 'Have a look.'

She hardly thinks her father is giving her anything booby-trapped but she does wonder why he won't open it himself.

'It was in the shed,' he says, regarding it with what looks like suspicion mixed with reverence.

The shed is tucked into the corner of the back garden and Cynthia has only been in it a couple of times. It was a temple to her father's – and, later, Kit's – attempts to make things for the house and its environs.

'Are you sure I should look at it?' Cynthia says.

He nods slowly. 'I think she'd want you to.'

'She? Mum?'

More nodding, and now Cynthia's heart is beating faster, although she has no idea why. What could possibly be in there that would make her nervous?

She unwraps the calico to reveal a leather-covered notebook. Rather, as she can see when she opens it, a sketchbook. The first page bears her mother's name: *Diane Scheffer.*

Cynthia swallows, perhaps with anticipation, perhaps because her past, her mother's past – all of their family's past – is stuck in her throat, awaiting whatever is in this book.

Turning a page, she sees a drawing of a plant. The shape of the leaves tells her it's a native – she knows enough about plants now to know that. And there's a tiny label: *White Beard.*

Another page over, another drawing: *Broad-leaved Geebung.* Then *Primrose Ball Wattle.*

The drawings are detailed and alive, and there are at least a dozen in the book. Yet there are no dates to help anchor her, and no sense of what it could all mean.

'Mum drew these?' Cynthia asks softly.

'She did,' her father affirms.

'But I never saw her draw, or do anything remotely arty.'

Was it just that Cynthia was a less-than-diligent daughter and didn't notice?

'She did them at night,' he says. 'After you children were asleep.'

That makes Cynthia feel marginally better.

'How did she know what to do?'

'She told me she took drawing classes when she was at school. And the plants she'd draw from memory, I think.' He raises his eyebrows. 'She spent enough time with them.'

'But they're so realistic. How could she remember all of that?'

'Maybe she took the book with her on weekends . . . You know.'

When she was a Sunshine Gardener, he means. While she was gardening she could check her work, or perhaps she drew while she was there. Or perhaps it was neither – she might have taken herself off to the national park or elsewhere to sit and draw, without any of her family members knowing.

'She had this whole big life,' Cynthia murmurs. 'And we knew nothing about it.'

'I knew a bit,' her father says gruffly. 'But not enough.'

Cynthia feels like placing the book on an altar and lighting candles around it, because it feels sacred somehow.

'Why didn't she tell us?' she says.

'Because it was private.'

Her father says it plainly, not like he's resentful. But Cynthia is resentful. She wanted more of her mother than Diane was clearly prepared to give, even if Cynthia has to acknowledge that she didn't express interest in anything her mother did. And by the time she figured out that mothers are people too, Odette was underfoot and she was wondering where her youth had gone.

'So why are you giving me this now?' she says.

'You're in that society too. You understand – or you might – her interest in these plants. These flowers.'

'Do you think she joined the society so she could draw? Or did the gardening introduce her to something she loved enough to draw?'

'I don't know.' There's a hint of sadness in his voice.

'And we never will.' Cynthia picks up the book and presses it to her chest. 'This is precious, Papa. Please don't take this the wrong way, but what was it doing in the shed?'

'Your mother put it there. Or she must have. I found it there after she died. I guess she didn't want it in the house in case . . .' He stops and looks into her eyes. 'In case someone was fossicking through her things and found her most precious thing. Someone who didn't know what to do with it.'

As Cynthia wouldn't have known a few months ago. Now, what might have seemed like a group of pretty drawings is a document of great historical importance. It's not just a record of the plants Diane observed but of the work of the Sunshine Gardening Society itself, for it's unlikely Diane would have known which plants were what, or where to find them in order to draw them, without that education. The same education her daughter is receiving now. Which leads her to think of one person.

'Von,' Cynthia breathes. 'I wonder if she knew about it?'

'Your mother was good at keeping secrets, so I wouldn't bank on it.'

'I'm going to ask her.'

'I figured you would.' He smiles wryly. 'Anyway, the book is yours to do as you wish with it. Even if your mother kept it secret all that time, I believe she'd know that you understand how special it is now.'

'I do.' Cynthia hugs it closer. 'I really do.'

He bends down and kisses the top of her head.

'You're a good girl,' he says, then he leaves her holding on to the sketchbook and all the stories she will never know about her mother.

CHAPTER THIRTY

Kathy hasn't realised how dismissive she is of native plants and bushes and trees until she is standing in the overgrown back garden of some old gent in Little Cove whose property backs on to the national park and her first thought is, *Yuck*.

In fact, it isn't a thought because she says it out loud and Cynthia, standing next to her, says, 'What do you mean?'

Kathy gestures to the hodgepodge of different plants in front of them. 'They're so ugly. Where are all the pretty flowers?'

She's chosen the wrong time to say that because Shirl has come huffing up behind her. Today she's wearing a Jefferson Airplane T-shirt. Kathy has been taking note, because the T-shirts all look worn enough to suggest that Shirl might have acquired them at concerts for these acts. Last weekend it was James Brown.

'Ugly?' she says. '*Ugly?*'

Kathy feels like she did in kindergarten when the teacher made her sit on a stool in the corner after some transgression or other. There was always something.

'Listen, my girl,' Shirl goes on. 'You're getting an education today.' She nods at Cynthia. 'She grew up not far from here so she can give it to you. All right?'

Shirl walks off, shaking her head and calling out to Barb, probably to tell her that Kathy is an ignoramus.

Cynthia looks slightly aghast and Kathy can't tell if it's because Shirl is forcing them to spend time together or because she too doesn't think much of native plants.

Now they're leaning into garden beds strewn with bracken, trying to sort out the difference between what's meant to be growing here and what could be classified as leaf litter. It's not a warm day but Kathy feels hot and scratchy, even more so because Cynthia looks as unruffled as she usually does.

'I'm sick of this,' Kathy mutters.

'Sick of what?' Cynthia turns and narrows her eyes.

'This . . . stuff.' She gestures to the tangle in front of them. 'Sorry. These beautiful native plants.'

There's a hint of a smile on Cynthia's lips as she pulls sticks away from living branches. 'We've barely started,' she says. 'Don't tell me you're a fair-weather gardener – only interested in daffodils and crocuses?'

'Um . . .' Kathy screws up her face, trying to figure out how not to admit the truth.

'It's all right if you are. Just because Shirl is rah-rah about natives doesn't mean you have to like them. Although I should do as she suggests and tell you about any I recognise.' Cynthia gestures to a low shrub. 'That's midyim. It flowers from spring so that's why it doesn't look like much at the moment, but the flowers are white, very delicate.'

She crouches and puts her fingers under green leaves on a plant that is dandelion-sized. 'Beach sow thistle. Again, doesn't flower until it's warmer.' She stands up. 'This garden would look pretty once everything flowers.'

Kathy nods. She realises she's rushed to judgement on something she knows nothing about, but can you blame a person for liking a pink rose? Or a blue iris? Maybe she's been brainwashed by the gardens she grew up with and the paintings she's seen – who doesn't love a bit of Monet? – but native flora just aren't her thing. They're clearly Cynthia's thing, though. Just maybe not as much as they're Shirl's thing.

'So, like Shirl said, you know this because you grew up around here?'

'No,' Cynthia says with a tight smile. 'I did grow up nearby, that's true.' She jerks a thumb over her shoulder. 'My dad's house is just back there and that's where I'm living at the moment. But I didn't know anything about the plants until I joined the society.'

Kathy frowns. 'So how did you . . .' She stops just as Cynthia starts to speak again.

'My friend Von has been teaching me. And my mum made drawings of native plants.' Cynthia looks away. 'I just found them. Well, Dad remembered he had them. I've spent some time with the drawings.'

'Your mum's not alive?'

'No.' Another tight smile. 'Although I really wish she were. She was a member of this society too.'

'Really? Wow! Is that why you joined?'

Cynthia appears to consider this. 'Partly. And partly because I thought Lorraine and I could do it together. I lived overseas for a long time and we lost touch.'

She smiles over her shoulder in the direction of Lorraine and Elizabeth, who are deep in conversation and pointing at something in the bush before them.

'Happy to be back in touch now, though,' Cynthia concludes.

'Yeah, Lorraine's great,' Kathy says. She always has a kind word for each of them and while Kathy sometimes thinks Lorraine looks tired, she is always positive. It's a quality she'd like to cultivate in herself if only she could find the motivation to do it. Or the reason.

'So this,' Cynthia says, leaning forwards and running her fingers over thin drooping stalks hanging from the branch of a large tree, 'is a coastal she-oak.' She looks up to the top of the tree, which is several metres above ground. 'It's probably been here for a long time. They get to be about ten metres high and I'd say this one's close to that.'

Kathy looks around at the property they're on and how there are no boundary fences. 'So is this house even meant to be here?' she says. 'It's pretty much right in the bush.'

'Kev's been here so long no one can remember when he wasn't here,' Cynthia says. 'It's possible he, uh, just went ahead and did what he wanted with the house.' She grins. 'He has a reputation for that. What brought you to the area?'

Cynthia might have asked this because she's genuinely interested, but Kathy wishes she hadn't because she doesn't feel ready to 'share'.

That's what Jemima used to ask her to do – 'share'. There were regular requests for Kathy to *share* her feelings, *share* her stories, *share* her dreams and aspirations and fears. And Kathy did share, more than she had with anyone, so that when Jemima left her it felt like she lost a huge part of her . . . self. She doesn't like to say 'soul' – that's a term for hippies and people who go to India to find enlightenment.

'It wasn't a trick question,' Cynthia adds gently.

'No.' Kathy licks her lips, stalling.

She should be able to just tell people and not feel ashamed that at fifty-four she got dumped, after dumping her husband, and ran away to a different state because she thinks she's made a mess of her life. But she can't. Not yet. Maybe not ever. The people she works with don't know a thing – she told them she moved to Queensland because she 'felt like a change', which is a version of the truth. It's a good line and she should stick to it.

'Oh, you know,' she says. 'Queensland has the best weather. Melbourne can be so cold and grey.'

'You're from Melbourne?'

'Yes. Anyway – what's this plant called?'

Cynthia gives her a funny look but Kathy knows enough about her to feel she's unlikely to pry further. Which gets Kathy off the hook, for now.

'Not sure,' Cynthia says. 'Shall I ask Shirl?'

'Ah – no.' Kathy smiles apologetically. 'We'll probably both get a lecture. Let's get stuck into that pile of sticks, shall we?'

'Sure.' Cynthia smiles. 'I'll go first.'

As Kathy watches Cynthia hauling out small and large fallen branches she doesn't feel the relief she'd expected at keeping her secrets to herself. Instead she feels as though something is starting to curdle within her, and it's not last night's wine. But she doesn't know how to identify it, and this is not the time or the place, so she takes the sticks from Cynthia and puts them in a pile on the lawn, over and over again.

The repetitive actions of their work are soothing; Kathy's noticed this before. They don't so much free her mind to wander as allow it to empty completely. Jemima used to rave about meditation and Kathy thought it was silly, but maybe this is what she was talking about.

'You have a daughter, don't you?' she says after a while. She might not be willing to offer up details about her own life but she can at least ask Cynthia about hers.

'I do,' Cynthia says. 'Odette.'

The clipped nature of Cynthia's answer makes Kathy wonder if she should ask anything more. It's hard to work out what other people want. Maybe Cynthia wants her to stop talking. Or maybe she doesn't want to talk too much so she's restraining herself. If neither one of them talks, though, they'll never get beyond a certain point of knowledge about each other, and Kathy is pretty sure she likes Cynthia, so she wants to know more. She's quite aware she's being hypocritical but it's not going to stop her.

'Why don't you tell me about her?' she says.

Cynthia stops work and sits back on her haunches, her face serious. 'We used to be close,' she says. 'She came with me when I moved to the States. She was five then. Her father, Pat, is from here, so he stayed here.'

From that description Kathy can't work out if Cynthia wanted him to come and he refused, or if they were never really together in the first place.

'I married Max when she was twelve, I think,' Cynthia continues. 'He was fine, at first. To her. Not to me. Once we were married, he thought it meant he could control everything I did and he was outrageous . . .' Cynthia squeezes her eyes shut, then opens them again and clears her throat. 'Then once Odette went through adolescence and got a bit rebellious, he hated that he couldn't control her either.'

There's a throat-clearing noise from Shirl and Cynthia starts picking up sticks again.

'So they fought. It was awful. A few years ago Odette decided to move back here to live with her father.' Cynthia sighs. 'I stuffed it up. Stuffed her up. I should have left my husband instead of letting her go, but . . .' She pauses. 'It was complicated.'

Kathy thinks about leaving her children in Melbourne and how she'd rationalised it away because they're adults. Yet there's Michelle feeling abandoned and Grant not that wild about her leaving either.

'It usually is,' she says. 'But here's how I see it: mothers put their children first so often that if there's the odd time they don't, the kids can act like it's a huge failure. Sometimes it's just because we don't have it all figured out either and we're trying our best.'

Cynthia stops what she's doing and turns around. 'Thank you for saying that.'

'But don't you think it's true? We're all just trying our best. Most of the time, anyway.'

A weak smile from Cynthia indicates her agreement. 'I'll tell myself that,' she says softly.

They go back to the sticks and the tossing, and after an hour has passed they've cleared enough of the garden to be able to make out distinct shapes of bushes and shrubs.

Kathy feels something like satisfaction, and it's not all about the gardening. She knows Cynthia better than she did at the start of the day, and that's a reward in and of itself.

CHAPTER THIRTY-ONE

There have been mornings – several of them, in fact – when Elizabeth has sat outside the doctors' surgery in her car and cried. Not because she doesn't want to go inside, because she doesn't mind it in there. Not because she doesn't want to do her job, because she quite likes it and it's paying her bills and for that she is very grateful. It's because the tears come whenever she has a few moments to herself.

As soon as she wakes up she gets herself ready for the day, and Charlie ready for school, then she puts him in the car for the short drive to the school entrance, then off he goes to his day and she drives on to Sunrise Beach and pulls up outside the building where she will spend her day, and if she's not quick enough at exiting the car – if she takes even a minute to turn off the radio and the engine because she's thinking about something or trying to remember something – she starts crying.

The tears aren't caused by anything in particular, although grief is the obvious culprit. It sounds so offhand now, though: she's *grieving*. She's a *widow*. Actually, yes, that's the word that can start her off if she lets it creep into her mind. She can manage the grieving part just fine when there's not a noun attached to it.

The other day at church, as she was trying to make a fairly quick exit, waving at Reverend Willoughby, one of the congregants grabbed her arm – a little forcefully, causing Elizabeth to frown.

'Oh, it's so sad. I heard that you're a *widow* now,' the woman said, and Elizabeth could see that she enjoyed performing pity. It was surprising that she hadn't accosted Elizabeth before.

Elizabeth had stared at her, mainly because that word, *widow*, hadn't yet been used in her presence. Her parents hadn't said it, nor had her friends. The people who were the most understanding didn't say anything at all about Jon being dead, they just kept him in the conversation in small ways that Elizabeth would only appreciate later, by referring to things he'd said or done. As if there might be more stories to tell about him one day, even though the subtext of every conversation is that there won't be. In short: no one who loves her categorises her as being anything other than Elizabeth. Certainly not as a widow.

Yet there the word was – in her face, literally. She tried to swallow it. To chew on it. After a few seconds she realised it was stuck in her throat and she wasn't going to be able to get rid of it, and for that she would never, ever forgive this woman she didn't know and hoped never to see again.

'Yes, I suppose I am,' she said, then she gripped Charlie's hand tighter and walked away.

That's what pops into her head in silent times now: that woman giving her a label. And Elizabeth really wishes she could get it out of her head but she has no idea how to do that, and so here she is, crying in her car, and her mascara will be running and she doesn't have a tissue to wipe it off her cheeks.

A knock on her window doesn't even make her jump because she's so caught up in being that awful W-word.

But the knocking comes again and here's Olive, peering in at her and motioning for Elizabeth to roll down the window like she won't take no for an answer.

'What's going on, duck?' she says once the window is down a few centimetres.

Elizabeth continues to roll it the whole way as it would be rude otherwise. She sniffs and it's one of those wet, snorty sniffs that happen when you're crying and it's running into your nose, and your sinuses feel like they're in on the act as well. Charming. And not something she wanted anyone else to witness.

'Um . . .' she says, wishing desperately for that tissue.

Olive fishes around in her handbag and brandishes a welcome white square. 'It's clean,' she says, thrusting it into the car.

'Thanks,' Elizabeth mumbles then blows her nose.

Olive lets out a noisy sigh and puts a hand on her hip. 'This is no good,' she says, and Elizabeth's heart contracts in fear: is she going to be sacked for crying before work?

'No good at all,' Olive goes on, shaking her head vigorously. 'Lovely young lass like you, sitting here in a mess.' She pulls on the door handle and opens the door wide. 'Come on, out you get.'

'But . . .' Elizabeth dabs under her eyes with the now-sodden tissue, and quickly grabs her handbag and the keys out of the ignition lest Olive physically remove her from the vehicle.

'Come inside and I'll make you a cup of tea and we're going to talk about it,' Olive says briskly, winding up the window before shutting the car door.

Once they're inside Olive dumps her bag on their desk and hastens to the small kitchen out the back. Elizabeth follows her slowly, and watches as she boils the kettle and makes a pot, not daring to say anything because Olive is quite clearly in charge of whatever is going on here. Instead she listens to the radio that is on almost constantly, to the end of that Whitney Houston song that everyone loves.

'Now,' Olive says as she sets the pot, cups, saucers and a small plate of Venetian biscuits on the table, 'out with it. Come on – first patient will be here in ten and I want a full confession before then, or I'm going to ask Marco to prescribe you some Valium. And you *don't* want to start down that road, *believe me.*' She rolls her eyes.

'It's noth—'

'Don't you dare say "It's nothing" – I'm no fool.'

Olive pours the tea and offers a cup to Elizabeth.

'All right,' Elizabeth says, swivelling the cup on the saucer. 'But it may sound ridiculous.'

'Sweetheart, I like to take holidays on cruise ships. Wait until you've been around four hundred people with gastro who are still trying to get free drinks, *then* talk to me about ridiculous.'

Elizabeth laughs involuntarily and she can tell from the smile on Olive's face that this was the intended outcome.

'All right,' she starts again. 'I . . . Well . . .' She stops and sighs. She's never said this to anyone and it really does sound silly when she thinks about it.

'Go on.' Olive sips her tea.

'I . . . I didn't think I was a widow. As in, I never use that word for myself.' Elizabeth sighs again. 'No one else called me that either. And it sounds so awful, doesn't it? *Widow*. It's so heavy. So . . . final.'

She looks down at her tea, as if it holds answers to questions she hasn't formulated yet. 'This woman at church said something the other day. You know how some people love to say things to upset people?'

'Oh yes.' Olive makes a face. 'After Morrie died this woman in my crochet group told me it was so sad that my life was over now he was gone. Imagine!'

'What did you say to her?'

'I said, "Like bloody hell! He's dead, I'm not!"' Olive nods once. 'I was sad. Course I was. But my life wasn't over, because it was *my* life, not his. He wasn't my entire world. I knew who I was without him.'

She looks Elizabeth hard in the eye. 'Widow is just a word, duck. I can't believe that someone as bright as you would let some idiot at church make her feel like this.'

Elizabeth's bottom lip starts to tremble and she's not sure why. Maybe it's because Olive understands and, as well-meaning

as her friends and family are, they don't. They can't. They're not
... Well, they're not widows.

'I don't mind you crying,' Olive continues. 'It's normal. Healthy.
But what I will not tolerate is you crying because someone else
said something stupid. Well, you can indulge it if you want to,
I suppose.' She flaps a hand. 'But what's the point?'

She takes another sip of tea. 'Unless you like to wallow.'
She narrows her eyes at Elizabeth. 'But you don't strike me as
the type.'

'I'm not,' Elizabeth says firmly, because it's the truth.

All those nights at home alone after Charlie has gone to bed
she could be wallowing, and certainly the temptation has been
there. She doesn't do it, though – she reads books, she plays
music, she listens to the radio. She stays in the world and doesn't
go under.

'I guess ...' She smiles weakly. 'I guess I was feeling like I was
doing fairly well. Then she said that and ... It's like the whole
thing started again.'

Olive nibbles on a Venetian, then puts the biscuit down.

'Here's a little tip for you,' she says. 'It never ends. So it can't
start again. I'd say you'd just reached a point where you weren't
thinking about it all the time, am I right?'

Elizabeth contemplates this, then nods slowly.

'And then *boom*, along comes Madam Busybody and she
gives you a word to latch onto. Because believe me, I know, our
little brains like latching onto things. So here's this word. *Widow*.
There – I said it.' She gives Elizabeth a mischievous smile. 'And
your brain's been having a rest, see, from all this grief. But it
grabs onto that word and doesn't want to let go. Know why?'

Elizabeth shakes her head.

'Because you were in the habit of grieving. It's like smoking,
right? If you try to give it up you have to stay away from other
smokers because otherwise, bang, one sniff of it and you're gone.'

Elizabeth isn't quite sure if there's a connection but she's not prepared to argue the point.

'What you haven't worked out, though, is what's good about this,' Olive says. 'You *weren't thinking about it* as often as you used to.'

Elizabeth's breath catches.

'And I know. I *know*.' Olive reaches over and pats her hand. 'That means you weren't thinking about *him*. And that makes you feel like you betrayed him. *That's* why you're sad.'

Now there's a shuddering in Elizabeth's chest because she knows Olive is right. Even if she's never acknowledged it to herself, that's exactly what's been happening.

Olive holds up a finger and wags it at her. 'You don't need to cry about that. You're not betraying him. You're doing *fine*. So drink your tea, eat a biscuit and get going. Marco'll be here shortly.'

The front door opens and closes.

'I mean now,' Olive says. 'He's here now. Come on, pick up your cup and saucer.'

Olive doesn't wait for her. Obviously she trusts Elizabeth to do as she's ordered.

And Elizabeth does, wiping a finger under each eye, sniffing back the tears that were threatening to appear, and carrying her tea and the plate of Venetians to the front desk.

SEPTEMBER 1987

WIDE BAY BORONIA

CHAPTER THIRTY-TWO

It's really hard for Lorraine to not get tetchy about the jobs that haven't been done around their house because Mike is busy doing jobs at other people's houses. Yes, yes, that brings in the money and they need the money, and it's great that Mike is so popular that he's booked out seven days a week. He and Lorraine talked about whether he should really work that much, but she said he'd best make hay while the sun shines – even if now she regrets saying it because their garden is a *mess* and it's not as if Terry will help her, or Cora. And she's not going to ask Simon because he actually would help and, even though she likes the idea of giving him jobs, he should enjoy being a kid for a while longer.

So, yes, Lorraine gets tetchy about the jobs that aren't done but she knows she shouldn't because if Mike's this busy he probably isn't going to the TAB. Also because her own work is part of the reason why the jobs aren't done. Because Mike has so many jobs, she's flat out doing the bookkeeping and taking the phone calls, and fitting in the odd lawn-mow when he can't.

She's considered offering other gardening services now that she's had a bit of practice with the Sunshine Gardening Society. Could be a bit cheeky – do some voluntary work then make money off it. But she enjoys it too. That's surprised her. All that rummaging around in leaf litter, getting her trousers dirty and herself sweaty, and she's feeling happier than she has in a while.

So that's why, when she was complaining to Cynthia about her own garden being a mess and Cynthia suggested the two of them do some work on it, Lorraine said yes. And that's also why they're sitting on their haunches in front of some maidenhair ferns doing some careful pruning while Cora's off at some church thingy and Terry and Simon are watching television.

The first time Cora started going to church – or saying that's where she's going, because who knows what old people get up to when no one's watching – Lorraine remarked to Mike that she didn't think there was a Greek Orthodox church anywhere on the Sunshine Coast. Mike said she was going to the local Catholic church, and Lorraine replied with, 'Any port in a storm, eh?' which didn't go down so well. He got upset, saying she wasn't taking his mother's faith seriously. Lorraine said that wasn't the case – in fact, she takes everything about Cora seriously because she has to live with the woman and it's no barrel of laughs. That bit she didn't say out loud, though. Instead she apologised and told Mike she'd make him beef Wellington, which is his favourite but which she can never be bothered with because it involves puff pastry and why would you make that if you don't have to? But she did, and he was happy.

Now every time Cora says she's going to church, Lorraine smiles sweetly and bids her goodbye and counts herself lucky for the reprieve. Which is why she's got Cynthia over here on a Sunday morning. She's determined to not inflict Cora on Cynthia. Or, rather, she wants to keep Cynthia to herself because almost everything else in her life seems to belong to her family.

'How often do you prune these ferns?' Cynthia says, peering at some brown, withered fronds.

'Um . . .' Lorraine smiles brightly to offset her slackness. 'Never.'

'Hm, well, I won't lecture you because you should know better now you've been doing some gardening.'

'Our garden is meant to be Mike's job,' Lorraine says, clipping off a frond and chucking it over her shoulder. 'But he's not going to get to do anything around here for a while, so I thought I'd do it. Good excuse to put you to work.' She nudges Cynthia, who smiles.

'How's your mum?' Cynthia asks.

When they were teenagers Cynthia would tell Lorraine that she wished Rose was her mother because she was kind and interested and Cynthia thought her own mother couldn't care less about what she was up to. When Cynthia got pregnant Lorraine wondered – for a disloyal second – if Cynthia did it partly to get her mother's attention. Although it did seem like a drastic manoeuvre if that was the case.

'She's well. Really well, I think.' Lorraine keeps pruning and chucking. 'I asked her a while ago if she wanted to move closer to a beach and she said she loves the hinterland, so she's staying. Although she mentioned some bloke was sniffing around, saying he was from a . . .' She screws up her face, trying to remember the term. 'Golf club consortium – does that sound right?'

'You're asking me? I wasn't there.'

'But *consortium* – is that a word?'

'It is.'

'Right. So some golf consortium bloke said they're looking at buying up all these properties and making a big golf resort. Would have thought it was too hilly for that but he told Mum no problem, they'd just level the hills.'

'Can they do that?'

Lorraine shrugs. 'I guess. If they have enough money.'

'I mean can they just do what they want to the land?'

'Mike says some owners just take the money from those sorts of fellows and close their eyes.'

'They lie back and think of England, you mean?'

'How rude!' Lorraine tosses a clod of earth at Cynthia, who laughs. 'I had no idea you had such a dirty mind.'

Then she stops and thinks about what it really means if people don't care about who does what to the land. 'But I guess that's bad, isn't it? If people can just do what they want to a hill.'

She remembers something Barb mentioned the other day – about how there'd been this plan to turn the whole of Noosa Heads into a giant resort, and it almost happened because the state government was going to give money for it. Then the government changed and Hastings Street didn't get bulldozed. Lorraine felt so relieved when Barb told her that, she wondered if she was turning into some kind of vegetarian person who likes incense and hugs trees.

These aren't issues that used to trouble Lorraine's mind. She's married to a man who likes his Holden Commodore to be the latest, and has a son who whinges when his friends get better Walkmans than he has. She thought that's just how it works: you get the best, most up-to-date thing you can. So if someone wants to build a shiny new resort, isn't that the best and most up-to-date? But after what Barb told her she's been thinking about how new isn't always good. New isn't always right. Old bush is bush that has hung on for a lot longer than Lorraine's been here, and digging it up to make a golf course or a resort or what have you would ruin something that is timeless and beautiful.

Because that's what she's realised these scrubby, oddly shaped, khaki and brown and golden and sometimes green bushes and shrubs and trees are: beautiful. All these weekends Shirl's been banging on about natives and Lorraine thought she was a bit touched, and now here Lorraine is, believing Shirl may be onto something. You wouldn't read about it.

'When it comes to development,' Cynthia is saying, 'it's generally not a good idea to let people do what they want. There has to be some oversight.' She turns her attention to a lavender that isn't as healthy as it should be, frowns, then starts making small cuts here and there. 'In Los Angeles some people seem to do what they want,' she says, her attention still on the lavender. 'They build these ugly office towers and apartment blocks. No one says anything. I guess because the city isn't that old and there's not much in the way of natural land left.'

She lifts her head and looks seriously at Lorraine. 'But we have a lot left here. So I hope your mother doesn't sell to that person.'

Lorraine grins. 'She told him to buzz off. Although I guess if he comes back with more money she might be tempted. Except she'd probably just buy somewhere else in the hinterland then complain about the golf course once they build it.'

'Papa's had offers,' Cynthia says. 'There are so few lots in Little Cove that I suppose they're appealing to certain types. But it's his home.'

'Your home too,' Lorraine murmurs.

Cynthia stops what she's doing and turns to face Lorraine. 'I guess it is, now,' she says, then she sighs. 'Am I home?'

Her face crumples a little and Lorraine reaches across and takes her gardening-gloved hand.

'Your daughter is here, your father is here. Von is here. Handsome Pat is here.' She winks. 'And I'm here. Plus I think Shirl and Barb are quite partial to you. To me that sounds like you're home.'

Cynthia sniffs and nods quickly, ducking her head, and Lorraine wonders if she's crying. She can't remember seeing Cynthia cry. It wasn't her thing when they were young.

'I think you're right,' Cynthia says when she lifts her head.

'It actually doesn't matter what *I* think, though.' Lorraine lets go of Cynthia's hand. 'It matters how you feel.'

Cynthia sits back and looks around the garden. 'My father gave me something the other day,' she says.

'A million dollars?' Lorraine teases and is rewarded with a flash of a smile from Cynthia.

'No. And I'm fine for money anyway because my attorney has wrung a substantial settlement out of Max.'

'Sounds like that's the least that could be wrung out of him.' Lorraine frowns. 'What an arsehole.'

Cynthia makes a face. 'I chose to marry him.'

'He wasn't who you thought he was!'

'No,' Cynthia concedes.

'Anyway, your dad gave you something?'

'Yes.' Cynthia clears her throat, which makes this announcement sound important, so Lorraine stops pulling dead leaves off the plant in front of her and pays attention.

'My mother had a sketchbook,' Cynthia goes on. 'Of native plants. Flowers.'

She exhales and looks to the sky, and for a second Lorraine wonders if she's praying or something, but that really isn't Cynthia's style.

'I had no idea she could draw. Or that she was interested in art in any way. Just like I had no idea that she was in the Sunshine Gardening Society.'

Now her eyes look into Lorraine's and there's sadness there, which makes Lorraine feel sad. Cynthia can't get to know her mother now. Lorraine doesn't take it for granted that she can see Rose whenever she likes.

'What kind of daughter does that make me? That I didn't know or notice?' Cynthia says. Her eyes are so wide that she looks startled.

'The kind her mother kept secrets from,' Lorraine says. 'And that was her choice, Cyn. It wouldn't have been anything to do with you. Who knows why we do what we do? I don't know half the time!'

A kookaburra swoops from the pine tree in the corner of the garden and picks up some creature that Lorraine can't see.

'Terry's been feeding that bird,' she says. 'That's why it hangs around.'

'Maybe it just likes it here,' Cynthia says.

'Here? With all the yelling and the complaining? Not likely.'

'I like it here too,' Cynthia says.

'Great,' Lorraine says. 'Then I'll book you in for some regular visits and you can help me keep this garden under control.'

Cynthia laughs. 'It's a deal.'

'Don't be too hard on yourself about your mum,' Lorraine says. 'She was kind of unknowable. Nice to me and all that, but there were walls up. I bet your dad would say the same.'

Lorraine hears the TV volume suddenly shoot up inside the house and the sound of an agitated boy. 'Kids!' she yells, then scrambles to her feet.

'I'll be back,' she says to Cynthia, and hurries inside to take care of whatever skirmish has broken out in her living room.

CHAPTER THIRTY-THREE

Kathy is listening for the sound of a car being parked outside her house, which means that anytime a car approaches she hops off the couch, then has to sit down again once she hears it drive by. She has no idea why she's so nervous about seeing her own child. Maybe because she doesn't know how they'll be with each other – if Michelle will be angry at her for leaving her father then leaving the state, even though she says she's not. Maybe she was faking it when she said she wanted to visit to see Kathy? Maybe she only wants to come here to air grievances?

It's a long way to drive if that is the case. Michelle called two days ago and said she was setting off, and Kathy told her not to take the coast road because it isn't as safe as the New England Highway, although she knows Michelle will do whatever she wants. That's what she's been like from infancy: if she didn't like a food Kathy would be unable to get her to eat it; if she didn't like a relative she would refuse to be hugged. She didn't like school, so that meant Kathy and Owen embarked on a major bribery campaign involving dolls and a bike. Bribery is Michelle's weakness.

No bribe has been deployed in this visit. Michelle is, therefore, coming because she wants to. So Kathy can relax. Or not. Her choice. And she does realise it's a choice, because she could switch off the thoughts running through her head and instead decide that it's such a lovely thing that her daughter whom she hasn't seen in months will be here shortly.

Another car drives by. No – this one is stopping. This one is Michelle's.

Kathy flings open the front door, which tells her that she's more excited to see Michelle than she's been prepared to admit to herself.

A white Corolla is parked behind her blue Laser, and as Michelle had a white Corolla the last time she saw her Kathy feels confident approaching the car.

She can see a hand waving from the driver's side, then the door opens and out steps her daughter: coppery hair tied in a ponytail, lots of make-up – as usual – and wearing a T-shirt that has shoulder pads and sequins, which seems an excessive amount of embellishment for such a simple garment.

'Mum!' Michelle is beaming. That's a good sign.

She slams the door shut and Kathy winces. Owen was always telling their daughter not to slam car doors but the advice has never taken.

Michelle hurries around the back of the car and before Kathy can utter a greeting she's been enveloped in a hug. She hugs back and remembers how good it is – how reassuring – to be held by someone who loves you unconditionally. If Michelle still does. No guarantees with children. Or girlfriends who tell you that they'll love you forever.

'Hello, my love,' she says into Michelle's ponytail and squeezes her a little tighter for a few seconds.

Michelle kisses her on the cheek, then stands back and looks down at her. She's the tall child. Grant is the same height as Owen – five foot nine – but Michelle takes after Kathy's father, who was six foot four. Although she's not that tall – five-eleven the last time they measured her.

'I like your haircut,' Michelle says and smiles.

Kathy runs a hand through the bob she got done a couple of days ago at the local hairdresser, feeling like a change then wondering if a woman her age should have a hairstyle that's better suited to a schoolgirl.

'Thank you. I thought I'd get ready for warm weather.' Kathy smiles and feels her shoulders and neck letting go of whatever tension she didn't know they were holding. 'I'll get your bag.' She nods towards the boot.

'That's okay, I've got it! You don't need to do that for me.'

Kathy wants to say that she likes to do things for her children, but Michelle could truthfully reply that Kathy left her children and moved half a country away, which doesn't suggest that she wants to do anything much for them. She probably wouldn't accept Kathy's reasoning that she moved *because* she believed she was doing something for her children: sparing them the shame and the shambles that her life had become. In Kathy's eyes, at least.

Michelle pulls a small suitcase from the car and Kathy gestures for her to walk ahead up the path to the house.

'Pretty flowers,' Michelle says, gesturing to the pink-dotted bed to her left.

'Pigface,' Kathy says. She didn't know their name when she moved in but she does now.

'Really? I wonder why they're called that.'

'I don't know.' Perhaps Shirl would; Kathy can ask her next weekend.

They enter the house, which is darker than Kathy likes but she rented it in a hurry. If she decides to stick around this part of the world she may look for something brighter. She has surprised herself by even thinking of staying, because when she moved here she thought it would be temporary. A place to change and move on – to where, she didn't know. Her emotions were all over the place and permanency not on her mind. It's grown on her, though, this coastal lifestyle. Melbourne has a bay and there are beaches further south, but it's not as if she or many people she knows grew up as 'beach people'. The Sunshine Coast is full of beach people, either by upbringing or choice, and there's a lot to be said for how relaxed it can make a person to live in a place where mild breezes and seagulls remind you that the ocean with its breathtaking vastness is so close by.

Michelle puts her bag next to the couch and glances around. 'It looks like you're camping,' she says.

'I suppose I have been.'

'You're not staying, then?' She sounds somewhat hopeful.

'I don't know. Maybe.' Kathy gestures to the couch. 'Take a seat. Can I get you a glass of water? Some food? When did you last eat?'

'Water would be lovely, thanks, Mum. But I ate not that long ago.'

After filling a glass in the kitchen, Kathy offers it to Michelle then sits next to her. She only has the couch; there aren't any chairs or beanbags or anything else to suggest she's planned for visitors.

Michelle takes a couple of sips of water then puts the glass down on the coffee table.

'Dad says hello,' she says, glancing at Kathy out of the corner of her eye.

'How is he?'

Michelle's jaw hardens, then she relaxes. 'He's, um . . . He's okay now.' Another glance. 'But he was pretty bad for a while. Upset, you know. More about you leaving Melbourne than anything.'

'I know it was a big shock. All of it.'

Kathy remembers the tumult when she told Owen she was leaving him. Nothing had happened with Jemima apart from a statement of intention – Kathy had no interest in being an adulteress. She told Jemima she had to leave her marriage before they could begin anything, so when she told Owen she'd fallen in love with someone else it was with a clear conscience, even if she didn't tell him who it was. That didn't stop the whole matter becoming wretched, though. He was devastated, telling her that he'd planned their retirement and everything. He didn't understand what someone else could offer Kathy that he couldn't.

Kathy didn't want to use the old clichés about how you can't help who you fall in love with, but in the end that was all she had. That and the knowledge that she'd never been in love with Owen, so when she fell in love with Jemima it was all the fireworks she'd heard about and that was impossible to walk away from.

There had been love in their marriage, of course – Owen was a lovable man. There just wasn't love in the way he wanted, not for her, and she felt terrible for denying him the opportunity to be with someone who might have really fallen for him too. Except she didn't know that she hadn't been in love with him, not until she met Jemima. She thought that the rush of affection she'd felt for him when he started courting her, then the thrill of being proposed to, were what 'in love' meant. It never once occurred to her that the thrill was because she felt like she'd achieved something she'd been trained for her whole life. Her job was to get married and have babies. Well . . . job done. Nowhere was there any consideration of how a woman might feel about it; of what satisfaction – or not – might come with it. Jemima made her believe there was a better way to live – a way that made you feel alive, like every day was singing with possibility. Until it wasn't.

'I think he's over the shock,' Michelle says. 'He's met someone.'

Now her body is turned towards Kathy and she's watching her mother's face. For the reaction, of course. All Kathy feels is happiness.

'That's wonderful,' she says.

'Don't you want to know who it is?'

Kathy considers this for a second. 'No. That's his business.'

From the look on Michelle's face Kathy wonders if that question was designed to enable Michelle to ask about Jemima. Kathy's never given much detail.

'And you?' Michelle says.

'Me?'

'Have you . . . ?' Michelle raises her eyebrows and Kathy knows why.

In the weeks after Kathy left Owen, her daughter had pressed her on the subject every time they spoke, asking how she could just leave the marriage when nothing seemed to be wrong. Sick of lying – to herself as much as anyone else – Kathy finally said that nothing was wrong with Owen except for the fact that he wasn't a woman, because she'd left him for a woman named Jemima. Michelle had made a sound like she was choking and ended the call, and the subject hadn't been raised since.

'Are you asking if I have a girlfriend?'

Kathy thinks that what Michelle really wants to know is if Kathy is still attracted to women or has now decided it was a passing fancy.

'Um . . .' Michelle bites her bottom lip.

'It's okay if you are,' Kathy says softly. 'I know that part was a shock to you.'

When Michelle's eyes meet hers Kathy can see the little girl who went off to her first day of school both scared and defiant.

'It really was,' Michelle says. 'And you didn't want to talk about it.'

'I know.' Kathy sounds defeated because she feels it. 'I know.'

She glances towards her meagre back garden. It really should be in better shape now that she has more knowledge about plants.

'I don't have a girlfriend.' She smiles sadly. 'Or a boyfriend.'

Another glance at the garden and she realises she has something else to say on the matter.

'But I have friends. I mean, I've made friends. We garden together.'

Now Michelle is looking at the garden too and Kathy sees it as she would: with a solitary drooping pandanus palm and a clump of sad strelitzia.

'Not out there, I hope,' she says and Kathy bursts out laughing.

'No. In other people's gardens. We help out people who need it.'

And they're also helping me. That's what she discovered last weekend: the women of the Sunshine Gardening Society have, simply by giving her an activity to do that helps her feel useful, offered her a community that she didn't know she was seeking.

'Don't you need it too?' Michelle points to the pandanus. 'That's on its last legs!'

'Don't be cheeky!'

'Take better care of your garden!'

'Michelle! I hope you didn't come here to lecture me.'

'What if I did?'

'Well . . .' Kathy pauses. 'Then I guess I deserve it.'

She sits gazing at her daughter, who looks as though she's not sure what to say.

Michelle takes another sip of water.

'No, you don't,' she says. 'No more than anyone.'

She stands. 'Show me your miserable garden?' She grins.

Kathy stands too. 'With pleasure.'

She slides open the glass door that leads to the garden and feels the afternoon sun on her cheeks. Out here she can still hear cars passing by. Now, though, she can relax: her girl is here. They can work their way back to each other, starting now.

CHAPTER THIRTY-FOUR

'Well, would you look at that!' Shirl is standing on the steps leading to Elizabeth's garden, hands on her hips, feet wide, and a look of satisfaction on her face. And Shirl is what Elizabeth calls her now, ever since it popped out of her mouth one day and she realised that they must be familiar enough with each other for it to fit.

Today she's wearing a singlet with a faded Eureka flag on it and Elizabeth wonders – not for the first time – where Shirl gets all of her tops. Last weekend she wore a different singlet bearing a cartoon of Joh Bjelke-Petersen with a handful of peanuts and she apologised for showing her 'flappy bits'.

'Don't worry, we can't see your boobs,' Lorraine had retorted and Elizabeth blushed.

'I was talking about the backs of my arms,' Shirl said, lifting a limb and shaking it. 'But thanks for the compliment.'

Elizabeth was mortified for Lorraine, who merely laughed.

'After two babies I know *mine* are flappy,' she'd said, then put on her gloves and got to work.

Shirl hadn't seemed the least bit offended, which made Elizabeth wonder if she reads too much into things. Or if she doesn't have a sense of humour. Both, of course, can be true at the same time.

Now Shirl is nodding and looking proud as she surveys the riot of colour in the garden. 'Gotta love spring,' she says. 'It was a bit slow this year but now . . .' She throws her hands in the air. 'Colour! A riot of it!'

'And here I was,' says Barb as she draws alongside, 'thinking you had no kind words for anything that isn't a native.'

'I have my principles,' Shirl says, picking up the plastic tub she uses to toss weeds into. 'Which include appreciating beauty where I find it.'

It is true that the garden is looking beautiful. The pansies are blooming purple and pink and yellow, and the magenta-coloured bougainvillea is cascading down one part of the fence as jasmine blooms in another, the scent carrying on the air, and the pink hibiscus nod alongside it all.

That jasmine was here when they moved in, and she and Jon would sit in the garden on a warm evening, before the sun set, and take in its aroma. They stopped doing that at some point Elizabeth can't recall; all she knows is that smelling it now reminds her so strongly of the times before he ailed – when he was strong and tall and hearty – that she gasps and bends over, putting her hands on her thighs.

Smell is the strongest sense – she has been told this. It's just never captured her as much as it has now. Never transported her so fully to a different dimension of time.

'You right?' Lorraine pats her on the back.

Elizabeth takes a deep breath through her mouth – avoiding the scent of jasmine – and stands up.

'I'm getting there,' she says, smiling as Lorraine frowns.

'You're crying,' Lorraine says, pointing to her cheek.

'Happy tears,' Elizabeth promises, and it's half-true. She's happy to be in this garden, smelling something that once gave her so much pleasure.

'Sure,' Lorraine says drily.

'I just . . .' Elizabeth exhales raggedly and shakes her head to try to rid herself of a display of emotion that is no doubt as unwelcome to her companions as it is to her. 'I haven't smelt the jasmine for a while. I haven't . . . been out here when it's been blooming.'

'It's been blooming for a few weeks,' Kathy says matter-of-factly, tucking her trowel into her waistband.

'Then I guess I haven't noticed,' Elizabeth murmurs.

'Can't keep up with everything.' Lorraine winks. 'But you must be happy with how this is turning out. Look at it! Colour everywhere. We should call one of those gardening mags. Like *Belle*, is it?'

'Do you read those?' Cynthia says archly and Lorraine makes a face.

'Cora does. She probably thinks I should do our backyard like one of those gardens. As if I have the time for that!'

She turns and marches towards the end of the garden, which she long ago declared to be her favourite spot. It's cooler there because the thick green leaves of the camellias seem to create their own little climate.

Elizabeth feels guilty that these women are all working on her garden when they could be working on their own. Lorraine doesn't have time to tend to hers because she's helping Elizabeth. That doesn't seem right. Not any more. Not while all the plants are blooming, because clearly everything is working the way it should.

'You in need of a job?' Shirl says in her direction.

'Probably,' Elizabeth says softly. The others seem to know exactly what they're doing in her garden and she's just standing here.

'I'm going to deadhead those azaleas.' Shirl nods to the side of the house, where shrivelled old flowers are still on the bushes.

'You shouldn't have to,' Elizabeth says, and Shirl's response is a look that is a cross between withering and pitying.

'What on earth is that supposed to mean?' she says.

'I should be able to look after this garden on my own. The plants are in such good shape, thanks to you all. It's just a matter of maintenance from now on.'

Shirl sighs heavily. 'If you think that, you haven't learnt nearly enough, my girl.' This time the look on her face is of pure pity.

'Gardens aren't just *maintained*,' she goes on. 'They're living works of art. Sure, this one looks great now, and once those gardenias open up it'll stink in the best possible way and you'll think it's all wonderful. Then what?'

Shirl looks at her pointedly and Elizabeth can only shrug in response, because she's not sure what she's meant to say.

'You stay *vigilant*,' Shirl says. 'Yes, there's maintenance, but you also have to keep assessing what you have here. Maybe the pansies don't look so good next year. What then? You might want to put something else in. Maybe the camellias don't produce flowers. Something's going wrong, isn't it? You have to diagnose it.'

She sighs again, but this time she smiles with it. 'This garden is in a relationship with you, and you with it.' Turning, she looks Elizabeth in the eye. 'Maybe that's what Jon wanted.'

It's said plainly and it has greater impact for it.

Barb said something to Elizabeth recently about how humans can often sense things far in advance of them happening – years, even. When they bought this house, Jon was so determined to create a garden that Elizabeth presumed he wanted, although he kept telling her it was so it 'will look beautiful, for you'. It was courteous; chivalrous, perhaps. An act of tribute was how he seemed to treat it and how she was prepared to take it. Now she wonders. Because as Jon faded, he kept asking her to work on the garden. She thought it was his way of clinging onto this world – still attached to his grand project – and possibly of distracting himself from the failures of his body by focusing on the flourishing of the garden he would never see again. She didn't consider that he might have had another motive: to keep *her* in this world by offering her this relationship with nature, with beauty. Perhaps because she wasn't ready to see it then.

She may not even be ready now – although she believes Shirl wouldn't accept that.

'We'll never know,' Elizabeth says.

'Oh, I do,' Shirl says firmly. 'I've got a hotline to heaven.'

She nods as if she's said the most logical thing possible, and Elizabeth starts to laugh.

'Really?' she says as her laugh turns into a giggle.

'Hasn't Barb told you?' Shirl looks around and Barb lifts her head from the buxus she's trimming, mischief in her eyes.

Shirl winks. 'I've always got the inside track. That's how I knew we'd get this garden right. Didn't I, Barb?'

'Something like that,' Barb murmurs, and Elizabeth isn't sure whether to take either one of them seriously.

'Anyway, we're not going anywhere,' Shirl says. 'You're in charge of this place – of course you are – but there's too much work for one. Your hubby might have had some nice ideas – just wish he'd thought about the load. It's too much when you're working and raising the kid.' She shrugs. 'So, time to deadhead. You with me?'

Elizabeth looks at the various Sunshine Gardeners dotted around her springtime wonderland and smiles, thinking of what they've all made together.

'I really am,' she says, and picks up the bucket she plans to fill with brown azalea flowers to make way for the new crop, next spring.

OCTOBER 1987

HAWKWEED

CHAPTER THIRTY-FIVE

'What do you *mean* she's not going to the hospital?' Cynthia shrieks into the phone because Pat has just called to tell her that Odette's in labour, and now he's saying something nonsensical about Odette not wanting to give birth in the hospital.

'She's giving birth at home,' Pat says calmly, and his passivity makes Cynthia want to throw something.

'I find it extraordinary that you can be so sanguine about our only child expelling a small creature from her loins *at home*! She needs a hospital! She may die!'

'Cynthia, try not to get too worked up. Women have been –'

'Don't you *dare* tell me that women have been giving birth in fields for millennia and that worked out all right, because a lot of them *died*, Patrick. They *died*. I have one child and I do not want her to *die*.'

'Odette wants the baby to have a peaceful entry into the world and she thinks that won't happen in hospital.'

Cynthia exhales loudly. It sounds dismissive of Pat and that's fine with her because she wants it to sound that way. *The idiot.*

'Patrick, let me clear up something for you: the only way birth is peaceful is if the mother has had a general anaesthetic, so she's not awake to be aware of the brutal reality of what goes on. Odette has been getting this claptrap about a peaceful birth from someone – is it you? *You*, the person with a *penis*, telling her how to give birth?'

She knows she sounds somewhat hysterical, and Pat will probably say that's because she wants to be in control of the situation – and he'll be right, because she does, because her child has gone into labour and any mother would feel tense about that, and now is not the time for lecturing about the merits of home birth. Especially when the lecturer has never given, and can never give, birth himself.

'No, Cynthia, not me. Listen –'

'I'm on my way,' she says and hangs up the phone.

'Papa!' she calls out, although she knows her father isn't here. That doesn't stop her wanting him to be here. She could do with his steadiness, and she's also not sure that she won't crash the car. Not that that will stop her driving to Pat's house. If Odette thinks she's going to give birth in that dilapidated beach shack that's probably still on a septic tank for sewerage, Cynthia is going to talk her out of it.

She drives as fast as the speed limit will allow towards Pat's home. When she gets there his front door is open and Cynthia can hear the gasps of pain from outside.

After she gave birth to Odette, her mother told her that she wouldn't remember the pain, and while she doesn't remember the actual pain itself she remembers the surprise of it and how nothing could have prepared her for it. Perhaps the surprise will propel Odette towards the hospital. Cynthia simply cannot countenance her daughter giving birth in a place where there are no doctors and no nurses and no help of any kind.

The first person Cynthia sees as she walks in is a tall young man with sun-bleached long hair and a T-shirt with holes in it. The baby's father, presumably, and he can't even be bothered showing up to the birth in proper clothes. Not a good sign.

'Darling,' Cynthia says as she spots Odette sitting on the floor, her legs wide, her face screwed up and her cheeks wet.

'Hi, Cyn,' Pat says as he enters the room carrying a glass of water.

'Patrick.'

Cynthia kneels next to Odette. 'Darling,' she says again and takes Odette's hand.

No matter what difficulties have been between them she knows that Odette will want her here, the way Cynthia wanted her own mother when Odette was born. Not that her mother came. Cynthia was alone at the house she shared with Pat when Odette arrived faster than she had been warned could happen. There was no time to tell anyone what was going on, and she was terrified. She would have given anything to be in a hospital with a nurse to reassure her about what was happening, for a doctor to check her baby, to feel safer than she felt as she pushed Odette out onto the kitchen floor and watched as blood followed her. She didn't know if that was normal or if something was wrong. Then Odette squawked and Cynthia burst into tears, and a few minutes later Pat came home.

He was calm then too. She'd continued crying as he wrapped towels around Odette, whose umbilicus was still attached to the cord, then picked them both up and carried them to the car, laying them so gently in the back seat before he sped to the local GP's surgery. Luckily the doctor had delivered several babies and, while Cynthia was still in a fog of fear and hormones, he took them into his treatment room, cut the cord, cleaned them both up and sent them home.

Cynthia doesn't want that for Odette. She wants clean sheets and antibacterial everything. It doesn't matter that events turned out well for her and Odette was fine; she doesn't believe they could be that lucky twice.

Odette sniffles and takes Cynthia's hand. 'Hi, Mummy,' she says, sniffling again. 'The baby's coming.'

'Your father told me. He also said you want to have it here.'

Odette nods but there's uncertainty in her eyes.

'Is that what you *really* want?'

Odette glances up at Ash, who looks more like a scared boy than a man about to become a father.

'It's not his decision to make, darling,' Cynthia says firmly.

'I think hospital is safer. But his mother said it's better –' Odette gasps and squeezes Cynthia's hand.

'*Odette*,' says Cynthia. 'The decisions made about a birth should be the business of the woman giving birth unless she needs medical intervention. These men have nothing to do with it.'

She glares at Pat, blaming him absolutely for what is happening, even though it was probably Ash's doing in the first place.

'Dettie,' says Ash, moving into Odette's line of sight, and Cynthia wants to growl at him for turning a perfectly lovely name into a charmless nickname.

'Dettie,' he repeats, crouching and putting his hand on Odette's leg. 'You told me that you want this. You said that if you told me you want to go to hospital that I should remind you that you don't really.'

'I've changed my mind!' Odette says, her eyes flashing.

'Yeah, but . . .' Ash looks stricken and Cynthia now feels sympathy, because he is in quite a spot. But not too much sympathy because he doesn't deserve it.

'Let's look at it this way,' Cynthia says as evenly as she can. 'Ash, you're interested in the wellbeing of your child, yes?'

He hesitates then nods.

'And I'm interested in the wellbeing of *mine*,' she goes on. 'Your child isn't here yet. Mine is. She says she's changed her mind about hospital. If she's angry at you later, you can blame me.'

Cynthia lets go of Odette's hand and stands up. 'We're going,' she says. 'Patrick, Ash, take her under the armpits and get her up.'

Without waiting to see how they manage it, Cynthia heads for the open door and her car.

'This is not about control, Pat,' she mutters as he passes. 'This is about our child being safe.'

'I understand,' he says, and she could swear his voice breaks.

When he turns to look at Cynthia after he's helped Odette into the back seat, he puts his hands on her cheeks.

'I understand,' he repeats. 'Because I'm scared too.'

Cynthia nods slowly. 'Then you and Ash go together in your car. I don't want Odette upset.'

She doesn't wait to hear his response as she closes the back door. She gets in the front, starts the car and drives off, breaking the speed limit just a little as she tries to remember where the hospital is.

CHAPTER THIRTY-SIX

For a while there Kathy thought Michelle would try to join her for this morning's gathering of the Sunshine Gardening Society. Her stay with Kathy has turned out to be a couple of weeks long already, which Kathy doesn't mind at all because they've been getting on the way they always used to, chatting about everything. Obviously Kathy was chatting a lot about the gardening because Michelle said she wanted to meet these women her mother was spending weekends with, and find out why, exactly, Kathy was prepared to spend time making other people's gardens beautiful while ignoring her own.

For that Kathy had no answer, but she promised to buy a couple of plants. Even if the property is a rental and she doesn't know how long she'll be there she could at least try to make it beautiful. As an act of self-respect – which she's starting to think she may have. Or have rediscovered.

As Cynthia had told her when Kathy asked why she always turned up on weekends looking groomed when they're all about to get dirty in a garden: 'Taking care of myself is an act of respect for myself. If I don't do it, no one will. Besides, you all have to look at me and I'd like to make the experience as pleasant as possible.'

In that moment Kathy was grateful that Cynthia hadn't appraised her own lack of effort in the grooming department.

The only time in her life she's felt like doing herself up was when she was with Jemima – because each time they saw each other it felt like a celebration. When it's just for her she's never seen the point. Except, as Cynthia said, she doesn't have to look at herself. Other people do. And she certainly has to look at her back garden.

At any rate, she'd managed to dissuade Michelle from joining them today, saying she'd need to be vetted by Shirl and Barb first, and sent her off to the Eumundi Market. Kathy hasn't been but her co-workers rave about it, saying you can find all sorts of arts and crafts, and Michelle loves that stuff. Kathy has no idea where she gets it from, because she's not artsy or craftsy herself. Mind you, Owen was handy at sewing on a button.

'Morning, Lorraine,' Kathy says as Lorraine arrives clutching a plastic shopping bag and tying a tracksuit top around her waist.

'Pineapple,' Lorraine says, holding up the bag. 'I cut some up. In case anyone wants morning tea.'

The others murmur their thanks and arrange their tools in front of the council garden bed next to the river. It's a nice spot to work; quite serene if you can ignore the dogs barking at each other as they pass by in the park and the boat motors chugging towards the ocean.

'Cynthia's not coming,' Lorraine announces as she puts the bag in a shady spot. 'Odette's had her baby.'

'Oh!' Barb says, getting to her feet. 'Is she all right?'

'Everyone's okay. Cynthia just wanted to help settle them in at home. I think Odette's boyfriend still hasn't decided if he wants to be a father so he's not doing anything. Luckily Pat's around.'

'Pat?' Barb asks.

'Odette's dad. Cynthia's ex.'

'Right.' Barb turns away and kneels down in front of the garden.

Kathy has noticed that Barb's not a gossip – she'll ask the pertinent questions but not engage further. Shirl, on the other hand, could gossip for Australia, although it's well meaning. She doesn't say nasty things, just likes to know what's going on – although that can mean asking if anyone knows if So-and-so is really leaving his wife for Whatsername, and does anyone know if it's true that the real estate agent in Noosaville is expanding to Coolum. Kathy learns more about the goings-on in the local area in one Saturday morning with Shirl than in a whole week at work.

'Hi, Elizabeth.' Kathy smiles as the young woman walks up. She's looking a little better these days, Kathy thinks. Not as sad around the eyes.

'Hello, all.' Elizabeth too holds up a plastic bag. 'Strawberries.'

'Well, isn't this a cornucopia,' says Shirl. 'Lorraine's brought pineapple.' She nods at the trees. 'Over there in the shade, love.'

Elizabeth smiles and drifts towards the trees.

Lorraine squats next to Kathy. 'So, what are we doing today?' she asks. 'Wait – let me guess. We're planting natives.' She glances slyly in Shirl's direction.

'You'll keep,' Shirl says, but she looks quite pleased. 'We're pruning these roses and tidying up these beds – you can see how the weeds are creeping back in. Bit of mulch on top. Although *yes*, Lorraine, planting natives would be a better solution.' She squints up at the tall eucalyptus close by. 'I swear those kooka-burras just sit there waiting for us to put mulch on because they want to swoop down and mess it up.'

'But natives don't go with the roses, right?' Kathy asks. 'From an aesthetic point of view, I mean.'

'Correct.' Shirl sighs loudly. 'If I had my way we'd pull out those roses.'

'The roses have been here for years, Shirley,' Barb says. 'They're staying in.'

'I know, I know.' Another loud sigh. 'Here I go, pruning them, see, Barb? Now they'll grow back nice and strong.'

Elizabeth moves to the other side of Lorraine and pulls on her gloves.

'How's work?' Lorraine asks her, and Kathy realises that she didn't even know Elizabeth had a job. She presumed Jon would have left life insurance or something so that Elizabeth didn't have to work straightaway. What a strain, having a young child and working and trying to manage on your own, all while you're grieving. Elizabeth is stronger than she looks.

'It's good.' Elizabeth's smile seems genuine. 'The days are busy. I like that.'

'And Charlie's managing the change in routine?'

'He is. I'm lucky that my parents can pick him up each day, because he loves spending time with them.'

'I think it's amazing that you say you're lucky,' Kathy pipes up. Her eyes meet Elizabeth's and she hopes they show that she's being serious. 'With what you've gone through . . . What you're going through. Not many people would say they're lucky.'

Elizabeth stares at her then she nods slowly. 'I guess not. And I haven't felt that way a lot of the time. But . . .' She looks around at their small gathering. 'Some days are better than others.'

She grins and it's the first time Kathy has ever seen her really smile. Normally there are quick little expressions that are on the way to a smile. If she's part of the reason why Elizabeth can smile – if they are, collectively, the reason – that makes her feel she's done something right.

For the next ten minutes or so they all work in silence. Chitchat is welcome but Kathy has found that some days they all naturally concentrate, and there's delicate work to be done in this garden. One random wrong prune and the rose may not recover – although from the way Shirl tells it, roses are like triffids and threatening to take over the earth one day because they're so hardy.

It's while Kathy is examining a soft pink rose, deciding where to cut the stem, that she notices the sunlight being blocked out and turns to see a sweaty man in a suit and tie whose gut is straining against his shirt and belt. He's grinning and rubbing his hands together.

'What have we here?' he says, and Kathy is fairly sure that's a leer he's throwing in Elizabeth's direction.

'Not your harem,' Shirl barks, holding up her secateurs. 'Buzz off.'

'Wow. *Unfriendly.*' He chuckles and Kathy is tempted to take her own secateurs to his goolies. What a creep. Why can't they just be left alone?

The last time they were in a council park there was some nob in running gear who thought they'd enjoy watching him stretch next to where they were working. They didn't and it was Barb who chased him off, telling him they had no interest in seeing his shrivelled little testes straining to make an impression on his nylon shorts. Those were the exact words she used. Kathy wrote them down afterwards in case she ever needs to use them in another context.

'Anyway, girls –'

'We're not girls,' Shirl says loudly. 'We're ladies. Women at a pinch.'

'All right, *ladies.*' He winks at Shirl, who makes a chopping action with the secateurs.

'Anyway,' he goes on, 'love what you're doing here. Looks great. But you won't have to do it again.'

Barb stands up, wielding her trowel as if it's a sword. 'Who are you?'

The man holds up his hands. 'Whoa, Tex, don't shoot me. I'm Vince.'

'Vince who?'

'Need-to-know basis.' He seems to think this is a hilarious response and Barb looks furious.

'I work in property,' he says. 'Aaaand . . .' He spreads his arms and half-turns around. 'Some mates and I have plans to develop this beautiful spot. Isn't that ace?' He puts his hands on his hips and nods. 'Just waiting on the paperwork. So, uh, it's nice you're keeping the place pretty and everything, but all this will be gone soon.'

Kathy feels a little sick, and from the look on the faces of the others, they do too. This spot? This public land on the water that people enjoy with their dogs and their kids? Where they have picnics and ride bikes? If it's developed, the walking trail will be severed at this point and no one will be able to continue around the river.

'Like hell it will!' Barb says, and Kathy's mouth drops open because Barb's volume has never before gone above lullaby level. 'This is public land!'

'Not for long.' Vince winks again. Now it's his eyelashes Kathy would like to sever. 'But if you don't like it, take it up with the council. Not sure how far you'll get, but.' With that he tucks his shirt further into his trousers, turns and walks away.

As Kathy glances around the group she sees mouths as open as hers.

'They can't do that, can they?' she murmurs.

'This has been happening,' Barb says darkly. 'Too often.' She glances at Shirl. 'But never on land like this.'

'Can we go to the council?'

'Only if you take a whacking great bribe with you,' Shirl mutters.

'Shirley,' Barb warns.

'All right, all right. Unfounded rumours.' Shirl purses her lips. 'But we're not going to solve anything this morning. These roses are still here. Let's get on with it.'

Kathy slowly restarts her examination of the rose branch but her mind is whirring. She hasn't lived in this area long but she knows how rare these public lands are when they're in this sort of housing area. Sure, there's the national park at Noosa Heads, but people need green space where they live too. There's a little park near her house and she likes just looking at it, even if she doesn't spend much time there.

Maybe she could ask the council if there's anything she could do. Yeah, right – not likely. She's one person and she's not a local. It doesn't sound like Shirl or Barb have much faith that anything would change. This could be something she just needs to accept.

Except she feels a niggle, in her belly. Like an itch on the inside. The feeling she gets when she knows something isn't right. She's familiar with it because she had it for a lot of her marriage; she doesn't want to live with it for that long again.

She glances at Shirl, whose face is like thunder as she digs into the dirt, and at Barb, who looks upset, and that decides it: Kathy's going to at least try to talk to someone. What kind of civic gardener is she if she doesn't even try?

Perhaps she can rope in some of the others. Not Lorraine – she's too busy. Elizabeth has enough on her plate.

Cynthia. She'll know what to do. Give it a few weeks so she's not spending as much time with Odette, then Kathy will give her a call.

CHAPTER THIRTY-SEVEN

Lorraine has been feeling out of sorts. It's a generalised feeling, in that it's with her all the time, but she thinks it has a few specific causes. One is the ongoing situation with Cora and the children. She's sure Cora's giving Simon extra food, because he's putting on weight and Lorraine isn't feeding him differently. It's not that she minds Simon having treats every now and again – it's that she thinks Cora's doing it just to get at her, to undermine her, to try to make her own son prefer his grandmother.

Lorraine said something to her mother about it and Rose said that Mike needed to sort it out, because it's his mother and his son and Lorraine shouldn't have to do everything.

Now she's waiting for Mike to come to bed and it's not really the time to bring up those sorts of subjects. It'd kill the mood. And she does like the mood. The mood is what keeps her going in the hard times when she wants to clobber Mike over the head for all the things he washes his hands of around the house. He probably knows it, too, that's why he's so good at creating that particular mood.

As he walks heavily into their bedroom, though, Lorraine can tell there will be no mood tonight. The corners of his mouth are turned down and his shoulders are sagging. Normally he stands up pretty straight, and he's fit from all the manual labour so he looks quite strong. The Mike in front of her now looks defeated. Weak.

'What's wrong?' she says as he sits on the side of the bed and rubs the back of his head.

'Ah . . .' He puts his elbows on his thighs and his head in his hands, which makes Lorraine feel alarmed. She's never seen him like this before. Not even when Terry fell off his bike and broke his arm when Mike was meant to be watching him.

She puts a hand on his shoulder blade and pats. 'Mike?'

She rubs circles, like she did with the kids when they were little. They always liked that right before they fell asleep.

'Are you okay?' she says softly.

He inhales noisily and sits up straight, then turns himself around so he's facing her. His eyes are bloodshot, almost as if he's been crying.

Nah, that isn't possible. She's never seen Mike cry.

'Mike? What is it?'

'You know what happened on Tuesday?' he says, not looking her in the eye.

'Tuesday?' She tries to think what happened on Tuesday. The kids went to school, she banked some cheques and did some shopping, took Cora to the dentist in Noosa Junction, cooked a . . . what did she cook for dinner?

'The stock market crash,' he says.

'The . . .' Now she remembers watching the news and how they were calling it Black Monday even though it was Tuesday here, and everyone was saying it was the end of the world or something, but she didn't see how it would affect her because she doesn't have stocks, she just has some money tucked away in a savings account and not much of it at that, but she saves what she can. So it was bad news for people on Wall Street, but not for Lorraine with a Commonwealth Bank savings account earning hardly any interest.

'What about it?' she says.

He squeezes his eyes shut then takes her hand, kneading it hard, and she winces.

'Ow,' she says, and she's starting to worry because she's never seen Mike like this, not even when the doctor said his father had only a few weeks to live. He was upset then, sure, but he knew he had to be strong for his dad so he held it together. Whatever's going on now has to be something bigger and harder than his father dying, which can only mean something's happened to one of the kids ... Except she checked on them not that long ago and they were asleep. Yes, she still checks on Terry, because even though he's a teenager he'll always be her baby and she likes to check. But he's fine. Simon's fine. So ...

'I invested money,' Mike says, almost choking on the words.

'What money?'

She knows he's been working so hard because they need extra cash to cover all the expenses. Or that's what he told her. He looks after their joint account and she looks after the business account.

'Some money.' Now he won't look her in the eye again.

'*What money?* We don't have any extra.'

'I, uh ... I took out a mortgage on the house.'

Her mind starts trying to work it out. The house is in Mike's name because he told her he could get the loan more easily that way – he went to school with the bank manager. But he also told her they'd pretty much paid it off.

'This house?' she says, because maybe Cora has a property she doesn't know about.

'Yes.'

He takes her hand again but she yanks it back, feeling her body become cold, with shock or fear or maybe both.

'This house I live in, your children live in and your mother lives in?'

'Yes.'

'And you didn't think to tell me?'

'It's my house!' he yells and now her spine goes rigid.

She doesn't recognise this man. Mike has never yelled at her. They have spats but they don't yell.

She takes a few seconds to think about how to handle him, because she doesn't want him flying off the handle and waking the kids. Or Cora. For some reason Lorraine wants to protect Cora from the knowledge that her son has done something dishonest and stupid.

'We've always made financial decisions together,' Lorraine says, her voice calm the way Rose's was once when an angry man tried to bully her out of a parking spot.

'I had an opportunity,' he says quickly, more quietly.

She looks at him and finally he looks back at her.

'To invest. In some shares,' he explains.

To gamble, he means. Investing in the stock market is a gamble. She should have known the TAB wasn't the beginning and end of it. Stupid – *stupid*. That's how she feels, for not asking him about those TAB receipts at the time. If he'd known she'd noticed maybe he wouldn't have kept going.

'So you mortgaged the house to do that?'

He nods and looks away again.

'And now . . . what? Because of this crash you've lost the money?'

Now he's definitely crying, and for a second she thinks he's going to try to hug her but she is not going to comfort him.

'I owe money,' he sobs.

Lorraine needs a few more seconds to think about this. To try to comprehend how much money he might be talking about if he took out a mortgage.

'So does that mean we lose the house?' she enquires with as little emotion as possible.

'I don't know,' he says, sniffing back his tears and whatever is streaming out of his nose.

Something else occurs to her. 'So you've been doing all that extra work to pay back the mortgage, not to cover our expenses?'

He nods.

'Don't tell Mum,' he says, his voice raspy. 'Or the kids.'

Lorraine pushes herself away from him on the bed and tucks her legs up against her chest.

'You don't have any right to tell me what to do and not do,' she says, and her voice is as icy as she feels.

Mike is surprised; she can see that. She's never stood up to him like this. Clearly she should have. When he said he was going to buy the house in his own name and her mother said she shouldn't let him, but Lorraine trusted him, didn't she? That's when the standing up should have started.

Too late now for that. Not too late for whatever comes next, and it's not going to be her bailing him out.

'Sleep somewhere else,' she says, turning her back to him.

'But –'

'Get out,' she hisses.

She closes her eyes and wraps her arms around her legs, then waits until she hears his loud tread on the stairs before she puts her head on her knees, wondering if it's too late to call Cynthia to ask her what she should do.

CHAPTER THIRTY-EIGHT

The morning has moved fairly swiftly after the hiccup at its start, when Charlie didn't want to go to school.

'I want to be asleep,' he said to Elizabeth, who wondered if this was a matter for concern or if he was genuinely tired.

Since Jon died, some nights she wakes up in the early hours, usually around two o'clock, and in the past few weeks she's seen Charlie's light on every now and again. She doesn't go in – her mother told her when he was a baby that children have their own sleep patterns and unless there's something going wrong, like he's chronically tired, she shouldn't try to change his. So the nights when his light has been on she has lain awake, feeling like a sentry, waiting for it to go out, which it always has.

There is part of her that wants to ask Charlie if he's waking up and thinking of his father, as she is; there might be shared comfort in that. It's not Charlie's role, though, to support her, to make her feel that she's not alone in this grief. That is her role for him. So when he says things like 'I want to be asleep' she feels as if she is failing him.

'Are you tired?' she asked him, trying to elicit some idea of what was really going on.

'No,' he said. Then he sat in the back seat of the car and hyper-ventilated as he looked out the window at the school building. The breathing was new.

'Why don't you want to go to school, Charlie?' she prodded gently.

'I want to be asleep!'

He looked as though he was trying not to cry, and that meant she had to try not to cry, because while parents are meant to be strong for their children she has always wanted to cry when he does, which feels more like the natural order of things than not crying.

'Is something going on at school?' she tried again.

His eyes were so big and sad as they looked into hers. 'I don't like the teacher,' he said.

This has come up before, and Elizabeth thinks it's because Charlie finds the schoolwork difficult, because when she had a meeting with the teacher in the middle of the year he seemed friendly and relaxed and quite happy with Charlie.

'I can't take you home, darling, I'm sorry,' she said.

Although she could probably take him to her parents' – she just doesn't want him to think that's an option, and won't use it unless she absolutely has to.

'Why not?' He sniffed.

'Because I have to work.'

'Stupid work!' He kicked the back of the passenger seat.

Elizabeth knew she should say something but she understood the sentiment: to him the work is stupid because it means he can't do what he wants.

'Come on, darling. I'm sure it will be fine once you're in there.'

She wasn't sure, obviously – no parent knows what their child goes through once they're inside the school gates. The tortures could all be inside the child's head as they try to navigate other children and difficult subjects and the politics of the playground. Elizabeth remembers it well and has always said she's glad she never has to go back to school – yet there she was, waiting outside her son's school, trying to force him to go inside.

After a few more minutes of stand-off Charlie went in, and she wasn't too late for work. Olive didn't even seem to notice because she was chatting on the phone, quite animatedly, and Doctor Lopes hadn't arrived yet.

There was patient after patient – Doctor Simpson is in today too, so they had a full house. Elizabeth has enjoyed the flurry, barely having time for a cup of tea let alone a word with Olive, who is always in her element when it's busy. Elizabeth has no idea what time it is when her stomach starts gurgling, but she hopes it's close to twelve thirty, which is when she's able to take a break.

'Hello, Lizzie,' says a voice from above and Elizabeth whips her head up to see Shirl beaming down at her.

'Shirl!' She stands up. It feels appropriate. Partly because Shirl isn't wearing a T-shirt and shorts – she's in quite a nice pink cotton dress.

'Olive.' Shirl nods at Olive and winks.

'You two know each other?' Olive says.

'Lizzie's in the Sunshine Gardening Society,' Shirl says, beaming like a proud parent. 'You know, Ol, that thing I tried to get you to join years ago and you told me you didn't want to ruin your nails.'

Olive looks at her perfectly lacquered red fingertips. 'Correct. I don't.' She turns towards Elizabeth. 'You haven't said anything about this society.'

Elizabeth feels nervous, like she's done the wrong thing by becoming a Sunshine Gardener. 'It's on weekends. It doesn't affect work.'

'I didn't think it would.' Olive looks at her as if she's odd. 'Silly girl, I just meant I like to *know* what's going on. You know I like a gossip! And if you'd mentioned it earlier I would have told you I know Shirl. We had our kids around the same time, didn't we, Shirl?'

Shirl has children? She's never said. Although there's probably been no reason to.

'Lost our husbands around the same time too,' Olive goes on. 'Although she kicked hers out.' Olive winks and Elizabeth takes that as approval of Shirl's action.

'No-good bum.' Shirl purses her lips. 'Him and the sheila he was dealing with. Anyway, how you been, Ol?'

'Good. Won fifty on number two in the fifth last weekend.'

'Doomben?'

'Eagle Farm. Want my tip for this weekend?'

'Maybe.' Shirl now appears to be chewing gum, and added to the other information presented to Elizabeth this morning it's all becoming too much for her to process.

'I didn't see a Shirley on the patient list,' she says, hoping to put herself on solid ground by working out what Shirl is doing here, apart from chatting to Olive.

'Fit as a fiddle, Lizzie.' Another wink. 'Don't need the doc. Just here to pick up my fella for lunch.'

Now this is really more than Elizabeth can handle: Shirl is Doctor Lopes's girlfriend? Olive never said anything about him seeing someone, and given the predilection for gossip Elizabeth thought she would. Elizabeth's mind whirls as she tries to remember if she's ever said anything about him while she's been around Shirl, and if so why didn't Shirl say something?

'Bob Simpson,' Shirl says, looking amused. Clearly Elizabeth's confusion is showing on her face.

'Oh.' Elizabeth exhales.

The door to Doctor Simpson's room opens and his smile is bright. 'There's my girl,' he says. 'Won't be long. Just writing up some notes.'

With a wave he closes the door again and Shirl stands there looking pleased.

'Good sort, isn't he?' she says, and Elizabeth hopes it's a rhetorical question because she has no intention of answering it. Although Shirl probably wants some kind of response.

'Where are . . . where are you going for lunch?' she says.

'My place.' *Chew chew.* 'It's not too far. He likes it there.'

There's a glint in her eye that makes Elizabeth blush.

'Anyway, Ol, I should tell you that Lizzie's a bit of a star on the gardening side of things.'

Olive now rotates fully towards Elizabeth. 'Is she?'

'Oh, I'm not,' Elizabeth interjects, because how could someone be a star at the sort of thing they're doing?

'She's a demon on the weeds. No one better at getting them out by the root. It's almost like she's got super-sensitive fingertips.'

Right as Shirl says the last part Doctor Lopes's door opens and Elizabeth is sure he's heard it, which is mortifying.

'I thought I knew that voice, Shirley,' he says, coming over and kissing her hello. 'Lovely to see you. Does Bob know you're here?'

'He does.' Shirl looks to be appraising Doctor Lopes, and Elizabeth wonders how well she knows *him*. 'You've lost some weight, Marco. Better put it back on. Girls like muscles.'

Elizabeth squeaks with surprise and hopes no one heard her.

Thankfully Doctor Simpson's door opens once more, and this time he comes to the front of the reception desk and greets Shirl with a kiss on the lips.

'Come on, chook,' he says, tapping her on the derrière. 'Limited time.'

'I've got my orders,' Shirl says, quite gleefully. 'See you on Saturday, Lizzie. Ta-ta, Ol – I'll call you about that tip. Marco, eat something.'

And with that Cyclone Shirl is gone and Elizabeth is left in her wake, trying to understand how these two parts of her life could so profoundly intersect. No doubt it's because she lives in a fairly small community, but still ... She had no idea how anonymous she was in Brisbane until now.

'She's a hoot, that Shirl,' Olive says, rolling some paper into the typewriter. Then she peers over the desk at the patient they all seem to have forgotten in the waiting room. 'Doctor Lopes won't be long, Mrs Graves.'

Elizabeth's stomach gurgles again and this time she's sure it was loud enough for Olive to hear.

'You choof off to lunch, love,' Olive says. 'It's almost time anyway.'

Elizabeth heads to the kitchen and takes her sandwich out of the fridge, although at first she's too enervated by the flurry of activity and revelation to eat. Then she feels sad that she doesn't have anyone to recount it all to later. If Jon were alive he'd have sat and listened to her, and laughed. But if Jon were alive she wouldn't even be here. She wouldn't be in this job; she wouldn't be in the gardening society.

It's a paradox she doesn't want to dwell on, so instead she starts to eat her sandwich and wonders if perhaps her mother won't find the story amusing when she sees her later today.

NOVEMBER 1987

PHEBALIUM

CHAPTER THIRTY-NINE

Even though she plainly knew Odette was pregnant, Cynthia hadn't considered what it would mean to become a grandmother. Especially not at the age of forty. In her mind, grandmothers are well into the grey-hair phase of their lives – possibly even white hair – and have started to take an interest in lawn bowls and baking scones. This is a generalisation, she realises, and her own mother never took up bowls or scones so Cynthia doesn't know how she came to have such thoughts. Yet they're in her brain and she can't reconcile them with the woman she sees in the mirror, whose face is still fairly unlined, her figure still defying gravity – in most areas – and her interests decidedly of the non-baking variety.

When she called Lorraine to tell her about the baby her oldest friend thought it was an opportunity to start teasing her.

'Can I call you Nana?' she crowed, and Cynthia realised she was possibly in for months, if not years, of Lorraine enjoying the use of as many names for 'grandmother' as she could think of, and probably inventing a few more.

The baby, a boy, has been named Jordan Patrick. Pat, of course, thinks this is wonderful and has been practically stopping people in the street to tell them that he has a grandson who is partly named after him.

At least Pat looks more grandparent-like, with grey creeping into his hair and years of sun damage catching up to him. Not that Cynthia feels any schadenfreude about that; not much, anyway. And it's not that she doesn't want people to know she's a grandmother – she just doesn't want the appellation. There's nothing she can do about it, however, because Odette is firmly in the Granny camp, while Pat gets to be Pa, which is so close to his actual name it seems almost like cheating.

One of the things Cynthia didn't particularly like about motherhood when it happened to her was that she was needed all the time. She was at an age when her own needs were still a priority and suddenly there was this small creature who needed her for absolutely everything and she couldn't hand her off to anyone else for most of it, for hers were the only breasts that were lactating. Now she is surprised to discover that she likes Odette needing her.

It's probably surprised Odette too – sometimes when she rings she sounds like she's not sure why, almost as if she simply wants to hear Cynthia's voice. She keeps turning up at the house, too, which is why she's camped today in the sitting room, Jordan in a bassinette in front of her, half a boob hanging out of her top and bags under her eyes.

Cynthia remembers the bags. Her mother told her to put haemorrhoid cream on them to help them deflate. Cynthia thought that was a strange suggestion, but when she moved to Los Angeles everyone was doing it. Too late: by then Odette was a child and Cynthia was sleeping through the night.

'Where's Ash?' Cynthia says, as she does every time Odette appears asking if she can spend a few hours at Wilfred's.

Odette shrugs. 'Surfing, I guess.'

'You guess? He doesn't tell you?'

'I don't really care, Mum. He's useless. I'd actually prefer it if he never comes back.'

Her big, round eyes are full of confusion and disappointment, and Cynthia wants to scoop her into a hug. They don't have that kind of relationship any more but Cynthia wonders if Odette becoming a mother will make them as tactile as they used to be.

'And your father?' she says.

'Working.'

Jordan snuffles and Odette's face cracks into a smile.

Cynthia feels relieved: at least she's happy with the baby. In the days after his birth Cynthia wondered if Odette would feel regret for what has happened to her life. Cynthia herself had the odd twinge of it, but she was always happy to be Odette's mother.

'It's so cute when he does that,' Odette coos, and Cynthia remembers all the little things Odette did that she thought were the best things in the world. She'd sit watching her for hours, it seemed, and wonder where the time went.

Luckily Pat felt similarly dotty, so they'd both sit and talk about how their baby was the best, the sweetest, the most adorable. Regardless of what happened between them as husband and wife, they were always united on the subject of Odette and how wonderful she was.

Cynthia doesn't know if she told Odette that enough in the years that followed; or if Pat told her more and that's why she felt comfortable moving back here to be with him. Sometimes she wants to ask, but maybe she doesn't really want to know the answer. It's not as if she can change the outcome, which is that she lost her daughter for a few years. And she doesn't wish to lose her again.

'He is *extremely* cute,' Cynthia says as she gets on the floor. All the squatting in gardens has made her more limber, just in time to crawl around after her grandson.

'Thanks for having us here all the time,' Odette says and her voice cracks, causing Cynthia to look up and frown.

Just then Wilfred enters the room. 'Ah, my beautiful grand-daughter,' he booms and that elicits a smile from Odette. He bends over to look at the baby. 'How is my great-grandson?'

'He's good, Pa.' Odette sniffs and wipes her nose with the back of her hand.

Wilfred straightens and scrutinises Odette's face. 'What's going on?'

'Nothing,' Odette chokes out, closing her eyes and wiping again.

Cynthia feels the way she always has when her daughter is in pain: she wants to simultaneously cry and attack whatever the cause of the pain is.

'Darling,' she says, putting her hand on Odette's knee.

'Don't, Mum,' Odette says, but it doesn't sound like she means it. In fact, it sounds like she wants nothing more than for Cynthia to comfort her.

'What is it?' Cynthia urges gently. 'I mean, apart from the fact that becoming a mother can be quite overwhelming.'

'It's not Jordan,' Odette says quickly, but now tears are rolling down her cheeks. 'I love him. He's the best.' Her smile shows that she means it, but then her face falls again.

'Then . . . ?' Cynthia says. She looks up at her father, who is frowning, his arms folded across his chest. He's never been that comfortable around emotional women and she's not sure how he's taking this.

'Is it Ash?' Another prod, and a fairly safe guess.

Odette blinks away some tears just as Jordan squawks. She picks him up and holds him against her chest.

'It's not just Ash,' she says, then sighs, and sighs again. 'It's going to sound bad,' she continues, and glances at Wilfred.

'We can handle it,' says Cynthia, although she's now wondering what's been going on to make her daughter feel this way. She's living with Pat – hasn't he noticed that she's so upset?

'That we can,' Wilfred affirms.

'I don't want to live with just men,' Odette says quickly. 'Dad's been great but . . .' Her eyes meet Cynthia's and Cynthia can see what's there: the desire to not betray her father coupled with a desire to not betray herself.

'But he's never given birth,' Cynthia finishes for her. 'And neither has Ash.'

She can guess what Odette wants to say and looks up at her father, whose face is now passive.

'And neither has your grandfather, but I suppose having raised two children to adulthood he understands a thing or two.'

Wilfred nods slowly.

There's a comfort, Cynthia thinks, in reaching a stage in life and in your connection to another human being that means you can communicate wordlessly. It makes moments like these a lot easier.

'You want to move in here, don't you?' Cynthia says and is rewarded with relief on Odette's face.

'Is that all right?' Odette says quickly.

'You're not even going to pretend to not like the idea?' Cynthia teases, because part of her can't believe it was so recently that Odette was acting as if she was the worst person in the world.

She'd think it was funny, except she well knows how profoundly motherhood can change a person and how things you thought were all fine and lovely beforehand become unacceptable, and vice versa. There is no preparation for the bomb of hormones and sleeplessness and need and pure, unselfish love that motherhood drops into your life and, therefore, no way of knowing how you'll feel once it happens.

Odette starts to laugh then it turns into crying. 'I need my mummy,' she whispers, and once again she is the baby Cynthia would cradle in the wee hours, just the two of them on the couch watching the sun rise, Cynthia feeling like she could never love anyone the way she loved Odette and resolving to never say it out loud, because Pat, for one, would wonder if that meant she didn't love him as much. And she didn't. Not in the same way. That was her secret, though; hers and her baby's.

'Of course you do,' Cynthia responds, and she reaches over to wipe away Odette's tears with her thumb.

'I'll go and talk to Pat,' Wilfred says. 'Collect your things.'

'No, Pa, that's okay,' Odette protests.

'Let us look after you, pet,' he says, then he bends down and kisses the top of her head. 'You have a big job to do.'

'What about Ash?' Cynthia says.

'What about him?'

The steely pre-motherhood Odette is back and Cynthia feels pleased to see that she hasn't lost that aspect of her personality. She's going to need it once she has to deal with parent–teacher nights and birthday party negotiations.

'You need to tell him.'

'He can come here,' Odette says defiantly. 'I'll talk to him then.'

Cynthia and Wilfred exchange glances because they both know it's unlikely to be that simple. But Cynthia also knows that her father feels as she does: Odette is their priority, and Jordan too, and Ash isn't really even running in that race.

'I'll get going,' Wilfred says, and within seconds Cynthia hears his keys being picked up from the kitchen bench and the back door closing.

'Thanks, Mum,' Odette says, holding Jordan out in front of her and wriggling her nose at him. 'Isn't he the best?'

'Close to it,' Cynthia says. 'I've always thought *you're* the best.'

They sit and smile at each other, and it seems so simple, right then, to be a mother: to love your child and support them and offer them help when they need it.

And maybe that's all it is. Maybe they complicate things by trying to score points against each other about who said what and did what when. Although Cynthia knows she needs to stand up for herself from time to time, to do what's right for her even if Odette doesn't like it – that's how she has shown Odette to do the same for herself. That's what has led Odette to be here today.

So it is simple and not. It is love, but self-love has to be there too. This is the back-and-forth of being human, and now, in this house she grew up in, in this small town with its beaches and palms and bush, Cynthia finally feels like she knows how to live.

CHAPTER FORTY

Kathy hasn't spent much time on Hastings Street since she moved to Noosa. It's over the hill from the junction and she usually doesn't have a reason to go – it doesn't have a supermarket or a fruit shop or anything else she needs. Like a grog shop. Although she hasn't been visiting her local as much lately. A psychologist – if she were to visit one, which she wouldn't, because she thinks they put ideas in people's heads and not usually good ones, just the kind that make you question your childhood and your adulthood and your whole identity – might say it's because she's a little more content than she was. That's because she's no longer worrying about her relationship with Michelle: by the time her daughter left they were as chummy as they ever were, and Kathy felt like she had her friend back, not just her child. They've been speaking every couple of days since, the chatty sort of conversations they always used to have.

So Kathy is feeling better about life and she's also busier. Distracted by activities. Certainly work is keeping her occupied, and she has the occasional outing with colleagues, even though she feels like their spinster aunt.

However, the Sunshine Gardening Society is what really keeps her brain whirring. She started thinking about what to do with the garden at home, then she moved on to thinking about gardens in general, and now when she walks past houses she looks at the gardens and considers how she might change them if she had time and pots of dough. Would she put aspidistras in that nook? What about a bromeliad here or there? She likes callistemons – what about those?

Sometimes when she's thinking about plants and gardens and what she'd do with them, it feels like her brain is expanding, although she knows that's rubbish. But it really does – as if her awareness is reaching far beyond her cranium. It's odd, and she likes it. It's becoming a hobby, almost.

She's never been a creative type – at school one of her teachers said Kathy was the least creative child she'd ever encountered and ever hoped to – but this feels a little like being creative. Like daydreaming, which is something she did a lot before teachers started telling her to stop looking out the window.

So today she's walked from the junction, up over the hill and down towards the beach, stickybeaking at gardens as she goes. Walking has become a new pastime too, and while she tells herself it's because exercise is good for you, mostly she likes it because she can stickybeak. And today she's also going to have a swim. That's another thing she wants to do more of – she's living in this beautiful place with all these beaches and she's barely been to them. So, towel over one shoulder, string bag over the other containing hat and some money and keys, and a book to read if she decides to stay a while, she's arrived on Hastings Street feeling smug about walking up that hill and quite content about her plans for the next few hours.

There aren't any gardens on this street, but there are some shops and some restaurants, so she decides to take a look at those just so she knows what's what. Maybe she'd like to eat out every now and again at a restaurant that isn't her workplace. It could happen. She's starting to have friends.

In fact, here's one of them now, walking towards her and smiling – and pushing a pram.

Kathy waves. 'Hi, Cynthia!'

Cynthia stops, looks surprised for a second then smiles.

'Hi,' she says, pushing the pram to one side so it's not between them. 'Have you come for a swim?'

Kathy nods. 'Thought I'd give it a go. So this is your daughter's baby?'

She peers into the pram to see a little scrunched-up face below a definite outline of hair.

'This is Jordan.' Cynthia smiles proudly. 'I just got him off to sleep – he likes to be moved. And Odette can't walk around jiggling him all day. I suggested she have a sleep too.' She bends down and peers in, then straightens up. 'Cute, isn't he?'

Kathy smiles and nods, although she rarely thinks babies are cute. Even her own didn't earn the epithet.

'How have the past weekends been?' Cynthia asks. 'I'll be back this Saturday.'

'They've been fun,' Kathy says, and means it. 'And I was going to call you about something – I just wasn't sure when you'd have time to chat.'

Cynthia narrows her eyes. 'Oh?'

'This bloke came up to us at the riverside park and said he'd bought the land and was going to develop it.'

'That . . . doesn't seem right.' Cynthia glances down and Kathy hears Jordan squawk. Maybe it's not a good time to talk to her – she's distracted.

'It's not right and I was going to ask your advice about it,' Kathy says in a hurry, 'but it can wait. You have enough to think about.'

'It's fine.' Cynthia smiles. 'We all have enough to think about and we fit more in, don't we?'

'Yeah.' Kathy smiles gratefully. 'Well, I'm just not sure if I should try to talk to someone at the council about it. To see if it can be stopped.'

Jordan squawks again and Cynthia bends towards him, checking quickly, then straightens.

'It's absolutely worth trying. Let me talk to my father about it – he's been involved in council on and off over the years, he might know someone.'

'That would be great,' Kathy says, relieved. 'Thank you.'

Cynthia smiles mischievously. 'Look at you, the gardening activist.'

Kathy laughs nervously. 'I wouldn't go that far! I just enjoy what we do. Seeing things become pretty. You know.'

'I do – although there's nothing wrong with being an activist. I'd say Shirl's one, wouldn't you?'

Kathy thinks of Shirl with her machete and her lectures about native plants. 'Yeah.'

'It's great you joined us. And while Barb and Shirl wouldn't say it, I'm sure they appreciate how much extra time you're putting in, doing that mowing for that gent in Peregian and – what's the other one? You're helping that old lady in Yandina with her front garden. That must be your Sundays all used up.'

Kathy shrugs. 'I have the time. And I enjoy it.'

Barb had told her that the Sunshine Gardening Society tend to take on projects rather than maintenance – unless it's for the council – but that individual members have, over the years and in certain circumstances, helped members of the community with odd jobs. Two calls had come in close together and Kathy had volunteered to attend to both. And she's found she likes to help people.

Just then Cynthia's gaze shifts to something over Kathy's right shoulder and Kathy feels a squeeze on her arm. Her first thought is that it's a co-worker – who else would she know around here, apart from Cynthia and Lorraine and Elizabeth? – so she turns with a smile prepared.

And sees Jemima. Standing with a woman around her age, their body language indicating the closeness of their connection.

'Kathy!' Jemima says, and as Jemima attempts to hug her Kathy's shoulders stiffen. Why is she trying to hug her? Why is she trying to be any kind of affectionate after what she did?

Kathy's eyes meet those of Cynthia, who is looking concerned, and Kathy wonders what expression she has on her face. Cynthia doesn't know her well enough to read subtle cues, but Jemima does and she's persisting with the hug.

As Kathy smells her perfume she wants to collapse, because Jemima's scent brings everything back, then she feels like screaming because Jemima keeps hugging her, then she wonders if she can fight her way out of this without it seeming violent. All of that probably takes twenty seconds but it feels like twenty minutes, and by the time Jemima lets her go Kathy's throat is tightening and her breathing is becoming rapid and she wonders what the hell is happening.

'Are you up here for a little break like the rest of Melbourne?' Jemima grins, showing that snaggle tooth Kathy once found endearing.

'Um . . .' Kathy's floundering, caught between wanting to appear as though her life is cool and wonderful and in control, and trying to work out why her chest is tight now too and the sound in her ears is going funny.

She and Jemima had talked about taking a holiday in Noosa Heads. Not just talked – planned. They'd booked accommodation and thought that driving up would be a great adventure. Kathy had never felt so carefree and giddy, like she'd been waiting her whole life to be with this woman and do things, go places, she would never have otherwise. That was just before Jemima left her, and after that Kathy realised the holiday discussion had been a con, that Jemima had been willing to go so far as to make a booking while already planning to leave. Or at least hadn't been interested enough in Kathy to stay long enough to take a holiday with her. So Kathy feels sick – stomach-churningly, bile-rising sick – to see Jemima here. It's almost like a taunt; not that Jemima would know she moved here. And how would she explain that? Would she say that Noosa represented everything that was beautiful and savage about their relationship and she came here to try to understand it?

'She's staying with me,' Cynthia says loudly – or maybe it just sounds loud to Kathy. 'We're old friends. And you are?'

'Jemima. And this is my *best* friend, Caroline.'

Jemima puts her arm around Caroline's shoulders and squeezes, and Kathy now feels like she could vomit all over their shoes. Maybe that's what she should do, to register her complete and utter discomfort at being here, forced to see the woman she loved so much so clearly not in love with her.

'Well, Jemima, nice to meet you.' Cynthia gives that fake bottom-half-of-her-face smile Kathy saw her use once on a nosy council ranger. 'Kathy and I are due to meet my daughter on the beach, so we'd best be off.'

Cynthia grips Kathy's wrist with one hand and with the other pushes the pram in the direction of the sand. And while Kathy still wants to vomit, she's also never felt so grateful and relieved in her life. She doesn't look back to see what Jemima's doing because there's a noise in her ears, like a pounding, and she can't quite get her breath.

'Stop,' Cynthia commands. 'Sit.'

She practically pushes Kathy onto a seat that's covered in small graffiti, right at the entrance to the surf club car park. Cars and people are going past but all Kathy can hear is her heart, and that noise in her ears.

'Head between your legs,' Cynthia says firmly and she puts her hand between Kathy's shoulder blades, which is the most comforting feeling in the world, then bends down so her head is next to Kathy's.

'Just keep your head down until your breathing comes back to something resembling normal,' she murmurs.

Seconds pass, then minutes. Kathy has no idea how long she has her head down, but eventually the noise in her ears subsides and her breathing has slowed, so she lifts her head.

'Take your time,' Cynthia says, her hand on Kathy's shoulder.

As Kathy sits up she sees that Cynthia is pushing the pram back and forth with the other hand, and she feels embarrassed. Cynthia was having a walk with her grandson and it's been completely derailed by Kathy's stupid behaviour. Then she starts to cry – she doesn't want to, it just happens – and she feels even more embarrassed.

Cynthia stops pushing the pram and sits next to Kathy, putting an arm around her shoulders.

'I don't know what that woman means to you,' she says quietly, 'but you need to never see her again.'

Kathy cries and nods and sniffs and nods again.

'I loved her,' Kathy says, because somehow she knows that Cynthia won't find that statement strange.

'Do you still?'

Kathy turns to look at her and blinks her tears away. This isn't a question she has dared to ask herself for quite a while now, scared of what the answer might be.

'Maybe a bit,' she says, because she knows there's truth in that. 'I try not to think about her.'

'I don't like her,' Cynthia says. 'I mean, I can see the appeal – she's very pretty and she seems quite outgoing. But she's a little too ... hm, what's the word? Up herself. That's it.'

She grins and Kathy laughs, feeling her chest release the tension it's been holding.

'Maybe,' she admits.

'Definitely.' Cynthia stands up. 'Come on, let's walk up to the end of the street and people-watch all the tourists and make comments about their swimwear.'

Kathy laughs again, and they set off for the river end of Hastings Street, where there's bush and a walking track. As they amble Cynthia talks about what it was like growing up in the area and how much she loves this beach.

By the time they return to their starting spot Kathy has forgotten about Jemima. And when she finally plunges into the water, having waved Cynthia goodbye, she feels like, just maybe, she is washing away the past, and now she can start her life over again and see where it takes her.

CHAPTER FORTY-ONE

Around the entrance of the national park there are Kombi vans that look like they haven't been washed in years, their back windows covered from the inside by tatty towels or draped pieces of cloth. The door of one is open and Lorraine can smell the reek from metres away. She spies an old mattress and can only imagine what else is inside the van. Joss sticks, that's for sure and certain, because she can smell those too. Probably being used to mask the stench of everything else. Well, *it's not working*.

'Yuck!' she says to Cynthia as they walk past, wrinkling her nose.

'Not your kind of vehicle?'

'Not my kind of squalor. How do people live like that?'

'I think they're on holidays more than living like that.' Cynthia peers more closely at the vehicle. 'On the other hand, you may be right, and they're living in the van.'

'I don't approve!' Lorraine says grumpily.

'Clearly.' Cynthia looks amused and they walk on.

'Why are we here?'

'Barb told me the other day that some tidying up is needed in here – not necessarily of the gardening variety. Of the rubbish variety. It would be an extra project, so the whole group wouldn't be there. And obviously the park is huge, so we'd only do a section at a time. I thought it would be interesting to have a look and see what the state of it is.'

Lorraine nods slowly. She likes the idea of having a walk – the only exercise she gets is the gardening. Still, this is something Cynthia could have done on her own.

'But why am *I* here?' she says.

Cynthia stops and angles towards her. 'Because you've been miserable and I think it'll do you good to get outside for a while.'

About to protest and say she's not miserable, just angry at Mike, Lorraine then remembers the nights she's spent crying in the upstairs bathroom, door locked, boys in their beds. Sometimes she calls Cynthia after she cries, sometimes before. So, yeah, she's miserable.

'What's so good about *outside*?' she grumbles.

Cynthia laughs, which irks Lorraine even as she understands why she's being laughed at.

'Take a look around,' Cynthia says, gesturing ahead of them to the path that leads into the park, then to the sea at their left, with the beach stretching all the way around for kilometres and kilometres, the sun on the water and surfers paddling out to the break.

She'd probably love it, Lorraine thinks, if dolphins could pop up right about now, thereby proving her point that outside is *great*.

There are dolphins here. Lorraine has seen them. She's seen whales too. So that's not a far-fetched idea. *But still* she wouldn't want Cynthia to have the satisfaction of being able to rave about how *amazing* outside is when all Lorraine wants to do is curl up in a ball and feel sorry for herself, preferably with a box of Roses chocolates and a Jackie Collins novel. They're her usual go-tos when she needs comfort.

'All right, I get it,' she concedes. 'It's full of life or something.'

'It is. And sometimes I think being in a place as glorious as this can at the very least be a distraction.'

They're silent for a while as they continue walking to Boiling Pot. There are plenty of pandanus palms and vines and things that Shirl would be able to identify but Lorraine has no idea. She can, however, identify the rubbish in the bush to their right: chip packets and aluminium cans and ice-cream sticks.

'So I guess that's what Barb's talking about,' Lorraine says, pointing to a small mound of rubbish. Lately Barb's been like a broken record on the subject of litter in the park and how someone needs to do something, but she doesn't have time at the moment.

'Yes, and it's the whole way along,' Cynthia says.

As they reach Tea Tree Bay they can see a cluster of surfers waiting for the next wave – although the surf isn't that big so Lorraine thinks they'll be waiting a while. Once winter is over the swell isn't nearly as impressive and nor are the opportunities for a good wave, although it would be nice to sit out there on a board, feeling the swell beneath you. Maybe seeing a dolphin.

So okay, Cynthia is right. Outside is pretty good.

Lorraine glances at her friend and finds her absorbed in their surroundings.

'It's beautiful,' she breathes as she catches Lorraine looking. 'When we were young I didn't pay attention.'

'Who pays attention to anything when they're young?' Lorraine says. 'I didn't either. We took it for granted, but that's what kids do.'

Ahead on the path there's a man walking towards them wearing a long T-shirt and . . . nothing else, which Lorraine can tell by the sideways movement going on.

'*Cyn! Cyn!*' she hisses as he passes, then she starts to giggle.

'What?' Cynthia looks at her quizzically.

'That bloke!' Lorraine jerks a thumb over her shoulder, then turns to look and sees the half-moons of his bum and giggles some more.

Cynthia looks too. '*No!*' she says.

'Yes! Bloody nude in the national park!'

'And big enough for us to tell,' Cynthia says with a wink. 'No doubt he's proud of himself.'

Lorraine laughs so hard that she starts to cough. 'Do you think there's any more of them in there? Because I'm looking to trade mine in.'

'I don't blame you,' Cynthia says, then presses her lips together in the universal expression of disapproval.

Lorraine appreciates the fact that Cynthia hasn't once suggested she 'work it out' with Mike, that it's her duty to forgive him to keep the family together. All she's been interested in is what Lorraine wants to do. How Lorraine is feeling. Sometimes she asks about the boys, but mainly she's focused on Lorraine.

The kids are in bits, of course, because their father's sleeping on a li-lo in the garage and Lorraine won't make meals for him, although neither parent has told them what's going on.

Cora asked Lorraine what was happening, which Lorraine found ridiculous – she couldn't ask her son, *the cause of the problem*? But no, Cora wouldn't do that because how could Mike ever be to blame for anything. It would have to be Lorraine's fault.

Well, let's see how Cora likes it when Lorraine kicks them both out, because if Mike goes for good Cora will have to go with him.

It's still an *if*, though. Lorraine hasn't kicked him out yet. Part of her likes keeping him guessing about what she's going to do next, but the reality is she's so angry most of the time she can't think straight, so she doesn't know what she wants to do.

Her mother's said she'll support her whatever. And she knows Cynthia will. It's good to have people who believe in you.

Lorraine doesn't believe in Mike any more and that's a sad situation after so many years of a good marriage. But how can she trust him? She still doesn't even know the true extent of their financial problems, which means she doesn't know what she'll have to do to get out of them. All she knows is that she'll have to take care of the kids financially, because Mike will be earning money to pay back his debt – Lorraine refuses to be responsible for that. That was the argument they had the day after he told her the truth: he'd insisted that because they're married all her money is his; she'd insisted that marriage doesn't mean lying to your wife and risking your children's stability and security by gambling on the stock market. That was the last time they had a conversation that lasted longer than two minutes.

Until this morning, and the content of that conversation is why Lorraine's actually glad Cynthia suggested they go for a walk, because she has something to tell her. It's taken thirty minutes of walking on this slender trail, where they can barely stay abreast, to work up the courage for it.

'Yours has been all right, though,' she says, then clears her throat as if it's just a casual remark.

'My what?' Cynthia says.

'Husband.'

Cynthia turns and frowns, but she put her sunglasses on a few minutes ago so Lorraine can't see her eyes.

'*Ex*-husband,' Lorraine hurriedly explains.

'Oh, yes.' Cynthia sounds completely uninterested.

'Pat's offered to loan Mike money to help with the debt.'

Cynthia stops and puts her hands on her hips before slowly rotating towards Lorraine. 'What?'

'You know they're friends.'

'Not really. Pat and I don't chat about much other than Odette.'

Lorraine feels a little sick, like she's betrayed her friend even though she hasn't, and wouldn't. Pat and Mike went off and had a beer, and next thing Lorraine hears is that Pat's the financial white knight. The source of the money is mysterious but Mike said something about a mine.

'It's none of my business, of course,' Cynthia says, her voice tight, and she starts walking again.

'It is.' Lorraine tugs on her arm to stop her just as a woman in a tie-dyed T-shirt pushes past them. Rude! And who wears tie-dye any more?

'I'll tell Mike to leave it alone,' she says.

'No,' Cynthia says, stepping to the side of the track as a surfer squeezes past, his board almost whacking Lorraine in the head. She had no idea that the national park track was basically a highway.

'You need the money,' Cynthia says.

'It's not for me,' Lorraine hastily explains.

'It should be. I mean, it should have an effect. If Pat lends Mike money that should take some pressure off you. Shouldn't it?'

Lorraine tries to calculate all the ways it may or may not help her and simply feels tired in response. 'Honestly, Cyn, I just wish I could close my eyes and make it all go away.'

She turns and looks beyond the swell. The ocean stretches out beyond them; there's a yacht further away, and a much larger ship near the horizon. Life is carrying on, goods and people are being moved, surfers are eternally trying to just get on a wave. There are moments when Lorraine thinks her situation isn't so bad in the grand scheme of things, and others when she thinks it's the worst thing that's ever happened to her, and other times when she believes both can be true at once.

'Perhaps Pat can make that happen,' Cynthia says, and she puts her arm around Lorraine, who is startled, because it's not really a Cynthia thing to do.

'Gee, you must be worried if you're trying to hug me,' she says.

'Or I just wanted to give you a hug.' She kisses Lorraine's temple. 'Mike should take the money. And if all else fails, you and I can move to a cheap property in the hinterland with our children and my grandson and make the best of what we have.'

More surprises from Cynthia, who's never struck Lorraine as the commune type, although she can't say she dislikes the idea.

'You're on,' she says.

Then their moment of affection is over because Cynthia drops her arm and steps ahead on the path, and keeps leading Lorraine until they reach Hells Gates, where they turn around and go back to town.

CHAPTER FORTY-TWO

Cynthia can see a cluster of men outside the Noosa Heads Surf Life Saving Club as she walks down the small hill from Little Cove and onto the beach. She's barefoot because she wants to put her feet in the water – maybe her whole self. She could have done it at Little Cove, as that beach is closer to home and it's a picturesque spot too, fringed by pandanus palms by the roadside and rocks on the beach, with a view across Main Beach towards the breakwater and beyond. It's too close, though, for someone who feels like a stroll, so she plans to amble along the sand on Main Beach for a while, then take a dip – or not – in front of the buildings of Seahaven before strolling back. It's early enough in the day for the flags to not be up on the beach, so anywhere is fair game for swimming as far as she's concerned.

When she left the house Odette was still asleep, Jordan in a bassinette beside her. Odette puts it on top of the bed, in the space where another adult might sleep if there was one. It seems to work for them both because he likes a long sleep, that baby, and his mother does too. Which Cynthia completely understands: she remembers those early months and how she felt like her life force had been sucked out of her, only occasionally topped up with food and a swim.

Her father, on the other hand, was awake as she tried to leave quietly.

'You're off early,' he said from the kitchen and she put a finger to her lips in the hope he'd lower his voice.

'It's a beautiful morning,' she said. 'And our babies are asleep, so I thought I'd take the chance to go for a walk.'

'And a swim.' He nodded at the towel.

'If I feel like it.' She smiled. 'Thank you for having them here,' she went on. 'I don't think I say that enough.'

'You don't need to say it at all. They can stay forever, if they want. It would suit me.'

He doesn't smile back but she knows that doesn't mean anything, because he can appear gruff and be far from it. 'Taciturn' her mother called him.

As Cynthia slipped out the back door to the garden and out the gate, the sun was already warm even though it was only six o'clock. By the time she arrives on the beach it feels like it's at full strength and she wonders how hot the day will become. They'll need to keep Jordan inside, sheltered.

Some of the men outside the surf club obviously think the water isn't quite as warm, however – they're wearing springsuits to go with the surfboards under their arms. As none of them is wet Cynthia imagines they're talking about whether or not the waves at First Point are worth their time, or if they should go into the park. It's a gamble, this surfing business: betting on where the waves will be good, taking the chance that they won't. It's always been her experience that even if the waves don't deliver, surfers are quite happy sitting out the back on their boards, enjoying the ocean.

She's about to pass the group when she hears someone cry 'Cyn!' That can only mean it's Pat.

He's one of the springsuited and he trots towards her across the sand, a big grin on his face, his hair uncombed and evidence of a beard-in-waiting.

'You're up early,' he says, driving his board into the sand.

'So are you.'

'Oh, yeah, well – I usually am.' He glances towards the surf. 'A few nice little waves this morning.'

'When I saw you all there I thought maybe you were deciding whether they were nice enough to stay for.'

His face clouds. 'So you saw me and didn't say hello?'

She wants to tell him not to be so delicate, but also has no wish to cause a fight so early in the day.

'No, I saw a group of middle-aged men, some of whom have pot bellies and no business surfing, standing on the sand instead of going into the surf.' She raises an eyebrow. 'I didn't know you were one of them until you called out.'

'You didn't recognise me?'

'Pat!' she cries, exasperated. 'I wasn't *looking* that closely. I had a quick glance. You could have been anyone.'

Now he looks hurt and she didn't mean to do that to him, so she scrambles to think of a way to make it up to him.

'Do I know any of them?' she asks, nodding towards the pack.

Pat had his surfing friends back in the day. They'd hang around the house at night, smoking and drinking, and Cynthia always wanted them gone because that lifestyle wasn't compatible with the infant Odette's. Usually Pat would tip them out – but only after a couple of drinks. He was young and she knew he wanted to enjoy being young; so did she. They had made the choice, though, to be parents and in her mind that meant they had to give up some of the activities of youth. She didn't mind him surfing; it was just everything that went along with it.

'Probably,' he says, squinting as if he's trying to recall information. 'Blue and Gull and Digger were around back then. Maybe Alby? I can't remember if you knew him or not.'

She doesn't remember an Alby, but the others she does: professional surfers without the professional part, so they lived off the dole and camped in Noosa Woods, cracking on to tourists and having a surprising amount of success because they were fit and good-looking.

'I suppose you think we're all Peter Pans,' Pat adds when she doesn't say anything.

'I don't think anything about you at all,' she says, and is rewarded with another hurt face.

'Collectively you, I mean,' she clarifies. 'The English language has its limitations.'

'I wouldn't know,' he says lightly. 'I only speak Surfer.' He looks wistful then. 'I wasn't the most attentive husband, was I?'

Cynthia frowns at the abrupt sentimental turn the conversation has taken. 'I don't know many who are. And I didn't begrudge you the surfing, if you remember.'

He nods. 'I do. But I didn't have to take advantage of it the way I did.'

She sighs and watches a couple of bodysurfers catching a neat wave, laughing as they end up in the white water. This beach has always had these lovely waves, just right for riding. So she understands why Pat would spend hours here and further around the point. It was the way he wanted to live. It just wasn't the way *she* wanted to.

'I don't know that you did,' she says. 'We just wanted different things.'

'Yeah.' He taps her arm lightly, as if they're mates and he can just do that. 'You wanted a husband who put his wife and child first.'

Her face tightens. 'It's not an unreasonable expectation. When children are small they're vulnerable and so are their mothers. Why do you think Odette wanted to move into Little Cove? Her grandfather and I can protect her.'

'And I can't?' he says, his voice hard.

'Clearly she didn't think so. And you can't blame a mother, Pat, for doing what she needs to do to protect her child. You also have to respect her decisions. We're happy to have them both living with us. That doesn't mean she won't come back to you, and I'll be happy about that too, if it's what she wants.'

Pat's name is called by one of the group – Blue, she thinks, given his red hair.

'Go,' she says. 'Your mates want you.'

He flashes her a look – of anger, or dismay, or regret, she's not sure. 'I'll pop round later,' he says. 'If that's all right with you.'

'You're welcome anytime. I mean that.'

He nods, then picks up his board and walks across the sand. She decides to walk back in the direction of the breakwater to have her swim, far from Pat and his feelings.

CHAPTER FORTY-THREE

Elizabeth's fondness for the Sunshine Gardening Society has somewhat crept up on her. Considering she never intended to join, even when Shirl and Barb were standing in her garden, looking at her expectantly, she is surprised by how much she looks forward to working with the others as well as having time for herself. Not time *to* herself – she has enough of that at night, after Charlie goes to bed and it's just her and the radio. But time in which she can do something that is not only meaningful but verging on joyful. For that's what she's found as she works in other people's gardens and in her own: joy in small, considered actions; in effecting change that will benefit others – even if that only means making a corner of a garden bed weed-free and knowing she'll have to come back another time and do it again.

When she told her mother how much she liked being part of the society and the work they were doing, her mother smiled and patted her cheek and said, 'You've always been kind-hearted.' Which took Elizabeth by surprise, because there are so many days she doesn't feel that way – when she feels mean-spirited and pessimistic; when she doesn't think she pays attention to other people at all and is instead wrapped up in the tiny dramas swirling inside her head, which she pushes aside reluctantly when Charlie needs something or when Doctor Lopes asks her to type up a letter or there's a load of washing to be done or dinner to make. Kindness has never been, or so she thought, in her character.

She certainly doesn't feel that it's kindness that's brought her to this garden in Doonan this morning, standing with her gloves on and secateurs in hand. It's selfishness. Because this is something she's doing just for her; the fact that it may help someone else is secondary. What she'll get out of it is company and laughter, and a sense of having achieved something other than just making it through the day.

'Dear me,' Shirl says, shaking her head as she comes up next to Elizabeth. 'Dear, dear me. This place is a mess, isn't it?'

Then she grins and her eyes shine, and Elizabeth knows it's because Shirl loves nothing more than a mess that she can transform into something lovely.

'Bit of work here, girls,' Shirl continues. 'It'll take us all day just to figure out if this is a garden or a jungle.' She clips on her tool belt and brandishes the machete. 'We few,' she says with a wink to Elizabeth. 'We happy few.'

Elizabeth laughs as Shirl plunges into the overgrowth that looks like forest oak and acacia, with some ferns and barbed wire grass thrown in. She wants to warn Shirl about the grass but that could be seen as condescending: Shirl knows more than any of them about the vegetation around here.

'Have you ever met anyone so happy to destroy things?' Lorraine says as she puts on her gloves. 'Then make something lovely afterwards?' She shakes her head as she smiles. 'She's a card, that Shirl.'

'I don't know where she gets the energy,' Elizabeth says. 'I think she's about thirty years older than me and I'm not that energetic now.'

'I know what you mean.' Lorraine's smile is swift and sad, and Elizabeth is taken aback. Lorraine is usually as lively as Shirl.

'Anyway, how are *you* going?' Lorraine says. 'And we can start over here, I think.'

She moves towards a part of the garden that hasn't yet been attacked by one of the others, then turns to look over her shoulder, as if to check that Elizabeth is still there.

Elizabeth isn't sure how to take the question: does Lorraine want to know the nitty-gritty, like how she still cries at night sometimes when she tries and fails not to think of Jon? Or does she want the superficial answer that goes along the lines of, 'I'm fine, work's good, Charlie's happy at school'?

The enquiring look on Lorraine's face tells her that she's waited too long to answer.

'It's a genuine question,' Lorraine says. 'I want to know. You're grieving. Sometimes it's good to talk about it.'

Elizabeth talks to her parents regularly about how she's feeling or coping or not coping, and Olive has been great, but she's not used to answering a direct question from someone she's not even sure is a friend. Or maybe this is Lorraine's way of making friends?

'I'll go first, if you like,' Lorraine says as she kneels down. 'Which is not why I asked you – to talk about myself, I mean. But sometimes it's easier to talk when someone else tells you something, right? So here's my situation: my husband's lost all our money and then some. *Poooof* – gone.'

She hacks into a climbing asparagus fern, which Elizabeth knows is a weed because Shirl gave them a lecture about it last week.

'And now –' *hack, hack* '– I have to work out whether I should divorce him and give myself the best chance of starting over before everything completely collapses, or stay for the kids.' She says this last bit in a tone that indicates how little she thinks of the idea. 'Because –' *hack, hack* '– we always have to think of the *kids*, don't we, Elizabeth?'

Lorraine stops, sweat on her forehead and a gleam in her eye. 'Why does no one stop to think that what's best for the *mother* might be what's best for the *kids* when it's the *mother* who has to look after the *kids* because the *father* usually won't do it or he'll stuff it up.' She huffs out a breath. 'That's all I have to say on the matter for now. That and Mike seems to think that dedicating songs to me on the local radio station will make me forgive him.'

Elizabeth knows her mouth is open because she can feel air on her tongue, so she closes it and swallows. 'Um . . .'

'That was probably a bit much, was it?' Lorraine wipes her forehead with her forearm. 'Sorry. Had to get it off my chest.' She snaps the secateurs. 'Your turn.'

'Oh . . .' Elizabeth isn't really the confessing kind. Although what would she be risking if she did share something of herself with an almost-stranger? Embarrassment. But she also risks not making this almost-stranger into a friend if she doesn't share that something. Because she likes Lorraine and for some reason she trusts her. She trusts them all, really. As they work away on the weekends – heads down and bums up, as Shirl says – there's no competition, no sniping, no one-upping. There's just care for the tasks at hand and respect for the places they're in and the people attached to them. Elizabeth thinks that, for many, the attraction of the Sunshine Gardening Society may be that their activities are ideal for people who want to show care for others yet would rather avoid those others if they can. Volunteering for introverts.

Except that doesn't explain Shirl. Sometimes she thinks Shirl just likes to cut things and that's why she's in the society.

Nor does it explain Lorraine, who is clearly no introvert. Lorraine's here because Cynthia's here, though – she told Elizabeth that once.

'See these weeds?' Lorraine says after Elizabeth has been silent for a while. 'We have to get them out so the garden can reach its full potential. And *yes*, Elizabeth, I'm trying to be really obvious here. It's a, um, whatsit – meta— meta— . . .' She frowns.

'Metaphor.'

'Yep. That's it. A metaphor. Get the weeds out and the garden can grow. Corny, isn't it? But true!' She laughs and it sounds genuine enough. 'So how are you going?' she asks again.

Elizabeth glances at the pile of asparagus fern at her feet and the secateurs in Lorraine's hand and thinks about weeds.

'I'm still very sad,' she admits. 'And I don't know if it will ever end.'

Lorraine nods and keeps cutting. 'It won't,' she says bluntly. 'But over time you won't notice it as much.' She glances back at Elizabeth. 'That may or may not help you.'

Elizabeth likes the fact Lorraine is so blunt about it.

'I just want to get up one morning and not feel like the day is going to be hard,' she says, then pauses. 'I mean, not every day does end up being hard. But they all start the same way. They feel like they'll be hard.'

'But you keep going,' Lorraine says, now focusing on pulling out the weeds at the root. 'You have *kept* going for a while now.'

'I guess I have.'

'No guess! It's been happening. You just haven't noticed.'

Lorraine stands and holds out the secateurs. 'Your turn to get stuck into it.'

'What do I do?' Elizabeth hasn't done this kind of work before. She's been happy to pick up the detritus and do the tidying.

'Just go for it,' Lorraine says. 'They're weeds. You can't hurt them.'

'All right.' Elizabeth tries the action of the tool.

'Go on,' Lorraine urges.

Elizabeth steps forwards and puts some effort into the first big hack and feels the satisfaction of watching the severed plant fall to the ground. So she keeps going, and after a few minutes the exertion has made her blood pump and her temperature rise, and soon she's lost in the hacking and tossing and clearing, and much happier for it.

DECEMBER 1987

LOLLY BUSH

CHAPTER FORTY-FOUR

Kathy knows she's going through menopause – who isn't by fifty-five? – but she's sure the hot flush she's experiencing is entirely to do with the weather. December has arrived and brought with it what feels like one hundred and twenty per cent humidity, if that's even a thing, which it probably isn't but it should be, because her T-shirt is already sodden and she's only just out of the car – although given that her version of air conditioning is winding down all the windows and hoping for the best, this should not be a surprise. She's wearing cotton shorts and she should have picked the navy pair instead of the light green because she's absolutely sure there's a sweat patch right across her bum and god knows where else. Ick.

It is at this point that she firmly believes coming to Eumundi Market wasn't her brightest idea. Except Michelle loved it when she visited, and told Kathy the other day during one of their now-regular phone calls that she's been wearing the tie-dye T-shirt and pants she bought and she's hung the small painting she bought too. Kathy isn't on the hunt for tie-dye. A painting is what she's looking for, maybe more than one, to add some nice touches to her home.

The market conveniently operates on a Wednesday as well as a Saturday. Kathy hasn't been able to make it here on a Saturday since the Sunshine Gardening Society is taking up her weekends, which she's happy about. It's keeping her in shape, all that bending and squatting and pulling and planting.

There are so many people here that Kathy immediately feels sweatier. How to avoid all the bodies? She aims for the row of stalls that looks least crowded and turns her head from side to side, assessing the wares. Some fine-looking pineapples – she might come back for one of those. Ceramics, honey, macadamias . . . and Lorraine. Chomping on a macadamia sample and offering one to an older woman beside her.

'Hi,' Kathy says as she walks up to them.

'Kath!' Lorraine looks delighted to see her and Kathy takes it as a great compliment. 'This is my mum, Rose. Mum, Kathy is one of the gardeners. And she moved here from Melbourne. Right, Kath?'

'I did. Hello, Rose, lovely to meet you.'

'I've heard about you,' Rose says, and as she smiles Kathy can see the resemblance, even though Lorraine is taller and more tanned and her hair isn't as neat. 'You're the lass who met them in the park.'

'I am.' Kathy feels quite chuffed to be the subject of a Lorraine family conversation.

'Do you come to the market often?' Rose asks, then she pops a macadamia into her mouth.

'First time.' Kathy eyes off the macadamias but decides against taking a sample. There may be other things she wants to eat here so she shouldn't get ahead of herself.

'Mum and I come here often,' Lorraine says. 'She lives close by.'

'I do my fruit and veg shopping here,' Rose says. 'The *best* pineapples.' She taps the side of her nose.

'Come on, there's a baker in the next row,' Lorraine says.

'You're not buying nuts?' Kathy asks.

'We may come back for them. They're pretty good. But the baker has these cinnamon –' She stops, her eyes wide. 'Oh. My. God,' she breathes, then she puts her hand over her mouth and starts to laugh.

'What is it, Loll?' Rose says.

Lorraine catches Kathy's eye and her shoulders shake with mirth. 'Kath!' she says, jerking her head towards a massive fig tree. 'Kath – look!'

Kathy tracks her gaze along the same line as Lorraine's and sees a card table under the tree covered in a purple cloth that's catching the sunlight – it must have sequins on it or something. There's a woman sitting behind the table, her spine ramrod straight, her hair neatly pulled up, and she's talking earnestly to the young woman across from her and tapping a pile of cards.

Taking a couple of steps closer – mindful that her long-distance vision isn't what it once was – Kathy can now see that the straight-spined woman is Barb, and she gasps.

'No!' she says, turning back to Lorraine.

'*Lorraine*, what is it?' Rose sounds irritated.

'Mum,' Lorraine says, still shaking with laughter, 'that woman under the tree, with the tarot cards, is Barb. She runs the gardening society. And she's the most *proper* bloody person you could ever meet – but there she is reading tarot! Kath, you wouldn't read about it, would you!'

Kathy shakes her head because the situation is indeed extra-ordinary and she's not sure whether she can believe her eyes. Barb, who seems like such a rule-follower, everything done right, not a hair out of place, is a psychic? Or clairvoyant? What's the term these days?

'Do you think . . .' Kathy starts but then laughter overtakes her.

Lorraine grabs her shoulder. 'Isn't it unreal?' she says, doubling over.

'Do you think she reads Shirl's tarot?' Kathy finally gets out, then she too doubles over.

It's the improbability of it that makes it so funny. The scenarios that are now filling Kathy's brain – wondering if Barb has this whole secret life that's completely different to anything she might suspect – make her laugh even harder.

'Sh-shhh,' Lorraine says. 'She'll hear us. Let's head back this way.'

She tugs on Kathy's T-shirt and, still giggling, they go past the macadamias, the honey and the pineapples, Rose not far behind.

'I can't wait to tell the others,' Lorraine says gleefully.

'Oh, we can't!' Kathy says. 'She's never told us so she mustn't want us to know.'

'Ah, come on, Kath, she's right there out in the open. Anyone could have seen her. It just happened to be us. Ha!' Lorraine does a little jig.

Rose looks from one to the other. 'I'm going to ask her to do a reading.'

'Mum, you can't!'

'Why not? I've never had one done. Maybe she'll tell me I'm going on a cruise.'

'Do you want to go on a cruise?'

'I wouldn't mind. And if this Barb says I'm going on one I'll have something to look forward to, won't I?'

'No, Mum.' Lorraine sounds like she's scolding a child. 'You won't be able to help yourself and you'll tell her that you know me.'

Rose makes a mischievous expression. 'So?'

'Kathy's right,' Lorraine says, sighing like the admission is a huge hardship. 'We need to leave her alone. It's her business.' She pinches Kathy's waist. 'But I'm keeping it in reserve just in case I need to earn gossip points.'

'All right, I'll let you,' Kathy concedes, and smiles to show she means it.

'Come on,' Lorraine says, 'let's head to the bakery stall this way. Then I'll take you to see my friend's paintings. They're really good.'

Kathy restrains herself from asking Lorraine if she too is psychic, given she hasn't said anything about wanting to look for paintings. Instead she follows Lorraine and Rose around the market for the next hour, and it's one of the most pleasant hours she has spent in a very long time.

CHAPTER FORTY-FIVE

Wallet, keys, something she's forgetting . . . No? Yes. Deodorant. Lorraine forgot to put deodorant in her bag and it's so stinking hot that she's going to sweat all day, which means the deodorant she's currently wearing will stop working in about an hour's time and then she's going to smell and who wants to be near that? Not that the others will say anything. They're too polite. Especially Elizabeth. Lorraine has a theory that if she stomped on Elizabeth's foot she'd be apologised *to* – Elizabeth would probably say she was sorry for getting in Lorraine's way. Honestly! She's going to have to teach that girl a thing or two about not making excuses for herself.

Actually, that's advice Lorraine can take as well. If she starts to pong she won't make excuses, she'll just say it's natural. If she says anything at all. Maybe it won't be that bad. Yeah, she had garlic for dinner last night and that always means a bit of seepage out of the pores, but garlic's good for you, isn't it? That's her excuse for putting it raw into the pasta sauce. Terry probably still hasn't forgiven her because after dinner he said he was too stinky to go to the movies with his mates. Lorraine said he was lucky to be fed at all. Not the best thing to say to a teenage boy who'll take any excuse he can get to never talk to his mother ever again.

'What's wrong?' Cynthia is standing by Elizabeth's gate, frowning at Lorraine.

'Huh?'

'You look like you've lost something.' Cynthia arches an eyebrow. 'Maybe your marbles?'

'Ha ha. No. Deodorant.' She can tell Cynthia. No judgement between them. Once, when they were at school, Lorraine's period arrived in the middle of lunch and she bled through her pale-blue uniform. Without a word Cynthia held out her hand and hauled Lorraine off to the toilets, where they scrubbed the dress, then Cynthia tied her cardigan around Lorraine's waist before taking her to the sick bay to ask for a pad. The only comment she made was that it was stupid to put teenage girls in light-coloured uniforms because the risk of bleeding was high. Lorraine was too busy being relieved that her friend was so capable to be embarrassed, and Cynthia was too much of a queen bee for anyone to say anything about it to Lorraine, if they'd even noticed.

'Oh, great,' Cynthia says, wrinkling her nose. 'You already smell like a deli.' Then she smiles, so Lorraine knows she doesn't really care.

'Do you have your gloves, at least?' Cynthia asks.

Lorraine panics momentarily, then puts her hands into the pockets of her shorts. Her gardening shorts as they've become. They're so ratty from her crawling through garden beds and bracken that she can't wear them anywhere nice. And no matter what Shirl says Lorraine has to wear shorts in weather like this. It's too humid for long pants – they just cling to her and she feels like she's encased in Glad Wrap.

'Yep,' she says, pulling them out with a triumphant smile. 'At least I got that right.'

Cynthia frowns briefly. 'Are you feeling like you don't get things right?'

'I married a liar,' Lorraine says quickly, sharply. 'So, yeah, I don't get things right.'

'That wasn't your fault.' Cynthia pauses and glances towards the house, where the back door is opening. 'And he's cleaning up the mess, isn't he?'

'Not quickly enough.' Lorraine thinks of the fight she and Mike had last night, when he told her he was doing his best to make things right and she said his best was never going to be good enough again. She wasn't even sure she meant it – because she still loves him – but it felt good to say it. Anger feels powerful. It's been surprising to discover that.

'Hello.' Elizabeth appears at the gate and pulls it open, ushering them inside.

'Charlie here?' Lorraine says, grateful to have the chance to think of someone other than Mike. She's fond of that little fellow – he's curious about things and not in that annoying-kid way. Probably going to be a scientist or something one day.

Elizabeth shakes her head. 'He's with a friend. They've gone to the Big Pineapple.'

That reminds Lorraine that she's been promising Simon she'll take him there. He went when he was younger but he can't remember it and he keeps seeing it on postcards. That gives her an idea.

'Maybe I should bring my Simon over one day?' she says. 'There's a bit of an age difference but Simon's great with other kids.'

Going by the look on Elizabeth's face, this is not a suggestion she's wild about. 'Oh,' she says. 'Well, yes. Perhaps.'

Then she smiles. 'I'm still getting used to Charlie's life carrying on as normal while mine . . .' She shrugs.

'The Sunshine Gardening Society isn't normal?' Lorraine says archly.

Elizabeth laughs. 'I guess you are now.'

As the three of them approach Kathy and Shirl, Lorraine and Kathy exchange a conspiratorial smile, and Lorraine almost bursts out laughing, thinking about their random sighting at the market.

'I saw that,' Shirl says briskly. 'What's going on?'

'Nothing!' Lorraine squeaks. 'Where am I today?'

Glancing around the garden it's clear that the best of the blooms is over. Most of the colour has gone and, not for the first time, Lorraine considers that there's not much rhyme or reason to their gardening caper. You grow things, they look great for a few days, then they don't for the rest of the year. Or they do, but it's different. So maybe that's the reason. A person has to learn to appreciate the ways in which any given plant looks nice and then there's always something to enjoy.

Shirl looks smug, which isn't her usual expression. 'We're planting,' she says.

'Planting what?' Cynthia asks, then her eyes widen. 'No!'

'Yes.' Shirl's smugness intensifies.

'What?' Lorraine asks.

'Natives,' says Cynthia.

Lorraine looks at Elizabeth, who shrugs. 'I didn't see a reason not to. As Shirl says, they're good for the garden and the birds and the insects. And she's suggested some plants that will work with what's already here.'

'And Jon won't mind?'

It's out of Lorraine's mouth before she realises how wrong it sounds. Except she thinks of Jon as being like Charlie in *Charlie's Angels* – he sets the task but they never see him. He's an idea of a man, yet also an actual man. Except not, of course, because he's dead. It wouldn't make sense to anyone but her, which is why she should have kept it to herself – except Elizabeth looks kind of relieved, like Lorraine has said out loud what she already thinks about.

'He liked beauty,' she says. 'So I think he would approve. Shirl and Barb have a plan for how it can work.'

Lorraine glances around. 'Where *is* Barb?'

'Not here.' Shirl waves a hand dismissively. 'Some event she had to go to in Brisbane. She took her big pink crystal so who knows what she's getting up to.'

Lorraine and Kathy catch each other's eye and grin.

'Right – that's it,' Shirl says. 'What is it?'

'Nothing,' Lorraine says quickly. 'What's her big pink crystal?'

'This big triangle of pink rock she keeps in her house. Something about love. Now, tell me.' Shirl's hands go to her hips and her eyes narrow.

It's not really appropriate for Lorraine to say anything – they've never been a gossipy bunch, mainly because they're too busy working – except she doesn't know if she can keep it in forever.

'We saw Barb,' Kathy says, saving her from having to make a decision. 'At Eumundi Market.'

'Oh yeah?' Shirl squints. 'I think I know where this is going.'

Cynthia and Elizabeth look bewildered and Lorraine feels momentarily proud that she at least kept her mouth shut around them. It's not like she picked up the phone and blurted out the news.

'Where is it going?' Cynthia says.

'She reads tarot,' Shirl says. 'That's what you saw, isn't it?' She glances at Kathy and Lorraine in turn. 'Don't see why it's funny.'

'It's not!' Lorraine cries, abashed now that it's been said openly and doesn't sound nearly as outrageous as she thought it was at the market. 'It was just . . . unexpected.'

'Why?'

'She seems so proper,' Kathy says. 'You know – not the type for . . . cards.'

Shirl nods slowly as Lorraine risks a glance at Cynthia, who looks mildly surprised.

'We're all the type for cards when we need some reassurance,' says Shirl. Her eyes drill into Lorraine's. 'I know it probably seems funny but she's been doing it for years and people come to her for all sorts of reasons. She's accurate, too. Told me I was going to meet a handsome fella with a stethoscope.' She winks in Elizabeth's direction.

Lorraine has no idea what to make of that, apart from wondering if Elizabeth has been keeping some secrets for Shirl.

'Anyway, she's off with her psycho mates. No – wait. Psychic?' Shirl frowns. 'Yeah, that's it. So let's get this planting done and next time she'll see what we get up to without her.'

Contrite, Lorraine smiles weakly at Kathy, who grins back as if to say they've done nothing wrong. Which they likely haven't, but Lorraine feels like she personally shouldn't have thought that what Barb does with her time was so weird. Some people might think that gardening is weird. Once upon a time Lorraine would have been one of them.

That's one of the things she's learnt, being a Sunshine Gardener: you have to keep turning over your own soil so that it doesn't get old and you don't stay stuck thinking and doing what you've always done. Barb clearly gets out there and does interesting things; Lorraine can do the same. Instead of finding Barb silly she should be taking inspiration from her. What a nice idea, to know people who are inspirational.

Not that she'll say anything to Barb. That would be awkward. Lorraine just wants to come to this garden, or someone else's garden, and forget about all that kind of stuff. That's something else she's learnt about gardening: it can be fun and rewarding. Nothing weird about that.

CHAPTER FORTY-SIX

Cynthia hasn't spoken to Kathy for any great length of time since the day she saw her on Hastings Street. At the next gathering of the Sunshine Gardening Society, Kathy looked at her as if she was scared of what Cynthia might do or say. Certainly Cynthia had no wish to discuss private matters in front of the others, yet she didn't feel as if she knows Kathy well enough to take her aside for a chat, or ask her to socialise. She does want to talk to her, however, because she's aware that Kathy is new to the area and likely doesn't have any close connections. And a person really needs to talk to another person about the sort of distress Kathy was in. So instead of attempting to socialise Cynthia asks if Kathy would like to spend an early Sunday morning helping her out in the national park.

When Barb had first suggested the park Cynthia had asked if their remit extended to Crown land. Barb waved off her concerns, saying, 'I've been in there dozens of times over the years and never seen anyone official. It's not like they care – they're not doing anything about the weeds or the litter! They should be grateful we are.' She did, however, tell Cynthia to say she's a 'concerned citizen' if anyone asks her what she's doing fossicking about in bushland and to not mention the Sunshine Gardening Society. Cynthia, a rule-follower by inclination if not always in practice, is happy to comply.

She gives Kathy the same instruction just before they set off for Tea Tree Bay, which is where Cynthia's decided to start work. There's more rubbish there than anywhere, so she thinks today will be mostly about rubbish collection and removal, although she's yet to break that to Kathy.

When it comes to bringing up what happened the other day, Cynthia decides to just plunge in. It's the only way to address hard subjects. Namby-pambying around tends to lead to confusion, distress and sometimes alienation – as happened when she left Pat. Instead of just saying what she wanted, she tried a circuitous route that made it sound as if he could have tried to salvage the situation when she already knew he couldn't.

'So,' she says, feeling the humidity rising as they move under the canopy.

'So,' Kathy says lightly, and Cynthia sees her smile.

'How are you feeling after the other day?'

Cynthia slows her walk to let a jogger get past them. She always thinks it's a shame to run on this track because its natural beauty can't be savoured that way.

'I wondered when you were going to ask.' Kathy doesn't sound upset, which is good.

'I couldn't not ask. But I wanted to wait until the others weren't around.'

'I probably should have said something to you.'

'There are no "shoulds" here, Kathy. We barely know each other. Which is why – look, I'll be frank, this is an awkward conversation to have, isn't it?' Cynthia flashes her a sympathetic smile. 'But I'm genuinely interested in your wellbeing and you were very distressed the other day.'

'Yes, I was,' Kathy says softly. 'Jemima . . .' She takes a breath. 'Broke my heart.'

Cynthia had figured as much, but it's always good to let people tell you their story in their own way and their own time. It would have been nice, of course, if she could have figured that out while her mother was still alive, because then Diane may not be such a mystery to Cynthia now. Cynthia so wishes she had known her mother better.

'I'm sorry,' she says. 'That's very hard to deal with.'

'I'm not a lesbian,' Kathy says quickly, and Cynthia stops and raises her eyebrows.

'I don't care if you are, but the evidence suggests otherwise.' She starts walking again, because she isn't sure if she's made Kathy uncomfortable, then feels her arm being grabbed.

'I mean . . .' Kathy starts, swallows and blinks. 'I wasn't. I was married. To a man. Owen. We have two children, Michelle and Grant.'

Cynthia is now forming an idea of how high the stakes of the relationship with this Jemima might have been, which would understandably add to Kathy's distress at the end of it.

'Did she sweep you off your feet?' Cynthia smiles to show Kathy that she would understand if that had been the case.

'Bowled me over,' Kathy says, sounding relieved. 'I was so shocked.'

'You must have been. That sort of thing tends to be a surprise, no matter who causes it.'

Cynthia gestures to the path ahead to show they should keep walking. She doesn't want them still out here picking up rubbish in the middle of the day, when it will feel like a wet blanket has been laid over everything.

'Was your . . .' Cynthia considers how to say the next bit.

'I left my husband for her,' Kathy supplies, saving her the trouble.

'Then she left you?'

Kathy nods quickly, trying to be brave, Cynthia can see, but failing.

She stops again and picks up Kathy's hand, patting it. 'I'm sorry to upset you.'

She releases the hand, never one for lingering gestures of affection. She's made her point and that's enough.

'No – it's fine.' Kathy wipes her eyes with the backs of her hands. 'I'm really glad you brought it up. I didn't know how to.'

Cynthia nods and walks on. 'It's funny,' she says, 'how these decisions of the heart can be so clear in the moment and so hard to talk about later.'

She glances at Kathy, who seems to be okay. Certainly there are no more tears.

'I was so sure that I fell in love with a surfer I met right about here,' she goes on, gesturing to the ocean and remembering the lanky American who walked up to her while she sat on the rocks with Odette, waiting for Pat to come in from a surf. He'd asked her name and Cynthia felt like the world had shifted off its axis. 'I left my husband for him. Moved countries.'

Kathy looks shocked.

'Once we were in the United States, though, I couldn't explain why I'd thought it was such a good idea to follow him. I still desired him. But it wasn't enough. What I felt for him only made sense while I was here. And by then it was too late. I'd changed too many lives to go back.' She glances quickly at Kathy. 'Not that I think you should go back to your husband. The circumstances are quite different.'

'I still changed a few lives, though,' Kathy says.

'We can do that even without trying, you know. And there's a lot to be said for trying, as a woman, to claim happiness for yourself. We're so often told our happiness only comes from serving other people. It's not true. Some things we have to take or create for ourselves.' Cynthia pauses. 'So I guess it's no wonder we sometimes make mistakes when we try. We don't have a lot of practice.'

They have reached the patch of bush that she chose the other day. 'Here we are,' she says, and she moves off the track and into the scrub.

She'd told Kathy to wear socks and sneakers and long pants if she could bear them, because their legs could get scratched otherwise.

'Not everyone is like Jemima,' Cynthia says as she takes a large plastic bag from her pants pocket, ready to put rubbish into it. 'I hope you won't give up on creating some future happiness for yourself.'

Kathy looks wistfully to the ocean, then back at Cynthia. 'I won't. Although I sometimes think I'm never going to meet someone I like as much.'

'It's a common problem,' Cynthia says. 'I have it myself.'

They both laugh and Cynthia feels relieved that the conversation hasn't gone as awkwardly as it could have.

'Do you have somewhere to go on Christmas Day?' she asks, which was something she had already planned to ask. Nothing quite as wretched as spending Christmas alone, as she knows.

'No,' Kathy says. 'I mean, I think my children will be in Melbourne. We haven't actually talked about it.'

'You're welcome to join my rabble,' Cynthia says. 'You know where the house is – we worked near it recently.'

Kathy nods.

'We eat lunch around two. Just come over whenever you feel like it before then. *If* you feel like it, that is.'

Kathy nods again. 'Thank you.'

'You're welcome.'

Cynthia points to some rubbish. 'Let's start there. I know it looks like a lot but we'll get through it.'

'I believe you.'

They squat and start plucking rubbish and throwing it in the big bag, working in silence but occasionally smiling at each other, used to a joint endeavour that doesn't require conversation so much as companionship.

CHAPTER FORTY-SEVEN

Kathy was told not to bring anything because there would be more than enough food and drink for everyone, but she wasn't brought up to go empty-handed to anyone's house, no matter what they said. Especially on Christmas Day. So she's made some of the rum balls that her mother had taught her to make when she was a teenager, and which Owen and their children always loved. Then she discovered what it's like trying to make rum balls in extreme humidity, which isn't a situation she's encountered before. In short: trying to form the balls was difficult. She didn't want to give up – partly because she didn't have anything else to take – so she dragged her little air-conditioning unit into the kitchen, closed all the doors and brought the temperature down. Then she put the balls in the fridge, which she usually tries not to do because the chocolate can bloom, except she couldn't leave the air con on overnight. If they bloom, they bloom.

That was her Christmas Eve: wrangling rum balls. And there was a phone call from Michelle saying she would miss having a family Christmas tomorrow. No rancour in it, which was nice; just a tinge of sadness.

In the morning Kathy takes the balls out of the fridge and drives the short distance over Motel Hill, down to Hastings Street, and around to Little Cove. 'Motel Hill' was what Cynthia called it – she said all the locals do, and the reason is obvious. Kathy doesn't mind having so many accommodation places close by. They remind her that she's not the only one who thinks this place is worth journeying to, even if she's staying a little longer than most.

As she opens Cynthia's side gate she hears Christmas music and a woman's voice – not Cynthia's – calling something about prawns.

Before Kathy can think how to approach the bustling gathering, Cynthia appears on the verandah, beaming. Her hair is blonder than Kathy remembers – which is because she's only ever seen it under a hat. Cynthia has make-up on – again, not something Kathy has seen. Plus she's wearing a dress. Another first. It's like there's a whole other version of Cynthia that exists far from Kathy's awareness. Although Cynthia may think the same of her, because she's not wearing a hat either, nor is she slopping around in an old T-shirt. She put on a nice linen shirt and linen pants, and she's even wearing shoes without dirt on them.

'Hello!' Cynthia says, coming halfway down the steps to greet her. 'It's so lovely you could join us!'

Kathy proffers the rum balls. 'They need refrigeration,' she says. 'Sorry.'

'It's summer.' Cynthia laughs. '*Everything* needs refrigeration.'

'I'll take those,' says a handsome man who looks to be around Cynthia's age, although he's more sunbaked than Cynthia and his hair is greying. He holds out his hand for the plastic container. 'Great to meet you, Kathy. I'm Pat.'

'Hi, Pat.' Kathy knows who he is – not from Cynthia so much as Lorraine, whose voice carries wherever they are. If she's working with Cynthia and the two of them are chatting, it's not uncommon to hear Pat-this and Pat-that.

'Please, come in.' Cynthia is still smiling as she gestures towards a light-filled sitting room with low couches covered in white, and pots of poinsettias on side tables which, Kathy is sure, have been acquired just for Christmas. Their bright-red leaves are certainly festive.

A tall, slightly stooped older man is laying cutlery next to a young blonde woman. No prizes for guessing that this is Odette and her grandfather.

'My father, Wilfred Scheffer,' says Cynthia. 'And my daughter, Odette. Papa, Odette, I'd like you to meet my friend Kathy.'

Kathy flushes with pleasure to hear herself described as a friend. It's been a while since anyone claimed her as that.

'Hi!' Odette says, grinning, then she glances towards the corner of the room where there's a bassinette on the floor. 'That's my little boy,' she explains. 'Just checking to see if he's still asleep.'

'Perfectly understandable,' Kathy says, then she shakes Wilfred's proffered hand.

'Champagne, Kathy?' Pat asks, and before she can reply there's a cold flute in her hand and Cynthia is clinking it.

Kathy has barely had a sip before she hears noise and turns to see an elderly woman at the verandah door.

'Von!' Cynthia cries, putting down her glass and almost flying across the room. 'I didn't hear you arrive.'

Von smiles mysteriously. 'I can still be stealthy when I want to be.'

Kathy isn't sure how, for Von wields a walking stick and the stairs would have required some effort.

She can't help feeling a little awed at Von's presence: although they met when the Sunshine Gardening Society worked in her garden, Kathy didn't know then the full extent of Von's involvement in the society. Cynthia filled her in while they were picking up rubbish in the national park. Kathy thinks it's not too much of a stretch to say that without Von she wouldn't be at this gathering, because she wouldn't have met Cynthia. She also wouldn't be feeling such purpose in her life, a sense that she's useful after so long feeling useless. Von could never have known, when she and her friends began the society, how far-reaching its effects would be. Or perhaps she did; perhaps it was her plan all along. The woman standing before Kathy looks wise enough to foretell all manner of things.

'Hello, Odette,' Von calls, raising her free hand and receiving a beaming smile in return. 'Where is your son?'

'He's sleeping,' Odette says, pointing to the bassinette then glancing towards the nearby clock. 'He'll probably be awake soon.'

'Von, you remember my friend Kathy,' Cynthia says, her hand in the crook of the older woman's elbow.

As Von holds out her hand Kathy feels like kissing it, but she doesn't, of course, because that would be quite odd. Instead she takes it and squeezes it.

'Thank you,' she says.

'What an interesting greeting,' Von says, her eyes twinkling.

'Yes.' Kathy clears her throat. 'I meant *hello*, of course. And . . . well, thank you too. For creating the society. I didn't say that last time. It has . . .'

She stops and sighs heavily, mainly to stop herself becoming too emotional, because she feels slightly embarrassed about it. She doesn't know these people, so they don't know how much the society and the companionship and sense of achievement it's brought mean to her.

'Oh,' Cynthia murmurs and puts her free hand on Kathy's arm. 'Are you all right?'

The movement and noise in the room have stopped and Kathy is conscious that the others must be observing the tears now rolling down her cheeks.

'I understand, dear,' Von says, and she pats Kathy's cheek. 'I felt the same.' She smiles at Cynthia. 'And you probably do too.'

Cynthia locks eyes with Kathy and nods. 'I do.' The smile that follows is relaxed and radiant. 'I'm so happy you could both be here. We have much to celebrate with our little gardening victories, don't we?'

'Is that champagne I see?' Von points her cane towards the barely drunk glasses.

'It is,' Cynthia says. 'And I'll pour you one too.'

'Wonderful.'

Cynthia lets go of Von's elbow, and Von offers it to Kathy. 'Would you mind?' she asks. 'I feel more stable with help.'

'Not at all.'

Kathy guides her towards a couch just as Cynthia bustles across holding a leather-covered book.

'I want to show you something,' she says. 'Both of you. Von, have you ever seen this before?' Cynthia has a funny look on her face as she says this.

'No,' Von says. 'Is it a diary?'

'Sketchbook.' Cynthia angles it so Von can see the first page. Kathy peers over and sees *Diane Scheffer* written on it.

'It was my mother's,' Cynthia says to her, and Kathy remembers Cynthia saying something about it, months ago.

She turns to a page in the middle, where there's a drawing of a plant labelled *Lolly bush*. The drawing is mostly clean lines with some smudges. Done with a 6B pencil, Kathy would bet.

'Your mother was an artist?' she asks.

'Not that I knew of.' Now Cynthia's staring at Von. 'So you didn't know? It looks like she might have been doing these while she was in the society.'

Von shakes her head. 'I didn't. Or I didn't see her doing any of these.' As Von smiles her eyes mostly disappear. 'But she was a creative person, Cynthia. You remember how she kept this house – always moving things around to create different tableaux. Arranging flowers and paintings. Surely these drawings don't surprise you?'

Cynthia's mouth opens, then she shakes her head. 'They shouldn't. But they do.'

'I used to paint,' Kathy says. 'When my kids were little. It was my outlet. They wouldn't know that I did.' She squeezes

Cynthia's arm. 'So your mum isn't the only one who keeps stuff like that to herself.'

'You don't paint any more?' Von says.

'No.' Kathy tries to remember the last time she did. Or where she put all those paintings. Owen probably has them now, since he's still in the house. Or did she throw them out years ago?

'Perhaps you should,' Von says.

The baby starts a soft cry.

'Odette!' Von calls. 'Would you bring me your son? I love a baby.'

'Bossy as always,' Wilfred says drily as he approaches and sits beside Von before pecking her cheek. 'Good to see you, Veronica.' He pats her hand. 'And good to have you here.'

Kathy notices his eyes cloud a little and he glances away before fixing his gaze on Odette, who is holding out her son to Von.

'Hello, Jordan,' says Von, staring down at the little bundle now in her arms.

Kathy is content to sit amongst the family activity, which now includes Pat chopping something noisily in the kitchen. Cynthia arrives bearing a champagne-filled glass.

'Cynthia,' Von says, 'remind me to tell you about the Noosa Parks Association. I think you should talk to them about whether you can help with some parks.'

'We already do.' Cynthia glances at Kathy and shrugs as if to say, *Don't we?*

'Some *lobbying* regarding parks.' Von stops to coo at the baby. 'There are rumblings about this and that person wanting to build on the parks. The society knows them better than most so you may be able to provide some information about why that would be a *bad idea.*'

More cooing and Kathy is impressed by Von's ability to switch between encouraging activism and coddling a baby. And she's curious about this Parks Association. Her determination to do something to stop the riverside park being developed waned after that episode with Jemima on Hastings Street. It took her a while to recover from that: she lost her motivation to do anything other than feel sorry for herself and simultaneously feel ashamed that she was caught up in her emotions like some teenager.

'I'll talk to Shirl and Barb,' Cynthia promises. 'But let's forget about it for now.'

Von looks slightly disgruntled but says no more, instead handing Jordan back to his mother.

Cynthia hauls Von off the couch and accompanies her to the table, where they sit and eat prawns and turkey and potatoes and salad and bread – a combination of traditional and tropical Christmas that Kathy has never experienced but which exemplifies her old and new life.

Hours pass as they talk about Noosa and how it's changed, about the national park and the shops on Hastings Street, about Pat's favourite surf break. Christmas cake is brought out and eaten, and by nightfall Kathy is on her way home, clear-eyed and clear-headed, and feeling like she could really settle into this place.

CHAPTER FORTY-EIGHT

Christmas Day had started well, with Charlie opening presents and generally being cheerful the way children are on that day. Elizabeth had managed to find several of the items on his list of requests for Santa Claus, although there were some whose absence she had to explain as Santa not having had enough time to make or find whatever it was. Charlie was understanding, which is in his nature – or so she thinks, because for all she knows her child is perpetuating a charade every day of his life to help keep her on an even keel. He's not once asked why it had to happen to him that his father died.

The good start is why the descent of the day into the maudlin nightmare it became was unexpected.

Her parents had seemed to anticipate that Christmas Day would be hard and after they arrived it was almost as if they were attempting to put on a vaudeville show, practically dancing and singing their way around the house. It was the most forced joy Elizabeth has ever seen, apart from at Jon's funeral when some well-meaning relatives thought Charlie might enjoy being entertained with ball sports. It had taken her a great deal of self-control to not tell them that Charlie isn't stupid and he realised his father was dead.

By lunchtime her parents were worn out from the effort of jollying their grandson along, and Elizabeth was so sick of cooking that she didn't want to eat, so they ended up going to the beach – along with half of the Sunshine Coast, it seemed. So then they were all irritated at having to park half a kilometre away from where they wanted to go, and their time on the beach was cursory and distinctly lacking in fun.

The experience left Elizabeth prone on the couch after Charlie had gone to bed, wondering what Boxing Day would be like. What the entire school holidays would, in fact, be like, because he'll have weeks in which to contemplate his father's permanent absence. She has, she can see now, kept him busy ever since Jon died, but these holidays are long and she can't fill every second of them. For one thing, she has to work and therefore her parents will be doing the filling.

Today, however, Elizabeth woke up determined that things will be better. The first Christmas Day without Jon was always going to be wretched, and she should have just accepted that and not become so upset when it didn't turn out to be the jolly-hockey-sticks affair of old.

Except is it so bad for a mother to want her son to have a good day? A really good day? Charlie's days have been fair, she would say, over the past few months. They haven't been good and certainly not great. She's still trying to figure out how to be a parent on her own while not always feeling like she's failing at it, because she's sure that sense of failure creeps into every-thing she does. And she's not a father; she can only ever be a mother. She worries that not having a father will cause Charlie harm that she can't see, even if her own father is a wonderful role model.

There are also things Jon used to do with Charlie that she can't, because she lacks the skills. Like now: Charlie is in the garden tossing a tennis ball in the air because he enjoys it, in the way that children often enjoy repetitive activities. Jon and Charlie used to toss the ball back and forth; she'd hear Charlie giggling and Jon making loud noises whenever he missed, pretending that he was upset. But her own hand–eye coordination has never been good, so when she tries to toss the ball she drops it at least half the time, which is frustrating for Charlie.

There are noises coming from the garden now – non-Charlie noises – and Elizabeth considers the possibility that she's hallucinating them. That remembering Jon in the garden has switched on a track in her brain.

The noises get louder and closer, and there's a female voice. So it's not Jon. She feels disappointed, then ridiculous for feeling it.

The voice belongs to Lorraine, as Elizabeth can see through the kitchen window, and she has a boy with her. Simon, most likely, as she's mentioned that Terry is in his mid-teens.

'Hi!' Lorraine calls, her voice wafting in through the open back door. Then she's in the room holding out a cake tin. 'My mother's Christmas cake,' she says. 'I thought you'd like some.'

'Thank you,' Elizabeth says, taking the tin.

'I know we're here uninvited but I thought you may be at a loose end.' Lorraine gestures to the boy beside her. 'Simon and Charlie aren't so far apart in age, and I thought they could play together. Si, why don't you pop out and see if Charlie would like to play cricket or something? Is that all right, Liz? We brought the backyard set.'

Lately Lorraine has taken to calling her Liz and while Elizabeth has never been fond of nicknames, she knows that using them is part of Lorraine's personality so she has accepted the new appellation without a murmur of dissent.

'It's fine,' she says. 'The grass has been getting churned up anyway. Charlie's out there a fair bit now the weather's so warm.'

'Warm! It's a bloody oven. Still doesn't put me off a cuppa, though.' Lorraine waggles her eyebrows, and Elizabeth laughs and takes the hint, turning to pick up the kettle.

'Can't have cake without a cuppa,' Lorraine says.

She smiles in the everything-is-going-to-be-all-right way she sometimes has and Elizabeth feels like she could dissolve, because that's all she ever wants anyone to express to her. That's the mantra she has created for herself to start each day and it has so rarely felt true.

Lorraine puts her handbag on the kitchen table. 'And in case you're wondering if I'm partly using you to get away from Mike, *yes*, I might be. He's hanging around the house like a bad smell, thinking if he says nice things about my cooking I'm going to like him again. As if! Cora's the only one who likes him at the moment. Even Mum got sick of him yesterday and wanted to go home before we had pudding, and she can put up with a lot.'

She exhales loudly.

'But I did really want to see you.' She swivels and looks out. 'And see the garden. Have you been spending some time out there?'

'Yes.'

'I hope you don't . . .' Lorraine stops and scratches the side of her head. 'I hope you don't treat it like a shrine. Does that sound bad? I don't mean it to. I just mean you should get out there and use it. Be in it. We all want it to be beautiful for you and I think . . .' Another scratch. 'I think it's meant a lot to everyone, to be working on it. We're bringing it back to glory and we hope we're bringing you back too.'

Elizabeth isn't sure how to take that, so although she wants to say something she doesn't know what.

'That sounds weird,' Lorraine hurries on. 'Didn't mean it to.'

'No, I understand,' Elizabeth says. 'And . . . I'm in it, I can assure you. After work I like to sit out there. I take the radio for company, or sometimes Charlie is pottering around. It's calming being out there. But . . .'

She stops, thinking of the times she's felt Jon's presence in the garden so strongly that she wanted to take his hand, and her sorrow when she remembered that she couldn't. So it has made her happier – to have achieved this for him – and more sorrowful, and trying to reconcile those opposites can make her feel like she's in an existential limbo she never asked for.

'You don't have to talk about it if you don't want to,' Lorraine says. 'I just wanted you to know that it's a special project.'

Elizabeth nods, grateful to not have to explain herself. In times gone past she wouldn't have really liked Lorraine. Actually, that's not right: she wouldn't have approved of her. If Lorraine thinks something is the right thing to do she just does it and doesn't ask permission. And because she's not at all malevolent, her right thing usually *is* the right thing and therefore no harm is done. She has blasted right through Elizabeth's baked-in layers of reserve – mainly by telling rude jokes while they're on duty with the society, a tactic Elizabeth knows is peculiar to her because she's never heard Lorraine tell them to anyone else. Not even Cynthia.

Those two have an interesting relationship. They look at each other with love yet barely speak while they're working, which makes Elizabeth wonder how much time they spend together outside of society hours. She knows they've been friends since childhood; perhaps that gives them a certain base level of trust and acceptance which means they don't have to talk much any more. Elizabeth wouldn't know: she doesn't have any friends from childhood. She was reserved even then and books were her companions. Her friendships were made in high school, but she feels like they're slipping away because she's not in Brisbane any more and her life no longer fits into a straightforward mould.

'Charlie's a beaut kid,' Lorraine says. 'You're doing a great job, Liz.'

'Is he?' Elizabeth gazes out the window and sees Charlie laughing. No – squealing! He and Simon are running rings around each other and pointing at something. The mysteries of childhood play.

'Sure. Mine's pretty good too, if I sit back and think about it,' Lorraine says. 'The times when they drive you mad are the times you can forget that, but overall he's good. Easy to be around. Not like Terry.' She makes a face.

'Teenagers can be tricky,' Elizabeth says.

'Just wait until Charlie's a teenager and he stops talking to you. It'll break your heart.'

Elizabeth feels an anticipatory pang of loss for the time when this happens to her. Or maybe it won't. Maybe Charlie will always want to talk to her. She just wishes she knew how to make that happen, because Lorraine seems like a loving, interested mother yet her eldest is doing what so many teenage boys do.

There's more squealing from the garden and Elizabeth's heart lifts.

'Maybe I should bring Simon around more often,' Lorraine says. 'If that works for you.'

Elizabeth nods slowly. Charlie has school friends but they're usually busy on weekends and during holidays, so the holiday weeks are stretching ahead of them both with few distractions booked in.

'It does,' she says.

'Great! I'll get my diary out.'

The next thing Elizabeth knows, Lorraine is suggesting all sorts of days and times and things the boys could do together, and she can't help but think that Lorraine's visit wasn't just to see her and bring cake but to take care of Charlie too. There is so much kindness and thoughtfulness wrapped up in all of it that Elizabeth can barely understand how Lorraine can manage it; and so much gratitude in her that she barely knows how she'll express it.

There's time, though. Time for them all to get to know each other better. And that makes Elizabeth feel, at last, like the weeks and months ahead of her may become bearable.

COASTAL
BOOBIALLA

CHAPTER FORTY-NINE

After Von mentioned the Noosa Parks Association on Christmas Day, Kathy had wonderful intentions of contacting them and telling them about the riverside park that's supposedly going to be bought by that developer who approached the Sunshine Gardening Society. The Sunshine Gardeners have been back in that park and heard nothing further, which makes Kathy think that Developer Vince was engaged in wishful thinking more than fact, but the more time she spends literally in this environment, the more she wants to protect it. Even if that development isn't going ahead, there will be others. In a place like this there are always others.

Melbourne is a constant fiesta for developers – or it was, before the stock market crash. Some of them are probably licking their wounds right about now. Maybe the same thing is happening on the Sunshine Coast, except wherever Kathy goes she sees tradesmen. Someone has money. That's usually the case even in down times – the people who have real money that isn't made of stock-market sandcastles just carry on as if nothing's happening. They're coming into the restaurant for dinner, they're booking to stay at Netanya in Noosa Heads.

Not having ever been one of those people, Kathy isn't sure how it works. What she is sure of is that she wants to stop them using that money to buy public land. So she looked up the Parks Association in the phone book and talked to a woman named Emma, who gave her an address in Peregian, a time and a date, and suggested she join.

'So what were they like?' Cynthia asks as she sits back in one of the director's chairs that Elizabeth has set up in her garden.

They don't call it 'Jon's garden' as much as they used to – it's Elizabeth's garden now, and Kathy was touched when she invited the members of the Sunshine Gardening Society around for drinks in the garden that they've all put so much time into. The society is taking a break from gardening for January and Kathy hadn't expected to see any of them for a month. Not that she's seeing Shirl and Barb – Shirl is on a cruise and Barb is visiting a friend in Sydney. So there's four of them here in the early evening. Four adults, that is, and Charlie and Simon are tearing up and down the street on their bikes.

'They're an interesting bunch,' Kathy says, sipping on her soda and lime.

Over the past little while she's found herself to be less interested in wine, which she puts down to having other things in her life and in her brain. When she's home alone now she's reading books and magazines about gardening and plants, which is something she never thought would happen. She's not even sure she consciously decided to do it, either – she simply found herself gravitating towards that material in the newsagent's and the local bookshop. It's a reminder that life still has the capacity to surprise and that we don't always know ourselves as well as we think. Which Kathy was aware of, obviously, given she fell in love with Jemima. She just forgets sometimes.

'Some of them are artists,' she goes on. 'I didn't know there were that many artists around here.'

'Just look at what's at the markets,' Lorraine says. 'Plenty of art. Not all of it great, of course.'

'Von's husband was a painter,' Cynthia says. 'Quite successful.' She gestures around her. 'I suppose there's lots of inspiration in this area. Lots of beauty.'

'Mmm.' Kathy takes another sip. The evening is hot and she'd rather be inside with the air con, but she's hardly going to leave her friends. 'And I guess they spend so much time looking at the trees and everything that they start to care about them. Anyway, they've been going since . . .' She screws up her face as she tries to remember. 'Nineteen sixty-one? Sixty-two? For a while, anyway. And they know all about how to lobby council about things like that developer wanting to buy the park.'

The side gate is flung open and Charlie and Simon enter, red-faced and panting.

'Can I have an Icy Pole, Mum?' Charlie asks.

Elizabeth looks like she's wavering, then she glances at Lorraine, who nods once.

'Sure, darling. You know where they are. Simon would probably like one too.'

'Thanks!'

The boys are up the steps and into the house before any of them can blink.

'It's his birthday in March,' Elizabeth says quietly. 'I should make a fuss this year. Last year I almost forgot it. It was so . . .'

'When did Jon die – December '86?' Lorraine says.

Kathy wonders how Lorraine knows that. *She* should know that. They've been working in Jon's garden for months now and she hasn't once asked Elizabeth about him.

'Yes.' Elizabeth sighs. 'On New Year's Eve.'

Kathy isn't sure if it's rude to ask questions about a man she will never know, but what would be ruder would be to ignore the subject altogether, since Lorraine has introduced it. She feels she knows Elizabeth well enough by now that if Elizabeth says she doesn't want to talk about Jon, Kathy wouldn't be offended.

'What was he like?' she says. 'If you don't mind talking about him.'

Elizabeth's eyes meet hers and they are alight, and immediately Kathy is glad she asked the question.

'I don't mind at all,' Elizabeth says. 'He was strong, that's the first word that comes to mind. And maybe that sounds strange, considering he died, but he didn't want to leave us.' Her voice catches and she glances down. 'He tried so hard not to. In the end, though, he was too tired to continue. When cancer is in your blood, it's not as if you can evict it. His whole body was sabotaging him.'

The boys reappear on the steps, Icy Poles in hand, then head back out to the street without a word and Elizabeth smiles faintly as she watches them go.

'So he was strong,' Elizabeth continues. 'He was one of those men who can fix things and make things, you know?'

Lorraine nods vigorously. 'I've got one myself.' She frowns. 'Had one. Damn. Now I'll have to hire a bloke to fix things for me.'

Kathy doesn't know much about what's happened to Lorraine's marriage, but Elizabeth laughs knowingly.

'I'll give you my handyman's number,' Elizabeth says, then she stops smiling. 'So, yes, Jon was my handyman. And my support – he always encouraged me to pursue my interests. After Charlie was born he made sure I had time to myself, so I didn't get too overwhelmed.'

Another sigh, although this one is gentler. 'He was a man of faith. Right until the end. I think it helped him accept what was happening.' She blinks a few times. 'Although I couldn't. I still can't.' She smiles quickly but there are tears on her cheeks.

'He was quite a serious person. Good sense of humour but . . . serious. He took the world seriously. Took other people seriously. Took his work seriously. He was cautious. And that's how I knew that when he said he loved me he really meant it. He never rushed into anything and he always meant what he said. So when he said he wanted to have a child, I knew he would embrace that. And he adored Charlie. I think . . .' Another catch of her voice. 'I think the hardest thing for me is knowing that Charlie won't have that in his life any more.'

'Rubbish!' Lorraine declares and Elizabeth looks startled.

'*You* adore him,' Lorraine says. 'And I think he's all right. Cyn probably does too, don't you, Cyn?'

'Indeed.' Cynthia smiles. 'He's a delightful young chap.'

'Kath?'

'No better child,' Kathy says and it's the truth. She's become very fond of Charlie, and given what Elizabeth has told her of Jon she'd say the boy has inherited his father's best qualities.

'So,' Lorraine says, 'that's a few of us. Shirl and Barb seem to like him too.'

Elizabeth laughs. 'Really? I thought he might be annoying them.'

'No more than I do.' Lorraine grins. 'Anyway, there you have it: the kid has three aunties and you didn't even realise it.'

'Oh.' Elizabeth's mouth is open and Kathy wonders if she's about to say something else.

'Don't get weepy,' Lorraine orders. 'We know we're not the same as Jon, but what I'm trying to tell you is that we care. And we care about you too. Don't get weepy about that either, though, please. I'm premenstrual and it'll set me off.'

Lorraine pats Elizabeth's hand and stands up. 'Kath, I put some cheese and biccies in the kitchen. Wanna help me with them?'

'Sure.' Kathy stands and follows Lorraine.

She shouldn't be as surprised as she is to hear Lorraine sniffing as if she's trying to hold back tears. Lorraine always seems like such a force – always moving forwards, never stopping to indulge in sentiment.

'Blast that Elizabeth,' Lorraine says, opening the fridge and pulling out a plate holding different types of cheese. 'I just want to give her a big hug and look what it's doing to me.'

Faced with Lorraine's unabashed emotion, Kathy decides there's only one thing for it. 'How about I give *you* a hug instead?'

Lorraine nods. 'Good on you, Kath,' she says, and they hug for a few seconds before Lorraine tears the Glad Wrap off the cheese and they set about arranging biscuits.

'It's nice, being here, isn't it?' Lorraine says as she picks up the plate.

Kathy nods. 'Elizabeth has made a lovely home.'

'And we made a lovely garden. Us and Jon, wherever he is.' Lorraine looks like she may need another hug. 'We do good, don't we?'

'I think so. Although I think the gardening does me more good than I'm doing for anyone else.'

'Debatable,' Lorraine says, then grins. 'It's doing us all good. I'm looking forward to getting back into it.'

'Me too.' Kathy stands back so Lorraine can walk ahead of her.

'For now, though – cheese!'

Kathy laughs as she follows her friend back to the garden and into the evening light.

CHAPTER FIFTY

The waves are small today, not pushed to their cyclonic potential as they sometimes are at this time of year. The sand on this beach at Little Cove has a tinge of grey in its brown. It's not golden or white, the way some sand can be; the way it is in glamorous photographs of exotic beaches. It's the sand made of the basalt rocks around it, up against the road; the same sand Cynthia walked on as a child, and Odette after her.

Since Odette has moved into Wilfred's house they haven't had many moments alone – and moments they are, snatched in between the squalls of a hungry baby and visits from Pat and from Odette's friends, who look at Jordan like they can't work out if he's real.

Cynthia wants to tell them that his cries in the middle of the night are real – and also that she doesn't mind them. When Odette was a baby she minded very much that her nights were always broken and that the baby seemed to need so much from her. Now she wakes and listens to Odette cooing to her child, sometimes turning on the radio softly, and she waits until she hears them going back to bed before closing her eyes again.

Some nights she thinks she should get up and sit with Odette, but it's the sort of thing that requires an invitation. Odette may not want Cynthia to witness the night-time feed and it would be awkward if she just started showing up. She wouldn't have wanted her own mother to watch her feeding Odette – it would have felt like an assessment was taking place.

Of course, Cynthia likes to think she's not her mother. We all like to think we're not our mothers, that we will do things differently because we're not happy with how our childhoods went – until our own child arrives and suddenly it becomes clear that there are so many little decisions to be made every day, so much weighing up of risk and reward, that there's no such thing as perfect parenting. When each day involves so much change – and that's just within the child alone – how can there be any template, let alone a measure of success? If the child stays alive that's a good day. If they smile, even better. If they hit their milestones and grow up and go to school and make friends and enjoy activities, that's the jackpot. And sometimes, in quiet hours, we can think about our own mothers and how they tried, every day, to do their best, because that's all there is.

These are things Cynthia wants to say to Odette except they're not at that point yet. They are not confidantes as they once were. Although today Odette has accepted Cynthia's invitation to cross the road to the beach at Little Cove and have a swim with her in the warm sea, leaving Jordan with Pat.

Odette sighs as they walk onto the sand. 'It's been ages,' she says, stretching her arms overhead and arching her back like she's trying to catch the sunlight.

'Since before Jordan, I imagine,' Cynthia says, because Odette hasn't been for a swim since she moved in.

'Yeah, ages before. I used to . . .' Odette's expression is rueful. 'I took it for granted. Going to the beach. It's always here, right? I used to think, yeah, yeah, I'll go for a swim. I didn't. But I've missed it.'

She kicks off her thongs and unties her sarong, dropping it on top of her towel. Cynthia does her own version, adding her hat and sunglasses. Then, with a shy smile in Cynthia's direction, Odette walks slowly towards the water.

This is the most Cynthia has seen of her daughter's body since the birth and it is clear how it's changed, as they all change. She loathed the changes in hers, convinced that they made her unattractive. Not that Pat ever said that; attraction was never part of their problem. But it was the era of Twiggy and Jean Shrimpton, and Cynthia felt the pressure – especially at her age – to be that shape. Breastfeeding made her breasts huge, and while it sucked the fat out of her too she felt wobbly. Jiggly. Uncontrollable. Like her body was having a life without her. That sense of disconnection possibly set her on the path she ended up taking, as she tried to find herself again. She doesn't want that to happen to Odette, and hopes Odette doesn't feel about her postpartum body the way Cynthia did about her own.

Ahead, Odette duck dives and pops up on the other side of a wave, grinning. 'It's beautiful!' she cries, then she's under again.

Cynthia lowers herself, dunking her head, opening her eyes and looking at the fuzzy underwater world around her, before she presses her feet down and emerges into the air.

'It is,' she agrees.

For a few seconds they are looking into each other's eyes and smiling and Cynthia feels her heart expanding. Then a wave hits Odette in the back of the head and she squeals.

'Let's go out a bit further,' Cynthia suggests.

They breaststroke beyond the waves. It's low tide so the water isn't too deep but they still need to tread water to stay afloat. Cynthia has always found treading water quite relaxing, even as it's hard work. Or perhaps that's why.

'Do you think we'll ever see Ash again?' she says, deciding to launch straight into the hardest topic.

Odette has barely mentioned her baby's father since she moved in, and Cynthia wants to know if it's a temporary schism while Odette adapts to motherhood – which she could completely understand – or a permanent rift. Which may mean Odette is intending to stay forever – and if so, that's something Wilfred really needs to be told.

Odette makes a face. 'Who knows.'

'I note that it wasn't Ash you asked to look after Jordan while we came for a swim.'

'Dad was coming over anyway,' Odette says quickly, like she's prepared the answer in case she was challenged.

'That's irrelevant.' Cynthia angles herself so the sun isn't in her eyes and so she can see Odette's grumpy face better. 'I am on your side, darling,' she says more kindly. 'Always. So if I ask about Ash it's because I want to work out how we can help you if you're going to raise Jordan on your own. Your father and grandfather and I want only the best for the two of you.'

'I don't know,' Odette says angrily. 'I don't know!'

Cynthia waits to see if Odette will say any more. When she was a child she'd blow off steam then settle down quickly.

'It's just . . .' Odette starts, then she kicks herself into a circle like she's a dolphin at play.

Cynthia understands: that freedom of being in the water, far from care, can make you believe you can leave worries behind. It's deceptive. And impermanent.

'I still love him,' Odette continues. 'But he's a kid.' She shakes her head. 'That sounds weird. It's . . . He seems to think Jordan isn't a person . . . you know? Like he's a toy who doesn't need looking after, so Ash can carry on doing whatever he wants and has no responsibilities whatsoever. But I don't get to do what I want.' For a second she looks intensely sad.

'So if Ash grew up, would you want to live together as a family?' Cynthia prompts.

'That's a fantasy, Mum. And even if he did, it's years away. By then I'll be used to not having him around.'

Cynthia turns herself again so she can gaze out along the expanse of water, where there are swimmers and surfers, and buy herself time to think about what Odette has said. It's what

Cynthia feared for her – being on her own as a parent – yet now that she has first-hand knowledge of Ash's inaction she realises it's the best course. Odette could try to force Ash to be more involved with his child but that won't benefit anyone, not even Jordan. So Odette will bear the bulk of the child-rearing alone. Although it's not ideal, Cynthia is proud of her for being so clear-eyed and so responsible.

'I'm sad that it's come to this,' she says as she turns back, 'but I will help you. Just so you know.'

'I always thought you would,' Odette says. 'But I don't assume it. Okay?'

'Okay.'

They smile at each other.

'Let's float for a while,' Cynthia says.

Without another word Odette pops up on her back, buoyed by the salt water. Cynthia watches her for a few seconds, remembering the time she taught Odette to do just that, then she arranges herself similarly and closes her eyes, feeling the sun on her face and listening to the waves.

CHAPTER FIFTY-ONE

'Mike, as I've said ten times already, you can't stay here.'
Lorraine is brandishing a wooden spoon, although she didn't anticipate having it in her hand when Mike turned up looking for forgiveness and dinner. She told him to take his li-lo elsewhere because she doesn't want him staying on the premises and since then he's been staying who-knows-where.

She wasn't planning to wear her 'Kiss the Cook' apron either, but that's what she's got on, over her house dress, as she likes to call it, which is really a favourite old sarong because who wants to wear anything more than a sarong at this time of year?

'But it's my house!' he says, with a little less force than he's used the past few days.

They've been through this routine several times, although usually he tries it after dinner when he's had a few and stumbled over from whichever neighbour's house she supposes he's staying in. He's been cultivating all of them for years, helping out with lawns, taking out bins when they're away. Maybe he was buttering them up in case he ever needed a place to stay because he knew he was likely to stumble sometime with all of his comings and goings.

'Not yours any more,' she says, putting the spoon back into the pasta sauce and regretting that she agreed to make the kids their favourite spaghetti dish for dinner, because she's sweating up a storm over this stove. 'The bank owns it now.'

'Then it's not yours either,' he fumes.

'That's for a lawyer or a judge to decide.' She gives him a fake smile. 'Since you cheated me out of money. Remember? You wanted the house in your name and now it looks like that was so you could use it however you wanted.'

There's a noise at the kitchen door, which Lorraine closed as soon as Mike snuck in the back way. She doesn't want the kids to hear them arguing. They know what's going on because she's told them everything – no interest in protecting Mike from his own mistakes – but knowing it is different to hearing your parents yelling it at each other.

'Dinner's not ready!' she calls to whoever is turning the handle.

'Michael,' says a feeble voice, and it's Cora standing there in the doorway. Of course it is. Cora come to pat her naughty son on the head and tell him everything will be all right.

Lorraine has barely been able to tolerate having Cora in the house. She's dealt with it by not talking about Mike at all, just going about her business making meals and beds, cleaning and tidying and giving Cora no opportunity to complain about anything. That worked while Mike wasn't turning up to plead his case until after Cora had gone to bed. Lorraine can't help thinking his earlier appearance tonight is tactical: he wants his mother to back him up and to get the kids on his side. Well, he can get stuffed if he thinks that's happening. He probably hadn't counted on Lorraine telling them how their father has arranged it so they're probably going to be chucked out of the house.

'Michael, what are you doing here?'

Cora's jaw looks set – but that can't be right. She's meant to take Mike's side and tell Lorraine off for being an unforgiving wife. Et cetera, et cetera, et bloody cetera.

'I want to come home, Mum,' Mike pleads.

As Lorraine watches the show she can see his eyes are bloodshot and he seems to have developed jowls in the past few days. *Good.*

'What is wrong with your hair?' Cora walks over to him and yanks one of his cowlicks. 'You have not brushed it?'

'Ow, Mum, get off me. I'm sleeping on couches, all right? It's hard to keep my hair looking good.'

Mike sounds like Terry when he whines like that and Lorraine raises an eyebrow.

Cora glares at him. 'Couches have nothing to do with it. Use a comb!'

Lorraine stifles a titter. Her mother-in-law has told off her husband before – usually for dressing like a slob – but it's a remark here or there, not the campaign this seems to be.

'I left it here,' Mike grumbles.

'Then get it,' Cora orders and points upstairs.

Mike's eyes widen. 'But I want to –'

'Get it,' Cora repeats, and it looks like she's clenching her jaw again.

Mike stares at her, then at Lorraine, as if Lorraine has given the order. But he leaves the kitchen and within seconds his heavy tread is on the stairs.

Through the open door Lorraine can hear the television on, which pleases her because it means the boys probably haven't heard their conversation. But now she's not sure what to do: is she meant to chat to Cora about the fact that Mike is in the house and expecting to stay, even though Lorraine has told him over and over again that she doesn't want him to? She and Cora have never had a chatting type of relationship. Or much relationship at all. It could be classified as a close-quarters acquaintance-ship. Sometimes Lorraine thinks of them as being in a platoon together: fighting for the same cause – the wellbeing of the boys – but under no obligation to get along.

'Um,' is all Lorraine can come up with.

'I do not like what he has done,' Cora says in a rush, like she's been waiting weeks to say it, which she probably has because Lorraine hasn't given her the chance to talk about it. Mainly because she's just been trying to cope with the financial mess and still doing the books for the business and working and running the household.

Lorraine grimaces. 'Me neither.' Then hot pasta sauce splatters on her face and she yelps, whipping around to turn down the heat, then busies herself putting water on to boil. She almost forgot the spaghetti part of the spaghetti dinner.

'His father,' Cora says, and Lorraine thinks she can hear something like a sneer in it, 'his father was like this. A risk-taker.' Cora makes a *pfft* sound.

'Did he lose all your money too?' Lorraine says blithely, as if what Mike and his father have in common is a penchant for brown socks.

'Yes.' Cora sniffs and pulls out a chair from the kitchen table, which Lorraine takes as a sign that she's planning to settle in for a long chat. Great.

Cora shakes her head. 'And Michael knows this. He hated it. And now . . .'

She inhales sharply and Lorraine recognises that sound: imminent crying. Not at all what she wants to deal with as she tries to remember if she put salt in the pasta water. Cora'd better not expect her to be sympathetic, not after being such a grumble bum all these years. More than that, she knew Mike had gambling and god knows what else in his veins and she told Lorraine nothing! *Nothing!* A warning would have been good. Lorraine probably still would have married him because he's a nice side of beef, but at least she could have managed her expectations about what the marriage would be like.

'It's done now, Cora,' she says flatly. She can hear Mike stomping down the stairs.

'He cannot move back,' Cora states. 'He does not deserve to.'

Lorraine glances at her and can't quite believe what she's hearing. Is Cora actually going to tell her own son to get lost?

Even if Terry and Simon did something this diabolical, Lorraine doesn't know if she'd have it in her. Or maybe she would. Hard to tell. If they were married to a woman like her, maybe she'd come down on the wife's side. Because she knows what she's done for that man over the years. How she's helped him. And it's only just occurring to her that Cora may have an idea about that too.

Mike re-enters the room with his gym bag. At least, that's the optimistic name for it. He doesn't go to the gym – he just calls it his gym bag in case he ever does.

'I don't think it's right,' he says, but he addresses his mother not Lorraine.

'You know what is right,' Cora says, 'and you have not done this for your wife and your boys.'

She sniffs and Lorraine is sure the tears are going to come, because they haven't appeared yet, but instead Cora stands and moves ever so slightly towards Lorraine.

'We have to look after those boys,' she says. 'And that means you must stay elsewhere, Michael. I will not have them learning how to do bad things from you the way you learnt from your father.'

She sniffs again, but this time it's accompanied by a lifting of her nose.

The water is boiling so Lorraine shoves spaghetti into it. Probably too much but she can always freeze leftovers.

'Mike,' she says over her shoulder, 'it's not that we don't love you. But you've made a huge mess. Clean it up, then we can talk.'

She has no idea how he can clean it up, but it's not her solution to find. Making dinner is preoccupying her right now, and it seems to her that these small jobs of running a life – and other people's lives – are more important to her than getting the money back. Or her husband back. As much as they can feel like a grind, these small jobs are, at this point in her life, not only how she keeps going day after day but how she shows the people she loves that she loves them.

Not that she's close to loving Cora. Not yet. Maybe soon. Especially if she keeps up this new attitude.

Stirring the pasta, it takes Lorraine a few seconds to realise Mike has gone.

CHAPTER FIFTY-TWO

'**B**lessed is the one who perseveres under trial because, having stood the test, that person will receive the crown of life that the Lord has promised to those who love Him.'

Elizabeth knows the verse – it is from James and she has gone to it often over the past year. She hasn't told Reverend Willoughby this so she doesn't believe the reading was chosen with her in mind, but it feels like it. Everything about today's service feels like it's designed to help her, just when she needs help. Before Jon died she would have believed she could see God's hand in that – that He knew her so well that He was providing succour through His words. She saw God in so many things: in her relationship with Jon and her luck in finding him, in being Charlie's mother, in having friends, in being a friend, in her parents, in her home. Now, each time she goes to that verse, she asks herself if it's not because it's reassuring but because she really wants a guarantee of a reward for what she's enduring. For grief is a trial, the worst she's ever gone through. And she thought a thirty-hour labour was bad.

She has asked herself what the test is – living without Jon? Or grief itself? Perhaps it's knowing that Charlie has lost his father, which at times is a more difficult awareness for her than knowing she lost her husband.

So the verse is a crutch, she thinks; a talisman, maybe. If she incants it often enough she will believe there's a reward for every day being hard.

Although some days are less hard. There is more distraction and satisfaction in gardening with the Sunshine ladies than she could have anticipated. At the end of their hours together she has – they have – achieved something. The same cannot be said for the rest of her life: she feels like there is no achievement, just maintenance.

She said something along those lines to her mother the other day and was swiftly reprimanded.

'How can you say that?' her mother said. 'When you have suffered a loss like this, *each day* is an achievement. Some people never recover! You have a job, you have a child, and you are still the lovely daughter we have always had.'

Logically, Elizabeth can see her mother's point. Emotionally, she can't understand it. Perhaps it's not for her to understand, though. Perhaps it is, in the final analysis of a life, for God alone. God may judge her more kindly than she's judging herself, and she knows she should give herself some leeway accordingly, but knowing and doing are separate matters.

The rest of the service seems to pass her by because she is wrapped up in her thoughts. Charlie is uncharacteristically still; probably because he knows there's a reward for *him* on the other side of this. They're going to visit Lorraine and that means he can play with Simon.

The drive to Lorraine's marks the first time Elizabeth has taken the Cooroy Noosa Road. It seems ridiculous, but in all the time she's lived on the Sunshine Coast her life has been mostly circumscribed by the area around the house.

It's a windy day and she keeps an eye on tree branches by the roadside that look as if they might snap off, finally turning onto Lorraine's street with relief.

Simon in the front garden indicates she's at the right house. 'Hi!' he calls, waving and grinning.

He's a sweet boy and Elizabeth is grateful to him for being kind to Charlie; because Simon is older it's not as though they would naturally be friends otherwise. After their first meeting Charlie talked about Simon for days, and now he leaps out of the car as soon as Elizabeth puts the brake on.

'Charlie! What did I say about waiting until the engine is off?' she calls after him, but he's too excited to hear her.

Lorraine is at the front door, wiping her hands on her dress as Elizabeth walks up.

'How was church?' she says, grinning then hugging Elizabeth.

'It was . . . fine.' Elizabeth holds up a pound cake. 'Fresh out of the oven this morning.'

'You made?'

'I did.'

'Lizzie!' Lorraine jostles her. 'Hidden talents! Don't tell Shirl or she'll get you baking morning tea.'

'I wouldn't mind,' Elizabeth says, and she really wouldn't, because she might find a sense of achievement in that if nothing else.

'So you hesitated when I asked you about church,' Lorraine says as she leads the way through the house towards the rear.

As they pass the stairs Elizabeth can hear music playing, and she thinks she sees someone out of the corner of her eye in the sitting room. Signs of life, of other people, that a house should have.

'Did I?' she says as they enter the kitchen.

'Yeah. You paused, then said "fine" like I was pulling out one of your teeth.'

Lorraine gestures for Elizabeth to sit down at the table. From here the sounds of the boys in the garden are audible and Elizabeth allows herself to relax into the chair.

'Did I?' she says again.

'Is that the only thing you're going to say?' Lorraine purses her lips. 'This isn't an interrogation, Lizzie, I'm just trying to find out how church went! And I think you're lying to me!'

Lorraine has a look of false outrage and Elizabeth starts to laugh. 'Why are you so interested in my church experience?'

'Because it's important to you and I'm trying to, y'know, be a friend or something. I'm looking out for you, all right? Just let me.'

Now she looks like she's satisfied she's said her piece.

'Today's service was about struggle,' Elizabeth says. 'And the readings, the hymns, were so on point ... I thought maybe the reverend had designed the service for me.'

'Did you ask him?'

'No.'

'Are you struggling?'

The question is so bare – so frank – that Elizabeth doesn't know if she's ready to answer it. Except Lorraine is, as she said, trying to be her friend and Elizabeth could use her friendship.

'Yes,' she says.

'You know what? I'd think something was off if you weren't. Your husband hasn't been dead that long.'

Elizabeth flinches.

'Sorry,' Lorraine says. 'I use the D word. "Passed away" always sounds like someone's dissolved rather than died.'

'No, it's all right.' Elizabeth sits with it. *Dead.* Said out loud. By someone other than her. Yes, he's dead. She's relieved that Lorraine has said it, because even her parents are given to saying 'passed away' and it's always felt too soft for what has actually happened.

'But I don't . . .' She closes her eyes and remembers a hymn from this morning. 'Jerusalem' – somewhat clichéd now, yet it almost invariably makes her cry. As the lines rang out, 'Bring me my bow of burning gold/Bring me my arrows of desire/Bring me my spear', she wished, in that instant, to have those weapons.

If she were so armed – by God, or by herself – she would have more courage to face each day. She doesn't know how to come by them apart from through prayer, and her wish for them isn't something she wants to share aloud. Not yet. And unless she can tell Lorraine that part of what went on in church, she doesn't think she should tell her any part.

'I don't think anything that happened in church today was particularly interesting,' she says. 'That's why I said "fine".'

Lorraine looks at her askance. 'Sure,' she says.

Elizabeth smiles. 'The boys sound like they're having fun.'

For another few seconds Lorraine stares at her, then she too smiles and pushes herself up to standing. 'They do. My version of fun is eating some of that cake you brought, so let's put on the kettle and get into it.'

Elizabeth stands too. 'If you give me a knife I'll cut it up.'

'And I suppose we should take some into Her Majesty in the sitting room,' Lorraine says with a sigh.

'Who?'

'Mike's mother. Don't worry, she won't bite – she likes strangers because they're people who don't yet know what she's really like.'

Elizabeth laughs. 'Is she that bad?'

'Only if you're her daughter-in-law!' Lorraine says with false cheer. 'Actually, we're getting along better now. She, uh . . . stood up for me, to Mike. Never thought I'd see the day.'

Elizabeth is tempted to ask what happened but Charlie and Simon appear at the door, breathing raggedly and asking for cordial.

Lorraine pours the cordial and prepares the tea as Elizabeth cuts the cake, working in tandem as they have done in gardens, no effort, just easy in each other's company, and it occurs to Elizabeth that this right here, these seemingly unremarkable moments, might be the crown of life she has been waiting for.

FEBRUARY 1988

GOLDEN EVERLASTING PAPER DAISY

CHAPTER FIFTY-THREE

T his room looks exactly the way your mother kept it,' Von says as she glances around the sitting room. 'I meant to say that on Christmas Day.'

All the doors to the outside are closed, to keep out the summer heat – not that it's really helping. There's a small fan going in one corner that provides not much relief, and Cynthia is holding a fan which she uses from time to time. She's talked to her father about installing air conditioning but he thinks it's 'unnatural'. After years spent living in Los Angeles, where everyone had every mod con, Cynthia thinks *not* having it is unnatural. But it's not her house – or 'not yet', as her father likes to say.

'I didn't realise you'd spent much time here when Mum was alive,' Cynthia says, searching her memory.

She always went to Von's house for piano lessons, although she had a piano here. *Has* a piano here, because it's still in this room, although she hasn't touched it since she returned. She's both scared she won't have any skills left and scared she will, because if she starts playing she may become as obsessed as she used to be, fixating on one Chopin piece after another until she got them 'right'.

'Your mother would sometimes have the society ladies over for . . .' Von raises an eyebrow.

'You were about to say "tea" when you meant something else, didn't you?'

'Drinks, Cynthia, that's what I was really going to say.' There's a twinkle in Von's eyes that Cynthia can't ever remember seeing in her mother's eyes. Perhaps she had it when the society ladies visited. 'We had some raucous times.'

'Where was I?' Cynthia says. 'Where was Kit? Or Dad?'

'School. Work. I never said they were evening drinks.' More twinkling.

Cynthia can only hope to still be that amused by life when she's Von's age.

'Because we did the gardening on weekends,' Von continues, 'and then we were always running off to do housework and cooking and preparing children – if they were still school age – for the week ahead, the occasional weekday slot was all we could find. Lunches, they were, although we didn't eat much.'

Cynthia can't remember her mother eating much of anything ever. Diane was rake thin, and always seemed disappointed that Cynthia didn't similarly starve herself. But try as she might Cynthia was usually too hungry for that.

'Hi, Mum,' says Odette as she walks into the room carrying Jordan.

'Darling.' Cynthia beams.

They've been getting on so much better lately; Cynthia can barely remember the distance between them.

'Hello, Odette,' Von says as Odette settles on the couch, holding the sleeping baby to her chest.

She narrows her eyes. 'You look a great deal like your grandmother. I meant to say that the other day too.'

Odette looks at Cynthia then back at Von. 'Thank you,' she says. 'No one's ever said that. But she was lovely.'

'She was,' Von says with a nod, then her gaze turns to Cynthia. 'No one's told the child she's the dead spit of Diane?'

'Well, we . . .' Cynthia isn't sure what to say.

When Odette was young the resemblance wasn't clear, and she doesn't know if Wilfred said anything when Odette came back six years ago. Cynthia herself feels so remorseful about not being here for Diane when she was dying that it's never felt appropriate to say anything to her father about the fact that a version of her mother is still walking around.

'You don't like to talk about her,' Von surmises.

'That's not true!' Cynthia says, too quickly, because they don't talk about her much.

'You don't, actually, Mum,' Odette says with a frown. 'Nan and I got quite close after I came back. But after she died Pa never wanted to talk about her. And you haven't said anything either.'

Cynthia gazes towards the garden. 'I suppose I haven't,' she murmurs. 'She was a complex woman. I don't know that we were ever friends.'

Cynthia realises this is why she's never really learnt how to be friends with Odette. She's mothered her, yes, because she knew how that went. Transitioning to friendship, however, isn't something she experienced herself.

'Diane was hard to know,' Von says. 'That's the way she liked it.' She pats Cynthia's hand. 'Not your fault. Or your doing. But she loved you.'

'She never said it,' Cynthia says softly.

'*You* don't say it either,' Odette adds, then she presses her nose into Jordan's tiny head. 'I'm going to say it all the time.'

'I say it!' Cynthia protests, although she can't remember the last time she did. Or the first. She never told Pat she loved him, just let him tell her.

'You don't, Mum.' Odette doesn't look upset about this; in fact, she looks slightly amused. 'I mean, it's fine. Dad says it all the time. *All* the time.' She rolls her eyes. 'In front of people. So it's not like I've never heard it.'

'I never told you I love you?' Cynthia could have sworn she said it when she kissed Odette goodnight, when she sent her off to school, when Odette was crying due to some hurt small or large. Or perhaps she only thought it, and the words have never formed on her lips because they were never said to her. Is that how families work – we repeat the patterns of each generation unless we find the fortitude to change them?

'I love you,' she says now, and the shape of the words in her mouth is familiar yet not.

'You don't have to say it,' Odette says as Jordan starts to stir.

'I know I don't have to. I want to. I love you, darling. Enormously.' Cynthia wants to hug her but that would be ostentatious.

'I love you too.' Odette grins. 'See – it's easy.'

'Does no one have a word for me?' Von says, looking from one to the other.

'I love you too, Von,' Cynthia says. 'And I mean that. I've always adored you – even when you scared me.'

'Why did she scare you?' Odette says, making a funny face at her son.

'Because she was brilliant. Commanding. I was terrified of making a mistake in a lesson because I didn't want to disappoint her.'

'You could never have disappointed me,' Von reassures her. 'And you made your mother proud. She'd be proud that you're in the society too.'

'Is this society what you get up to on weekends?' Odette asks. She hasn't paid that much attention to Cynthia's comings and goings, but that's normal for a preoccupied new mother.

'Yes. The Sunshine Gardening Society. Saturdays and some Sundays. Von was one of the women who founded it.'

'Really?' Odette looks impressed. 'Cool. Mum always seems happier when she comes home afterwards so it must be good.'

'Happier?' Cynthia frowns.

'Yeah. You always seem tense in the mornings, then you go off to that society thingy and come back happy.'

It's an unsettling feeling to realise you've been so closely observed that another person has detected things in your demeanour you didn't even realise were there. And Cynthia remembers thinking the same about her mother: how unhappy she seemed in the mornings, as if each day was bound to be a burden. Except she didn't think it was unhappiness at the time so much as just the way her mother was.

'I was like that,' Von says. 'The prospect of all that housework and mothering used to drive me mad. The society was something I could do that benefited others but also benefited me. Part of its charm.'

She glances at Cynthia as if seeking her agreement, and Cynthia nods in response.

'Do we really need to get away from our lives so much?' Cynthia wonders, thinking of what her father said about how her mother had nearly left them. He has never defined exactly what that meant.

'It's a good thing,' Von says. 'We can't escape the drudgery of being here – the work of it. Relentless. It falls on some of us more than others. But if we can find something that brings joy, even for a short period of time – well . . .' Von smiles, her wrinkles dancing. 'Those are the moments of our greatest humanity.'

Cynthia thinks of the pleasure of putting her hands in the soil, of planting a young tree, of removing weeds that serve no purpose other than to irritate, of joint enterprise, knowing she's working with others for a common good. Of being with friends and with Lorraine in particular. Of laughter and sunshine and a kookaburra's call and a cockatoo's screech, of the shape of a gum leaf and the delicate beauty of its blossom. Those, indeed, are the moments when she feels most human. Most *here*. If that's what her mother felt, she is glad and she is grateful.

'Now, let me have a cuddle,' Von says, gesturing to Odette, and as Odette stands and moves to put Jordan in Von's arms, Cynthia sits back and enjoys the moment.

CHAPTER FIFTY-FOUR

Some days Elizabeth feels like she's moving through mud, like today as she's digging up dirt in a garden bed attached to a house not far from her home. She notices her movements are slow and that it's almost like she's witnessing them instead of doing them. She's an observer of her own life, she guesses, except there isn't much to observe. Especially not this week.

It's been a year and two months since Jon died and although that shouldn't mean anything – each day is a remembrance of him just as it's a difficulty being without him – she has been surprised by how much she's focusing on it. *It was over a year ago.* That could be because the passing of one year makes her think of two years. Three. More. Forever. How can she bear this *forever*?

If she forecasts the rest of her life, as Charlie grows up and moves out of home and on with his life, it's bare. Which is not to say that she's nothing without Jon, only that she's not sure what's to become of her. She's not used to being alone. To feeling alone. Or lonely. She's both a lot of the time, even with well-meaning people around her.

'Get yourself a fella,' Lorraine said the other day, then added, 'Probably not good advice coming from a woman who's chucked out her husband.'

Elizabeth couldn't disagree. And getting herself a fella is not on her agenda, even though it's a solution several people have suggested, as if it's the fella per se – any fella, doesn't matter which – that's the goal, as opposed to the one fellow in particular whom she misses. Her Jon. Telling her to get another fella is like suggesting she gets a different son. They're not interchangeable.

Which is not to say that she doesn't appreciate certain men if they cross her field of vision. Doctor Lopes is nice to look at; she even admires the much older Doctor Simpson's compact muscularity. She's still human, after all. But she's not in the market for a Jon replacement, as she told Lorraine.

It's Lorraine who's squatting next to her in this garden today, picking up a snail to inspect it. Elizabeth hopes Lorraine won't notice that she's slower than usual and is sighing more; that today is one of those days when it's hard to get out of bed and harder still to stay out of it.

Yet she's here. She's doing something positive for someone else, and by extension herself.

'It's good to move,' her father said – somewhat pointedly, she thought – when he came to pick up Charlie this morning and found Elizabeth sitting on the kitchen chair, staring into space. 'You'll enjoy being outside in that garden.' When he said it, all she could think about was going back to bed. She'd be letting down the ladies but they'd forgive her.

'So what's going on?' Lorraine asks as she looks at the limp hydrangea in front of them.

'Hm?'

'Hell-*ooooo*.' Lorraine taps lightly on Elizabeth's skull. 'I said your name three times and you didn't answer.'

'Oh.'

Lorraine frowns. 'The lights are on but nobody's home – is that it?'

Elizabeth isn't sure what she means and hasn't the energy to try to figure it out.

'Having a hard day?' Lorraine asks in a softer tone.

'Yes,' Elizabeth says. 'I think I am.'

'If you think you are then I'd say you are.'

Lorraine moves along to the next part of the garden bed, which is Elizabeth's cue to follow her, because there's nothing left to do in the portion in front of her. Lorraine has done it all while she's been sitting there thinking of everything and nothing all at once.

'Is there something about today that's harder than other days?' Lorraine says, digging somewhat aggressively into the dirt.

No point withholding information when Lorraine has already correctly guessed that something's up.

'Not especially,' Elizabeth replies. 'I mean, I don't really understand why memories work the way they do. For some reason I keep thinking about what it was like after Jon died and before the funeral. It was . . . so hard and strange.'

She was in limbo that week. Jon's parents were barely functioning so her own parents swept in and took care of the house and food and phone calls while Elizabeth preoccupied herself with Charlie and writing some notes for what she wanted to say during the service. Actually, that's not correct: she didn't *want* to say any of it. She didn't want to be there; she didn't want the occasion to exist; she didn't want to have to use the past tense speaking about her husband. And she especially didn't want to see her young son sitting on his grandfather's knee in the front row, because no child that young should have to be at their parent's funeral.

In some ways it was a week like any other – keeping Charlie's life as normal as possible demanded that – but that added to the strangeness. To her sense that time had fractured on the day Jon died, and there was one timeline in which she could properly grieve without distractions and another in which she was cutting up banana and tidying up toys and trying to fit in her grief around it all. The timelines interwove at night; sometimes they still do, although mostly she's on banana-and-toys now.

'I can't imagine it,' Lorraine says. 'I mean – I can. Because I have an imagination. But I haven't gone through it. So I could say all the usual stuff people say or I could just say this: yeah, it's hard. Harder than anything else, I reckon.'

Elizabeth nods mutely.

'Is there anything you can do to make it easier? Because that's what I'd be looking at. Y'know, if I were you.' Lorraine digs into the dirt. 'And feel free to ignore anything I say because it's really none of my business.'

'The house is making me sad.' It's out of Elizabeth's mouth before she has a chance to censor it.

Lorraine keeps digging and Elizabeth wonders if she finds her ungrateful, given all the work the Sunshine Gardening Society has put into the place.

'I can see how it would,' Lorraine says. 'Everywhere I turn in *my* place there's evidence of Mike and it makes me want to scream because I'm so cross at him. I'm not going to move but I know why you'd want to. It's hard to move on when they're all around you.'

'I love the garden,' Elizabeth says, just in case Lorraine is in any doubt. 'I sit out there sometimes and really enjoy it.'

'But he's not in it.'

'I wasn't going to say that.'

'Don't have to.' Lorraine sits back and smiles kindly at her. 'If you want to move, just move. You don't owe it to anyone to stay.'

'But it's Charlie's home. He's had enough disruption.'

This is the argument Elizabeth has been using on herself, because although she has odd, random thoughts about moving she knows how hard it will be to pack up a life that no longer really exists.

'He's a kid! Have you seen how much kids' bones grow in a year? Disruption is all he knows, Lizzie. Don't worry about him, he'll be fine. As long as he has you he won't care. All kids want is someone to love them and give them food. Mine'd squawk if

I said we were moving but they'd get over it. They did when we moved a few years ago. It lasted about a night.'

Elizabeth contemplates this for a minute or so. 'Maybe I'll think about it,' she says eventually.

'Sounds like you already have.' Lorraine grins. 'Let me know if I can help with anything. Terry's strong enough to lift stuff.'

'I thought you weren't getting along?'

'Funny that – now his dad's not at home he's decided he's the man of the house. He's like a different boy.'

'Do he and Mike get along normally?'

'Well, I have to say I didn't notice. We were all running around like blue-arsed flies most of the time. Me and Mike in particular. Terry was just . . . surly. To me. Can't say I noticed what he was like with Mike. Mike never said anything, but now I just think he was too busy playing the stock market to notice me, his mum or the kids.'

'How is Cora?'

'Good.' Lorraine makes a face. 'Actually, really good. She's making lunches for the boys, she's doing some washing.' She scratches her head. 'I can't quite work out why Mike turning out to be a dickhead has made her nicer, but there we go.'

'Maybe she feels bad.' When Elizabeth met Cora she perceived her to be a woman unsure of her position in the house and also slightly scared of Lorraine. Not that Lorraine would believe her if she said that.

'Oh, I'm sure she does. Mike's father was a gambler too – don't think I've told you that bit. So she could have warned me. Or warned Mike off gambling.'

'So she's making it up to you now?'

'Guess so. Life's funny, isn't it?'

Elizabeth nods slowly. 'It can be.'

'And sad.'

'It can be that too.' It's something of a relief to have it acknowledged.

'Sorry,' Lorraine says. 'I should probably not say anything about Jon.'

'No, I appreciate it. After someone dies people tend to not mention their name or ask how you are because they're worried about upsetting you. But it's not as if I've forgotten about Jon and that mentioning him is going to bring back a bad memory. He's always here.'

Even if sometimes she wishes he wasn't, but she hasn't worked out how to program her brain to eliminate random repeated memories of him.

'That's a good thing,' Lorraine concludes. 'For you and for Charlie.' She picks up the little hoe she brings with her to society gatherings. 'Time to see what's in this dirt.'

Elizabeth takes up her trowel and they investigate the soil together.

CHAPTER FIFTY-FIVE

'Honestly, Mum, I've told you and told you that the path needs to be fixed.'

Lorraine huffs and puffs as she plumps the pillows behind her mother's back. Pillows that are usually on Lorraine and Mike's bed, but now they're in Simon's room where Rose is recovering from a fall. It's not like Mike uses his any more. Lorraine doesn't know where he's sleeping these days and she doesn't care.

Well, she does care because she can't just turn off her feelings about the bloke, but to anyone who'll listen she's saying she doesn't care. He still seems to care, because he left a bunch of flowers on the doorstep with a note asking her to forgive him because the worst thing he can imagine is losing her. All Lorraine could think about was where he got the money for the flowers.

'I can't afford to get it fixed,' Rose says meekly.

'I've offered to pay!' Lorraine practically yells, as much as you can yell at a mother who looks like she's shrunk five centimetres in the past couple of days.

The path in the back garden has been a subject of contention between them for a while. Lorraine has said she'll either pay for the repair of it or deploy Mike to fix it, and Rose has repeatedly refused, saying it's her home and she'll take care of it – except now she's gone and tripped on one of the bigger cracks and come down on her arm, with a busted radius to show for it.

At her age, thinks Lorraine, she'll be lucky to get the full use of the arm back. *And* it's her writing hand. How's she going to do crosswords? That was the first thing Lorraine thought when they called her from the hospital to say her mother was there. Rose doesn't know how to live without crosswords.

'I have my pride,' Rose almost whispers and that *really* gets on Lorraine's goat.

'*Mum*, pride does you no bloody good when you break your arm because of it. You're elderly!'

'I'm not!'

'Technically you are!'

'I don't care, I don't feel elderly!'

That stumps Lorraine, because you can hardly argue with how a person says they feel. Something inside her lets go a little.

'All right, I understand. But how does it hurt your pride to have me help you?'

'I've always managed,' Rose says. 'Whatever you needed, I've managed.'

'I'm not saying you haven't. But can't you see that *I* may want to give *you* what you need now?'

'You have enough on your plate.'

'You're not on my plate. You're my mum.'

Rose's bottom lip quivers, but then, like the stoic Lorraine knows her to be, it stops. Not a fan of crying, her mum. Which maybe isn't healthy but that's the way she is. Rose's dad served in World War I and he probably never cried, because if you were in that war you'd probably never stop if you started. Imagine how bad it was. Anyway, Lorraine thinks that's where Rose gets it.

'But I don't want to add to your worries,' Rose says.

That makes Lorraine dig her fingernails into her palms, because having her mother here with a broken arm for an indefinite amount of time adds more to her worries than fixing the blasted path would have.

She's meant to be taking care of the books today because even though Mike's not around she's still looking after his business. It's her business too, even if her name isn't on it. Just like her name isn't on the house. Talk about adding to worries. Rose knew what she was talking about when she warned Lorraine about the finances, but oh no, Lorraine knew better because she loved Mike and he loved her and all that ridiculousness. No doubt if she asked her mother – which she won't, because she'd never hear the end of it – Rose would say that if Mike really loved her he would never have put her in this position. And she'd be right, and that would make Lorraine cross, then they'd argue and Rose would get worked up and that's not good for an elderly person with a broken arm.

Breathe, breathe, Lorraine, don't have a tizzy. It won't help anyone.

'Anyway, it's done now,' she says, because what else can she say? No point going over the past. Again.

There's a knock on the door, which is open, so that means it's Cora. The boys would just come barrelling in if they were here, but they're at school.

Cora peers into the room and Lorraine wishes she'd come in properly, or say something, instead of lurking like she's waiting for permission. Which is polite, Lorraine admits, but Cora's never been one to hold back and she can't believe her mother-in-law's suddenly developed manners around Rose. Or maybe she has. People can change.

'Hello?' Cora calls softly.

'Come in, Cora,' Lorraine says. And yes, she's read vampire stories so she knows that by issuing the invitation she's giving Cora permission to bite her in the neck.

'I just came to see how Rose is feeling.' Cora is fully in the room now and the grandmothers are staring at each other.

When Lorraine told Rose that she'd have to move in here for a little while – because she can't cook or do much of anything with a broken arm – Rose's only protest was about having to live with Cora. But as Lorraine said at the time, 'Nothing I can do about it, Mum. You can't go home and she doesn't have another home.'

'Rose is feeling fine,' Lorraine's mother says loudly, sitting up straighter.

'Your arm . . .' Cora gestures towards it. 'Is it sore?'

'Not while she's on painkillers,' Lorraine says. 'And she'll let me know when they start to wear off.'

'I can answer for myself, Lorraine,' Rose snaps.

Great, now Lorraine has *two* old ladies on her back.

'Sorry, Mum,' she says, because that's the only thing for it. You can't chastise your mum in front of her mortal enemy.

'It was painful at first, Cora,' Rose explains carefully. 'But Lorraine is right – I'm not in pain at the moment.'

Lorraine rolls her eyes but not in view of either woman.

'Can I help with anything?' Cora says.

Like you've ever helped Mum with anything, Lorraine wants to say, then she's suspicious. Cora isn't naturally nice, so when she adds this offer to the help Cora's been giving her around the house it seems like her mother-in-law must want something.

'No, we're fine,' Lorraine says, then of course her mother scowls because she's answered for her again.

'Sorry,' she amends. 'I mean *I'm* fine.' She glances at her mother, who looks satisfied.

'And I'm fine too,' Rose adds.

Cora looks nervously from Rose to Lorraine and back.

'What's wrong, Cora?' Lorraine snaps. Time to end this pantomime.

'I just . . .' Cora takes a breath. 'I am wondering if Rose is here to stay.'

Lorraine frowns, trying to work out why Cora is asking. Then it hits her: with Mike gone, Cora must think her position isn't certain. So if Rose moves in, she has to move out. The idea hadn't actually occurred to Lorraine until right now and it's kind of tempting . . .

'No,' Rose says. 'Once I'm fixed up I'll be straight back home.'

So that's that.

Cora looks so relieved that Lorraine feels slightly guilty for hoping for a better outcome. They've been getting along okay, sure, but Cora isn't *her* mother so Lorraine doesn't feel the same obligations she does to Rose. Besides, for all she knows Cora is feeding info to Mike. About what, Lorraine doesn't know, because life around here is pretty routine, but Cora can't be trusted. Not as much as Rose can.

'Oh,' Cora says. 'Well, if you need some company while you are here I would be only too pleased.'

That's a turn-up for the books. She must *really* be happy that Rose will be going home.

'Do you play cards?' Rose asks and Lorraine's mouth drops open.

'I like gin rummy,' Cora replies.

'A game a little later on would be good,' Rose says.

Lorraine narrows her eyes, suspicious of the cahoots these two now seem to be in, but she can hardly tell her mother what to do. *That* has been clearly established.

'Very well,' says Cora. 'After lunch?'

A nod from Rose, a wave from Cora and the rest of their day is sorted.

Lorraine, meanwhile, feels a slight sense of unease and an awareness that there will be no gin rummy for her.

MARCH 1988

YELLOW BUTTONS

CHAPTER FIFTY-SIX

'Right, see, what you want to do is not cut that one back.' Shirl is pointing to something but Kathy can't tell what. 'Which one?'

'The thyme.' Shirl puts the secateurs back on her tool belt. 'If you go too hard it'll never recover and it's a nice bit of ground cover there. Plus it smells good.'

It's a turn-up for the books that Shirl would in any way endorse the growth of a non-native plant, but as this is Elizabeth's garden and she's long since accepted defeat on the natives front, perhaps Kathy shouldn't be surprised.

The dedication they all have is to making sure that this garden is what Elizabeth wants, or what she believes Jon wanted, since it's still his garden. They're the guardians of it, and holding it in trust for Charlie. Or that's how Kathy likes to think of it. And today they're making sure it looks as lovely as possible for Charlie's birthday party, which is looming.

Elizabeth has invited them all and Kathy was really touched to be included, given she feels like much less of a local than the others. Cynthia and Lorraine have deep roots on the coast, and Elizabeth is emotionally rooted here because it's where her son was born and her husband died. Kathy was agonising over what to buy Charlie as a present until Cynthia suggested a book – 'Children can never have too many of them,' she said, and Kathy remembers her kids borrowing the maximum number of library books each time and ploughing through them.

'So, er, what would you like me to do?' she asks Shirl, since she's not yet at the stage where she feels confident doing garden work without instruction.

'Why don't you give Cyn a hand inspecting for pests?' Shirl gestures towards the hydrangeas, where Cynthia is squatting down scrutinising leaves.

Kathy nods her assent and moves in that direction.

'I'm with you,' she says to Cynthia.

Lorraine is scrabbling around in the dirt next to them, while Elizabeth is pruning the roses. Roses seem to need pruning around two hundred and fifty times a year by Kathy's calculation, and it's always so brutal: the blooms are lopped off and the bushes are cut back to a bunch of sticks.

'Bug watch,' Cynthia says with a smile.

'I guess we do all the jobs.' Kathy gets down on her haunches with a wince.

'What's going on there?' Cynthia murmurs.

'Sore hips. I've been walking a bit for exercise and maybe I pounded the pavement a bit too hard.'

Cynthia nods. 'How's the Parks Association going? You haven't given us an update for a while.'

Kathy smiles as she thinks of the motley crew of regulars at the association meetings: young, old, from money, no money, all sorts of professional backgrounds, people who've lived here for decades, and some recent blow-ins like her. If she thought the Sunshine Gardening Society was a good introduction to her new home, the association has opened her world further.

'They like to disagree about biscuit choices,' she says, chuckling as she remembers the most recent stoush.

'No one likes squashed-fly biscuits?'

'I do. But I think I'm the only one. Peter, one of the older blokes, said he prefers a Spicy Fruit Roll but we didn't have any so . . .' Kathy raises her arms in surrender. 'There was a lot of disappointment.'

'Any group over the size of three, I believe, will result in that kind of thing,' Cynthia says with a laugh. 'But you feel like it's worth going?'

'Absolutely. I've found out a lot about the area and about how close they've come sometimes to losing the land to development. And don't tell Shirl but . . .' She looks over her shoulder to where Shirl is in a heated discussion with Barb. 'I appreciate her point of view more now.'

Cynthia grins. 'Scandal!'

'I know, I know. I can't tell her because she'll do a victory dance or something.' Kathy peers at a leaf. 'Is this anything?'

Cynthia bends closer. 'It was something. I'd say the pest has done its damage and moved on.'

'So . . .'

'You can pull it off. No point leaving it there using energy the plant could put somewhere else.'

Kathy looks at her sideways. 'Is that how it works?'

'If leaves are dying it's best to get rid of them – they're going to die anyway and the plant doesn't need to try to keep them alive.'

There's probably a metaphor for life in there somewhere; maybe Kathy's already applied it by ending her marriage. Not that she would ever have thought of Owen as a dying leaf, and she didn't get rid of him so much as rid herself of the situation.

'Does that sound cruel?' Cynthia says after Kathy has been silent for a while.

'What? No. I was just thinking about pruning things. Pruning life.'

Cynthia strips off a few leaves. 'It can be tough but necessary. It means you can grow something better. Or is that being too grandiose?'

'I'd say it's appropriately grandiose,' Kathy replies with a laugh. Then she stops to think about its practical application:

about the things she's grown in place of the leaves – branches, if she's being honest – she's pruned.

'On Christmas Day,' she starts.

'Mm?'

'Your mother's sketchbook.'

'Yes.' Cynthia pulls off some more leaves.

'It got me thinking.'

Cynthia is silent, which is fine, because Kathy really should just get on with her story.

'About my painting,' she continues. 'So I got talking to Emma at the Parks Association. She's a painter.'

More silence, but some nodding this time along with a smile.

'She teaches painting – she has a little class at home. Monday nights, which I have off. So . . .'

Kathy sits back and tosses some dead leaves behind her onto the grass, where Charlie picks them up and puts them in a bucket. He knows they're working on the garden ahead of his party and he told Elizabeth he wanted to help, so Shirl assigned him to rubbish duty.

'I'm painting again.' Kathy can hear the note of triumph in her own voice.

Cynthia whips her head around. 'That's wonderful!'

'What? Painting?' It's Lorraine, who's obviously heard the whole exchange. 'Did you know she painted, Cyn?'

'Kathy mentioned it once. But as something from the past.'

'You need to have a show,' Lorraine declares.

'Lorraine, honestly –'

'No, you must. I bet you're really good. I can feel it in me waters. Cyn and I will organise it.'

'Will we now?' Cynthia says, amused.

'Course we will. This is a big deal! Kath's an artist!'

'Shh,' Kathy says, not ready to share it with Shirl in particular, because Shirl probably knows Emma and she'll start asking questions about Kathy's ability or something. It would be better to develop her art in her own time – if Lorraine doesn't intervene first.

'Be proud of yourself, Kath.' Lorraine nudges her. 'Some people would talk about it forever and never do a thing. You're on your way.'

'We'll see,' Kathy mutters.

'Now.' Lorraine puts her hands on her hips and surveys the garden. 'We need to work out where to put the tables and chairs for the party. Lizzie! Let's have a chat.'

She charges off in Elizabeth's direction and Kathy once more turns her attention to the hydrangeas.

'I'm glad Elizabeth's having this party,' Cynthia says softly. 'It turns this garden into a place of celebration. Not . . .'

'A mausoleum?' Kathy makes a face. 'I know what you mean.'

'I was going to say "shrine" but it's probably not much different.'

They both turn to look at Lorraine, now pointing and talking like she's a general giving orders, which is not that far from the truth.

'It's a turning point,' Cynthia says. 'Elizabeth should be proud of herself. And you should be proud of *yourself* for painting again. I can't wait to see what you're working on.'

Kathy smiles and nods, although she's determined not to show Cynthia anything unless she's sure it's very good. Because she's painting native plants – not at all in Diane's style, but taking inspiration from the sketchbook – in honour of all the women in this gardening society that has changed her life in ways that initially seemed small but have turned out to be very big indeed.

CHAPTER FIFTY-SEVEN

'Si made the card himself, didn't you, darling?' Lorraine is holding out a brightly coloured-in offering to Charlie, who looks delighted.

Elizabeth feels herself relax. She's been so worried about this party – the first proper gathering she's had in this house, and its garden, since Jon's wake. Worried about being around all those people; worried that she won't remember how to be sociable; worried that the food won't be right or enough. Then Lorraine knocked on the door, Simon in tow, being her bright self, and the worries went away.

'Happy birthday, Charlie!' Simon says, then without another word the two boys run in the direction of the garden.

Elizabeth smiles gratefully at Lorraine. 'Thanks for coming,' she says, accepting Lorraine's noisy kiss on her cheek.

'As if I'd miss it!' Lorraine holds out a plastic plate full of chocolate crackles. 'I know you did all the food but I figured I'd bring something extra for the kids. Simon'll eat you out of Cheezels in five seconds so it's good to have more supply.'

'Thank you.' Elizabeth takes the plate and walks towards the kitchen, knowing Lorraine will follow her. The Sunshine Gardeners are all very familiar with this house now, in and out to the bathroom and the kitchen.

'Are the others here yet?' Lorraine says. 'Sorry we're late.'

'You're not late,' Elizabeth says as she puts the plate on the kitchen bench and turns around. 'It's a party. You're only late if it's already over when you arrive.'

'True!' Lorraine looks out the window and her eyes widen. 'Don't tell me,' she breathes.

'What?'

'Shirl's in a *dress*!'

Elizabeth grins. 'I know. I almost didn't recognise her – she's not wearing her tool belt either.'

She hasn't told anyone, not even Lorraine, about seeing Shirl out of uniform at the surgery so has to pretend to be as surprised as the others to see her in civvies.

Lorraine squints. 'Who's the bloke with her? They look a bit cosy.'

'That's, uh, Doctor Simpson.'

'*Your* Doctor Simpson?'

'Yes.'

Lorraine puckers her mouth and raises her eyebrows. 'Woo-ee, Shirl has a boyfriend!'

With a laugh Elizabeth starts to move towards the back door, then she hears the front doorbell ring.

'That'll be Cyn,' Lorraine says. 'She called to say she was running a little late because Odette had to get back from class or something.'

'Class?'

'She's doing some course. Secretarial, maybe?'

Cynthia hasn't said anything about Odette studying. Then again, Cynthia doesn't say much about Odette at all; nor has Elizabeth asked, so that's probably on her.

'Hello,' she says as she opens the door to see Cynthia holding a frame under her arm.

'Hi.' Cynthia steps inside. 'I almost went via the side gate but then I remembered we're not gardening.'

She holds the frame out to Elizabeth, who sees under its glass a fine-lined drawing of small round flowers clustered together on long stems, and in small cursive the words *Yellow buttons*.

She hears Lorraine gasp behind her.

'This is for you,' Cynthia says. 'I thought . . .' She pauses. 'My mother drew it. And it's dated – if you look down the bottom, it says *March 1963*. As it's a March drawing and Charlie was a March baby, I thought it would be appropriate to give you that one.'

'But . . .'

Elizabeth doesn't know what to say, first because she is sure this drawing is precious. She knows that Cynthia's mother died last year and also knows that they weren't close, and the other day she and Lorraine were talking about a sketchbook that was recently found. And also because it's not her birthday, so she doesn't know why she'd be given a present.

'You made it, Elizabeth,' Cynthia says, and although she's smiling Elizabeth can see a certain weariness in it. Or perhaps it's recognition of the long road they have both been on as mothers. 'You have raised your son in the most trying of circumstances and here you are, over a year later, throwing him a party and creating wonderful memories for him in Jon's garden. That deserves recognition. That deserves a *present*.'

Cynthia gestures to the frame. 'I could have kept my mother's sketchbook as it was and pulled it out every now and again, but I think the drawings deserve to be looked at. Especially by a member of the Sunshine Gardening Society. I think she'd approve.' Cynthia pulls a face. 'Actually, I don't really know, but I hope she would. My father did when I asked if he minded me taking one of them out.'

Lorraine sniffles.

Cynthia laughs. 'Loz approves.'

'How dare you make me cry at Charlie's party!' Lorraine says.

Elizabeth feels like crying herself – at the unexpectedness of the gift as much as for its sentiment – but she has a party to run.

'This is so special I don't know how to thank you enough,' she says, putting one arm around Cynthia and hugging her.

There's resistance for a second then Cynthia relaxes into it.

'Just hang it on the wall where you can see it every day and that will be thanks enough for me,' she says softly.

Releasing her, Elizabeth nods. 'I'll just put it safely away.'

Stashing it in her bedroom, she returns to the sitting room and gestures for Cynthia and Lorraine to descend to the garden they know so well.

Children from Charlie's class are running around after a tennis ball being thrown by Simon, narrowly missing the table that is laden with popcorn and red frogs and chips and Simon's favourite Cheezels.

Elizabeth's parents are helping two girls choose food, and her mother smiles in her direction. They have been here for hours, helping with everything, and yet again Elizabeth wonders how she'd cope without them. When she said something along those lines her mother said, 'Darling, there's nowhere else we'd rather be than with you and Charlie', and that made Elizabeth falter a little because there have been times when she's wanted to be anywhere else but here. They're fewer now, though.

'Lorrie! Cyn!' Shirl calls, holding up a plastic glass that Elizabeth filled with wine not long before. 'Kath's just telling us that she's in the Parks Association with my mate Emma.'

Elizabeth drifts over to where Barb is sitting in a director's chair, one leg crossed over the other, smiling serenely.

'Isn't this wonderful?' Barb says. 'A garden full of life, in all ways.'

Charlie squeals as the tennis ball hits him, then he giggles and grabs it, brandishing it in the air.

'The lawn may not recover,' Elizabeth mutters and Barb waves a hand.

'It will,' she says. 'And it's for using, not looking at. There is no better use than this.'

'I guess not.'

While the garden's flowers aren't in bloom, it looks lush and orderly enough to be the haven Jon created and dreamed of continuing. Elizabeth may never have the same interest and passion in gardening as he had but she understands now that it's not just about the result – about looking at something lovely. The ongoing work of maintaining the garden creates the connection to it, which in turn increases the enjoyment of it when it blooms. Which means that a garden can provide rewards year round, not just in spring. This is knowledge she likely could have lived her whole life without and not missed it, but she's glad to know it now. Glad too for the small community of women who have taught it to her or learnt it with her.

'Congratulations, my dear,' Barb says. 'You have created beauty – in this garden, in this day, in your son. I applaud you.'

'Thank you, Barb,' Elizabeth says, then she sees Lorraine barrelling towards her holding two glasses.

'Drinks, Liz!' Lorraine calls. 'Then let's get the party pies into the oven.'

Elizabeth laughs and takes the proffered glass of white wine before making her way back into the house, Lorraine at her heels chattering about how they should take the boys to Maleny on the weekend and how she's thinking about putting Simon into Nippers next summer and maybe Charlie should join too. The sounds, and signs, of life continuing, just as she knows it should.

CHAPTER FIFTY-EIGHT

'Terrr-rrrryyyy! Biiiiinnnnsss!'

Lorraine pokes her head out the back door and looks around the garden but can see no sign of her eldest son. Of course. It's rubbish night and he's meant to put the bins out but he's probably on his skateboard somewhere. Or smoking behind a shed like she did when she was a teenager. She always thought Rose didn't know but *of course* she knew. Like she knew Cora was tricky the second she met her. Except now Rose and Cora have become thick as thieves, and it's left Lorraine feeling like she's in some horror movie, except it's not the usual sort of horror – it's an unnamed creeping sensation of not being able to name your worst fear but suspecting it's about to come true.

Actually, she can name it – now. It wasn't something that existed a few weeks ago, because never in her wildest dreams would she have imagined that her mother and Mike's mother would become so clubby, yet there they are, playing gin rummy in the living room, telling Lorraine to go off and have fun while they watch Simon. Except they're so rapt with each other she's convinced Simon could crack his head open and they wouldn't notice until blood dripped on their cards.

Revenge, that's what it is. Cora's revenge for all those years Lorraine grumbled about her. She's captivated Rose and Lorraine is now second fiddle in her own mother's life. Outrageous!

'Terrr-rrrryyyy!' It's worth another crack.

'Yeah?'

Lorraine jumps because the voice seems to come from nowhere. She turns around and sees him leaning in the kitchen doorway.

'Where were you?'

'Talking to Nana and Gran.'

Whispering, more like it, because she didn't hear them.

'It's bin night.'

He rolls his eyes. 'I know.'

'So . . . ?'

'I'll take them, I'll take them.'

Lorraine feels like patting him on the head as he slouches past her, but she's sure that would earn her more eye-rolling and she just wants to bask in the glow of her eldest son doing his chores for once. Well, twice. She screws up her eyes as she thinks. *Three times.* Gawd, that's the third week in a row he's taken out the bins. She hesitates to think it's because he likes being the 'man of the house' now Mike isn't around, but maybe he does.

She and Mike are in negotiations. Rather, she and Mike and her mother are in negotiations. Because Rose came up with a suggestion.

'Is your marriage over?' she asked the other day as Lorraine was folding towels.

'Dunno,' Lorraine answered.

'How can you not know?'

'Because I don't want it to be over, Mum,' Lorraine had snapped, although that wasn't a thought she'd said out loud before that point. Or even admitted to herself, really.

'I still love him. He's still the kids' father,' she'd gone on, as if she had to explain herself to her mother, the only person alive who loves her without wanting anything from her other than for her to be herself and be happy.

'I understand that, Lorraine,' Rose had said patiently. 'Why do you think I asked instead of presuming?'

'Well, if you're going to *make sense* . . .' Lorraine had smiled weakly. 'I just need to give it a bit more time, Mum. I'm upset. And I think he needs to pay for that. I just don't know for how long.'

'And he doesn't have anywhere to stay yet, does he?'

'He's moving around, I guess. Looks like hell.'

Mike popped up every now and again, looking for a piece of clothing or a tool or to see the kids. Or kid. Simon was usually the only one around. Mainly he visited to try to convince Lorraine to take him back and he probably had no idea how close she was to doing just that. Because it's hard when you miss the way someone smells and feels and kisses you, even though you know they've done something to hurt you. You feel weak wanting them back but you can't help it. That's the state she's been in.

'I have an idea,' Rose said – then she suggested that Mike move into her house and she'd stay with Lorraine for a while. The boys were already sharing a room so she could sleep in Simon's.

Simon thought it was great; Terry was mortified. And he remained that way when Lorraine told him that Rose was going to be with them for a while. Nevertheless, he's been hanging around the house a little more now he has two grandmas telling him that the sun, moon and stars shine out of him.

Lorraine tries not to watch him as he slides the bins up the driveway. Part of her will always be at the school gate that first day, watching her little boy go off into the world without her and already missing him. Parenthood is odd that way: you're meant to bring them up so they can be capable and independent, but all you want to do is keep them close and never let anything bad happen to them. Maybe that's why Terry goes off on his skateboard – because he knows that she wants to keep an eye on him all the time. Or maybe he does it because he wants her to worry about him, because being a kid is odd too.

Lorraine remembers thinking Rose was the worst in the world for wanting to know where she was going and what she was doing, but when her mother stopped asking – sick, no doubt, of Lorraine brushing her off – she missed it. She still misses it. Which is why she loves the idea of Rose staying a while longer. It's been so nice having her around, and she's let herself be mothered again while she still tries to wrangle her own two.

'Thanks, sweetie,' she says as Terry returns.

'Anything else I can do?' he asks and she almost faints from the shock. But she gets herself together because this is an opportunity that may never be repeated.

'How do you feel about peeling potatoes?'

He grins then it's gone too quickly. 'I can probably handle that,' he mumbles.

'I'll just check on your grandmothers and see if they need anything,' she says.

Mainly she wants to jump up and down with glee because her son isn't trying to run away from her, and she doesn't want to do it in front of him.

'How're you going?' she says as she enters the living room and sees them hovered over the coffee table with their cards.

The sight of these two being companions still gives her pause, although her mother explained it to her the other day. 'We both love the boys,' she said. 'It's pretty simple.'

Why couldn't you have worked that out years ago, Lorraine wanted to ask, because there'd been plenty of Christmas lunches and kiddie birthdays that were a little uncomfortable. Still, she needs to make herself be glad they've sorted it out, especially since they're under one roof.

'We're fine, love,' Rose says, beaming.

'I am enjoying this game.' Cora smiles nervously, almost as if she's waiting to see how Lorraine reacts.

'That's great, Cora,' she says. 'I'm just about to get dinner ready. Terry's helping me.'

The grandmothers glance at each other, then Rose beams again. 'Wonderful,' she says. 'Anything I can do to help?'

Simon appears just then with a book under his arm.

'You could help Simon with his reading homework,' Lorraine says.

'My pleasure,' Rose says, and she puts down the cards and shifts over on the couch. 'Simon, sit here, darling.'

As her youngest son sits next to one grandmother, and the other smiles as if it's the cutest thing she's ever seen, and her eldest son is in the kitchen preparing to peel potatoes, Lorraine can't help but feel that something is wrong. This household never runs so smoothly.

And it probably never will again if Mike comes back. Which is okay, she thinks. In fact, whichever way it turns out is okay. She's had enough change over the past few months to feel like a human washing machine and she's survived it. Some days she's even enjoyed it. What she's learnt is that she just has to show up each morning and do her best, and if she can laugh and tell people she loves them, even better.

'I'll give you a yell when we're close,' she says to the grandmothers before turning to go back into the kitchen.

There she finds Terry, so tall now he needs to stoop over the bench, already peeling. She didn't even have to get the potatoes and the peeler out for him. That, out of everything, is enough to make her feel like she could unravel but it's pathetic to start crying over something so small, so she pulls herself together and gets the chops out of the fridge.

APRIL 1988

AUSTRALIAN
BLUEBELL

CHAPTER FIFTY-NINE

The letter came first – no stamp, so it had been hand delivered. Then there was a knock on the door just as Elizabeth was trying to get out of it to drop off Charlie at a swimming lesson. A strange man in a suit, smiling toothily, his hair layered and slicked back.

'G'day,' he said as she pulled the door open a fraction, not willing to open it wide to someone she didn't know. 'I'm John Patterson. I dropped off a letter recently.'

His name was why Elizabeth had thrown the letter out straightaway. It seemed too eerie that a man named John wanted to encourage her to sell the house that her Jon had been so keen to buy.

That day on her doorstep he reiterated what was in the letter: that he was a real estate agent who had a buyer *very* interested in her house. 'It's a large block,' he explained, glancing towards the garden side of the house. 'Not many of them around in this area.'

Elizabeth wanted to tell him that she didn't care and that she wasn't interested . . . but ever since Charlie's birthday party she's had the strangest, strongest feeling that her business with the house and its garden might be complete. She has brought the garden back to life with the help of her friends, and she isn't sure what more can be done to it or for it. She no longer needs to prove anything to Jon or to herself. Still, if she is to leave she wants to do it on her own terms.

Then the agent told her how much the prospective buyer was willing to pay. It was far more than Elizabeth had thought she might receive. Enough for her to pay off the mortgage in one fell swoop and have money left over. That's when the house started to seem as Jon had intended, what he'd told her as he was dying: financial security for her and Charlie, and she should do whatever she wanted with it.

She told her parents, and while they were subdued – as is their wont with any big news – she could tell they were pleased for her.

'He's making it easy for you, isn't he,' her father said, and Elizabeth couldn't disagree.

Yet she hasn't completely made up her mind. Some afternoons when she sits in Jon's garden she feels like she could never leave, because she would be leaving him behind for good. Then a voice pops up in her head, telling her that perhaps that would be for the best. She has a life to live; she needs to move forwards.

Yet she's hesitated – because of the garden, not because of Jon. The garden is what brought the Sunshine Gardening Society into her life and she feels as though she owes the ladies some loyalty. Which is why she has brought the decision to them on this Saturday morning as they carry out maintenance work in a garden in Tewantin.

Elizabeth arranges to work alongside Lorraine so she's the first person she can tell.

'Reallllly?' is Lorraine's response, then she tilts her head like an enquiring pup. 'That's interesting. Are you thinking about it?'

'I am.' Elizabeth pulls up a clod of dirt that flies into her face.

'Brush it off,' Lorraine commands.

'Hm?'

'Don't let that dirt get in your nose and eyes. You don't know what's in it. All sorts of bugs can come out of the soil.' Lorraine twinkles her gloved fingers. 'That's why we wear these.'

'Oh.' Elizabeth brushes off as much as she can and Lorraine does the rest.

'Hey, Cyn,' Lorraine calls. 'Liz is going to sell the house.'

'I haven't decided yet!' Elizabeth says, slightly panicked. She doesn't want the news announced before she's ready, although she could have guessed Lorraine would say something – and perhaps she wanted her to.

Cynthia shuffles across, then sits and crosses her legs like she's settling in for a chat.

'That lovely house?' she says. 'Why?'

'I know it's lovely,' Elizabeth says quickly. 'It's nothing to do with the house itself.'

Cynthia frowns.

'I mean,' Elizabeth adds, 'the house is perfectly functional and we like living in it. And the garden – I so appreciate it. But . . .' She pauses and closes her eyes, hoping that when she just says it straight they'll understand. 'But it feels like Jon's house,' she says, her eyes open again. 'He chose it. He loved it. I have loved it too. It's not that.'

Now she worries that she's going to sound brutal, like she's moved on too quickly. Should she even be concerned about that? These aren't people who knew Jon.

'It's that you want to move on with your life,' Cynthia says. 'Because it's *your* life, not his.'

There's a hint of sadness around her eyes then it's gone, and Elizabeth is grateful she's been saved having to give an explanation.

'Makes sense,' says Lorraine. 'What do you reckon, Kath?'

Kathy has now joined them, glancing enquiringly from one to the other. 'About what?'

'Liz is planning to sell the house.'

'Oh.' Kathy's face falls.

'Are you thinking about the garden?' Cynthia asks.

'Maybe.' Kathy looks sheepish.

'We did a job, that's all,' Cynthia says. 'It's always been Elizabeth's to do with as she wishes.'

'I know.' Kathy shrugs. 'It just seems . . . sad, I guess. Sorry, Elizabeth – that probably sounds mean.'

It's nothing Elizabeth hasn't thought herself, except she's past it now. So past it that the other morning, just before she woke – which is when she always has the most intense dreams – she dreamt she was flying. Soaring, actually. She was over Brisbane then the Sunshine Coast, over rivers and beaches. While she was flying she felt she could go anywhere and do anything, and it was so thrilling that she cried when she woke because her waking life doesn't feel that free. Not that she'll share that with the others because they'll probably think her a little odd. But it planted the idea in her head that she could, one day, be that free. That she could go wherever she wants to, if only she's unencumbered by the worries that weigh her down. Like the house, because it feels like it is the entire weight of her past, and she now believes that she deserves to look to the future.

'It's not mean,' she replies to Kathy. 'Because you're right, it is sad. The whole situation is sad. But the house and the garden have served their purpose and Charlie and I need to leave them behind. It's just the two of us now. We need to make a new home that can be ours alone.'

'That makes sense,' Kathy says.

'Can we have a send-off party?' Lorraine says, waggling her eyebrows.

'I'm sure we can,' Elizabeth says, and as she laughs she can hear air in it. Light. Happiness, maybe.

'So is it already on the market?' Cynthia asks.

'No, but an agent has approached me saying someone wants to buy.'

'They always say that,' Lorraine says with a snort. 'That's to get you to list it.'

Elizabeth feels a twinge of disappointment in herself for being so gullible. But even if it turns out to be true, the agent did something for her by forcing her to consider the possibility of leaving. Now the next question she has for herself is whether she leaves the area altogether. Her old life is in Brisbane. Jon's family is there too, and it could be time for them to see Charlie more, as much as she wishes she didn't have to deal with them. And if her parents stay put, well, they're not too far away.

She has options. These haven't seemed possible – let alone available – to her for a very long time.

'We'll see,' is what she says to Lorraine. 'And now I'd better get working before Shirl says something.'

'Oops,' Lorraine says. 'Too late.'

Shirl is almost upon them, squinting. 'What are you talking about?' she says.

'Liz is thinking of selling the house,' Lorraine tells her.

'What?' Shirl squawks. 'Barb! *Barb!*'

'Mm?' Barb lifts her head from her stooped position.

'Liz is going to sell the house.' Shirl whips her head back and narrows her eyes further.

'I'm only thinking about it!' Elizabeth protests, because it's technically true.

'Nah.' Shirl presses her lips together. 'You've decided.' She looks crestfallen. 'I was hoping to see another spring in that garden.'

She sighs and Elizabeth feels terrible. She really hadn't considered that some of the others might put up resistance to her selling.

'Still,' Shirl says, her tone matter-of-fact, 'it's a house. And a garden. Not an arm or a leg. You have to take arms and legs with you, right? Houses and gardens can be left. Besides . . .' She glances towards Barb. 'Maybe we can ask whoever buys it if they mind us doing a bit of work. Just so we can keep an eye on the place.'

'I'm sure they won't,' Elizabeth says, relieved that the resolution appears to be so neat.

'We won't make you come along.' Shirl pats her on the shoulder. 'You need to fly free.'

Elizabeth starts, wondering if Shirl knows about her dream. Except she couldn't. Could she?

'Come on, then,' Shirl says. 'Weeds are going to waste.'

Lorraine waggles her gloved fingers at Elizabeth, who nods and crouches down next to her, a feeling of bittersweet relief washing over her.

CHAPTER SIXTY

As much as Cynthia has resisted the word 'grandmother' she has embraced grandmotherhood. After she turned forty Odette teased her that maybe, finally, she could be called Granny, but Cynthia's response was to say that the issue is moot until Jordan learns to talk, and she'll make up her mind then.

Not that she has alternatives in mind. Her maternal grandmother had been Nana and Wilfred's mother was Grand-mère. She wasn't French but she wished she was, so she tried to arrange her world accordingly – a somewhat confusing state of affairs for Cynthia and her brother given she often spoke to them in French, a language they didn't understand.

Pat, on the other hand, loves being referred to as Pa, talking to Jordan in a baby voice and telling him 'Pa loves you'. Which is sweet, Cynthia has to admit, but given she and Pat are the same age she wishes he would reconsider.

This afternoon, Pat is sitting on a rug in Wilfred's garden, dangling a small toy over the baby, provoking giggles. It's a scene that makes Cynthia pleased and resentful all at once as she observes it from her own spot on the lawn.

'I don't remember you being this interested in Odette when she was a baby,' she says. He really only became engaged once Odette could walk.

She's held in this particular observation for a while but she's growing tired of being polite about it, probably because Odette keeps going on about how 'great' Pat is with the baby and how he's such a 'cool grandpa'. When Pat's eyes meet hers, though, she can see that her arrow has found its mark and she feels slightly ashamed. The past could have been left in the past. Couldn't it?

'Yeah,' he says. 'I was more interested in waves when she was tiny.' He looks away then back to her. 'I'm sorry.'

It's the apology she's waited years for but it doesn't feel like a victory. Instead she feels sad that Odette missed out on the affection her father is showing her son. And, since he's opened the door to it, she also feels like making a point.

'You made it hard for me,' she says. 'You were always off at dawn, right when she was waking up. Gone for hours.'

'I was young,' he says, as if that's the get-out-of-jail-free card.

'And what was I?' she snaps.

His mouth opens slightly and she can see, with awful clarity, that he has not once stopped to consider this. Even though she left him. No doubt he thought her leaving was just something that happened to him rather than taking any time to examine his role in it. No time like the present, then.

'You were her mother,' he says softly. 'I didn't . . .'

'You didn't think I needed to exist outside of that.' Cynthia clenches her jaw. 'Except for when *you* wanted things from me.'

She remembers being so tired from waking up during the night to feed Odette, and spending the days cleaning, washing, cooking, then he'd want her to be his lover and never understood how she simply didn't have the energy. Once she tried to explain that if he just helped her more she'd have more enthusiasm for him, but he'd looked at her as if she'd asked him to pole vault to the moon. It was hard – too hard, in the end – to sustain interest in him when he didn't seem to have any in her. He adored Odette, but mainly he wanted to be what he was, which was a young man, and didn't much care – or didn't seem to – that she was a young woman and wanted to be that too. Odette was a child they both wanted but only one of them took responsibility for her.

'Yes,' Pat says, and she's been so lost in her anger at the him of twenty years ago that she's not sure if he's really speaking to her now. 'I wasn't fair on you,' he goes on. 'On us. I was . . .' He sighs heavily. 'Selfish.'

'*Quelle surprise*,' she says drily, and it's as if Grand-mère has resurrected herself. It's not the first time Cynthia has heard phrases her mother or grandmothers used to say pop out of her mouth; Jordan's arrival has opened some kind of vortex to the past that is both unsettling and reassuring.

'Huh?' Pat frowns.

'Don't worry about it, Patrick,' Cynthia says. 'Don't worry about anything.'

Jordan makes some of his cute baby noises and Pat's face relaxes into a smile.

'I was an idiot,' he says as he tickles the tiny tummy, 'to think surfing was more fun than this.'

As he looks up she can see sadness in his eyes. Her first inclination is to tell him to grow up; her second is to realise that maybe that's what he's doing. And her third is to wonder how long she can hold on to this resentment she's been carrying for two decades, given it's already propelled her away from this place and to another hemisphere, from one marriage to a silly love affair to a badly chosen second marriage.

At least that second marriage has now been officially dissolved. The settlement has come through and Cynthia can – without letting on to anyone else, because it's none of their business – not worry about money for the foreseeable future. Her latest ex, Max – or, rather, his lawyer – had the good sense to realise that Cynthia had, as her lawyer said, contributed considerably to his business and that was worth something. She was worth something.

Maybe that's what Cynthia has been trying to establish all along. Becoming a mother so young locked her into one definition of being – bestowed on her by others – and she has struggled ever since to find out who she is. That could be a large part of her resistance to being called a grandmother. Because she is many other things: a friend and a daughter, a gardener now, a woman with dreams of creating beauty who is still searching for the right outlet for them. A reader, a crossword solver, a cook, a dancer. All those things and, yes, a grandmother too. It may be all right, she thinks, to allow herself to be called that if she can feel she truly embodies all those other titles too.

And that's part of why she's here, in the place she loves more than any other: to rediscover who she was before it all changed. That may be the work of a lifetime, but at least she's started on it.

'Surfing is fun too,' she says, because it is – she used to surf as a teenager, but deemed it too risky once Odette arrived, even if Pat never did. 'But once responsibilities turn up, fun has to be managed around them. They're not managed around it. That's boring, I know, but that's adulthood. I didn't get a choice in that and you shouldn't have had one either.' She pauses to consider how to phrase what she needs to say. 'You let us both down.'

'I did,' he concedes quickly. 'And I paid for it.'

That gets her colour up. 'Do you expect me to feel sorry for you? I gave it a few years – and I loved you, Pat. I never stopped. But I had to do something for me. I had to be with someone who could *see me*. You treated me as your servant and Odette as an afterthought. I was still a person. *A woman.*'

There. That's the concise version of what she's always wanted to say to him. At the time she left she didn't bother because she knew he wouldn't understand.

His cheeks are red and he's pressing his lips together; whether from anger or sadness she doesn't know.

'I don't expect that,' he says after a minute or so has passed. 'I felt sorry enough for myself. But I didn't deserve to.'

Jordan starts to cry and Pat picks him up, cradling him in the crook of his elbow the way the baby likes.

'I wish we could start again,' he says, and as his eyes meet hers she sees the kind young man she fell in love with. 'I would do things so differently.'

'And maybe I would too,' she replies, but she doesn't mean it in the way he probably thinks she does.

'Is there . . . ?' He glances away.

She can guess what he was going to ask: *Is there any chance for us?* So she decides to answer him.

'I don't know, Pat,' she says softly. 'Why don't we just try getting along first?'

He nods and looks down at the baby, his face transforming as he shows himself to be as besotted with Jordan as Cynthia is.

If she and Pat are to find a way back to each other, it will be because of this baby, and the paradox is not lost on her because it was their own baby who sent them off in different directions. That's life, though, full of bad timing and good, missed chances and opportunities taken, coincidences and deliberation. It can all seem like it was meant to be when we try to make sense of it, but maybe none of it is. Maybe it's just humans floundering away in confusion, making the best of each day. Which in itself is worthy of recognition.

'Would you like to come for a walk?' Pat asks her. 'I think Jordan's getting restless. And you know how he likes the pram.'

She smiles. 'Sure. Let's promenade.'

He walks over and offers her his hand to help her up from the grass. She takes it.

CHAPTER SIXTY-ONE

When Cynthia suggested that they walk into the national park as far as Alexandria Bay, Lorraine was tempted to tell her to get stuffed. What is she, a marathon runner? It's hard enough doing all the squatting for the gardening let alone going on a walk that will take them *at least* an hour return to Cynthia's place. And that's walking at a Cynthia pace. Lorraine is going to need to stop for a rest every now and again. Not that she thinks she's too unfit, because she runs around after the kids and does the housework – she read somewhere that vacuuming can really burn off the calories. There's a difference, though, between folding washing and going on a long walk.

'Can't we just walk on the beach?' she countered.

'No,' came the answer, and long experience has taught her that Cynthia's word is final.

Which is usually okay because Cynthia tends to have good ideas – like joining the Sunshine Gardening Society. Lorraine doesn't know what she'd have done without it, especially lately with all the worrying she's been doing. At least when she's there on a weekend she can focus on their work and have a bit of chitchat with the others, and she doesn't have to be anywhere else or do anything else. It's great. She has a few hours of not wondering if she'll ever forgive Mike, or if her mother and Cora are going to suddenly remember that they don't like each other very much and stop their cosy games of gin rummy and taking their turns with issues of *The Australian Women's Weekly*. Last week she caught them comparing cake recipes.

Cynthia thinks it's hilarious that they're getting along so well, because Lorraine had told her about the cold war that came before it. But Lorraine isn't finding it so funny because now she can't complain to Rose about Cora, and she doesn't really want to put all of her complaining onto Cynthia. Although maybe Cynthia wouldn't mind.

'Don't you have better shoes?' Cynthia says as Lorraine arrives at her house so they can set off from there.

Lorraine looks down at her old Volleys with mismatched laces. 'No. What's wrong with them?'

'They don't look very sturdy.'

'They'll do. They have to.' Lorraine makes a face at her.

'All right, don't get cross,' Cynthia says. 'I have only your feet's interests in mind.'

Lorraine shrugs. 'It's a dirt track, isn't it? Not too tough on feet.'

Cynthia raises an eyebrow. 'I suppose not.'

They set off, down the hill towards the entrance to the park and past the usual collection of vans and utes belonging to surfers who are already in the water off First Point or even deeper in the park at Tea Tree or Granite Bay.

Lorraine grew up around surfers but she was never tempted to try it. Actually, not true: she was, but the boys at school all said surfing wasn't for girls and she believed them. Then Pam Burridge started to win titles and she realised she'd been duped. She mentioned to Elizabeth recently that she had wanted to learn to surf and Elizabeth asked why she didn't. Lorraine had no good answer to that, other than fear. Of looking stupid not of hurting herself. Or maybe they're the same thing.

She sniffs as they pass a panel van. 'Bit early for that, isn't it?' she mutters to Cynthia.

'What?'

'Gangajang.'

'What?' Cynthia laughs.

'You know . . .' Lorraine looks around to see if anyone might be listening. 'Marijuana.'

'Why do you call it that?'

'Mike does.'

'Does he . . . ?' Cynthia wrinkles her nose.

'No. Can't hang that on him. His mates do, though.'

Cynthia nods and they walk a few steps in silence.

'Have you seen him lately?' she asks.

'He pops around to see the kids and Cora. Keeps asking when I'm taking him back.' Lorraine sighs. 'Sometimes he brings me chocolates. The other day it was a cake. He's wearing me down.'

'Do you want him to?'

'I don't know.' She huffs. 'I miss him sometimes.'

'That's to be expected.'

A jogger passes them, and Lorraine catches a whiff of BO and remembers the parts about men she *doesn't* like.

'Try some deodorant!' she calls and the jogger looks back and gives her a wink. Big hairy bloke. Bit like Mike . . . Oh yeah, she misses him.

'Did you ever miss Pat?' she asks Cynthia, keen to move on from thinking about Mike.

'Yes,' Cynthia says, and Lorraine is surprised because in the letters they exchanged, before everything petered off, Cynthia never mentioned it. Although why would she? By then she was shacked up with the surfer in California.

'So why did you . . .' Lorraine trails off because there's no good way to say 'dump him'.

'I missed myself more,' Cynthia replies and Lorraine thinks that's as good an answer as any.

'Pat's life kept going the way it was before Odette was born,' Cynthia goes on. 'Mine didn't. And I didn't expect it to be the

384

same – but I also didn't expect *his* to be the same. He didn't even try to adjust to help me. And I was just . . . overtaken.' She turns her head briefly towards Lorraine. 'I'm sure you remember what that's like.'

'Yeah, but I had my mum to help. And . . .' Lorraine doesn't really want to admit the next part. 'Cora was pretty good too. I don't think your mum was around as much.'

Cynthia's mouth turns down. 'It was more that I felt like she didn't approve of me having a baby at that age and she didn't try to understand. She loved Odette – it was hard not to. But I felt like she didn't love me any more.'

Another jogger goes past and this time there's no BO, which is a relief, but he kicks up some dirt that hits Lorraine in the calves. She *knew* this walk was a bad idea.

'How much further?' she mutters, and Cynthia laughs.

'We've just started!'

'Oh. Right.'

Lorraine tries to make the best of it by looking to her left, at the ocean and the stretch of Noosa's Main Beach, with rolling waves that are so perfect it's like they were ordered out of a catalogue.

'I enjoy walking,' Cynthia says, 'but I really wanted to chat to you about something.'

She sounds so serious that Lorraine scans her memory for a clue: is Cynthia mad at her after all because Pat lent Mike money? Or did she do something in high school that Cynthia's still worried about? Or maybe she did something silly last weekend while gardening. That's entirely possible.

'I want to buy Elizabeth's house,' Cynthia says.

Well, that makes Lorraine stop and she hears swearing behind her. Another bloody jogger. Don't get so close, mate, if you don't like surprise stops!

'Why?' Lorraine asks and continues walking.

'She's going to sell it regardless, by the sound of it,' Cynthia says. 'And we put all that work into the garden. I would hate for it to be destroyed.'

Lorraine can't argue with that logic, but she also feels a twinge of protectiveness towards Elizabeth – would she feel weird about Cynthia buying her house? Can Cynthia even afford it? They don't talk about money unless it's Lorraine's, and because Cynthia's been living with Wilfred Lorraine just thought she couldn't afford anywhere else.

'And thanks to my divorce settlement,' Cynthia continues, 'I can pay cash for it.'

Lorraine lets out a sigh of relief – so that's it!

Cynthia laughs. 'You thought I didn't have the money, didn't you?'

'Well . . .' Lorraine shrugs.

'I've been living with Papa because I wasn't sure if I was going to stay.'

That makes Lorraine stop again, except this time she pulls to the side to do it. Just in case.

'So you were planning to go again?'

She puts her hands on her hips because this makes her cross, it really does. Cynthia has been getting all involved in life around here, with the gardening and the chatting and whatnot. A person could presume she was staying for good. A person like Lorraine.

'Not planning,' Cynthia says. 'I just didn't know. Odette might have really wanted to get rid of me.'

Lorraine drops her hands and lifts her chin. 'I'll accept it.'

'Oh – good.' Cynthia laughs. 'I was living and dying on your approval.'

'Shut up,' Lorraine says but she nudges her gently. 'If you're staying put that's going to make my day. Month. Year. Possibly my life.' She glances sideways. 'I know my kids love me and Mum loves me, but they don't know all the bad stuff the way you do. And you stick around.'

'The bad stuff is just life, Loz.' Cynthia wraps an arm around her and kisses her cheek. 'And so is the good. And all of your stuff is interesting to me.'

Lorraine feels a little emotional, which is embarrassing when you're in a public place, but no one's looking so she lets a couple of tears roll down her cheeks.

'Great,' she says. 'Because Simon has silkworms and I want to tell you about them. And Mum and Cora want to take the boys to Expo 88 and I'm scared they'll get lost in Brisbane.'

Cynthia laughs and it's big and hearty, which makes Lorraine smile long enough to forget that they still have about forty-five minutes left of this walk.

MAY 1988

SWEET WATTLE

CHAPTER SIXTY-TWO

For all the Saturdays and the occasional Sunday they've spent together, this is the first time Elizabeth and Cynthia have had a proper conversation – and it feels apt that it's about the house, and its garden, that caused them to meet in the first place.

Cynthia went about the purchase in the appropriate way, contacting the real estate agent with whom Elizabeth had decided to list the house, since he was so firm about the prospects of sale. She didn't ever find out if there really was a potential buyer when he approached her, but it didn't matter, because the approach itself helped her make up her mind: it was time to find a place that was just for her and Charlie.

Her parents said that if necessary she and Charlie can stay with them while she looks for a new home, whether that's to buy or to rent. Elizabeth has toyed with the idea of returning to Brisbane, although as winter starts to lightly touch the Sunshine Coast, changing it only so as to enhance it, she thinks, the prospect of returning to a city where she may lose this connection with the natural world has less and less appeal.

That's something she's realised since she moved here, and more since she's been spending time close to the bush and the gardens of this area: she is not as much of an urbanite – even a suburbanite – as she thought. As her mood has waxed and waned over the past year or so, she has increasingly found that the remedy is to be in nature. Some days when she needs a lift she simply sits in the garden for ten minutes and she feels better. This is nothing that anyone has prescribed for her; it's something she has discovered, but she has wondered why more people don't know about it.

'You're looking well,' Doctor Lopes said to her the other day, and she told him it was because she'd been spending more time with trees and flowers.

He'd looked at her quizzically. 'I haven't heard of that before.'

'Maybe no one's mentioned it,' she replied. 'Because it's not an official medical treatment. But it works. Or it's worked for me.'

'Do you have a favourite spot?' he asked, and she was about to say 'Jon's garden' when she realised that it wasn't his any more. It was hers and Charlie's.

'Our garden,' she said.

'I'd like to see this garden,' he'd said with a slight smile. 'Since it's such a tonic.'

'You'll have to be quick,' she said, 'because I'm selling the house.'

That was the moment at which she knew she'd made up her mind.

So when the real estate agent called and said he had a real potential buyer, she was interested. Then when Cynthia told her it was her, she felt so relieved she wondered what kind of worry she'd been holding onto.

She asked Cynthia to come over and have a proper look at the house, like any prospective buyer would want to do, because she doesn't want to take Cynthia for granted just because she knows the house already. The agent would no doubt have preferred to be there, but their friendship entitles Cynthia to a private showing.

'I could have come straight to you, I suppose,' Cynthia says as they sit in the living room looking out onto the garden. 'But having the agent involved means that if there are other interested parties you will receive the price you should.'

'I don't know if there are,' Elizabeth says. 'I appreciate you doing that, though.'

Cynthia smiles. 'This is a business transaction, Elizabeth. It needs to be done fairly. So I don't want you thinking I need to be treated differently.' She turns up her palms. 'Apart from today's visit, obviously.'

'It would mean a lot if the house goes to you. I'd feel like . . .'

Her gaze drifts to the garden, to the ordered beds, to the lavender bushes in pots closer to the glass doors that were Cynthia's suggestion, actually, over Shirl's loud protests. The lawn is neatly mown; Elizabeth has been paying a local lad to do it each couple of weeks because the humidity makes it grow quickly. She hopes Cynthia will keep him on.

'I'd feel like it will be taken care of,' she concludes.

'I'd make sure of that,' Cynthia says. 'Although I plan to ask Odette if she'd like to move in too. The house is big enough, and Jordan will enjoy that lawn once he starts crawling. So while I'll definitely take care of it, it may not be kept as neatly as it is now.'

Elizabeth smiles sheepishly. 'It's only neat because I made Charlie pack away his toys this morning.' The place is usually strewn with schoolbooks and LEGO and anything else Charlie finds of interest.

'I'd love to think another little boy will grow up here,' she continues.

She's tempted to ask if Jordan's father will also be living here but it's none of her business. Cynthia only mentioned him around the time of the birth, and she hasn't heard of him living at Cynthia's father's. Initially Elizabeth found herself starting to judge this: that Odette would be a single mother, and how Jordan really needed a father. Then she remembered her own circumstances. It's not for her to say that Odette has any more choice over being on her own than she does. For all she knows Jordan's father has disappeared.

'And I'd love to think that you and Charlie will visit,' Cynthia says. 'If you wouldn't find that odd.'

'That would be wonderful,' Elizabeth says, even if she doesn't know that it will happen. Once she's left here – regardless of where she moves to – she may wish to seal it up in her memory.

After Jon died she was encouraged to 'talk about it'. One of her Brisbane friends is very keen on seeing psychiatrists and thought Elizabeth should have one. The thing is, though, Elizabeth doesn't believe that talking about it is for everyone.

Her father served in New Guinea in World War II. She knows he was shot at; she knows he survived. That's all she knows. She believes it's all her mother knows. Her psychiatry-mad friend once opined that Elizabeth's father undoubtedly had shell shock and that's why he never mentioned the war, but Elizabeth's view has always been different: he simply doesn't want to talk about it. That may be because it's how he manages to live with the memories so he can be a good husband and father, and he has certainly been both. Or it may be that he doesn't even like to think about it.

If a psychiatrist were to ask her father to lie on a couch, she wonders what he or she would make of the man – would he be someone avoiding reality, or someone who is so keen to live in reality that he doesn't wish to live in the past? Is he an example of a man who isn't coping just because he won't 'talk about it' or, rather, as she believes, a man who shows every day that he is coping?

Her conclusion about her own experience – based on what she has seen of her father's – is that when faced with a traumatic event each person has to manage the way that works best for her or him. If Elizabeth is getting out of bed each day, feeding her son, getting him to school, going to work, *functioning*; if she has moments of joy and wonder as well as sadness, isn't that just what it means to be alive? So many people have terrible things happen to them. They walk around and no one knows, because the victory over those terrible things is the walking around. It's the showing up, the being present for people and in places. It's not for anyone else to say that this is the wrong method, that 'talking about it' is preferred. And, for that matter, why should there be a preference at all? Sadness and tragedy are part of the gamble of being alive, and everyone rolls their dice differently.

That's why she thinks she won't ever come back to this house. Which is not to say she wouldn't want to see Cynthia socially – she would. They'll just have to meet on neutral ground.

'So,' Cynthia says, gazing around the room, 'I don't really need a tour to be convinced of the value of this place, but let's do one anyway. Then I'll drive straight to the agent and put in my offer.'

Elizabeth knows she's been given a nudge because she was probably sitting there in silence. That happens sometimes – in lieu of talking. Not that Cynthia seems to mind. When you spend hours next to someone in a garden without speaking, it makes other non-verbal interactions easier.

Elizabeth gets to her feet. 'Let's start with the bedrooms.'

'After you,' Cynthia says, gesturing for Elizabeth to lead.

CHAPTER SIXTY-THREE

The day is outrageously bright and sparkling, as Kathy can see when she looks out of the restaurant's glass front to the river. A yacht goes past with two men on it clad in T-shirts and shorts; they're laughing and pointing at something on the other side of the river, and Kathy wishes she could be out there with them, soaking up the day.

Late autumn in Melbourne involves ominous portents of winter, but here it's still weather for light clothing and outdoor activities, and she doesn't know that she'll ever get used to it – in a good way. In a grateful way. Although she is a born-and-bred Melburnian Kathy knows she can't go back to the cold and the grey; to winters when a football match is the only thing worth leaving home for, other than work; where the advent of springtime means that everyone emerges and turns their faces to the sun, like it's a god. And it is, of sorts – one she's taken to worshipping now she lives on the Sunshine Coast.

The real estate agent called her yesterday to ask if she's staying on. Her lease was up a while ago and she's been going month to month, but the owner wants to know if she's thinking of leaving anytime soon because they might do a new coat of paint and some other maintenance. It made Kathy realise that she hasn't thought about the future because she's been living so much in the present.

That also means, of course, that she hasn't been thinking about the past. Jemima hasn't crossed her mind in weeks. She's been free; freer than she's felt in . . . well, ever. Since she was a young woman Kathy's worried about other people – what they think of her, what she can do to help them, where she fits in the world in relation to them. Since moving to Noosa she's been able to concentrate on the things she needs to do each day and not worry about anything or anyone else. And it's glorious. Stress has fallen out of her life since she did something that was in her own best interest, and that's a lifestyle she intends to continue.

So she has something to tell the real estate agent – and Hans too, since when she started the job she said she wasn't sure how long she'd be here. He'd been relaxed about it; pleased, he said, to have someone with her experience. It would be nice, though, to give him some certainty.

As Kathy watches the river for a minute more, enjoying the spectacle of birds and humans and boats on the waterway, she can hear the chefs chatting loudly as they do their prep for what looks to be a fully booked lunch service.

'It's a beautiful day,' Hans says from behind her. 'We are lucky to have such a view.'

'We really are,' Kathy says as she turns around. She checks her watch. 'I'm dawdling, sorry – patrons will be arriving soon.'

'It's fine. We are ready.'

He smiles so kindly at her – as he always does – that Kathy wants to ask why. Certainly she's never done anything special to deserve it; she's been a fairly standard employee. No above-and-beyond. Just turning up on time, doing her job. Or maybe that's so rare these days that he thinks she's the bee's knees.

'But I do have a question about next week,' he says, indicating that they should walk to the front desk. 'We have two staff taking two days off. I do not expect you to cover all of their shifts, but if you are able to cover some I would appreciate it.'

'Sure,' Kathy says, because all the freedom she has now also means she's available to cover people's shifts. Extra money doesn't hurt.

'And while we're talking about shifts,' she goes on, 'I should mention that I'm, ah . . .'

She was about to just blurt it out, that she's staying, but it feels momentous all of a sudden. It's a commitment. To this area. To herself. All these years – this lifetime – of letting things happen to her and never really deciding what she wants, and here she is in her fifties doing it and it feels both too late and too early. Like she's finally growing up. Her mother used to say that when she was seventy she still felt thirty; Kathy feels like she's nineteen or something, finally figuring out what she wants to study at uni. Except this uni is her life. And really, it's about time she made some decisions. That's what adults do.

'I know when I started here,' she continues, 'I said it might be temporary.'

Hans looks amused. 'It has been a long temporary.'

'I know.' She laughs. 'Very long. And now it's permanent. I'm not going back to Melbourne. I'm staying up here.'

'Really?' He looks delighted. 'That is wonderful news. Because I need another manager here and I was hoping to offer it to you.'

'Another manager?' She didn't think anyone had resigned.

'We will be starting dinner service more nights of the week,' he explains. 'Although the position won't necessarily be for those sittings. It's just that another manager will be required. We can talk, yes? Perhaps after service today?'

'Sure.' Kathy blinks, slightly stunned at this news – she wasn't expecting her announcement to lead to a better job prospect.

'And you can also tell me about your parks people,' Hans says. 'The Sunshine Gardening Society?'

She's told him a little about the others and their work, but not enough for her to feel like it isn't still a bit of a secret society, because she quite likes that idea.

'No – the parks . . . association? Is that it?'

'Oh, yes.'

His question makes her think about something she's been contemplating for a little while, related to the Gardening Society as well as the Parks Association. Without her completely realising it, she's developed more than an interest in the local environment. It's become almost a second job.

It took Michelle to point it out, the other night when they had one of their regular phone calls. 'Mum, you're obsessed,' she said. 'If you're that into it, why don't you get a job doing it or something?'

That got Kathy thinking. And now she needs to tell Hans of the intention she's formed.

'About that,' she goes on. 'There's something that may affect which shifts I take.'

'Oh?' He frowns.

'I'm thinking of running for council,' she says quickly, not sure what he'll make of the idea.

Now that she's a permanent resident it has occurred to her that she could commit to the area in other ways. She can see that one encounter with a property developer in a park has started a cascade of notions: to get more involved in protecting the local land, which means staying in Noosa, which means telling Hans she wants to be permanent. She fully intends to maintain her commitment to the Sunshine Gardening Society, and maybe – if the conditions are right – see what else she can do to preserve the land she's grown to love.

An outsider – someone who knows bare details of her life – might think she's a middle-aged woman meddling in other people's business because her children have grown up and she doesn't have much else in her life. That might all be true. Even if it is, her decisions now are sincere and valid: she wants to stay because this place makes her happy, and so do its people, and its sand and waves and trees and – yes, Shirl – its native plants.

When Kathy moved here, happiness wasn't in the plan. She was escaping, pure and simple, and she never kidded herself about that. Happiness is a by-product and a bonus and, now, a powerful motivation to remain here.

She's been alive long enough to know that happiness isn't permanent. There will be hard days caused by reasons she doesn't even know yet. But, gee, the other days are so good. When the sun shines on her back while she's bent over a garden bed, new friends chatting around her and a sense of purpose in her veins, or bent over a canvas with a brush in her hand and a picture in her mind, there's nothing better.

'What a wonderful idea,' Hans says. 'I think the council would be very lucky to have you.' He smiles at her in such a way that it seems like a benediction, and she'll take it.

'I don't want it to muck up anything here, though,' she says.

'Not to worry. We will talk about it.' He checks his watch. 'Now, let us prepare ourselves for hungry people.'

Kathy smiles her agreement and glances around the restaurant – one last check that everything is in place. And it is.

CHAPTER SIXTY-FOUR

As Elizabeth turns on the kettle and waits for Olive to join her for lunch, she starts to think about the million and one things to check and organise and tick off before she leaves the house. It's been years since she moved, and she and Jon didn't seem to have as much stuff together as Charlie alone has accumulated in his short life. So many books, so many toys; baby clothes that she should really have thrown out except for a while she hoped she'd use them again. Part of her still hopes that, although she has no idea how it would happen. She has no thoughts of marrying again let alone bearing the children of a man other than Jon.

Although Reverend Willoughby said something interesting the other day after the service.

'You're looking well,' was how he started the conversation. 'Much better than I've seen you in . . . years. I don't mean that unkindly.'

'I don't take it that way,' she said, and meant it.

'And I hear you're moving.'

'I am. Well, I'm selling. The garden is looking just the way Jon wanted it. I guess I have you to thank for that, for sending Shirl and Barb to me.'

'Shirley tells me that you have done as much work as any of them.' He smiled. 'I gave it all a mere nudge.'

'I've learnt a lot from Shirl,' she said, although she'd never formed that thought before that moment. 'Not just about gardening. She really . . . embraces life, doesn't she?'

He nodded. 'That she does. And I think she'd believe – as I do – that embracing life is exactly the course you should take now.'

His eyes held hers in a way that made it clear he was trying to tell her something he wanted her to take seriously.

'We can hold more than one person in our hearts,' he went on. 'You may find there's capacity in yours for someone else.'

Elizabeth was surprised at that, perhaps because the Bible doesn't have many stories of women moving on after their husbands have died. If he'd told her that sackcloth and ashes were her destiny she'd have been more inclined to believe it. Yet she could see he was sincere.

'Thank you, Reverend,' she said, because there was nothing else to say.

Then this morning, standing in this very same kitchen at work, Olive came into the room, plonked her handbag on the table and announced, 'I have a fella for you.'

'What?' Elizabeth stopped dunking her tea bag.

'A fella. Nice looker. Has his own business. Mechanic along the river.' She jerked her thumb to the west.

'I, um . . .' Elizabeth felt her cheeks colouring. 'Thank you, but I'm not looking for a fella.'

Olive peered at her. 'Not yet.'

It took a great deal of self-control for Elizabeth not to say that she wished everyone would stop trying to pair her off. She's starting to get the impression that she unsettles them by being single. Except Olive understands her situation better than most and is generally well intentioned, so her pronouncement was no doubt meant to be helpful.

Now Olive's back in the kitchen as Elizabeth is putting her sandwich on a plate.

'How's the packing-up going?' Olive asks, looking down at the sandwich. 'Egg and lettuce again?'

'I like it,' Elizabeth says. 'And it's going slowly because there's only one of me.'

At that moment Doctor Lopes walks in, looking harried.

'What's wrong, Marco?' Olive enquires.

'I'm trying to get a patient into a specialist and there's just *no one* around here,' he says. 'I'll have to send them to Brisbane.'

'You often do.' Olive opens the fridge and pokes her head inside it.

'I know. I just wish . . . Sorry, Elizabeth, you're probably tired of hearing me go on about things like that.'

'Not at all.' Elizabeth's stomach rumbles but she suspects the eating of her sandwich is a while off.

'Young Liz is moving,' Olive announces, closing the fridge and turning towards Doctor Lopes.

'Oh?' He smiles. 'When?'

'Very soon.' Another rumble and Elizabeth folds her arms over her midriff, as if that will keep her stomach quiet.

'She needs help packing.' Olive picks up her handbag and puts it over her shoulder, winking at Elizabeth.

'I don't!' Elizabeth squeaks but Olive is already gone. 'Honestly, I don't.'

Doctor Lopes leans against the door. 'I'd be more than happy to help,' he says, his voice soft.

'Really, Olive shouldn't have said that. Sorry.'

He smiles and glances towards the front of the surgery, where Olive has no doubt positioned herself so she can hear everything.

'She likes to orchestrate things,' he says, looking back at Elizabeth. 'It's one of her better qualities.'

Now he's staring at her and Elizabeth's cheeks feel even hotter than before.

He steps closer. 'Please, let me help you. You don't have to manage everything on your own.'

She knows it's true – and also knows she hasn't been managing on her own. Her parents have always helped her, and the ladies of the Sunshine Gardening Society have made sure that the biggest project of her life – other than motherhood – wasn't conducted alone. Not that she's going to rebut what Doctor Lopes has said because that would be churlish. Besides, there is still so much that she is managing alone, including this move. And there's so much relief bound up in the idea of letting someone else assist her that she feels like handing over the whole project.

'All right,' she says at last. 'Thank you, I'd appreciate it.'

The sound of something like a whoop comes from the front desk and Doctor Lopes grins.

'Of course she's listening to every word,' he says. 'We'll work out a time before you leave today, all right?'

Elizabeth nods quickly.

Just as Doctor Lopes heads back to his room, her stomach grumbles once more. Except this time she takes a big bite of her sandwich and tries to swallow it while smiling.

JUNE 1988

WEDDING BUSH

CHAPTER SIXTY-FIVE

Now that Kathy has signed a new lease for twelve months and Hans has confirmed her promotion, she's been looking at getting a cat – an animal Owen loathed but one Kathy's always wanted. She's also decided to fully embrace the Sunshine Coast lifestyle and become one of the swimmers she sees off Noosa's Main Beach each time she's there. They go up and down the length of the beach, way out beyond the breakers, obviously unafraid of sharks.

Occasionally Kathy's had a dip right when they set off, so she's seen a group of them go out together and noticed the same faces. And she saw a sign at the surf club saying there's a Sunday morning group that meets at 5.30 a.m. in summer and 6.30 a.m. in winter. When the Sunshine Gardening Society convenes on Sundays – which isn't every weekend, but often enough for it to be a consideration – it's usually not until ten o'clock, because Shirl likes to sleep in. So that gives Kathy time to hop in the water and become one of those people who can pretend she's going to be Shane Gould one day.

Never too late – Kathy's come to realise that this appears to be her new motto. Never too late to leave her husband, move cities, try a new activity, make new friends . . . and be a fantastic swimmer. Along with the cat, the swimming is something she's wanted for a while but there just never seemed to be enough time to fit it all in, nor was Melbourne the epicentre of ocean swimming. Now she has time and freedom. It's a heady mix.

So she has a new Speedo costume and cap, and new goggles that the helpful young man in the surf shop on Hastings Street told her should do the trick. 'These ones don't leak,' he said, which made her wonder how many do. And she's standing in front of the surf club, feeling about as nervous as she used to be before school dances, wondering if any boy would like her. Ha! She needn't have bothered.

Her nervousness today, though, isn't about whether the swimmers will like her so much as whether she'll be allowed to join the group at all, because despite the 'all welcome' on the sign, she's lived in this area just long enough to realise there are cliques – she's in one or two herself. A gardening one and an art one. Which may mean she's not welcome in a swimming one. Because for sure someone will know Shirl or Barb – or Cynthia or Lorraine or Elizabeth – and if it's not a pleasant association Kathy will be cut before she even has a chance to get wet. Hence the nerves. She really wants to swim with this group. Swimming on her own will, she is sure, make her shark bait. Swimming in a group means there are other potential baits. Harsh, but true.

There's a group of three women slowly walking towards where she's waiting in front of the surf boats on their racks. It's too early for the lifesavers because the flags are hours away from going up, which means they must be swimmers. The fact they're in swimming costumes also suggests this.

One of them catches Kathy's eye and gives her a curious smile. Her eyes are bright and blue, and her hair is a shade of grey Kathy wishes hers would go but instead she's stuck with dun mixed with the occasional whitish stripe.

'Hi,' Kathy says, deciding to be brave. 'Are you in the swimming group?'

'Yep.' The woman smiles. 'I'm Sharon. This is Doreen and Kaye.'

Introductions seem like an invitation. Kathy feels slightly relieved.

'I'm Kathy,' she says. 'I, uh, I saw the sign.' She nods in its direction. 'Thought I'd see if I can join you.'

'In winter?' Sharon says. 'Not many people start then!' She laughs.

'Yeah, well . . . I hadn't thought about it earlier.' The truth is always easier than a lie.

'Of course you're welcome,' Sharon says. 'Have you done much ocean swimming?'

'No. Lots of pool swimming – I was a state swimmer at school. But I'm, uh, from Melbourne. Not a lot of ocean unless you live on the peninsula.'

'Really? Me too.'

Doreen mutters something Kathy doesn't hear.

'Sure, go ahead,' Sharon says. 'That looks like Davo already on the sand.' She squints. 'Maybe Gazza too. I won't be long.'

She turns back to Kathy. 'You can leave your stuff here, or on the sand. No one'll nick it. We've been doing it for years.'

Kathy nods and watches as Sharon swiftly takes off her track-suit pants and folds them up, puts her towel on top and tucks them both beside a tree trunk. She looks fit – no surprise, of course. Her body is lean and toned and . . .

Kathy looks away. A swimming club is not an opportunity to check out women. She's here for fitness. That's all.

After stowing her own clothes and towel she follows Sharon onto the sand, tucking her hair into her cap.

'So are you here to escape your family like everyone else is?' Sharon asks over her shoulder, then slows so she's walking alongside.

'Ah, no.' Kathy smiles quickly. 'No family up here. They're in Melbourne.'

'Oh?' Sharon glances at her. 'Are you here temporarily?'

'No. I live here. They live there. My kids are grown up. My husband is an ex.'

'Best way for them to be,' Sharon says drily. 'Never bothered myself.'

Kathy's surprised – Sharon looks to be in her forties, and in her experience women tend to have been married at least once by then. Or maybe that's only in her cloistered world.

That's something else she's learnt since moving to the Sunshine Coast: her life was narrow. She had friends she'd known since childhood, and so did Owen, and they never strayed outside those parameters. Everyone was married; everyone went to work and to the footy during the season, and watched test matches in summer and *Hey Hey It's Saturday* every week. No wonder Jemima felt like an earthquake.

'You're not going to say I just have to meet the right fella?' Sharon says teasingly.

'No,' Kathy replies quickly. 'It's none of my business.'

'That's a relief. Because fellas aren't my business either.'

As they reach the water Sharon angles herself towards Kathy. 'Just so you know,' she adds, and Kathy can't tell if it's a dare or a hint.

'Right,' she says.

Sharon grins and puts her goggles on. 'Last one in is a rotten egg!' she cries.

Kathy lets her run ahead. The water is cool and she needs to take some time to adjust, plus the waves are dumping and she has to figure out how to get past them. Added to that, her heart is beating faster than it was a few minutes ago and she can't tell if it's because she's nervous about the swim or about Sharon.

'Come on, Kathy!' Sharon calls just before she disappears under a wave.

So maybe Kathy won't get that time, but as she's learnt lately: opportunities need to be grasped when they present themselves to you. So she wades in, puts on her goggles, and lets the sea take her in.

CHAPTER SIXTY-SIX

It's already eight o'clock – oh, wait, it's almost eight thirty, which means Lorraine has to get out the door in ten minutes if she's going to make it to the garden in Noosa Heads by nine. It's a house up on Motel Hill, which is starting to have fewer motels and more of those holiday apartments.

Everywhere you look in Noosa someone's building. Which Lorraine understands, because it's beautiful and if her parents had been smarter and more fond of the ocean they could have bought closer to Hastings Street when Lorraine was young and she'd be looking forward to inheriting a motza. But no, they had to go and buy in the hinterland, and now only greenies want to live there and they don't usually have a lot of cash. It's that whole living-on-principle thing. Good for them, having convictions. Not for her, though. She likes money. She likes it even more now that Mike has lost theirs.

He's been working on paying back the mortgage, thanks to Pat. It's something she hasn't discussed with Cynthia since Pat made the offer, although they both know it's hanging there. The ex-husband who let Cynthia down has saved Lorraine's bacon. Funny how life works out.

Cynthia seems to be softening towards Pat now that he's such a devoted grandpa. What's also funny is thinking of either of them as grandparents, because they're young enough to have another kid together if they wanted. There's a thought. Cynthia wouldn't, though, would she? That'd be mad, having a baby when you're already cruising into early middle age. Lorraine's finding it hard enough having schoolkids at their age.

Here comes one of them now, his hair unbrushed even though she's told him he can't go to his friend's house if he looks like he's been dragged through a hedge backwards – it's akin to saying to his friend's parents that he can't be bothered getting tidy to come to their place. Rude.

'Couldn't find the hairbrush, Si?' she says, and is rewarded with that confused little face he makes when he knows he's done something wrong but can't quite pinpoint it.

'Your hair, baby. It's all over the place.'

'Oh.' He squints. 'The brush wasn't in the bathroom.'

A noise behind Lorraine turns out to be Rose, who is brandishing said missing item.

'Here it is, darling,' she says.

'Thanks, Mum. Come on, Si, get ready,' Lorraine says impatiently. 'I have to drop you on the way.'

'We'll take him,' Rose says.

Clearly there's some kind of support-Simon movement on in this house today.

'We?'

'Cora and I were planning to go for a walk. Simon's little friend is only a few streets away. We'll take him. Don't make yourself late.'

'I wasn't planning to. That's why I was hurrying him up.'

Lorraine feels a few different ways about the fact her mother and mother-in-law are so cosy. She knows Rose is on her side in all things, but this sort of caper makes her feel a little ganged up on. Which she told Rose the other night and Rose just winked and said, 'You know what they say: keep your friends close and your enemies closer.' Lorraine said, 'That's just an excuse you're making because you've decided you *like* Cora now.' Rose didn't deny it. So Lorraine has to live with it.

'We'll take care of him, sweetheart,' Rose says. 'By the way, I sewed up Terry's shirt.'

'Thanks, Mum.'

That's an advantage of having two grandmothers in the house: clothing repairs are taken care of swiftly. Cooking, too, because that's another thing Rose and Cora are ganging up to do. Suits Lorraine – she was never that wild about it in the first place. It's relentless, and she's constantly frustrated that it takes her hours to make dinner and it's gone in five minutes.

Terry himself ambles into the kitchen and rubs his eyes.

'Did you have a good sleep-in?' Lorraine asks and he nods slowly.

'What's for breakfast?' he mumbles.

'Whatever you make,' she answers and Rose shoots her a look.

'What, Mum? He's old enough to get it himself. Simon got his own.'

'I am making pancakes,' Cora says as she enters the room.

And now Lorraine really feels like she's being ganged up on – mainly because the kitchen isn't big enough for all of them. Or for the cloud of irritation that's building over her head, because lately Cora has decided that Terry is her new favourite, and while Lorraine would have thought Simon would be upset about that, Rose has taken to cosseting him. So her sons get a grandma each and she, Lorraine, the one keeping it all together, has no one.

Although she is grateful about the cooking, especially as she's taken on a new job after telling Mike to run things himself. She's bookkeeping for some local businesses – her friend Jane asked if she'd be interested because she couldn't keep up with the work herself. The hours are good and now there's actual money coming in, as opposed to Lorraine saving Mike money by doing his books and admin.

'Wish you could have made *me* pancakes,' she grumbles, because she had a piece of toast and a cup of tea.

'Next time, Lorraine!' Cora says brightly, and Lorraine can't tell if she means it or if she's sucking up for some reason yet to be revealed.

She still doesn't trust Cora, no matter how much she loves the boys – Mike is her son and he'll always come first. Lorraine knows this because her sons will always come first. If one of them did what Mike has done, she'd try to understand then try to help, and she'd always be hoping he'd come good.

'Where are you off to today, Loll?' Rose asks.

'Motel Hill. Some old bloke carked it and the garden was a mess by the time that happened. His daughter's inherited and she's not coping with all the work. So in we swoop.'

'People around here are lucky to have you,' Rose says, patting her cheek.

'I guess. It's not like there's a medal in it for us. But . . . I suppose that's not why we do it.'

'Why *do* you do it?'

It's Terry asking the question, and as this is the first time he has shown *any* interest *whatsoever* in the Sunshine Gardening Society Lorraine will give him a proper answer.

'I like feeling useful. In a way I don't . . .' She was about to say 'in a way I don't around here', but that wouldn't sound too good.

'It's different,' she says instead. 'We're helping people who want to take care of their gardens but they just can't, for whatever reason. And when I'm there, I'm really there. I don't think about anything else. I'm not worrying about . . .' She makes a face. 'About you wandering off on your skateboard or your brother being unhappy at school.'

'Or Dad being a dickhead.'

'Terry!'

'What? It's true.' He looks cross.

Lorraine glances at Cora, who appears stricken.

'He made a mistake, that's all,' Lorraine says, because even though she agrees with Terry she wants the boys to have a relationship with their father. The boys are probably the only reasons Mike has to set things right, given that upsetting Lorraine and his mother didn't seem to be a deterrent.

'It's a pretty big mistake.'

She can't argue with that.

'Being an adult isn't all that easy,' she says softly. 'We don't always get it right. But he loves you and he loves Simon. Just remember that.'

Terry bites his lip and glances quickly at his brother, who is kicking at the floor with his heel.

Ah, adults and the things they do to kids. Lorraine has tried all these years to protect her children from harm and the major cause of it was in the house the whole time.

'Anyway, the Sunshine Gardening Society gives me . . . well, sunshine,' she goes on, hoping to steer the conversation to safer ground. 'I have fun. I see my friends. And I've learnt a lot about plants. About respecting the land. Plus I get to see a lot of the coast and it's pretty bloody beautiful, I have to say.'

'Maybe I could join you sometime,' he says, and that makes her even happier, even if she has to refuse, because the society is sacrosanct, even from her boys.

'Sorry, mate – ladies only. But you could always start your own little garden gang.'

'As if!' he says, then smiles. There's the boy she remembers from before puberty.

She checks the clock on the kitchen wall. 'Shoot – I have to go.'

A glance at Rose and a nod in return tells her that things will be taken care of, and she's grateful that their parent-and-child shorthand is intact despite Cora's incursions.

'See you!' she calls as she slings her handbag over her shoulder, then swears and doubles back to the laundry to get her gardening gloves before hurrying out the back door to the car, to the road, to her few hours of sunshine with her society ladies.

CHAPTER SIXTY-SEVEN

Marco Lopes was as good as his word, only too happy to help Elizabeth move the little bits and pieces she didn't want to put in the hands of indelicate moving men. Now she's thinking about how to arrange those bits and pieces in her new sitting room, and considering which box to open first.

She decides to unpack the stereo so she can have Bach playing as she decants their lives into the small house in Sunshine Beach, two streets away from her parents.

Elizabeth didn't need to impose herself and Charlie on them, as it turned out, because they have a friend who's moved interstate and wanted to rent out their home. The timing was perfect – things came together as if they were meant to.

In the end, it wasn't hard to leave the old house. Elizabeth packed up each room calmly and quietly, Charlie playing in another room as she'd asked him to do. It's not a little boy's job to pack up his life. That's her responsibility, as his parent. His only parent.

As Elizabeth comes to the box containing the framed photos of Jon she smiles and thinks about how he must have helped with the move, making sure they were looked after. It all happened so smoothly – Cynthia made the offer, it was accepted, the settlement was quick because Cynthia paid in cash – that Elizabeth can't help but think she had assistance from elsewhere.

That's what Reverend Willoughby thought too when she told him the news.

'I know God works in mysterious ways,' he said, with a warm hand on her shoulder, 'but so do our loved ones. And who are we to say they are not one and the same?'

Elizabeth knows what he means. Since making the decision to sell the house, she has felt lighter than she has in a long time. Since Jon's diagnosis, she thinks, although that was so long ago she can barely remember who she was then.

That's the *Minuet in G Major* playing now. A simple piece and one Elizabeth has loved since she learnt it as a child. Jon regularly encouraged her to return to playing piano and she thought about it, then he became ill and she didn't think about it much, apart from towards the end, when she felt she needed the comfort of her fingers on the keys, the sense of satisfaction and accomplishment that came with creating something beautiful with her fingertips simply because she could follow little black dots on a page.

'Knock *knoooock!*'

Even over the Bach Elizabeth can tell that's Lorraine's voice.

'In here!' she calls. When Lorraine asked for the address she knew that an appearance was likely – why else would she need it?

'Beaut place,' Lorraine says as she enters the room, Cynthia not far behind her. 'Hope you don't mind but Cyn and I thought we'd help you unpack. I asked Kathy too. Gee, that was a bit bold of me, wasn't it? Inviting people to *your* house.'

She cackles and Elizabeth knows that Lorraine doesn't feel at all bold. No doubt she cooked up this scheme before she asked for the address and Elizabeth is the only one who didn't know.

'Hi, Charlie!' Lorraine calls, and Elizabeth hears her son's muffled response. She deposited him with a book in his new room.

'Hi, Elizabeth,' Cynthia says, smiling. 'Is it all right I'm here? I don't want it to be strange since . . . you know.'

'It's wonderful,' Elizabeth says, and means it. Cynthia provided her with an easy escape route from the maze she was in. She wants to tell her that she's grateful but Elizabeth knows her well enough to believe that Cynthia might think it flowery.

'I found you,' Kathy says triumphantly as she appears proffering a pot plant. 'Here – for *your* new garden.'

It's a maidenhair fern – a plant that even Elizabeth would find hard to kill, which Kathy likely knows.

'Thank you,' she says, taking it. 'I'll find just the right spot for it.'

'Hello, Cyn,' Kathy says, kissing Cynthia on the cheek. 'Loz,' and Lorraine gets a kiss too.

'Aren't you being affectionate?' Lorraine teases.

Kathy shrugs. 'We don't have gardening gloves on so I'm treating it like a social gathering.'

She opens her arms to Elizabeth. 'And *you* get a hug.'

As Kathy embraces her Elizabeth relaxes into it, and it feels like a hug from her mother, which Kathy is probably old enough to be: reassuring, not smothering, and over fairly quickly.

'Congratulations,' Kathy says proudly. 'You did it.'

'I did,' Elizabeth acknowledges.

'And in case you're wondering, Barb and Shirl aren't coming,' Lorraine says. 'Barb is reading tarot at some party, and Shirl says she has a gig to go to. I've brought dinner.' She holds up a heavy plastic bag. 'We're going to get you unpacked then we'll have a roast chook and some salads. Sound good?'

She doesn't wait for a response before heading off, presumably in search of a place to leave the food.

Kathy bears the pot plant towards the back deck as Elizabeth hears Lorraine opening and closing cupboards in the kitchen.

'Love the bench space!' Lorraine calls. 'Can I take some with me?'

'One day she'll get a bigger kitchen bench,' Cynthia says quietly as she kneels next to the box marked *Books*.

'May I?' she asks, and Elizabeth nods.

Cynthia gestures to the empty bookcase next to the stereo. 'If you'd like them in any particular order let me know.'

Jon used to have fiction and non-fiction separate, then categories within those, because he was often looking for something – a fact or a phrase that he was trying to remember. There was no order in the box, though. Elizabeth had put them in any way they'd fit, and she didn't think Jon would mind.

'No, there's none,' she says.

Cynthia takes out history books and an atlas, some big literary novels and slender crime stories.

'There are some serious books here,' she says with a curious glance in Elizabeth's direction.

'Jon liked knowledge,' Elizabeth says.

'And you?'

Elizabeth looks at the silver jug in her hands, a wedding present from Jon's sister. So much of what she's unpacking in this house comes from other people; they're not things she's chosen for herself. Perhaps that's why it started to feel important that she chose this new house – or, rather, that she chose to leave the house Jon chose for them. If she's to walk this path alone, with only Charlie for company, she has to decide how the path is paved – and where it goes. That can only happen one step at a time.

'I don't know,' she replies honestly. 'I read what Jon suggested. I suppose the books are good.'

'They are,' Cynthia says, 'but you don't have to keep them if you don't want them. This may sound tough but . . . he's not here, Elizabeth. You make the decisions now.'

Her tone is pointed and Elizabeth is taken aback, mainly because she feels exposed. As if Cynthia knows what she's been thinking, even though she's hidden it because she thinks she'll appear disloyal.

'I know that can be hard,' Cynthia continues. 'Because it would be nice, wouldn't it, if someone else could decide for you? Just once?'

Elizabeth nods. 'Yes,' she admits. 'I'm really tired of making all the decisions.'

They sit in silence for a few seconds, staring at each other, until Cynthia clears her throat.

'Then I'm going to be the bold one,' she says, 'and make the decisions for you when it comes to these books. I'll leave what I think you'll like and take the rest away. How's that?'

Elizabeth lets out a long breath. 'That is . . . perfect.'

'Your fridge isn't on?' Lorraine yells from the kitchen.

'Not yet,' Elizabeth yells back, then Lorraine re-enters the room, as does Kathy.

'Well, let's get on to that. Kath, check the powerpoints. I'll start looking for cords. Cyn, you right? You got a job?'

Cynthia's and Elizabeth's eyes meet, then Cynthia smiles at Lorraine. 'I do,' she says.

'Great. Okay, well, we can knock this over quickly.' Lorraine turns to go. 'Charrrliiieee! Can you give me a hand?'

Elizabeth hears chattering as Lorraine reaches Charlie's room and feels her body relax with the relief of other people making decisions.

She and Cynthia work mainly in silence until they have a filled room and empty boxes, and Elizabeth considers that Cynthia's thoughtfulness – Lorraine's and Kathy's too – is something else she is grateful for, and if she's not careful she'll find herself unravelling with all this kindness that she doesn't really feel she deserves.

Except perhaps she does. Perhaps now it is time, finally, for her to acknowledge that she hasn't done so badly, really. She's still here, so is Charlie, they have friends and a home, she has work and gardening and *meaning* in her life, and all of that is more than she imagined a year ago. It may be nothing to do with what she deserves so much as what she makes of what life presents to her – and if that is the case, she is deserving indeed.

CHAPTER SIXTY-EIGHT

'So I pull this one out? Really?' Odette bends over the bright green leaves covering the ground.

It's Odette's first tour of duty with the Sunshine Gardening Society. When she expressed an interest in joining Cynthia thought Wilfred might have put her up to it; and in a way he did, by talking to Odette about her grandmother and the fact that there is now a family line of Sunshine Gardeners. These conversations happened while Cynthia was scrabbling around in some patch of park or garden, so she didn't know about them until Odette asked her a couple of weeks ago if she could join the society.

Cynthia ran it past Shirl and Barb at the next meeting.

'So there'll be seven of us,' Barb said, and glanced at Shirl. 'I think that's the most since . . .'

'Since Fraser got into government,' Shirl said with a tight-lipped smile. 'For some reason, the end of Gough was the death knell of volunteering round here.'

'That's a little dramatic, Shirley,' Barb said, although Cynthia noted she didn't disagree.

'Is it too many people?' she asked.

'No!' Barb and Shirl said together.

'We're happy to have more, dear,' Barb said. 'Especially the younger ones.' She'd nodded towards Elizabeth. 'It reassures me that the work may continue after we decide to retire.'

So, after the approval from on high, Cynthia told Odette the news and was pleased to see her daughter's eyes light up.

'Great!' she said. 'I've already asked Dad if he'll watch Jordy.'

Cynthia was taken aback because Pat hadn't mentioned anything when they'd seen each other earlier that day. They've taken to having breakfast together every now and again, mainly to talk about their daughter and grandson, sometimes in tones that suggest they can hardly believe they're lucky enough to have them both.

She was glad, however, that Odette was so keen about gardening that she'd made arrangements. And now her daughter is pointing out a weed to Shirl, who is frowning at it.

'That's trad – yes, out! Little bugger!' Shirl huffs. 'It'll grow anywhere there's a spare patch of dirt, and sometimes where there's not.'

'But it looks okay.' Odette fingers some of the leaves. 'Is it really a weed?'

Shirl inhales sharply and Cynthia decides to intervene.

'Yes, darling, because it's not native to Australia,' she says, 'and it will grow over and around native plants, which means they have a harder time growing. So it's definitely a weed.' She points to a plant with pink flowers. 'That's a periwinkle and it has to come out too.'

'But it's so pretty!' Odette frowns. 'I don't get it.'

'They don't all look ugly!' Lorraine says from a larger patch of periwinkle nearby.

Cynthia sees Shirl's shoulders lift and her jaw set. 'Just do what Shirl tells you, all right?' she says to her daughter. 'She knows more than anyone else here.'

'And I've been in this group since the *Vietnam War*,' Shirl adds.

'Have you?' Cynthia asks. 'I didn't know that.'

Shirl arches an eyebrow. 'You didn't ask.'

Because you don't make it easy, Cynthia wants to say, but she also knows the same could be said of her. Shirl tried to prise details out of her early on – about why she had returned to Noosa, why she'd left 'that nice Pat', because everyone seems to know Pat. The only subject they had in common was Von and her role in the society.

She could have asked anyway, of course, but she's learnt most about Shirl through the way she teaches them how to care for the earth, for the gardens they tend and the environment they live in.

Cynthia decides to leave Odette to Shirl's tutelage and joins Kathy, who is swearing at the trad as it snaps off when she tries to pull it from the root.

'It's so hard to get the whole thing out,' Cynthia sympathises. 'It's almost as if it's designed to not be eradicated.'

'Yeah, weeds,' Kathy says drily. 'Who'd believe they want to stick around?'

'Very funny.' Cynthia peers at her more closely. 'Is that salt on your eyebrows?'

Kathy blushes. 'Yes. Why? How did you know?'

'Pat gets that. Anyone who spends a lot of time in the ocean tends to. So you . . . ?' She lifts her eyebrows.

'I've been swimming. Each morning,' Kathy says but she won't meet Cynthia's eye.

'And?'

'And what?' Still no eye contact.

'And *something*.' Cynthia grins. Kathy is usually so frank with her that she can detect her subterfuge a mile off.

'I have a new friend,' Kathy says lightly.

'Oh, a *friend*.' Cynthia nudges her, then reaches in and makes her best attempt to pull out a whole weed. 'Well, I won't press now but I expect to know her name in due course.'

Now Kathy allows herself a little smile. 'Okay.'

'Shirl!' Elizabeth calls from deeper in the patch of land, under a gum. 'Can you please tell me if this can stay or go?'

Looking like nothing would please her more, Shirl treads only on the weeds as she makes her way towards Elizabeth.

Cynthia glances over to where Odette is carefully plucking out weeds and inspecting each one; the same way Cynthia did when she started, not wanting to pull out something that actually belongs. Cynthia learnt by trial and error – often Lorraine's error, and her subsequent guilty face as she held up a native grass she hadn't meant to rip out along with a weed.

It pleases Cynthia immeasurably that Lorraine is with them now as they work together. Lorraine doesn't know Odette well, but Cynthia likes to think that will change. There are aspects of Cynthia that have never been revealed to Odette, and if something were to happen to Cynthia it's nice to think her old friend could fill in the gaps. Lorraine is like Shirl's beloved native plants: taking up space where weeds used to be, enriching the soil as she goes.

Over this past year and a bit, Cynthia has learnt to tend to the people who belong in her life, and the people who belong in her memory, too. She never knew her mother was a Sunshine Gardener, but she remembers everything else about her. Odette will, by contrast, have memories of *her* mother with her gardening gloves on, her knees dirty from a day's work.

The Sunshine Gardening Society and its activities are not grand events in the span of a life, Cynthia knows. Being here, amongst friends, with her daughter, is not a wedding or a graduation or a promotion. She knows, too, that people remember those grand events because they're rare. But isn't what they have here rarer still? Small acts, consistent attention, respect and care.

Cynthia couldn't have realised, before this, what her mother was clearly a part of: that they may save plants in this society, but they save lives too. Her own has come back to her, one weed, one tree, one precious native bush at a time. No matter how long she turns up on weekends, whether it's for months or years to come, she will never take that for granted.

'Oops.'

Cynthia turns around to see Odette standing behind her, looking upset.

'I think I pulled out the wrong thing,' she continues, holding up a stringy stem.

'No, darling, you didn't.' Cynthia smiles. 'That's meant to come out. And don't worry too much – we don't always get it right. You'll learn how to tell the natives from the weeds in time.'

Odette's face relaxes. 'Thanks, Mum.'

'Barb! Need your help with this one!' Lorraine calls just as Odette turns away.

Cynthia watches as Barb calmly approaches Lorraine and her quandary, then she turns back to pluck at the plants in front of her, tossing the weeds behind her as she goes.

ACKNOWLEDGEMENTS

It was only after I started writing this novel that I realised that the Sunshine Coast has such a rich history of residents who were interested in, and documented, its flora. I found some out-of-print books online, and a couple still in print, and had a lovely time reading the following for research:

Noosa's Native Plants (fourth edition) by Stephanie Haslam
Weeds of the Sunshine Coast (second edition) by Joan Heavey and Sonia MacDonald
Wildflowers of the Noosa Cooloola Area by Arthur Harrold
Noosa Nature (three-part series) by Cecily Fearnley
A Living River: The Noosa by Kathleen McArthur

The following books also provided information and inspiration:

The Noosa Story by Nancy Cato
The Shaping of Noosa by Michael Gloster
Place of Shadows: The History of Noosa by Phil Jarratt
Noosa . . . What's Your Point? by Rob Black
Wild About Noosa by Tony Wellington
Hastings Street: Stories from Noosa's Past by Emma Freeman

Many thanks to Fiona Hazard, Rebecca Allen, Louise Stark and all at Hachette Australia for their support of my writing, and to editors Celine Kelly and Nicola O'Shea, and proofreader Julia Cain.

Christa Moffitt has once again created a glorious cover – thank you.

Thank you to my agent, Melanie Ostell, for bearing with me through all the stages of my novels.

Thanks and love for their support to my parents, Robbie and David, and my brother, Nicholas; to my cherished friends Jen Bradley and Isabelle Benton; to Marg Cruikshank, Anna Egelstaff, Chris Kunz, Neralyn and Col Porter, Tammie Russell, Kate Sampson and Jill Wunderlich.

The artists of Australia's country music community never cease to provide inspiration and motivation, as well as wonderful music.

During the course of writing this novel I became a Bushcare volunteer in my local council area and have been so happy to have the company of Ruth, Diana and Brynley as I discover just how lovely it can be to pull out weeds and plant natives.